LITERAT

FOR ADVEI

In the Human Spirit

VOLUME II

edited by

Philip E. Bishop

Valencia Community College

PRENTICE HALL, Upper Saddle River, New Jersey 07458

Library of Congress Cataloging-in-Publication Data
(Revised for vol. 2)
Literature for Adventures in the human spirit.
 I. Bishop, Philip E. II. Bishop, Philip E.
Adventures in the human spirit.
CB245.B57L58   1995   909'.09821   94-28737
ISBN O-13-141269-8

Editorial/production supervision: Tina M. Trautz
Interior design: Jordan Ochs and Patricia V. Amoroso
Acquisitions editor: Bud Therien
Editorial assistant: Lee Mamunes
Manufacturing buyer: Robert Anderson
Cover design: John Judy

*Credits and copyright acknowledgments appear on pages ix–x,
which constitute an extension of the copyright page.*

Printed in the United States of America

10   9   8   7   6   5   4   3   2   1

0-13-141269-8

Prentice-Hall International (UK) Limited, London
Prentice-Hall of Australia Pty. Limited, Sydney
Prentice-Hall Canada Inc., Toronto
Prentice-Hall Hispanoamericana, S.A., Mexico
Prentice-Hall of India Private Limited, New Delhi
Prentice-Hall of Japan, Inc., Tokyo
Pearson Education Asia Pte. Ltd., Singapore
Editoria Prentice-Hall do Brasil, Ltda., Rio De Janeiro

Contents

Preface

Literature for Adventures in the Human Spirit is a two-volume companion to my survey of the humanities, *Adventures in the Human Spirit* (Prentice Hall, 1994), offered to instructors and students who wish to enrich the basic text with primary readings. The two volumes are divided to accommodate the most common organization of multisemester humanities courses: Volume 1 covers the ancient world, classical Greece and Rome, and the Middle Ages; Volume 2 extends from the seventeenth century to the present.

My selections in *Literature for Adventures* have been guided by simple principles. I have tried to represent fairly and concisely the literary and philosophical traditions of Western civilization; to explore the central concepts of Western thought by judicious choice of excerpts; and, most of all, to provoke students to examine and discuss these traditions in light of contemporary experience. Our determination to offer students a convenient and affordable format has limited the scope of these volumes. Still, we have managed to include some representative texts from non-Western traditions and to include a fair sampling of women and minority authors.

In Volume 1, "The Ancient World" draws on myths of Egypt and Mesopotamia that offer pointed comparison to the Hebrew Bible stories in Chapter 4. The inclusion of selections by Confucius and Buddha opens possibilities for comparison with classical and Christian religious and ethical teachings.

With ancient Greece and Rome (Chapters 2 and 3), I have included entire chapters of Homer's *Iliad* and *Odyssey* and of Virgil's *Aeneid* in the hopes of rendering some quality of the whole works. We offer the whole text of Sophocles' *Oedipus the King*, that primal drama of the Western imagination, and of Plato's *Apology of Socrates*. Other selections of classical philosophy—from Plato, Aristotle, Lucretius, Marcus Aurelius—make for fruitful connections to the Asian texts.

Readings from the Christian era include key passages of the Hebrew Bible, New Testament, and Qur'an, emphasizing these religions' common origins. In the Middle Ages, I have sought a balance between the secular and sacred traditions. Both the epic tradition (*Song of Roland*, Dante's *Inferno*) and the lyric mode are represented, while Chaucer's "Wife of Bath's Tale" epitomizes the medieval romance. With the Wife of Bath and Christine de Pisan, medieval womanhood is heard with a strong and distinctive voice.

Volume 2 begins with the Renaissance and the humanist writings of Petrarch, Machiavelli, and Pico. Shakespeare's *Hamlet* was chosen for its archetypal Renaissance hero and Montaigne for his skeptical view of Renaissance humanism. From the Baroque and Enlightenment, Cervantes' idealizing hero Don Quixote is set against Voltaire's naive young Candide, while the era's philosophical tensions are revealed by Descartes and Hobbes.

Two of romanticism's great literary heroes, Faust and Frankenstein, open Chapter 3, which includes a generous selection of romantic and symbolist poetry. The nineteenth century closes with the tortured figure of Dostoevsky's Grand Inquisitor, the brilliant portrait of ambivalence. The twentieth century stretches from Eliot's Prufrock to Ellison's invisible man. It includes such pivotal voices of the modern era as Freud, Virginia Woolf, and Sartre. Again, a selection of poetry mirrors the spirit of modernism and the insurgent contemporary voices from groups and cultures long denied a voice in the literary and philosophical tradition.

In shaping this collection, I am deeply grateful for the advice of reviewers and colleagues, many of them named below. I have thoughtfully considered their suggestions, even where the limitations of space or budget kept me from following them.

ACKNOWLEDGMENTS

For their advice in choosing selections, I am grateful to Andrew Alexander, Don Andrews, Elizabeth Eschbach, Carol Foltz, Rosita Martinez, Diane Maxwell, Lois McNamara, Mary Jo Pecht, Querentia Throm, and others unnamed here. For their unstinting assistance, I would like to thank Judy Clark, Karin Bonilla, Vicki Pipkin, Mary Beth Elkin, Bunnie Jackson, and the Word Processing staff. Thanks also to my editor Norwell F. Therien, Jr., for his enduring patience and good will. Thanks to Shaughna and Aaron, my marvelous children, and to Kira, the perpetual surprise, for reminding me that there are other things than books.

For inspiring me always by their courage in the face of difficult truths, I dedicate these volumes to my students. With this book, let them make their own truths anew.

PHILIP E. BISHOP

CREDITS

1

The Renaissance and Reformation

The impetus for the age called the Renaissance came from Europe's growing cities, where the bustle of commerce was replacing the slow rhythms of the rural medieval manor. City and town life loosened the individual's ties to the community, and, not surprisingly, the literature created by these city dwellers placed new emphasis on individual thought and action. From the mournful poems of Petrarch to the ruminations of Shakespeare's Hamlet, to the skeptical reflections of the essayist Montaigne, Renaissance intellectuals located moral and aesthetic values in the individual consciousness.

Renaissance humanism, specifically its enthusiasm for classical literature and philosophy, expresses the desire to free individual thought and creativity from restrictive medieval traditions. In *Hamlet*, this struggle is explicit: The Renaissance courtier cannot bring himself to obey the feudal obligations of blood vengeance. The insistently individualist spirit of the Renaissance is heard everywhere in its poetry and philosophy. Even the most skeptical voices, such as Erasmus and Montaigne, believe that true piety and wisdom are the province of the individual, reflective soul.

Still, as the doubts of Montaigne demonstrate, individual consciousness brings necessarily individual responsibility. Because Machiavelli believes the powerful and ruthless leader can save Italy, he must also believe the same kind of ruler can destroy his nation. Pico proclaims triumphantly that humans differ from other creatures in that God has not defined their nature. Free to be the most noble creatures in God's world, humans are also free to stoop to the most idiotic folly or evil barbarism. By dissolving the comforting intellectual strictures of the Middle Ages, Renaissance thinkers ushered Western civilization into a daring and daunting new era.

FRANCIS PETRARCH

The poet and scholar Francis Petrarch (1304–1374) helped inaugurate the Renaissance by championing classical learning and absorbing the lessons of the Greeks and Romans into his own time. Petrarch lived at courts and in university towns throughout Europe but styled himself a true citizen of "the republic of letters," the realm of ideas and literature that included the ancient Greeks. Most of Petrarch's major writings were consciously imitated from the Latin, including an epic modeled after Virgil's *Aeneid*. By his rigorous study and translation of classical texts, Petrarch successfully defined the ideal of the humanist scholar, seeking always to adapt the wisdom and beauty of antiquity to his own day.

As a poet, Petrarch is best known for his sonnets, the most famous dedicated to Laura, the woman he loved according to the idealized conventions of courtly love. Although these conventions themselves are medieval, Petrarch's verbal inventiveness, his delight in the sensuous beauty of language, and the almost confessional absorption with his own suffering mark these as works of the Renaissance.

For analysis and interpretation:

1. Evaluate Petrarch's complaint in "It Was the Morning" that his grieving mood on Good Friday made him more vulnerable to Laura's beauty. Is there a psychological truth to this notion?

2. In "The Eyes That Drew from Me," analyze the shift in the poem's structure from Laura's beauty to the poet's own grief and desolation. How does the poem's beauty contradict the poem's last lines?

3. Do you find the poet's grieving dedication to Laura in "Go, Grieving Rimes of Mine" emotionally exaggerated? How does the poet's eloquent wish to die also assure his (and Laura's) immortality? Might this grieving poet also be accused of vanity?

It Was the Morning

It was the morning of that blessed day
Whereon the Sun in pity veiled his glare
For the Lord's agony, that, unaware,
I fell a captive, Lady, to the sway

Of your swift eyes: that seemed no time to stay
The strokes of Love: I stepped into the snare
Secure, with no suspicion: then, and there
I found my cue in man's most tragic play.

Love caught me naked to his shaft, his sheaf,
The entrance for his ambush and surprise
Against the heart wide open through the eyes,

The constant gate and fountain of my grief:
How craven so to strike me stricken so,
Yet from you fully armed conceal his bow!

—Translated by Joseph Auslander

The Eyes That Drew from Me

The eyes that drew from me such fervent praise,
The arms and hands and feet and countenance
Which made me a stranger in my own romance
And set me apart from the well-trodden ways;

The gleaming golden curly hair, the rays
Flashing from a smiling angel's glance
Which moved the world in paradisal dance,
Are grains of dust, insensibilities.

And I live on, but in grief and self-contempt,
Left here without the light I loved so much,
In a great tempest and with shrouds unkempt.

No more love songs, then, I have done with such;
My old skill now runs thin at each attempt,
And tears are heard within the harp I touch.

—Translated by Edwin Morgan

Go, Grieving Rimes of Mine

Go, grieving rimes of mine, to that hard stone
Whereunder lies my darling, lies my dear,
And cry to her to speak from heaven's sphere.
Her mortal part with grass is overgrown.

Tell her, I'm sick of living; that I'm blown
By winds of grief from the course I ought to steer,
That praise of her is all my purpose here
And all my business; that of her alone

Do I go telling, that how she lived and died
And lives again in immortality,
All men may know, and love my Laura's grace.

Oh, may she deign to stand at my bedside
When I come to die; and may she call to me
And draw me to her in the blessèd place!

—Translated by Morris Bishop

PICO DELLA MIRANDOLA

Giovanni Pico della Mirandola (1463–1494) was notable for his audaciously ambitious defense of Renaissance humanism. He once offered to defend in philosophical disputation no less than nine hundred propositions on philosophical and theological truth. Suspected of heresy by the Church, he took refuge in the Florence of Lorenzo de' Medici. Though Pico was not an original thinker, especially when compared to Petrarch or Machiavelli, his *Oration on the Dignity of Man* is a summation of Renaissance humanism with its scholarly allusions and bold statement of the nobility of human character.

For analysis and interpretation:

1. Describe the hierarchy of creation and human beings' place in it, as conceived by Pico.

2. How does the undetermined nature of human character grant to humans a great freedom of choice, according to Pico? How is his thesis consistent with the writings of other Renaissance humanists, including Machiavelli and Erasmus?

From *Oration on the Dignity of Man*

I have read in the records of the Arabians, reverend Fathers, that Abdala the Saracen, when questioned as to what on this stage of the world, as it were, could be seen most worthy of wonder, replied: "There is nothing to be seen more wonderful than man." In agreement with this opinion is the saying of Hermes Trismegistus: "A great miracle, Asclepius, is man." But when I weighed the reason for these maxims, the many grounds for the excellence of human nature reported by many men failed to satisfy me—that man is the intermediary between creatures, the intimate of the gods, the king of the lower beings, by the acuteness of his senses, by the discernment of his reason, and by the light of his intelligence the interpreter of nature, the interval between fixed eternity and fleeting time, and (as the Persians say) the bond, nay, rather, the marriage song of the world, on David's testimony but little lower than the angels. Admittedly great though these reasons be, they are not the principal grounds, that is, those which may rightfully claim for themselves the privilege of the highest admiration. For why should we not admire more the angels themselves and the blessed choirs of heaven? At last it seems to me I have come to understand why man is the most fortunate of creatures and consequently worthy of all admiration and what precisely is that rank which is his lot in the universal chain of Being—a rank to be envied not only by brutes but even by the stars and by minds beyond this world. It is a matter past faith and a wondrous one. Why should it not be? For it is on this very account that man is rightly called and judged a great miracle and a wonderful creature indeed.

2. But hear, Fathers, exactly what this rank is and, as friendly auditors, conformably to your kindness, do me this favor. God the Father, the supreme Architect, had already built this cosmic home we behold, the most sacred temple of His godhead, by the laws of His mysterious wisdom. The region above the heavens He had adorned with Intelligences, the heavenly spheres He had quickened with eternal souls, and the excrementary and filthy parts of the lower world He had filled with a multitude of animals of every kind. But, when the work was finished, the Craftsman kept wishing that there were someone to ponder the plan of so great a work, to love its

beauty, and to wonder at its vastness. Therefore, when everything was done (as Moses and Timaeus bear witness), He finally took thought concerning the creation of man. But there was not among His archetypes that from which He could fashion a new offspring, nor was there in His treasure-houses anything which He might bestow on His new son as an inheritance, nor was there in the seats of all the world a place where the latter might sit to contemplate the universe. All was now complete; all things had been assigned to the highest, the middle, and the lowest orders. But in its final creation it was not the part of the Father's power to fail as though exhausted. It was not the part of His wisdom to waver in a needful matter through poverty of counsel. It was not the part of His kindly love that he who was to praise God's divine generosity in regard to others should be compelled to condemn it in regard to himself.

3. At last the best of artisans ordained that that creature to whom He had been able to give nothing proper to himself should have joint possession of whatever had been peculiar to each of the different kinds of being. He therefore took man as a creature of indeterminate nature and, assigning him a place in the middle of the world, addressed him thus: "Neither a fixed abode nor a form that is thine alone nor any function peculiar to thyself have we given thee, Adam, to the end that according to thy longing and according to thy judgment thou mayest have and possess what abode, what form, and what functions thou thyself shalt desire. The nature of all other beings is limited and constrained within the bounds of laws prescribed by Us. Thou, constrained by no limits, in accordance with thine own free will, in whose hand We have placed thee, shalt ordain for thyself the limits of thy nature. We have set thee at the world's center that thou mayest from thence more easily observe whatever is in the world. We have made thee neither of heaven nor of earth, neither mortal nor immortal, so that with freedom of choice and with honor, as though the maker and molder of thyself, thou mayest fashion thyself in whatever shape thou shalt prefer. Thou shalt have the power to degenerate into the lower forms of life, which are brutish. Thou shalt have the power, out of thy soul's judgment, to be reborn into the higher forms, which are divine."

4. O supreme generosity of God the Father, O highest and most marvelous felicity of man! To him it is granted to have whatever he chooses, to be whatever he wills. Beasts as soon as they are born (so says Lucilius) bring with them from their mother's womb all they will ever possess. Spiritual beings, either from the beginning or soon thereafter, become what they are to be for ever and ever. On man when he came into life the Father conferred the seeds of all kinds and the germs of every way of life. Whatever seeds each man cultivates will grow to maturity and bear in him their own fruit. If they be vegetative, he will be like a plant. If sensitive, he will become brutish. If rational, he will grow into a heavenly being. If intellectual, he will be an angel and the son of God. And if, happy in the lot of no created thing, he withdraws into the center of his own unity, his spirit, made one with God, in the solitary darkness of God, who is set above all things, shall surpass them all. Who would not admire this our chameleon? Or who could more greatly admire aught else whatever? It is man who Asclepius of Athens, arguing from his mutability of character and from his self-transforming nature, on just grounds says was symbolized by Proteus in the

mysteries. Hence those metamorphoses renowned among the Hebrews and the Pythagoreans.

—Translated by Elizabeth Livermore Forber

MACHIAVELLI

Niccolò Machiavelli (1469–1527) was one of the Renaissance's most profoundly original thinkers and is recognized today as an originator of the modern science of politics. As a diplomat and secretary to the Florentine republic, Machiavelli learned the inner workings of politics in Renaissance Italy. As an exile, he reflected on Italy's political divisions and drew comparative lessons from his study of classical history.

In his masterful analysis of political realism, Machiavelli coolly analyzed successful government as it was really practiced: disciplining an army by cruelty, betraying promises in the interest of maintaining the state, impressing common people with appearances of virtue. The goal toward which Machiavelli directs his analysis is the effective government of the Italian city-state. He wrote *The Prince* partly out of despair that Italy would be dominated by powerful foreign rulers who were more willing to practice ruthless politics than Italy's own princes.

For analysis and interpretation:

1. Apply Machiavelli's advice on cruelty and compassion to other occupations of governance: Must a parent or teacher, for example, sometimes balance cruel sternness against compassion in governing a family or a classroom?

2. Would most citizens today be willing to accept Machiavelli's principle that politicians must sometimes lie to govern effectively? What aims in government might justify the sacrifice of truthfulness?

3. Evaluate Machiavelli's assessment of the nature of fortune. Do people succeed in today's world because they are virtuous? To what extent should one "adapt one's policy to the time" in order to prosper?

From *The Prince*

XVII. Cruelty and compassion; and whether it is better to be loved than feared, or the reverse

Taking others of the qualities I enumerated above, I say that a prince must want to have a reputation for compassion rather than for cruelty: nonetheless, he must be careful that he does not make bad use of compassion. Cesare Borgia was accounted cruel; nevertheless, this cruelty of his reformed the Romagna, brought it unity, and restored order and obedience. On reflection, it will be seen that there was more compassion in Cesare than in the Florentine people, who, to escape being called cruel, allowed Pistoia to be devastated. So a prince must not worry if he incurs reproach for his cruelty so long as he keeps his subjects united and loyal. By making an example or two he will prove more compassionate than those who, being too compassionate, allow disorders which lead to murder and rapine. These nearly always harm the whole community, whereas executions ordered by a prince only affect individuals. A new prince, of all rulers, finds it impossible to avoid a reputation for cruelty, because of the abundant dangers inherent in a newly won state. Vergil, through the mouth of Dido, says:

> *Res dura, et regni novitas me talia cogunt*
> *Moliri, et late fines custode tueri.*

> [Harsh necessity and the newness of my kingdom force me
> To do such things and to guard my borders everywhere.

Virgil, Aeneid]

Nonetheless, a prince must be slow to take action, and must watch that he does not come to be afraid of his own shadow; his behaviour must be tempered by humanity and prudence so that over-confidence does not make him rash or excessive distrust make him unbearable.

From this arises the following question: whether it is better to be loved than feared, or the reverse. The answer is that one would like to be both the one and the other; but because it is difficult to combine them, it is far better to be feared than loved if you cannot be both. One can make this generalization about men: they are ungrateful, fickle, liars, and deceivers, they shun danger and are greedy for profit; while you treat them well, they are yours. They would shed their blood for you, risk their property, their lives, their children, so long, as I said above, as danger is remote; but when you are in danger they turn against you. Any prince who has come to depend entirely on promises and has taken no other precautions ensures his own ruin; friendship which is bought with money and not with greatness and nobility of mind is paid for, but it does not last and it yields nothing. Men worry less about doing an injury to one who makes himself loved than to one who makes himself feared. The bond of love is one which men, wretched creatures that they are, break when it is to their advantage to do so; but fear is strengthened by a dread of punishment which is always effective.

The prince must nonetheless make himself feared in such a way that, if he is not loved, at least he escapes being hated. For fear is quite compatible with an absence of hatred; and the prince can always avoid hatred if he abstains from the property of his subjects and citizens and from their women. If, even so, it proves necessary to execute someone, this is to be done only when there is proper justification and manifest reason for it. But above all a prince must abstain from the property of others; because men sooner forget the death of their father than the loss of their patrimony. It is always possible to find pretexts for confiscating someone's property; and a prince who starts to live by rapine always finds pretexts for seizing what belongs to others. On the other hand, pretexts for executing someone are harder to find and they are less easily sustained.

However, when a prince is campaigning with his soldiers and is in command of a large army then he need not worry about having a reputation for cruelty; because, without such a reputation, no army was ever kept united and disciplined. Among the admirable achievements of Hannibal is included this: that although he led a huge army, made up of countless different races, on foreign campaigns, there was never any dissension, either among the troops themselves or against their leader, whether things were going well or badly. For this, his inhuman cruelty was wholly responsible. It was this, along with his countless other qualities, which made him feared and respected by his soldiers. If it had not been for his cruelty, his other qualities would not have been enough. The historians, having given little thought to this, on the one hand admire what Hannibal achieved, and on the other condemn what made his achievements possible.

That his other qualities would not have been enough by themselves can be proved by looking at Scipio, a man unique in his own time and through all recorded history. His armies mutinied against him in Spain, and the only reason for this was his excessive leniency, which allowed his soldiers more licence than was good for military discipline. Fabius Maximus reproached him for this in the Senate and called him a corrupter of the Roman legions. Again, when the Locri were plundered by one of Scipio's officers, he neither gave them satisfaction nor punished his officer's insubordination; and this was all because of his having too lenient a nature. By way of excuse for him some senators argued that many men were better at not making mistakes themselves than at correcting them in others. But in time Scipio's lenient nature would have spoilt his fame and glory had he continued to indulge it during his command; when he lived under orders from the Senate, however, this fatal characteristic of his was not only concealed but even brought him glory.

So, on this question of being loved or feared, I conclude that since some men love as they please but fear when the prince pleases, a wise prince should rely on what he controls, not on what he cannot control. He must only endeavour, as I said, to escape being hated.

XVIII. How princes should honour their word

Everyone realizes how praiseworthy it is for a prince to honour his word and to be straightforward rather than crafty in his dealings; nonetheless contemporary experience shows that princes who have achieved great things have been those who have given their word lightly, who have known how to trick men with their cunning, and who, in the end, have overcome those abiding by honest principles.

You must understand, therefore, that there are two ways of fighting: by law or by force. The first way is natural to men, and the second to beasts. But as the first way often proves inadequate one must needs have recourse to the second. So a prince must understand how to make a nice use of the beast and the man. The ancient writers taught princes about this by an allegory, when they described how Achilles and many other princes of the ancient world were sent to be brought up by Chiron, the centaur, so that he might train them his way. All the allegory means, in making the teacher half beast and half man, is that a prince must know how to act according to the nature of both, and that he cannot survive otherwise.

So, as a prince is forced to know how to act like a beast, he must learn from the fox and the lion; because the lion is defenceless against traps and a fox is defenceless against wolves. Therefore one must be a fox in order to recognize traps, and a lion to frighten off wolves. Those who simply act like lions are stupid. So it follows that a prudent ruler cannot, and must not, honour his word when it places him at a disadvantage and when the reasons for which he made his promise no longer exist. If all men were good, this precept would not be good; but because men are wretched creatures who would not keep their word to you, you need not keep your word to them. And no prince ever lacked good excuses to colour his bad faith. One could give innumerable modern instances of this, showing how many pacts and promises have been made null and void by the bad faith of princes: those who have known best how to imitate the fox have come off best. But one must know how to colour one's actions and to be a great liar and deceiver. Men are so simple, and so much creatures of circumstance, that the deceiver will always find someone ready to be deceived.

There is one fresh example I do not want to omit. Alexander VI never did anything, or thought of anything, other than deceiving men; and he always found victims for his deceptions. There never was a man capable of such convincing asseverations, or so ready to swear to the truth of something, who would honour his word less. Nonetheless his deceptions always had the result he intended, because he was a past master in the art.

A prince, therefore, need not necessarily have all the good qualities I mentioned above, but he should certainly appear to have them. I would even go so far as to say that if he has these qualities and always behaves accordingly he will find them harmful; if he only appears to have them they will render him service. He should appear to be compassionate, faithful to his word, kind, guileless, and devout. And indeed he should be so. But his disposition should be such that, if he needs to be the opposite, he knows how. You must realize this: that a prince, and especially a new prince, cannot observe all those things which give men a reputation for virtue, because in order to maintain his state he is often forced to act in defiance of good faith, of charity, of kindness, of religion. And so he should have a flexible disposition, varying as fortune and circumstances dictate. As I said above, he should not deviate from what is good, if that is possible, but he should know how to do evil, if that is necessary.

A prince, then, must be very careful not to say a word which does not seem inspired by the five qualities I mentioned earlier. To those seeing and hearing him, he should appear a man of compassion, a man of good faith, a man of integrity, a kind and a religious man. And there is nothing so important as to seem to have this last quality. Men in general judge by their eyes rather than by their hands; because everyone is in a position to watch, few are in a position to come in close touch with you. Everyone sees what you appear to be, few experience what you really are. And those few dare not gainsay the many who are backed by the majesty of the state. In the actions of all men, and especially of princes, where there is no court of appeal, one judges by the result. So let a prince set about the task of conquering and maintaining his state; his methods will always be judged honourable and will be universally praised. The common people are always impressed by appearances and results. In this context, there are only common people, and there is no room for the few when the many are supported by the state. A certain contemporary ruler, whom it is better not to name, never preaches anything except peace and good faith; and he is an enemy of both one and the other, and if he had ever honoured either of them he would have lost either his standing or his state many times over.

XXV. How far human affairs are governed by fortune, and how fortune can be opposed

I am not unaware that many have held and hold the opinion that events are controlled by fortune and by God in such a way that the prudence of men cannot modify them, indeed, that men have no influence whatsoever. Because of this, they would conclude that there is no point in sweating over things, but that one should submit to the rulings of chance. This opinion has been more widely held in our own times, because of the great changes and variations, beyond human imagining, which we have experienced and experience every day. Sometimes, when thinking of this, I have myself inclined to this same opinion. Nonetheless, so as not to rule out our free will, I believe that it is probably true that fortune is the arbiter of half the things we do, leaving the other half or so to be controlled by ourselves. I compare fortune to one of those violent rivers which, when they are enraged, flood the plains, tear down trees and buildings, wash soil from one place to deposit it in another. Everyone flees before them, everybody yields to their impetus, there is no possibility of resistance. Yet although such is their nature, it does not follow that when they are flowing quietly one cannot take precautions, constructing dykes and embankments so that when the river is in flood they would keep to one channel or their impetus be less wild and dangerous. So it is with fortune. She shows her potency where there is no well regulated power to resist her, and her impetus is felt where she knows there are no embankments and dykes built to restrain her. If you consider Italy, the theatre of those changes and variations I mentioned, which first appeared here, you will see that she is a country without embankments and without dykes: for if Italy had been adequately reinforced, like Germany, Spain, and France, either this flood would not have caused the great changes it has, or it would not have swept in at all.

I want what I have said to suffice, in general terms, on the question of how to oppose fortune. But, confining myself now to particular circumstances, I say that we see that some princes flourish one day and come to grief the next, without appearing to have changed in character or any other way. This I believe arises, first, for the reasons discussed at length earlier on, namely, that those princes who are utterly dependent on fortune come to grief when their fortune changes. I also believe that the one who adapts his policy to the times prospers, and likewise that the one whose policy clashes with the demands of the times does not. It can be observed that men use various methods in pursuing their own personal objectives, that is glory and riches. One man proceeds with circumspection, another impetuously; one uses violence, another stratagem; one man goes about things patiently, another does the opposite; and yet everyone, for all this diversity of method, can reach his objective. It can also be observed that with two circumspect men, one will achieve his end, the other not; and likewise two men succeed equally well with different methods, one of them being circumspect and the other impetuous. This results from nothing else except the extent to which their methods are or are not suited to the nature of the times. Thus it happens that, as I have said, two men, working in different ways, can achieve the same end, and of two men working in the same way one gets what he wants and the other does not. This also explains why prosperity is ephemeral; because if a man behaves with patience and circumspection and the time and circumstances are such that this method is called for, he will prosper; but if time and circumstances change he will be ruined because he does not change his policy. Nor do we find any man shrewd enough to know how to adapt his policy in this way; either because he cannot do otherwise than what is in character or because, having always prospered by proceeding one way, he cannot persuade himself to change. Thus a man who is circumspect, when circumstances demand impetuous behaviour, is unequal to the task, and so he comes to grief. If he changed his character according to the time and circumstances, then his fortune would not change.

Pope Julius II was impetuous in everything; and he found the time and circumstances so favourable to his way of proceeding that he always met with success. Consider his first campaign, against Bologna, when messer Giovanni Bentivogli was still living. The Venetians mistrusted it: so did the king of Spain; and Julius was still arguing about the enterprise with France. Nonetheless, with typical forcefulness and impetuosity, he launched the expedition in person. This move disconcerted and arrested Spain and the Venetians, the latter because they were afraid and the former because of the king's ambition to reconquer all the kingdom of Naples. On the other hand, he drew the king of France after him. This was because the king, seeing Julius go into action, and anxious for his support in subduing the Venetians, decided he could not refuse him troops without doing him a manifest disservice. With that impetuous move of his, therefore, Julius achieved what no other pontiff, with the utmost human prudence, would have achieved. Because had Julius delayed setting out from Rome until all his plans and negotiations were completed, as any other pontiff would have done, he would never have succeeded. The king of France would have found a hundred and one excuses, and the others would have inspired Julius with a hundred and one fears. I shall not discuss his other deeds, which were all like this and which all met with success. The brevity of his pontifical life did not let him experience the contrary. If there had come a time when it was necessary for him to act with circumspection he would have come to grief: he would never have acted other than in character.

I conclude, therefore, that as fortune is changeable whereas men are obstinate in their ways, men prosper so long as fortune and policy are in accord, and when there is a clash they fail. I hold strongly to this: that it is better to be impetuous than circumspect; because fortune is a woman and if she is to be submissive it is necessary to beat and coerce her. Experience shows that she is more often subdued by men who do this than by those who act coldly. Always, being a woman, she favours young men, because they are less circumspect and more ardent, and because they command her with greater audacity.

—Translated by George Bull

ERASMUS

Desiderius Erasmus (1466–1536) was the leading voice of the Northern Renaissance, who shaped the Reformation through his biblical translations but kept his distance from Martin Luther's reforms. Erasmus shared the reformers' disgust for the Church's corruption and hypocrisy, but refused to join the Lutheran secession from the "mother Church."

This forthright ambivalence suffuses Erasmus's most popular work, *The Praise of Folly*. Erasmus speaks through the allegorical figure of Folly, who wittily defends human foolishness to her imaginary audience. Erasmus plays the intellectual ventriloquist, his own opinions veiled in the irony of Folly's "praises." Clearly Erasmus is mocking the vanities of ordinary people who perpetually violate the rules of common wisdom. Folly's praise of madness anticipates the heroic idiocy of Cervantes's great novel *Don Quixote*. But neither does Erasmus favor the opposite extreme of folly, the dry, lifeless reason of the Stoics. Through Folly, Erasmus may be affirming the fallible but forgivable nature of humanity. Only the pious, described in the last of the excerpts which follow, seem to escape the bite of Erasmus's wit.

For analysis and interpretation:

1. Evaluate Folly's assertion that the "fountain of life" is not wisdom or reason, but the folly of sexual desire and the pursuit of pleasure.

2. According to Folly, what kind of people are the happiest? How does Folly's answer to this question compare to classical philosophy? (Compare especially Aristotle.)

3. Describe the life of the pious, according to Folly. In what do the pious find happiness? Do you find their virtues more appealing than the errors of folly?

From *The Praise of Folly*

[*Folly as the "cause of life"*]

You have now heard of my birth, education, and companions. Now that it may not seem that I call myself a goddess without good reason, please give me your undivided attention while I tell how many advantages I bestow on gods and men alike. For if someone has written that to be a god is to help men, and if they have deservedly been admitted to the company of gods who show the use of wine or grain or some other commodity to men, then why cannot I be called and considered in truth the alpha of all the gods who alone am the dispenser of all goods to men?

In the first place what can be sweeter or more precious than life itself? And by whose assistance except mine is life conceived? Certainly not by the spear of potently fathered Pallas; not by the shield of cloud-gathering Jove is life propagated. Even the Father of the Gods and King of men who makes Olympus tremble by his least nod must set aside his three-pronged firebolt and that Titanic visage with which he terrifies the gods whenever he chooses, if he wishes to do that which he is forever doing, namely begetting children. Now, indeed, the Stoics think themselves very close to the gods; but give me a person who is Stoic three or four or even six hundred times over and see if he, though not putting aside his beard, an insignia of wisdom (but also common to the goat), will not surely put off his gravity, smooth his frowning brow, abandon his rockbound principles, and for a few minutes be silly and act the fool. In the end the wise man must come to me, me I say, if he wants to be a father; but why not speak more frankly, as I usually do? Now, I ask you, is it the head, the face, the breast, the hands, or the ear—all considered honorable parts—that bring forth gods and men? No, I think not; rather it is that foolish and ridiculous part that cannot even be named without laughter—the generative organ of the human race. It is the sacred fountain from which all things take life, more truly than from the tetrad of Pythagoras.

Tell me now, what man would wish to put himself in the trap of matrimony in the manner that these so-called wise men do, if he had considered beforehand the inconveniences of married life? What woman would give herself to a man if she pondered or foresaw the dangerous pangs of childbirth and the harassment of motherhood? Since you owe your existence to the marriage bed and marriage to my handmaid, you can now see how very much indebted to me you are. Then, too, would a woman who has gone through this experience repeat it again without the power and influence of Lethe? And Venus herself, Lucretius not withstanding, would not deny that without my powerful assistance her influence would be weakened and enfeebled. Thus from this silly and ridiculous game of mine come forth those supercilious philosophers (whose places have now been taken by those who are commonly known as Monks), kings in purple robes, pious priests, and thrice-holy Popes; also that whole company of the gods of the poets which is so numerous that Olympus itself, spacious as it is, can hardly hold the crowd.

However, let it be thought a small thing to be the cause of all life, if I do not show you that whatever good there is in life comes from me. Would life without pleasure be called life at all? You applaud! I knew that no one of you was so wise, or should I say foolish—no, wise is right—that you would err in that matter. The Stoics, however, spurn pleasure, or at least they carefully pretend to; they attack it assiduously in public but only so that they might enjoy it the more once they have deterred all others. But let them tell me, by Jove, what part of life is not sad, troublesome, graceless, flat, and burdensome unless you have pleasure, the seasoning of Folly, added to it. There is sufficient proof to this fact in that beautiful tribute given to me by Sophocles, a man not sufficiently appreciated, which states that ignorance is bliss. . . .

[*The happiness of fools*]

Suppose, then, that a man could look down from a great height as the poets say Jove does, how many calamities he would see in man's life! How miserable and sordid his birth and how laborious his education! He would see the many injuries he is subject to in childhood, the laboriousness of his youth, the oppressiveness of his old age, and the hard inevitability of death for him. This man would observe the army of diseases man is plagued with; the misfortunes that wait for him at every turn; the inconveniences that assault him. He would see nothing without some touch of gall, and this is without mentioning those things man does to man. Things of this type are: poverty, imprisonment, disgrace, shame, torture, plots, slander, lawsuits, and fraud. In doing this, however, I am clearly trying to count the grains of sand. It would not be right for me to relate right now for what offenses men have deserved these things or to say what angry god caused them to be born into such misery. Yet will not anyone who ponders these things approve the example of the Milesian virgins, even if it is pitiable? But what kind of people have committed suicide because of the tedium of life? Were they not neighbors of wisdom? Besides Diogenes, Xenocrates, Cato, Cassius, and Brutus, there is Chiron who chose death above immortality. Now you see, I warrant, what would happen if all men became wise: there would be a need for new clay and another potter like Prometheus.

But with a mixture of ignorance, thoughtlessness, forgetfulness of evil, hope of good things, and sometimes a sprinkling of pleasure, I bring relief from troubles so that men are loath to give up their lives even when, their thread of life having been cut by the Fates, their lives are ready to leave them. The tedium of life is so far from touching them that the less reason they have for living, the more they enjoy life. Certainly it is because of my gift that you see those old men of Nestor's age whose appearance is hardly human: babbling, silly, toothless, white-haired, bald—or even better, let me describe them in Aristophanes' words: dirty, stooped, wrinkled, bald, toothless, and toolless. Yet they are so delighted with life and desire so much to be young again that one dyes his hoary hair, another covers his bald spot with a toupee, another uses false teeth he obtained from heaven knows where, and still another is desperately in love with some young girl and acts sillier than any adolescent. For it is becoming fashionable and the usual thing for these old sticks and dry bones to marry some tender young wife who has no dowry and is sure to be enjoyed by others in the future. However, it is even more hilarious to watch the old women, almost dead with age and so like corpses that they seem to have returned from the dead. Still, they go around saying: "How good it is to be alive." They are always in heat, and they hire some Phaon to escort them about for a large sum. They painstakingly make up their faces. They can hardly pull themselves away from a mirror. They pluck out hairs from the strangest places. They show their withered and flabby breasts. And, with a quivering voice, they try to stir up a faint desire. They drink, go around in the company of young girls, and write love letters. They are laughed at by everyone because of their great foolishness. But they are pleased with themselves. They are bathed in delights and completely immersed in honey—all this happiness because of my gift! Of those who scorn this type of folly, I would only ask that they consider whether it is not better to lead a pleasant life of folly like this than to look for, as they say, the rope and rafters. Anyway, that their actions are scorned by people means nothing to my fools, for they either do not realize that anything is wrong or, if they do realize it, they easily shrug it off. If a rock falls on your head, that is certainly painful; but shame, disgrace, insult, and curses are only harmful in so much as they are realized. If there is no realization, there can be no harm done. What harm is done if the whole world hisses you, so long as you applaud yourself? Folly is what helps a person to do this.

However, I seem to hear the philosophers disagreeing. They say that it is misery itself to live in folly, to err, to be deceived, and to be ignorant. On the contrary, however, this is what it is to be human. I cannot see why they call this kind of life miserable when it is the common lot of all men to be born, brought up, and constituted in such a way. Nothing is miserable that is constant with its own nature. If so, then who would argue that man should be pitied because he cannot fly like a bird, walk on four feet with the rest of the animals, or be fitted out with horns like the bulls? In the same way the finest horse could be called unhappy because it is neither a grammarian nor a gourmet. Therefore, a foolish man is no more unhappy or ill-fated than an illiterate horse for the simple reason that each defect belongs to the particular nature.

The casuists argue next that men are naturally imperfect and support and strengthen themselves by the peculiarly human device of study. As if to make it appear that nature, who was so careful in making the flowers and herbs, should have dozed in making man so that he would need the sciences; but these were really thought up by Theuth, the evil genius of the human race, for the hurt of mankind. Instead of being instruments for the happiness of mankind, they hinder it. That is what that most prudent king of Plato also says about the discovery of letters. Therefore, studies crept in along with the other trials of men and from the same instigators who brought all the ills into man's life. Their name is "demons," from the Greek δαἱμ ουας, which means "those who know."

The people of the golden age lived without the advantage of learning and lived under the influence of instinct and nature. What need was there for a grammar when everyone spoke the same language and speech was only needed so that one person could communicate with another? What use was there for dialectic when there was no conflict of opinion? What place was there for rhetoric when no one wished to take advantage of another? What need for skill in law since all those evil practices that brought forth our good laws were non-existent? Furthermore, they were too religious to peer with irreverent curiosity into the secrets of nature, to measure the size, movement, and influence of the stars, or to seek the hidden causes of things. They considered it a sacrilege for a man to try to know more than he should. That insane inquiry as to what is beyond the heavens never even came into their minds. However, man slowly fell from the innocence of the golden age and soon the arts were invented, as I have said, by evil spirits; at first there were only a few of them, and only a few people took them up. Later, hundreds more were added by the superstition of the Chaldeans and the idle speculation of the Greeks. This was simply looking for trouble, since even one grammatical system is enough to make life one endless moment of torture.

Among these arts the ones closest to common sense (that is, to folly) are valued most highly. Theologians go hungry, scientists are given the cold shoulder, astrologers are laughed at, and logicians are ignored.

"The doctor alone," they say, "is worth more than all the rest"; and to the extent that this doctor is unskilled, audacious, and ignorant, the more is he honored among the rich and noble men. However, medicine as it is now practiced by so many is no less a part of the art of flattery than rhetoric is. The lawyers take second place behind the doctors; perhaps they should even be first but I hesitate to join the philosophers who usually laugh at lawyers for being such asses. Their estates grow, while the theologian who has examined and pondered over trunkfuls of manuscripts lives on beans and wages an arduous war against lice and fleas. As those arts are more pleasant that have the greater affinity with folly, so those people are far more happy who abstain from any traffic with learning and follow nature alone as their guide. She lacks nothing, unless perchance man wants to overrun the boundaries placed for him. Nature hates counterfeits; the less something is touched by art, the happier it is.

For, do you not see that those species of living things are happiest that are the furthest away from any mental discipline and are led by no other guide than nature? What could be happier or more wonderful than the bees? They do not have all the senses of the body; but what architect can be found to equal them in building and what philosopher is there who could frame a republic to match theirs? The horse, on the other hand, does have some human senses and travels around with men and, and as a result, shares some of their ills. He feels ashamed if he is defeated in a race, and while seeking glory in war he is run through and bites the dust with his rider. Along with this he endures the hard bit, the sharp spurs, the prisonlike stable, the whips, the sticks, and straps, the rider—in short, all the tragedy of servitude that he adds to himself when he tries to imitate brave men and zealously seeks vengeance against the enemy. How much more desirable, except for the treacheries of men, is the life of flies and birds, who live for the moment and by the light of nature. Birds, however, if they are shut up in a cage and taught to sing, soon lose all the luster of their natural beauty. For in every sphere what is nature is happier than what is falsified by art.

Therefore, I can never praise enough that cock (really Pythagoras) who had been all things: philosopher, man, woman, king, subject, fish, horse, frog, and perhaps even a sponge; and who concluded that no animal was as miserable as man. All other animals are content with their natural limitations. Man alone tries to overstep his. Among men, furthermore, the foolish are in many respects placed before the learned and great. Gryllus was more wise than the crafty Odysseus when he preferred to grunt in a sty rather than to expose himself to further dangers. Homer, the father of fiction, does not seem to disagree with this, since he often observes that men are wretched and miserable and very often describes Ulysses, the exemplar of wisdom, as wretched, but he never speaks in this way of Paris, Ajax, or Achilles. The reason for this lies in the fact that sly and artful Ulysses never did anything without the counsel of Pallas, the goddess of wisdom. Is that not having too much wisdom and getting too far away from nature? Among men, those who seek wisdom are the furthest from happiness. They are fools twice over because they forget that they were born men and try to affect the life of gods, after the example of the giants. They use their arts as instruments with which to attack nature. It follows, therefore, that they are least unhappy who are closest to the folly of brute beasts and who never attempt anything beyond their capacity as men.

There is no need for us to argue this out of Stoic syllogisms, however, when we can prove it by an evident example. By the immortal gods, I ask you, is there anyone happier than that class of people who are commonly called morons, fools, nitwits, and simpletons—most beautiful names in my opinion? I may seem to be speaking foolishly and absurdly at first, but it is profoundly true. First of all they have no fear of death—not an insignificant evil, by Jove! They are free from the pangs of conscience. They are not terrified by stories of the dead nor frightened by ghosts and hobgoblins. They are not tortured by the fear of approaching evils nor filled with hope for future goods. To sum up, they are not troubled by the thousand cares this life brings to all men. They feel no shame, fear, ambition, envy, or love. If they were any closer to brute beasts, they would not even be able to sin—or so the theologians say. I would like you to count the cares that trouble your soul day and night, O foolish philosopher, and then you would understand how much I do for my followers. They are not only always rejoicing, playing, singing, and laughing but even spread these things wherever they go, as if they were given the favor of the gods to lighten the sadness of human life.

In a world where men are mostly at odds, everyone together recognizes, seeks out, feeds, favors, embraces my followers as their friends. They even permit them to do and say what they wish with impunity. No one wants to hurt them, not even the wild beasts who sense their harmlessness and do not attack them. They are certainly sacred to the gods, especially to me, and therefore everyone honors them. Why, kings cannot eat or travel or endure an hour without their fools who give them the greatest delight. In fact, they regard them more highly than the crabbed counselors whom they keep around for appearances. I do not think this preference is so strange, and it can easily be explained. Counselors, depending on their wisdom, bring to kings only the unpleasant truth, and they are not afraid of sometimes scraping the tender ears of princes. Fools, however, present only what the rulers want: jokes, laughter, scoffing, and other delights.

Fools also have this not insignificant virtue: they alone are candid and truthful. What is more praiseworthy than truth? Even though Alcibiades thought that only children and drunkards speak the truth, all the praise is really owed to me as is proved by this line of Euripides: "The fool speaks foolish things." Whatever a fool has in his heart shows itself in his expression and speech. A wise man, however, has two tongues, as Euripides mentions, one of which speaks the truth, the other speaking what happens to be expedient at the moment. He changes white into black and cold into hot in the same breath; and he speaks what is far from being in his heart. For this reason kings seem to me to be the most unhappy because they lack people from whom they can get the truth and are forced to have flatterers for friends. Someone might say that kings hate wise men and avoid them because they fear that one of them might dare to speak the truth rather than what is pleasant; and this is true, kings hate the truth. It is quite admirable, then, that kings will listen with relish to not only a truth but quite a sharp truth from my fools. If this same statement were spoken by a wise man, however, he would surely die. But coming from a fool, it gives great pleasure. A truth, if it gives no offense, has a certain genuine spirit of pleasure, but the gods give this power only to fools. It is for these reasons, too, that these same fools are taken up by women who are naturally inclined to pleasure and frivolity. Moreover, they can explain away whatever they do with these fools as good clean fun, even when the sport becomes serious; for this sex is ingenious, especially at covering up its own lapses.

Now let us return to the subject of the happiness of fools. They live a life filled with happiness, with no fear of death, or sense of it, and then go straight to the Elysian fields. There they entertain the pious and idle shades with their tricks. Let us now compare the life of a wise man with that of a fool. Think up some model of wisdom to oppose this fool, someone who spent his boyhood and youth laboring in the classroom, who dissipated the best part of his life with sleepless nights, cares, and worry and who never tasted a bit of pleasure for the rest of his life. He was always abstemious, poor, unhappy, and crabby. He is harsh and unjust to himself, oppressive and hateful to others. He is pale, emaciated, sickly, sore-eyed, prematurely old and gray, and dying before his time. What difference does it make when he dies, since he never really lived? This is your glorious image of a wise man for you. . . .

I do not say, however, that every delusion or wandering of the mind should be called madness. A shortsighted man who thinks a mule is an ass is not considered insane; nor is someone who thinks that a trite poem is a very good one immediately thought to be insane. However, if a person is continually and extraordinarily deceived not only by his senses but even his judgment, then people will think him, at least, very nearly mad. For example, suppose he thinks he is listening to a symphony orchestra whenever an ass brays; or, if he is a pauper, suppose he believes he is Croesus, King of Lydia. This is surely insanity; but if it gives pleasure, as it usually does, it is extremely enjoyable both for those who are possessed by it and for those who watch it and are not mad in the same manner. For this type of madness is more widespread than the ordinary man realizes. One madman laughs at another, and they each give enjoyment to one another. If you watch closely, you will see that the maddest one gets the biggest laugh.

If Folly is any judge, that man is the happiest who is most thoroughly deluded. May he remain in that state which comes from me alone and is so widespread that I doubt whether there can be found one person in the whole race of man who has been wise for every moment of his life and has never been touched by some madness or other. The reason a person who believes he sees a woman when in reality he is looking at a gourd is called crazy is because this is something beyond usual experience. However, when a person thinks his wife, who is enjoyed by many, to be an ever-faithful Penelope, he is not called insane at all because people know that this is a common thing in marriage. . . .

[*The wisdom of the pious*]

In the first place Christians agree in many respects with the Platonists in that they hold that the soul is submerged and tied down with earthly chains. It is so impeded by what is crass that it hardly has a chance to contemplate or enjoy the truth. It is for this reason that Plato defined philosophy as the contemplation of death, because like death it leads the mind away from visible and corporeal things. As long as the soul uses the physical organs only, it is called sane; when, however, breaking its bonds, it attempts to assert its liberty, breaking away, as it were, from its imprisonment, it is called insane. When this condition is due to some physical ailment, then there is no doubt that it is called insanity. Yet we see people so afflicted, predict the future, understand foreign languages hitherto unknown, and give every evidence of some divine quality. There can be no doubt that now that the mind is somewhat liberated from the contagion of the body it begins to exercise its native abilities. We see the same thing in the case of those who are near death. They speak, as if inspired, of things beyond the ordinary. If this happens as a result of studied piety, though not identical with insanity, it is nonetheless so close to it that most will consider it madness. This is particularly true since only a few unimportant individuals stand apart in this respect from the common herd in their way of life.

In my opinion, what happened in the cave of Plato's myth, where he who escaped told the others bound within that the outside held realities rather than shadows, is the fate of most men. Just as they continued to believe in the shadow, thinking him deceived, so he thought them mad to be captivated by such an error. The masses do the same thing in admiring only what is corporeal and holding all else as being almost lacking in existence. Religious individuals take the opposite position and are being wrapped up in the invisible to the detriment of the physical. The majority of mankind attributes the greatest importance to riches, bodily comforts, and finally the soul, which many of them do not even believe in, as it is not seen with the eyes. The pious agree in directing their efforts first toward God, the purest of all existence, and in the second place, in what comes closest to Him, namely the soul. The care of the body they neglect. Money they disdain as husks and avoid. If they are obliged to engage in money matters, they do so unwillingly, possessing as if they did not possess.

—Translated by John P. Dolan

WILLIAM SHAKESPEARE

Shakespeare's dramas are a catalog of the Elizabethan age's rich language, graceful custom, and philosophical sensibility. Of Shakespeare's works, the tragedy of *Hamlet* most succinctly expresses the tensions of Renaissance individualism and the drama of Renaissance moral consciousness.

Young Hamlet is called back to medieval Elsinore from his humanist studies in Germany, where he has acquired the grace and education of a Renaissance courtier. Like Sophocles's Oedipus, young Hamlet must play the detective; as he seeks confirmation of the ghost's allegation, Hamlet's alienation from the other courtiers deepens. His madness is not entirely feigned, and he finds kindred spirits only among the roving players, who deal in the artifice of language and disguise. In the end, Hamlet avenges his father, but in his anguished self-consciousness has shown his unsuitability for the ruthless work of governing. As Machiavelli might have said, Hamlet was called by fortune to a ruthless task for which his own intelligence and sensitivity made him ill-suited.

For analysis and interpretation:

1. Drawing on several scenes and speeches, analyze the conflict between Hamlet's Renaissance humanist sensibility and his medieval obligation to avenge his father's death.

2. Discuss the play's use of the masque and theater as metaphors for life. Compare the analogy between theater and life to examples from other writings of this period (for example, Erasmus, Machiavelli, Cervantes).

3. In what ways does Hamlet's moral sensitivity retard his ability to act? Compare Hamlet to other characters able to act boldly through greed (king), folly (Laertes), or ruthlessness (Fortinbras).

4. To what degree is *Hamlet* a humanist play, in the sense of that term that is developed in other examples of Renaissance writing?

Hamlet, Prince of Denmark

[*Dramatis Personae*
CLAUDIUS, King of Denmark.
HAMLET, *son to the late, and nephew to the present king.*
POLONIUS, *lord chamberlain.*
HORATIO, *friend to Hamlet.*
LAERTES, *son to Polonius.*
VOLTIMAND,
CORNELIUS,
ROSENCRANTZ   } *courtiers.*
GUILDENSTERN,
OSRIC,
A Gentleman,
A Priest.
MARCELLUS, } *officers.*
BERNARDO,
FRANCISCO, *a soldier.*
REYNALDO, *servant to Polonius.*
Players.
Two Clowns, *grave-diggers.*
FORTINBRAS, Prince of Norway.
A Captain.
English Ambassadors.

GERTRUDE, Queen of Denmark, *and mother to Hamlet.*
OPHELIA, *daughter to Polonius.*

Lords, Ladies, Officers, Soldiers, Sailors, Messengers, *and other* Attendants.
Ghost of Hamlet's Father.

SCENE: *Denmark.*]

[ACT I.
SCENE I. *Elsinore. A platform before the castle.*]

Enter BERNARDO *and* FRANCISCO, *two sentinals.*

BER.   Who's there?

FRAN.   Nay, answer me: stand, and unfold yourself.

BER.   Long live the king!

FRAN.   Bernardo?

BER.   He.

FRAN.   You come most carefully upon your hour.

BER.   'Tis now struck twelve; get thee to bed, Francisco.

FRAN.   For this relief much thanks: 'tis bitter cold,
And I am sick at heart.

BER.   Have you had quiet guard?

FRAN.   Not a mouse stirring.   10

BER.   Well, good night.
If you do meet Horatio and Marcellus,
The rivals of my watch, bid them make haste.

Enter HORATIO *and* MARCELLUS.

FRAN.   I think I hear them. Stand, ho! Who is there?

HOR.   Friends to this ground.

MAR.   And liegemen to the Dane.

FRAN.   Give you good night.

MAR.   O, farewell, honest soldier:
Who hath reliev'd you?

FRAN.   Bernardo hath my place.
Give you good night.   *Exit* FRAN.

MAR.   Holla! Bernardo!

BER.   Say,
What, is Horatio there?

HOR.   A piece of him.   19

BER.   Welcome, Horatio: welcome, good Marcellus.

MAR.   What, has this thing appear'd again to-night?

BER.   I have seen nothing.

MAR.   Horatio says 'tis but our fantasy,
And will not let belief take hold of him
Touching this dreaded sight, twice seen of us:
Therefore I have entreated him along
With us to watch the minutes of this night;
That if again this apparition come,
He may approve our eyes and speak to it.

HOR.   Tush, tush, 'twill not appear.

BER.   Sit down awhile;
And let us once again assail your ears,   30

> That are so fortified against our story
> What we have two nights seen.

HOR.   Well, sit we down,
> And let us hear Bernardo speak of this.

BER.   Last night of all,
> When yond same star that's westward from the pole
> Had made his course t' illume that part of heaven
> Where now it burns, Marcellus and myself,
> The bell then beating one,—

Enter GHOST.

MAR.   Peace, break thee off; look, where it comes again!   40

BER.   In the same figure, like the king that's dead.

MAR.   Thou art a scholar; speak to it, Horatio.

BER.   Looks 'a not like the king? mark it, Horatio.

HOR.   Most like: it harrows me with fear and wonder.

BER.   It would be spoke to.

MAR.   Speak to it, Horatio.

HOR.   What art thou that usurp'st this time of night,
> Together with that fair and warlike form
> In which the majesty of buried Denmark
> Did sometimes march? by heaven I charge thee, speak!

MAR.   It is offended.

BER.   See, it stalks away!   50

HOR.   Stay! speak, speak! I charge thee, speak!   *Exit* GHOST.

MAR.   'Tis gone, and will not answer.

BER.   How now, Horatio! you tremble and look pale:
> Is not this something more than fantasy?
> What think you on 't?

HOR.   Before my God, I might not this believe
> Without the sensible and true avouch
> Of mine own eyes.

MAR.   Is it not like the king?

HOR.   As thou art to thyself: 60
> Such was the very armour he had on
> When he the ambitious Norway combated;
> So frown'd he once, when, in an angry parle,
> He smote the sledded Polacks on the ice.
> 'Tis strange.

MAR.   Thus twice before, and jump at this dead hour,
> With martial stalk hath he gone by our watch.

HOR.   In what particular thought to work I know not;
But in the gross and scope of my opinion,
This bodes some strange eruption to our state.

MAR.   Good now, sit down, and tell me, he that knows,   70
Why this same strict and most observant watch
So nightly toils the subject of the land,
And why such daily cast of brazen cannon,
And foreign mart for implements of war;
Why such impress of shipwrights, whose sore task
Does not divide the Sunday from the week;
What might be toward, that this sweaty haste
Doth make the night joint-labourer with the day:
Who is 't that can inform me?

HOR.   That can I;
At least, the whisper goes so. Our last king,   80
Whose image even but now appear'd to us,
Was, as you know, by Fortinbras of Norway,
Thereto prick'd on by a most emulate pride,
Dar'd to the combat; in which our valiant Hamlet—
For so this side of our known world esteem'd him—
Did slay this Fortinbras; who, by a seal'd compact,
Well ratified by law and heraldry,
Did forfeit, with his life, all those his lands
Which he stood seiz'd of, to the conqueror: 90
Against the which, a moiety competent
Was gaged by our king; which had return'd
To the inheritance of Fortinbras,
Had he been vanquisher; as, by the same comart,
And carriage of the article design'd,
His fell to Hamlet. Now, sir, young Fortinbras,
Of unimproved mettle hot and full,
Hath in the skirts of Norway here and there
Shark'd up a list of lawless resolutes,
For food and diet, to some enterprise
That hath a stomach in 't; which is no other—   100
As it doth well appear unto our state—
But to recover of us, by strong hand
And terms compulsatory, those foresaid lands
So by his father lost: and this, I take it,
Is the main motive of our preparations,
The source of this our watch and the chief head
Of this post-haste and romage in the land.

BER.   I think it be no other but e'en so:

      Well may it sort that this portentous figure
      Comes armed through our watch; so like the king   110
      That was and is the question of these wars.
HOR.   A mote it is to trouble the mind's eye.
      In the most high and palmy state of Rome,
      A little ere the mightiest Julius fell,
      The graves stood tenantless and the sheeted dead
      Did squeak and gibber in the Roman streets:
      As stars with trains of fire and dews of blood,
      Disasters in the sun; and the moist star
      Upon whose influence Neptune's empire stands
      Was sick almost to doomsday with eclipse: 120
      And even the like precurse of fear'd events,
      As harbingers preceding still the fates
      And prologue to the omen coming on,
      Have heaven and earth together demonstrated
      Unto our climatures and countrymen.—

Enter GHOST.

      But soft, behold! lo, where it comes again!
      I'll cross it, though it blast me. Stay, illusion!
      If thou hast any sound, or use of voice,
      Speak to me!   *It spreads his arms.*
      If there be any good thing to be done,   130
      That may to thee do ease and grace to me,
      Speak to me!
      If thou art privy to thy country's fate,
      Which, happily, foreknowing may avoid,
      O, speak!
      Or if thou hast uphoarded in thy life
      Extorted treasure in the womb of earth,
      For which, they say, you spirits oft walk in death,

                                  The cock crows.

Speak of it: stay, and speak! Stop it, Marcellus.
MAR.   Shall I strike at it with my partisan?   140
HOR.   Do, if it will not stand.
BER.   'Tis here!
HOR.   'Tis here!
MAR.   'Tis gone!   [*Exit* GHOST.]
      We do it wrong, being so majestical,
      To offer it the show of violence;
      For it is, as the air, invulnerable,
      And our vain blows malicious mockery.
BER.   It was about to speak, when the cock crew.

HOR.   And then it started like a guilty thing
  Upon a fearful summons. I have heard,
  The cock, that is the trumpet to the morn,   150
  Doth with his lofty and shrill-sounding throat
  Awake the god of day; and, at his warning,
  Whether in sea or fire, in earth or air,
  Th' extravagant and erring spirit hies
  To his confine: and of the truth herein
  This present object made probation.

MAR.   It faded on the crowing of the cock.
  Some say that ever 'gainst that season comes
  Wherein our Saviour's birth is celebrated,
  The bird of dawning singeth all night long: 160
  And then, they say, no spirit dare stir abroad;
  The nights are wholesome; then no planets strike,
  No fairy takes, nor witch hath power to charm,
  So hallow'd and so gracious is that time.

HOR.   So have I heard and do in part believe it.
  But, look, the morn, in russet mantle clad,
  Walks o'er the dew of yon high eastward hill:
  Break we our watch up; and by my advice,
  Let us impart what we have seen to-night   170
  Unto young Hamlet; for, upon my life,
  This spirit, dumb to us, will speak to him.
  Do you consent we shall acquaint him with it,
  As needful in our loves, fitting our duty?

MAR.   Let's do 't, I pray; and I this morning know
  Where we shall find him most conveniently.   *Exeunt.*

[SCENE II. *A room of state in the castle.*]

Flourish. Enter CLAUDIUS, KING OF DENMARK, GERTRUDE *the* QUEEN, COUNCILORS,
POLONIUS *and his Son* LAERTES, HAMLET, *with others* [*including* VOLTIMAND
and CORNELIUS].

KING.   Though yet of Hamlet our dear brother's death
  The memory be green, and that it us befitted
  To bear our hearts in grief and our whole kingdom
  To be contracted in one brow of woe,
  Yet so far hath discretion fought with nature
  That we with wisest sorrow think on him,
  Together with remembrance of ourselves.
  Therefore our sometime sister, now our queen,
  Th' imperial jointress to this warlike state,

Have we, as 'twere with a defeated joy,—   10
With an auspicious and a dropping eye,
With mirth in funeral and with dirge in marriage,
In equal scale weighing delight and dole,—
Taken to wife: nor have we herein barr'd
Your better wisdoms, which have freely gone
With this affair along. For all, our thanks.
Now follows, that you know, young Fortinbras,
Holding a weak supposal of our worth,
Or thinking by our late dear brother's death
Our state to be disjoint and out of frame,   20
Colleagued with this dream of his advantage,
He hath not fail'd to pester us with message,
Importing the surrender of those lands
Lost by his father, with all bands of law,
To our most valiant brother. So much for him.
Now for ourself and for this time of meeting:
Thus much the business is: we have here writ
To Norway, uncle of young Fortinbras,—
Who, impotent and bed-rid, scarcely hears
Of this his nephew's purpose,—to suppress   30
His further gait herein; in that the levies,
The lists and full proportions, are all made
Out of his subject: and we here dispatch
You, good Cornelius, and you, Voltimand,
For bearers of this greeting to old Norway;
Giving to you no further personal power
To business with the king, more than the scope
Of these delated articles allow.
Farewell, and let your haste commend your duty.

COR. ⎫
VOL. ⎭ In that and all things will we show our duty.   40

KING.   We doubt it nothing: heartily farewell.
                    [*Exeunt* VOLTIMAND *and* CORNELIUS.]
And now, Laertes, what's the news with you?
You told us of some suit; what is 't, Laertes?
You cannot speak of reason to the Dane,
And lose your voice: what wouldst thou beg, Laertes,
That shall not be my offer, not thy asking?
The head is not more native to the heart,
The hand more instrumental to the mouth,
Than is the throne of Denmark to thy father.
What wouldst thou have, Laertes?   50

LAER.   My dread lord,

Your leave and favour to return to France;
From whence though willingly I came to Denmark,
To show my duty in your coronation,
Yet now, I must confess, that duty done,
My thoughts and wishes bend again toward France
And bow them to your gracious leave and pardon.

KING.   Have you your father's leave? What says Polonius?

POL.   He hath, my lord, wrung from me my slow leave
By laboursome petition, and at last
Upon his will I seal'd my hard consent: 60
I do beseech you, give him leave to go.

KING.   Take thy fair hour, Laertes; time be thine,
And thy best graces spend it at thy will!
But now, my cousin Hamlet, and my son,—

HAM.   [*Aside*] A little more than kin, and less than kind.

KING.   How is it that the clouds still hang on you?

HAM.   Not so, my lord; I am too much in the sun.

QUEEN.   Good Hamlet, cast thy nighted colour off,
And let thine eye look like a friend on Denmark.   70
Do not for ever with thy vailed lids
Seek for thy noble father in the dust:
Thou know'st 'tis common; all that lives must die,
Passing through nature to eternity.

HAM.   Ay, madam, it is common.

QUEEN.   If it be,
Why seems it so particular with thee?

HAM.   Seems, madam! nay, it is; I know not 'seems.'
'Tis not alone my inky cloak, good mother,
Nor customary suits of solemn black,
Nor windy suspiration of forc'd breath,
No, nor the fruitful river in the eye,   80
Nor the dejected 'haviour of the visage,
Together with all forms, moods, shapes of grief,
That can denote me truly: these indeed seem,
For they are actions that a man might play:
But I have that within which passeth show;
These but the trappings and the suits of woe.

KING.   'Tis sweet and cómmendable in your nature, Hamlet,
To give these mourning duties to your father:
But, you must know, your father lost a father;   90
That father lost, lost his, and the survivor bound
In filial obligation for some term
To do obsequious sorrow: but to persever

In obstinate condolement is a course
Of impious stubbornness; 'tis unmanly grief;
It shows a will most incorrect to heaven,
A heart unfortified, a mind impatient,
An understanding simple and unschool'd:
For what we know must be and is as common
As any the most vulgar thing to sense,
Why should we in our peevish opposition   100
Take it to heart? Fie! 'tis a fault to heaven,
A fault against the dead, a fault to nature,
To reason most absurd; whose common theme
Is death of fathers, and who still hath cried,
From the first corse till he that died to-day,
'This must be so.' We pray you, throw to earth
This unprevailing woe, and think of us
As of a father: for let the world take note,
You are the most immediate to our throne;
And with no less nobility of love   110
Than that which dearest father bears his son,
Do I impart toward you. For your intent
In going back to school in Wittenberg,
It is most retrograde to our desire:
And we beseech you, bend you to remain
Here, in the cheer and comfort of our eye,
Our chiefest courtier, cousin, and our son.

QUEEN.   Let not thy mother lose her prayers, Hamlet:
I pray thee, stay with us; go not to Wittenberg.

HAM.   I shall in all my best obey you, madam.   120

KING.   Why, 'tis a loving and a fair reply:
Be as ourself in Denmark. Madam, come;
This gentle and unforc'd accord of Hamlet
Sits smiling to my heart: in grace whereof,
No jocund health that Denmark drinks to-day,
But the great cannon to the clouds shall tell,
And the king's rouse the heaven shall bruit again,
Re-speaking earthly thunder. Come away.

Flourish. Exeunt all but HAMLET.

HAM.   O, that this too too sullied flesh would melt,
Thaw and resolve itself into a dew!   130
Or that the Everlasting had not fix'd
His canon 'gainst self-slaughter! O God! God!
How weary, stale, flat and unprofitable,
Seem to me all the uses of this world!
Fie on 't! ah fie! 'tis an unweeded garden,

That grows to seed; things rank and gross in nature
Possess it merely. That it should come to this!
But two months dead: nay, not so much, not two:
So excellent a king; that was, to this,
Hyperion to a satyr; so loving to my mother   140
That he might not beteem the winds of heaven
Visit her face too roughly. Heaven and earth!
Must I remember? why, she would hang on him,
As if increase of appetite had grown
By what it fed on: and yet, within a month—
Let me not think on 't—Frailty, thy name is woman!—
A little month, or ere those shoes were old
With which she followed my poor father's body,
Like Niobe, all tears:—why she, even she—
O God! a beast, that wants discourse of reason,   150
Would have mourn'd longer—married with my uncle,
My father's brother, but no more like my father
Than I to Hercules: within a month:
Ere yet the salt of most unrighteous tears
Had left the flushing in her galled eyes,
She married. O, most wicked speed, to post
With such dexterity to incestuous sheets!
It is not nor it cannot come to good:
But break, my heart; for I must hold my tongue.

Enter HORATIO, MARCELLUS, *and* BERNARDO.

HOR.   Hail to your lordship!

HAM.   I am glad to see you well: 160
         Horatio!—or I do forget myself.

HOR.   The same, my lord, and your poor servant ever.

HAM.   Sir, my good friend; I'll change that name with you:
         And what make you from Wittenberg, Horatio?
         Marcellus?

MAR.   My good lord—

HAM.   I am very glad to see you. Good even, sir.
         But what, in faith, make you from Wittenberg?

HOR.   A truant disposition, good my lord.

HAM.   I would not hear your enemy say so,   170
         Nor shall you do my ear that violence,
         To make it truster of your own report
         Against yourself: I know you are no truant.
         But what is your affair in Elsinore?
         We'll teach you to drink deep ere you depart.

HOR.   My lord, I came to see your father's funeral.

HAM.   I prithee, do not mock me, fellow-student;
    I think it was to see my mother's wedding.

HOR.   Indeed, my lord, it follow'd hard upon.

HAM.   Thrift, thrift, Horatio! the funeral bak'd meats   180
    Did coldly furnish forth the marriage tables.
    Would I had met my dearest foe in heaven
    Or ever I had seen that day, Horatio!
    My father!—methinks I see my father.

HOR.   Where, my lord?

HAM.   In my mind's eye, Horatio.

HOR.   I saw him once; 'a was a goodly king.

HAM.   'A was a man, take him for all in all,
    I shall not look upon his like again.

HOR.   My lord, I think I saw him yesternight.

HAM.   Saw? who?   190

HOR.   My lord, the king your father.

HAM.   The king my father!

HOR.   Season your admiration for a while
    With an attent ear, till I may deliver,
    Upon the witness of these gentlemen,
    This marvel to you.

HAM.   For God's love, let me hear.

HOR.   Two nights together had these gentlemen,
    Marcellus and Bernardo, on their watch,
    In the dead waste and middle of the night,
    Been thus encount'red. A figure like your father,
    Armed at point exactly, cap-a-pe,   200
    Appears before them, and with solemn march
    Goes slow and stately by them: thrice he walk'd
    By their oppress'd and fear-surprised eyes,
    Within his truncheon's length; whilst they, distill'd
    Almost to jelly with the act of fear,
    Stand dumb and speak not to him. This to me
    In dreadful secrecy impart they did;
    And I with them the third night kept the watch:
    Where, as they had deliver'd, both in time,
    Form of the thing, each word made true and good,   210
    The apparition comes: I knew your father;
    These hands are not more like.

HAM.   But where was this?

MAR.   My lord, upon the platform where we watch'd.

HAM.   Did you not speak to it?

HOR.   My lord, I did;
              But answer made it none: yet once methought
              It lifted up it head and did address
              Itself to motion, like as it would speak;
              But even then the morning cock crew loud,
              And at the sound it shrunk in haste away,
              And vanish'd from our sight.

HAM.   'Tis very strange.   220

HOR.   As I do live, my honour'd lord, 'tis true;.
              And we did think it writ down in our duty
              To let you know of it.

HAM.   Indeed, indeed, sirs, but this troubles me.
              Hold you the watch to-night?

MAR.   ⎫
              ⎬   We do, my lord.
BER.   ⎭

HAM. Arm'd, say you?

MAR.   ⎫
              ⎬   Arm'd, my lord.
BER.   ⎭

HAM.   From top to toe?

MAR.   ⎫
              ⎬   My lord, from head to foot.
BER.   ⎭

HAM.   Then saw you not his face?

HOR.   O, yes, my lord; he wore his beaver up.   230

HAM.   What, look'd he frowningly?

HOR.   A countenance more in sorrow than in anger.

HAM.   Pale or red?

HOR.   Nay, very pale.

HAM.   And fix'd his eyes upon you?

HOR.   Most constantly.

HAM.   I would I had been there.

HOR.   It would have much amaz'd you.

HAM.   Very like, very like. Stay'd it long?

HOR.   While one with moderate haste might tell a hundred.

MAR.   ⎫
              ⎬ Longer, longer.
BER.   ⎭

HOR.   Not when I saw't.

HAM.   His beard was grizzled,—no?   240

HOR.   It was, as I have seen it in his life,
              A sable silver'd.

HAM.   I will watch to-night;

Perchance 'twill walk again.

HOR.   I warr'nt it will.

HAM.   If it assume my noble father's person,
I'll speak to it, though hell itself should gape
And bid me hold my peace. I pray you all,
If you have hitherto conceal'd this sight,
Let it be tenable in your silence still;
And whatsoever else shall hap to-night,
Give it an understanding, but no tongue: 250
I will requite your loves. So, fare you well:
Upon the platform, 'twixt eleven and twelve,
I'll visit you.

ALL.   Our duty to your honour.

HAM.   Your loves, as mine to you: farewell.

Exeunt [all but HAMLET].

My father's spirit in arms! all is not well;
I doubt some foul play: would the night were come!
Till then sit still, my soul: foul deeds will rise,
Though all the earth o'erwhelm them, to men's eyes.

Exit.

[SCENE III. *A room in Polonius' house.*]

Enter LAERTES *and* OPHELIA, *his Sister.*

LAER.   My necessaries are embark'd: farewell:
And, sister, as the winds give benefit
And convoy is assistant, do not sleep,
But let me hear from you.

OPH.   Do you doubt that?

LAER.   For Hamlet and the trifling of his favour,
Hold it a fashion and a toy in blood,
A violet in the youth of primy nature,
Forward, not permanent, sweet, not lasting,
The perfume and suppliance of a minute;
No more.

OPH.   No more but so?

LAER.   Think it no more: 10
For nature, crescent, does not grow alone
In thews and bulk, but, as this temple waxes,
The inward service of the mind and soul
Grows wide withal. Perhaps he loves you now,
And now no soil nor cautel doth besmirch

The virtue of his will: but you must fear,
His greatness weigh'd, his will is not his own;
For he himself is subject to his birth:
He may not, as unvalued persons do,
Carve for himself; for on his choice depends   20
The safety and health of this whole state;
And therefore must his choice be circumscrib'd
Unto the voice and yielding of that body
Whereof he is the head. Then if he says he loves you,
It fits your wisdom so far to believe it
As he in his particular act and place
May give his saying deed; which is no further
Than the main voice of Denmark goes withal.
Then weigh what loss your honour may sustain,
If with too credent ear you list his songs,   30
Or lose your heart, or your chaste treasure open
To his unmast'red importunity.
Fear it, Ophelia, fear it, my dear sister,
And keep you in the rear of your affection,
Out of the shot and danger of desire.
The chariest maid is prodigal enough,
If she unmask her beauty to the moon:
Virtue itself 'scapes not calumnious strokes:
The canker galls the infants of the spring,
Too oft before their buttons be disclos'd,   40
And in the morn and liquid dew of youth
Contagious blastments are most imminent.
Be wary then; best safety lies in fear:
Youth to itself rebels, though none else near.

OPH.   I shall the effect of this good lesson keep,
As watchman to my heart. But, good my brother,
Do not, as some ungracious pastors do,
Show me the steep and thorny way to heaven;
Whiles, like a puff'd and reckless libertine,
Himself the primrose path of dalliance treads,   50
And recks not his own rede.

Enter POLONIUS.

LAER.   O, fear me not.
I stay too long: but here my father comes.
A double blessing is a double grace;
Occasion smiles upon a second leave.

POL.   Yet here, Laertes? aboard, aboard, for shame!
The wind sits in the shoulder of your sail,

And you are stay'd for. There; my blessing with thee!
And these few precepts in thy memory
Look thou character. Give thy thoughts no tongue,
Nor any unproportion'd thought his act.   60
Be thou familiar, but by no means vulgar.
Those friends thou hast, and their adoption tried,
Grapple them to thy soul with hoops of steel;
But do not dull thy palm with entertainment
Of each new-hatch'd, unfledg'd comrade. Beware
Of entrance to a quarrel, but being in,
Bear 't that th' opposed may beware of thee.
Give every man thy ear, but few thy voice;
Take each man's censure, but reserve thy judgement.   70
Costly thy habit as thy purse can buy,
But not express'd in fancy; rich, not gaudy;
For the apparel oft proclaims the man,
And they in France of the best rank and station
Are of a most select and generous chief in that.
Neither a borrower nor a lender be;
For loan oft loses both itself and friend,
And borrowing dulleth edge of husbandry.
This above all: to thine own self be true,
And it must follow, as the night the day,
Thou canst not then be false to any man.   80
Farewell: my blessing season this in thee!

LAER.   Most humbly do I take my leave, my lord.

POL.   The time invites you; go; your servants tend.

LAER.   Farewell, Ophelia; and remember well
What I have said to you.

OPH.   'Tis in my memory lock'd,
And you yourself shall keep the key of it.

LAER.   Farewell.   *Exit* LAERTES.

POL.   What is 't, Ophelia, he hath said to you?

OPH.   So please you, something touching the Lord Hamlet.

POL.   Marry, well bethought: 90
'Tis told me, he hath very oft of late
Given private time to you; and you yourself
Have of your audience been most free and bounteous:
If it be so, as so 't is put on me,
And that in way of caution, I must tell you,
You do not understand yourself so clearly
As it behoves my daughter and your honour.
What is between you? give me up the truth.

OPH.   He hath, my lord, of late made many tenders
       Of his affection to me.   100

POL.   Affection! pooh! you speak like a green girl,
       Unsifted in such perilous circumstance.
       Do you believe his tenders, as you call them?

OPH.   I do not know, my lord, what I should think.

POL.   Marry, I will teach you: think yourself a baby;
       That you have ta'en these tenders for true pay,
       Which are not sterling. Tender yourself more dearly;
       Or—not to crack the wind of the poor phrase,
       Running it thus—you'll tender me a fool.

OPH.   My lord, he hath importun'd me with love   110
       In honourable fashion.

POL.   Ay, fashion you may call it; go to, go to.

OPH.   And hath given countenance to his speech, my lord,
       With almost all the holy vows of heaven.

POL.   Ay, springes to catch woodcocks. I do know,
       When the blood burns, how prodigal the soul
       Lends the tongue vows: these blazes, daughter,
       Giving more light than heat, extinct in both,
       Even in their promise, as it is a-making,
       You must not take for fire. From this time   120
       Be somewhat scanter of your maiden presence;
       Set your entreatments at a higher rate
       Than a command to parley. For Lord Hamlet,
       Believe so much in him, that he is young,
       And with a larger tether may he walk
       Than may be given you: in few, Ophelia,
       Do not believe his vows; for they are brokers,
       Not of that dye which their investments show,
       But mere implorators of unholy suits,
       Breathing like sanctified and pious bawds,   130
       The better to beguile. This is for all:
       I would not, in plain terms, from this time forth,
       Have you so slander any moment leisure,
       As to give words or talk with the Lord Hamlet.
       Look to 't, I charge you: come your ways.

OPH.   I shall obey, my lord.   *Exeunt.*

[SCENE IV. *The platform.*]

Enter HAMLET, HORATIO, *and* MARCELLUS.

HAM.   The air bites shrewdly; it is very cold.

HOR.   It is a nipping and an eager air.

HAM.   What hour now?

HOR.   I think it lacks of twelve.

MAR.   No, it is struck.

HOR.   Indeed? I heard it not: then it draws near the season
        Wherein the spirit held his wont to walk.

                          A flourish of trumpets, and two pieces go off.
        What does this mean, my lord?

HAM.   The king doth wake to-night and takes his rouse,
        Keeps wassail, and the swagg'ring up-spring reels;
        And, as he drains his draughts of Rhenish down,   10
        The kettle-drum and trumpet thus bray out
        The triumph of his pledge.

HOR.   Is it a custom?

HAM.   Ay, marry, is 't:
        But to my mind, though I am native here
        And to the manner born, it is a custom
        More honour'd in the breach than the observance.
        This heavy-headed revel east and west
        Makes us traduc'd and tax'd of other nations:
        They clepe us drunkards, and with swinish phrase
        Soil our addition; and indeed it takes   20
        From our achievements, though perform'd at height,
        The pith and marrow of our attribute.
        So, oft it chances in particular men,
        That for some vicious mole of nature in them,
        As, in their birth—wherein they are not guilty,
        Since nature cannot choose his origin—
        By the o'ergrowth of some complexion,
        Oft breaking down the pales and forts of reason,
        Or by some habit that too much o'er-leavens
        The form of plausive manners, that these men,   30
        Carrying, I say, the stamp of one defect,
        Being nature's livery, or fortune's star,—
        Their virtues else—be they as pure as grace,
        As infinite as man may undergo—
        Shall in the general censure take corruption
        From that particular fault: the dram of e'il
        Doth all the noble substance of a doubt
        To his own scandal.

Enter GHOST.

HOR.   Look, my lord, it comes!

HAM.   Angels and ministers of grace defend us!

Be thou a spirit of health or goblin damn'd,   40
Bring with thee airs from heaven or blasts from hell,
Be thy intents wicked or charitable,
Thou com'st in such a questionable shape
That I will speak to thee: I'll call thee Hamlet,
King, father, royal Dane: O, answer me!
Let me not burst in ignorance; but tell
Why thy canoniz'd bones, hearsed in death,
Have burst their cerements; why the sepulchre,
Wherein we saw thee quietly interr'd,
Hath op'd his ponderous and marble jaws,   50
To cast thee up again. What may this mean,
That thou, dead corse, again in complete steel
Revisit'st thus the glimpses of the moon,
Making night hideous; and we fools of nature
So horridly to shake our disposition
With thoughts beyond the reaches of our souls?
Say, why is this? wherefore? what should we do?

                                        [GHOST] *beckons* [HAMLET].

HOR.   It beckons you to go away with it,
        As if it some impartment did desire
        To you alone.

MAR.   Look, with what courteous action   60
        It waves you to a more removed ground:
        But do not go with it.

HOR.   No, by no means.

HAM.   It will not speak; then I will follow it.

HOR.   Do not, my lord!

HAM.   Why, what should be the fear?
        I do not set my life at a pin's fee;
        And for my soul, what can it do to that,
        Being a thing immortal as itself?
        It waves me forth again: I'll follow it.

HOR.   What if it tempt you toward the flood, my lord,
        Or to the dreadful summit of the cliff   70
        That beetles o'er his base into the sea,
        And there assume some other horrible form,
        Which might deprive your sovereignty of reason
        And draw you into madness? think of it:
        The very place puts toys of desperation,
        Without more motive, into every brain
        That looks so many fathoms to the sea
        And hears it roar beneath.

HAM.   It waves me still.
Go on; I'll follow thee.

MAR.   You shall not go, my lord.

HAM.   Hold off your hands!

HOR.   Be rul'd; you shall not go.   80

HAM.   My fate cries out,
And makes each petty artere in this body
As hardy as the Nemean lion's nerve.
Still am I call'd. Unhand me, gentlemen.
By heaven, I'll make a ghost of him that lets me!
I say, away! Go on; I'll follow thee.

                                        Exeunt GHOST *and* HAMLET.

HOR.   He waxes desperate with imagination.

MAR.   Let's follow; 'tis not fit thus to obey him.

HOR.   Have after. To what issue will this come?

MAR.   Something is rotten in the state of Denmark.

HOR.   Heaven will direct it.

MAR.   Nay, let's follow him.   *Exeunt.*

[SCENE V. *Another part of the platform.*]

Enter GHOST *and* HAMLET.

HAM.   Whither wilt thou lead me? speak; I'll go no further.

GHOST.   Mark me.

HAM.   I will.

GHOST.   My hour is almost come,
When I to sulphurous and tormenting flames
Must render up myself.

HAM.   Alas, poor ghost!

GHOST.   Pity me not, but lend thy serious hearing
To what I shall unfold.

HAM.   Speak; I am bound to hear.

GHOST.   So art thou to revenge, when thou shalt hear.

HAM.   What?

GHOST.   I am thy father's spirit,
Doom'd for a certain term to walk the night,   10
And for the day confin'd to fast in fires,
Till the foul crimes done in my days of nature
Are burnt and purg'd away. But that I am forbid
To tell the secrets of my prison-house,
I could a tale unfold whose lightest word
Would harrow up thy soul, freeze thy young blood,

Make thy two eyes, like stars, start from their spheres,
Thy knotted and combined locks to part
And each particular hair to stand an end,
Like quills upon the fretful porpentine: 20
But this eternal blazon must not be
To ears of flesh and blood. List, list, O, list!
If thou didst ever thy dear father love—

HAM.   O God!

GHOST.   Revenge his foul and most unnatural murder.

HAM.   Murder!

GHOST.   Murder most foul, as in the best it is;
But this most foul, strange and unnatural.

HAM.   Haste me to know 't, that I, with wings as swift
As meditation or the thoughts of love,   30
May sweep to my revenge.

GHOST.   I find thee apt;
And duller shouldst thou be than the fat weed
That roots itself in ease on Lethe wharf,
Wouldst thou not stir in this. Now, Hamlet, hear:
'Tis given out that, sleeping in my orchard,
A serpent stung me; so the whole ear of Denmark
Is by a forged process of my death
Rankly abus'd: but know, thou noble youth,
The serpent that did sting thy father's life
Now wears his crown.

HAM.   O my prophetic soul!   40
My uncle!

GHOST.   Ay, that incestuous, that adulterate beast,
With witchcraft of his wit, with traitorous gifts,—
O wicked wit and gifts, that have the power
So to seduce!—won to his shameful lust
The will of my most seeming-virtuous queen:
O Hamlet, what a falling-off was there!
From me, whose love was of that dignity
That it went hand in hand even with the vow
I made to her in marriage, and to decline   50
Upon a wretch whose natural gifts were poor
To those of mine!
But virtue, as it never will be moved,
Though lewdness court it in a shape of heaven,
So lust, though to a radiant angel link'd,
Will sate itself in a celestial bed,
And prey on garbage.

But, soft! methinks I scent the morning air;
Brief let me be. Sleeping within my orchard,
My custom always of the afternoon,   60
Upon my secure hour thy uncle stole,
With juice of cursed hebona in a vial,
And in the porches of my ears did pour
The leperous distilment; whose effect
Holds such an enmity with blood of man
That swift as quicksilver it courses through
The natural gates and alleys of the body,
And with a sudden vigour it doth posset
And curd, like eager droppings into milk,
The thin and wholesome blood: so did it mine;   70
And a most instant tetter bark'd about,
Most lazar-like, with vile and loathsome crust,
All my smooth body.
Thus was I, sleeping, by a brother's hand
Of life, of crown, of queen, at once dispatch'd:
Cut off even in the blossoms of my sin,
Unhous'led, disappointed, unanel'd,
No reck'ning made, but sent to my account
With all my imperfections on my head:
O, horrible! O, horrible! most horrible!   80
If thou hast nature in thee, bear it not;
Let not the royal bed of Denmark be
A couch for luxury and damned incest.
But, howsomever thou pursues this act,
Taint not thy mind, nor let thy soul contrive
Against thy mother aught: leave her to heaven
And to those thorns that in her bosom lodge,
To prick and sting her. Fare thee well at once!
The glow-worm shows the matin to be near,
And 'gins to pale his uneffectual fire: 90
Adieu, adieu, adieu! remember me.   [*Exit.*]

HAM.   O all you host of heaven! O earth! what else?
And shall I couple hell? O, fie! Hold, hold, my heart;
And you, my sinews, grow not instant old,
But bear me stiffly up. Remember thee!
Ay, thou poor ghost, whiles memory holds a seat
In this distracted globe. Remember thee!
Yea, from the table of my memory
I'll wipe away all trivial fond records,
All saws of books, all forms, all pressures past,   100
That youth and observation copied there;

And thy commandment all alone shall live
Within the book and volume of my brain,
Unmix'd with baser matter: yes, by heaven!
O most pernicious woman!
O villain, villain, smiling, damned villain!
My tables,—meet it is I set it down,
That one may smile, and smile, and be a villain;
At least I am sure it may be so in Denmark: [*Writing.*]
So, uncle, there you are. Now to my word;   110
It is 'Adieu, adieu! remember me.'
I have sworn't.

Enter HORATIO *and* MARCELLUS.

HOR.   My lord, my lord,—

MAR.   Lord Hamlet,—

HOR.   Heavens secure him!

HAM.   So be it!

MAR.   Hillo, ho, ho, my lord!

HAM.   Hillo, ho, ho, boy! come, bird, come.

MAR.   How is 't, my noble lord?

HOR.   What news, my lord?

HAM.   O, wonderful!

HOR.   Good my lord, tell it.

HAM.   No; you will reveal it.

HOR.   Not I, my lord, by heaven.

MAR.   Nor I, my lord.   120

HAM.   How say you, then; would heart of man once think it?
But you'll be secret?

HOR. ⎫
MAR. ⎭   Ay, by heaven, my lord.

HAM.   There's ne'er a villain dwelling in all Denmark
But he's an arrant knave.

HOR.   There needs no ghost, my lord, come from the grave
To tell us this.

HAM.   Why, right; you are in the right;
And so, without more circumstance at all,
I hold it fit that we shake hands and part:
You, as your business and desire shall point you;
For every man has business and desire,   130
Such as it is; and for my own poor part,
Look you, I'll go pray.

HOR.   These are but wild and whirling words, my lord.

HAM.   I am sorry they offend you, heartily;
    Yes, 'faith, heartily.

HOR.   There's no offence, my lord.

HAM.   Yes, by Saint Patrick, but there is, Horatio,
    And much offence too. Touching this vision here,
    It is an honest ghost, that let me tell you:
    For your desire to know what is between us,
    O'ermaster 't as you may. And now, good friends,   140
    As you are friends, scholars and soldiers,
    Give me one poor request.

HOR.   What is 't, my lord? we will.

HAM.   Never make known what you have seen to-night.

HOR. ⎫
      ⎬ My lord, we will not.
MAR. ⎭

HAM.   Nay, but swear 't.

HOR.   In faith,
    My lord, not I.

MAR.   Nor I, my lord, in faith.

HAM.   Upon my sword.

MAR.   We have sworn, my lord, already.

HAM.   Indeed, upon my sword, indeed.

                      GHOST *cries under the stage.*

GHOST.   Swear.

HAM.   Ah, ha, boy! say'st thou so? art thou there, truepenny?
    Come on—you hear this fellow in the cellarage—   150
    Consent to swear.

HOR.   Propose the oath, my lord.

HAM.   Never to speak of this that you have seen,
    Swear by my sword.

GHOST.   [*Beneath*] Swear.

HAM.   Hic et ubique? then we'll shift our ground.
    Come hither, gentlemen,
    And lay your hands again upon my sword:
    Swear by my sword,
    Never to speak of this that you have heard.   160

GHOST.   [*Beneath*] Swear by his sword.

HAM.   Well said, old mole! canst work i' th' earth so fast?
    A worthy pioneer! Once more remove, good friends.

HOR.   O day and night, but this is wondrous strange!

HAM.   And therefore as a stranger give it welcome.
There are more things in heaven and earth, Horatio,
Than are dreamt of in your philosophy. But come;
Here, as before, never, so help you mercy,
How strange or odd soe'er I bear myself,   170
As I perchance hereafter shall think meet
To put an antic disposition on,
That you, at such times seeing me, never shall,
With arms encumb'red thus, or this head-shake,
Or by pronouncing of some doubtful phrase,
As 'Well, well, we know,' or 'We could, an if we would,'
Or 'If we list to speak,' or 'There be, an if they might,'
Or such ambiguous giving out, to note
That you know aught of me: this not to do,
So grace and mercy at your most need help you,   180
Swear.

GHOST.   [*Beneath*] Swear.

HAM.   Rest, rest, perturbed spirit! [*They swear*]. So, gentlemen,
With all my love I do commend me to you:
And what so poor a man as Hamlet is
May do, t' express his love and friending to you,
God willing, shall not lack. Let us go in together;
And still your fingers on your lips, I pray.
The time is out of joint: O cursed spite,
That ever I was born to set it right!   190
Nay, come, let's go together.   *Exeunt.*

[ACT II.

SCENE I. *A room in Polonius' house.*]

Enter old POLONIUS *with his man* [REYNALDO].

POL.   Give him this money and these notes, Reynaldo.

REY.   I will, my lord.

POL.   You shall do marvellous wisely, good Reynaldo.
Before you visit him, to make inquire
Of his behaviour.

REY.   My lord, I did intend it.

POL.   Marry, well said; very well said. Look you, sir,
Inquire me first what Danskers are in Paris;
And how, and who, what means, and where they keep,
What company, at what expense; and finding   10
By this encompassment and drift of question
That they do know my son, come you more nearer
Than your particular demands will touch it:

Take you, as 'twere, some distant knowledge of him;
As thus, 'I know his father and his friends,
And in part him:' do you mark this, Reynaldo?

REY.   Ay, very well, my lord.

POL.   'And in part him; but' you may say 'not well:
But, if 't be he I mean, he 's very wild;
Addicted so and so;' and there put on him
What forgeries you please; marry, none so rank   20
As may dishonour him; take heed of that;
But, sir, such wanton, wild and usual slips
As are companions noted and most known
To youth and liberty.

REY.   As gaming, my lord.

POL.   Ay, or drinking, fencing, swearing, quarrelling,
Drabbing: you may go so far.

REY.   My lord, that would dishonour him.

POL.   'Faith, no; as you may season it in the charge.
You must not put another scandal on him,
That he is open to incontinency;   30
That's not my meaning: but breathe his faults so quaintly
That they may seem the taints of liberty,
The flash and outbreak of a fiery mind,
A savageness in unreclaimed blood,
Of general assault.

REY.   But, my good lord,—

POL.   Wherefore should you do this?

REY.   Ay, my lord,
I would know that.

POL.   Marry, sir, here's my drift;
And, I believe, it is a fetch of wit:
You laying these slight sullies on my son,   40
As 'twere a thing a little soil'd i' th' working,
Mark you,
Your party in converse, him you would sound,
Having ever seen in the prenominate crimes
The youth you breathe of guilty, be assur'd
He closes with you in this consequence;
'Good sir,' or so, or 'friend,' or 'gentleman,'
According to the phrase or the addition
Of man and country.

REY.   Very good, my lord.

POL.   And then, sir, does 'a this—'a does—what was I about to say? By the mass, I
was about to say something: where did I leave?   50

REY.   At 'closes in the consequence,' at 'friend or so,' and 'gentleman.'

POL.   At 'closes in the consequence,' ay, marry;
      He closes thus: 'I know the gentleman;
      I saw him yesterday, or t' other day,
      Or then, or then; with such, or such; and, as you say,
      There was 'a gaming; there o'ertook in 's rouse;
      There falling out at tennis;' or perchance,
      'I saw him enter such a house of sale,'
      Videlicet, a brothel, or so forth.
      See you now;   60
      Your bait of falsehood takes this carp of truth:
      And thus do we of wisdom and of reach,
      With windlasses and with assays of bias,
      By indirections find directions out:
      So by my former lecture and advice,
      Shall you my son. You have me, have you not?

REY.   My lord, I have.

POL.   God bye ye; fare ye well.

REY.   Good my lord!

POL.   Observe his inclination in yourself.

REY.   I shall, my lord.   70

POL.   And let him ply his music.

REY.   Well, my lord.

POL.   Farewell!   *Exit* REYNALDO.

Enter OPHELIA.

               How now, Ophelia! what's the matter?

OPH.   O, my lord, my lord, I have been so affrighted!

POL.   With what, i' th' name of God?

OPH.   My lord, as I was sewing in my closet,
      Lord Hamlet, with his doublet all unbrac'd;
      No hat upon his head; his stockings foul'd,
      Ungart'red, and down-gyved to his ankle;
      Pale as his shirt; his knees knocking each other;
      And with a look so piteous in purport   80
      As if he had been loosed out of hell
      To speak of horrors,—he comes before me.

POL.   Mad for thy love?

OPH.   My lord, I do not know;
      But truly, I do fear it.

POL.   What said he?

OPH.   He took me by the wrist and held me hard;
Then goes he to the length of all his arm;
And, with his other hand thus o'er his brow,
He falls to such perusal of my face
As 'a would draw it. Long stay'd he so;
At last, a little shaking of mine arm   90
And thrice his head thus waving up and down,
He rais'd a sigh so piteous and profound
As it did seem to shatter all his bulk
And end his being: that done, he lets me go:
And with his head over his shoulder turn'd,
He seems to find his way without his eyes;
For out o' doors he went without their helps,
And to the last, bended their light on me.

POL.   Come, go with me: I will go seek the king.
This is the very ecstacy of love,   100
Whose violent property fordoes itself
And leads the will to desperate undertakings
As oft as any passion under heaven
That does afflict our natures. I am sorry.
What, have you given him any hard words of late?

OPH.   No, my good lord, but, as you did command,
I did repel his letters and denied
His access to me.

POL.   That hath made him mad.
I am sorry that with better heed and judgement
I had not quoted him: I fear'd he did but trifle,   110
And meant to wrack thee; but, beshrew my jealousy!
By heaven, it is as proper to our age
To cast beyond ourselves in our opinions
As it is common for the younger sort
To lack discretion. Come, go we to the king:
This must be known; which, being kept close, might move
More grief to hide than hate to utter love.
Come.   *Exeunt.*

[SCENE II. *A room in the castle.*]

Flourish. Enter KING *and* QUEEN, ROSENCRANTZ, *and* GUILDENSTERN [*with others*].

KING.   Welcome, dear Rosencrantz and Guildenstern!
Moreover that we much did long to see you,
The need we have to use you did provoke
Our hasty sending. Something have you heard
Of Hamlet's transformation; so call it,

Sith nor th' exterior nor the inward man
Resembles that it was. What it should be,
More than his father's death, that thus hath put him
So much from th' understanding of himself,
I cannot dream of: I entreat you both, 10
That, being of so young days brought up with him,
And sith so neighbour'd to his youth and haviour,
That you vouchsafe your rest here in our court
Some little time: so by your companies
To draw him on to pleasures, and to gather,
So much as from occasion you may glean,
Whether aught, to us unknown, afflicts him thus,
That, open'd, lies within our remedy.

QUEEN. Good gentlemen, he hath much talk'd of you;
And sure I am two men there are not living 20
To whom he more adheres. If it will please you
To show us so much gentry and good will
As to expend your time with us awhile,
For the supply and profit of our hope,
Your visitation shall receive such thanks
As fits a king's remembrance.

ROS.   Both your majesties
Might, by the sovereign power you have of us,
Put your dread pleasures more into command
Than to entreaty.

GUIL.   But we both obey,
And here give up ourselves, in the full bent 30
To lay our service freely at your feet,
To be commanded.

KING. Thanks, Rosencrantz and gentle Guildenstern.

QUEEN. Thanks, Guildenstern and gentle Rosencrantz:
And I beseech you instantly to visit
My too much changed son. Go, some of you,
And bring these gentlemen where Hamlet is.

GUIL. Heavens make our presence and our practices
Pleasant and helpful to him!

QUEEN.   Ay, amen!
   Exeunt ROSENCRANTZ *and* GUILDENSTERN [*with some* ATTENDANTS].

Enter POLONIUS.

POL. Th' ambassadors from Norway, my good lord,
Are joyfully return'd. 41

KING.   Thou still hast been the father of good news.

POL.   Have I, my lord? I assure my good liege,
I hold my duty, as I hold my soul,
Both to my God and to my gracious king:
And I do think, or else this brain of mine
Hunts not the trail of policy so sure
As it hath us'd to do, that I have found
The very cause of Hamlet's lunacy.

KING.   O, speak of that; that do I long to hear.   50

POL.   Give first admittance to th' ambassadors;
My news shall be the fruit to that great feast.

KING.   Thyself do grace to them, and bring them in.

                                                        [*Exit* POLONIUS.]

He tells me, my dear Gertrude, he hath found
The head and source of all your son's distemper.

QUEEN.   I doubt it is no other but the main;
His father's death, and our o'erhasty marriage.

KING.   Well, we shall sift him.

Enter AMBASSADORS [VOLTIMAND *and* CORNELIUS, *with* POLONIUS].

                Welcome, my good friends!
Say, Voltimand, what from our brother Norway?
Volt. Most fair return of greetings and desires.
Upon our first, he sent out to suppress   60
His nephew's levies; which to him appear'd
To be a preparation 'gainst the Polack;
But, better look'd into, he truly found
It was against your highness: whereat griev'd,
That so his sickness, age and impotence
Was falsely borne in hand, sends out arrests
On Fortinbras; which he, in brief, obeys;
Receives rebuke from Norway, and in fine
Makes vow before his uncle never more
To give th' assay of arms against your majesty.   70
Whereon old Norway, overcome with joy,
Gives him three score thousand crowns in annual fee,
And his commission to employ those soldiers,
So levied as before, against the Polack:
With an entreaty, herein further shown,   [*Giving a paper.*]
That it might please you to give quiet pass
Through your dominions for this enterprise,
On such regards of safety and allowance
As therein are set down.

KING.   It likes us well;   80
And at our more consider'd time we'll read,
Answer, and think upon this business.
Meantime we thank you for your well-took labour:
Go to your rest; at night we'll feast together:
Most welcome home!   *Exeunt* AMBASSADORS.

POL.   This business is well ended.
My liege, and madam, to expostulate
What majesty should be, what duty is,
Why day is day, night night, and time is time,
Were nothing but to waste night, day and time.
Therefore, since brevity is the soul of wit,   90
And tediousness the limbs and outward flourishes,
I will be brief: your noble son is mad:
Mad call I it; for, to define true madness,
What is 't but to be nothing else but mad?
But let that go.

QUEEN.   More matter, with less art.

POL.   Madam, I swear I use no art at all.
That he is mad, 'tis true: 'tis true 'tis pity;
And pity 'tis 'tis true: a foolish figure;
But farewell it, for I will use no art.
Mad let us grant him, then: and now remains   100
That we find out the cause of this effect,
Or rather say, the cause of this defect,
For this effect defective comes by cause:
Thus it remains, and the remainder thus.
Perpend.
I have a daughter—have while she is mine—
Who, in her duty and obedience, mark,
Hath given me this: now gather, and surmise. [*Reads the*] *letter.* 'To the celes-
tial and my soul's idol, the most beautified Ophelia,'—   110
That's an ill phrase, a vile phrase; 'beautified' is a vile phrase: but you shall
hear. Thus: [*Reads.*]
'In her excellent white bosom, these, &c.'

QUEEN.   Came this from Hamlet to her?

POL.   Good madam, stay awhile; I will be faithful.   [*Reads.*]
                    'Doubt thou the stars are fire;
                    Doubt that the sun doth move;
                    Doubt truth to be a liar;
                    But never doubt I love.
'O dear Ophelia, I am ill at these numbers; I have not art to reckon my groans: 119
but that I love thee best, O most best, believe it. Adieu.
'Thine evermore, most dear lady, whilst this machine is to him, HAMLET.'

This, in obedience, hath my daughter shown me,
And more above, hath his solicitings,
As they fell out by time, by means and place,
All given to mine ear.

KING.   But how hath she
Receiv'd his love?

POL.   What do you think of me?

KING.   As of a man faithful and honourable.

POL.   I would fain prove so. But what might you think,
When I had seen this hot love on the wing—   130
As I perceiv'd it, I must tell you that,
Before my daughter told me—what might you,
Or my dear majesty your queen here, think,
If I had play'd the desk or table-book,
Or given my heart a winking, mute and dumb,
Or look'd upon this love with idle sight;
What might you think? No, I went round to work,
And my young mistress thus I did bespeak:
'Lord Hamlet is a prince, out of thy star;
This must not be:' and then I prescripts gave her,   140
That she should lock herself from his resort,
Admit no messengers, receive no tokens.
Which done, she took the fruits of my advice;
And he, repelled—a short tale to make—
Fell into a sadness, then into a fast,
Thence to a watch, thence into a weakness,
Thence to a lightness, and, by this declension,
Into the madness wherein now he raves,
And all we mourn for.

KING.   Do you think 'tis this?

QUEEN.   It may be, very like.   150

POL.   Hath there been such a time—I would fain know that—
That I have positively said ''Tis so,'
When it prov'd otherwise?

KING.   Not that I know.

POL.   [*Pointing to his head and shoulder*] Take this from this, if this be otherwise:
If circumstances lead me, I will find
Where truth is hid, though it were hid indeed
Within the centre.

KING.   How may we try it further?

POL.   You know, sometimes he walks four hours together
Here in the lobby.

QUEEN.   So he does indeed.   160

POL.   At such a time I'll loose my daughter to him:
      Be you and I behind an arras then;
      Mark the encounter: if he love her not
      And be not from his reason fall'n thereon,
      Let me be no assistant for a state,
      But keep a farm and carters.

KING.   We will try it.

Enter HAMLET [*reading on a book*].

QUEEN.   But, look, where sadly the poor wretch comes reading.

POL.   Away, I do beseech you both, away:
                       Exeunt KING *and* QUEEN [*with* ATTENDANTS].
      I'll board him presently. O, give me leave.
      How does my good Lord Hamlet?   170

HAM.   Well, God-a-mercy.

POL.   Do you know me, my lord?

HAM.   Excellent well; you are a fishmonger.

POL.   Not I, my lord.

HAM.   Then I would you were so honest a man.

POL.   Honest, my lord!

HAM.   Ay, sir; to be honest, as this world goes, is to be one man picked out of ten thousand.

POL.   That's very true, my lord.   180

HAM.   For if the sun breed maggots in a dead dog, being a good kissing carrion,— Have you a daughter?

POL.   I have, my lord.

HAM.   Let her not walk i' the sun: conception is a blessing: but as your daughter may conceive—Friend, look to 't.

POL.   [*Aside*] How say you by that? Still harping on my daughter: yet he knew me not at first; 'a said I was a fishmonger: 'a is far gone, far gone: and truly in my youth I suffered much extremity for love; very near this. I'll speak to him again. What do you read, my lord?

HAM.   Words, words, words.   190

POL.   What is the matter, my lord?

HAM.   Between who?

POL.   I mean, the matter that you read, my lord.

HAM.   Slanders, sir: for the satirical rogue says here that old men have grey beards, that their faces are wrinkled, their eyes purging thick amber and plum-tree gum and that they have a plentiful lack of wit, together with most weak hams: all which, sir, though I most powerfully and potently believe, yet I hold it not honesty to have it thus set down, for yourself, sir, should be old as I am, if like a crab you could go backward.

POL.   [*Aside*] Though this be madness, yet there is method in 't.—Will you walk out
     of the air, my lord?   201

HAM.   Into my grave.

POL.   Indeed, that's out of the air. [*Aside*] How pregnant sometimes his replies are!
     a happiness that often madness hits on, which reason and sanity could not so
     prosperously be delivered of. I will leave him, and suddenly contrive the means
     of meeting between him and my daughter.—My honourable lord, I will most
     humbly take my leave of you.

HAM.   You cannot, sir, take from me any thing that I will more willingly part withal:
     except my life, except my life, except my life.

Enter GUILDENSTERN *and* ROSENCRANTZ.

POL.   Fare you well, my lord.   210

HAM.   These tedious old fools!

POL.   You go to seek the Lord Hamlet; there he is.

ROS.   [*To* POLONIUS] God save you, sir!   [*Exit* POLONIUS.]

GUIL.   My honoured lord!

ROS.   My most dear lord!

HAM.   My excellent good friends! How dost thou, Guildenstern? Ah, Rosencrantz!
     Good lads, how do ye both?

ROS.   As the indifferent children of the earth.

GUIL.   Happy, in that we are not over-happy;
     On Fortune's cap we are not the very button.   220

HAM.   Nor the soles of her shoe?

ROS.   Neither, my lord.

HAM.   Then you live about her waist, or in the middle of her favours?

GUIL.   'Faith, her privates we.

HAM.   In the secret parts of Fortune? O, most true; she is a strumpet. What's the
     news?

ROS.   None, my lord, but that the world's grown honest.

HAM.   Then is doomsday near: but your news is not true. Let me question more in
     particular: what have you, my good friends, deserved at the hands of Fortune,
     that she sends you to prison hither?

GUIL.   Prison, my lord!   230

HAM.   Denmark's a prison.

ROS.   Then is the world one.

HAM.   A goodly one; in which there are many confines, wards and dungeons,
     Denmark being one o' the worst.

ROS.   We think not so, my lord.

HAM.   Why, then, 'tis none to you; for there is nothing either good or bad, but think-
     ing makes it so: to me it is a prison.

ROS.   Why then, your ambition makes it one; 'tis too narrow for your mind.

HAM.   O God, I could be bounded in a nutshell and count myself a king of infinite
space, were it not that I have bad dreams.   240

GUIL.   Which dreams indeed are ambition, for the very substance of the ambitious
is merely the shadow of a dream.

HAM.   A dream itself is but a shadow.

ROS.   Truly, and I hold ambition of so airy and light a quality that it is but a shadow's
shadow.

HAM.   Then are our beggars bodies, and our monarchs and outstretched heroes the
beggars' shadows. Shall we to the court? for, by my fay, I cannot reason.

ROS. ⎫
      ⎬ We'll wait upon you.
GUIL. ⎭

HAM.   No such matter: I will not sort you with the rest of my servants, for, to speak
to you like an honest man, I am most dreadfully attended. But, in the beaten
way of friendship, what make you at Elsinore?   251

ROS.   To visit you, my lord; no other occasion.

HAM.   Beggar that I am, I am even poor in thanks; but I thank you: and sure, dear
friends, my thanks are too dear a halfpenny. Were you not sent for? Is it your
own inclining? Is it a free visitation? Come, come, deal justly with me: come,
come; nay, speak.

GUIL.   What should we say, my lord?

HAM.   Why, any thing, but to the purpose. You were sent for; and there is a kind of
confession in your looks which your modesties have not craft enough to colour:
I know the good king and queen have sent for you.   260

ROS.   To what end, my lord?

HAM.   That you must teach me. But let me conjure you, by the rights of our fellow-
ship, by the consonancy of our youth, by the obligation of our ever-preserved
love, and by what more dear a better proposer could charge you withal, be even
and direct with me, whether you were sent for, or no?

ROS.   [*Aside to* GUIL.] What say you?

HAM.   [*Aside*] Nay, then, I have an eye of you.—If you love me, hold not off.

GUIL.   My lord, we were sent for.   268

HAM.   I will tell you why; so shall my anticipation prevent your discovery, and
your secrecy to the king and queen moult no feather. I have of late—but
wherefore I know not—lost all my mirth, forgone all custom of exercises;
and indeed it goes so heavily with my disposition that this goodly frame, the
earth, seems to me a sterile promontory, this most excellent canopy, the air,
look you, this brave o'erhanging firmament, this majestical roof fretted with
golden fire, why, it appeareth nothing to me but a foul and pestilent congre-
gation of vapours. What a piece of work is a man! how noble in reason! how
infinite in faculties! in form and moving how express and admirable! in action how like an angel! in apprehension how like a god! the beauty of the

world! the paragon of animals! And yet, to me, what is this quintessence of dust? man delights not me: no, nor woman neither, though by your smiling you seem to say so.   281

ROS.   My lord, there was no such stuff in my thoughts.

HAM.   Why did you laugh then, when I said 'man delights not me'?

ROS.   To think, my lord, if you delight not in man, what lenten entertainment the players shall receive from you: we coted them on the way; and hither are they coming, to offer you service.

HAM.   He that plays the king shall be welcome; his majesty shall have tribute of me; the adventurous knight shall use his foil and target; the lover shall not sigh gratis; the humorous man shall end his part in peace; the clown shall make those laugh whose lungs are tickle o' the sere; and the lady shall say her mind freely, or the blank verse shall halt for 't. What players are they?   291

ROS.   Even those you were wont to take delight in, the tragedians of the city.

HAM.   How chances it they travel? their residence, both in reputation and profit, was better both ways.

ROS.   I think their inhibition comes by the means of the late innovation.

HAM.   Do they hold the same estimation they did when I was in the city? are they so followed?

ROS.   No, indeed, are they not.

HAM.   How comes it? do they grow rusty?   299

ROS.   Nay, their endeavour keeps in the wonted pace: but there is, sir, an aery of children, little eyases, that cry out on the top of question, and are most tyrannically clapped for 't: these are now the fashion, and so berattle the common stages— so they call them—that many wearing rapiers are afraid of goose-quills and dare scarce come thither.

HAM.   What, are they children? who maintains 'em? how are they escoted? Will they pursue the quality no longer than they can sing? will they not say afterwards, if they should grow themselves to common players—as it is most like, if their means are no better—their writers do them wrong, to make them exclaim against their own succession?   309

ROS.   'Faith, there has been much to do on both sides; and the nation holds it no sin to tarre them to controversy: there was, for a while, no money bid for argument, unless the poet and the player went to cuffs in the question.

HAM.   Is 't possible?

GUIL.   O, there has been much throwing about of brains.

HAM.   Do the boys carry it away?

ROS.   Ay, that they do, my lord; Hercules and his load too.

HAM.   It is not very strange; for my uncle is king of Denmark, and those that would make mows at him while my father lived, give twenty, forty, fifty, a hundred ducats a-piece for his picture in little. 'Sblood, there is something in this more than natural, if philosophy could find it out.   319

A flourish [of trumpets within].

GUIL.   There are the players.

HAM.   Gentlemen, you are welcome to Elsinore. Your hands, come then: the appur-
tenance of welcome is fashion and ceremony: let me comply with you in this
garb, lest my extent to the players, which, I tell you, must show fairly outwards,
should more appear like entertainment than yours. You are welcome: but my
uncle-father and aunt-mother are deceived.

GUIL.   In what, my dear lord?

HAM.   I am but mad north-north-west: when the wind is southerly I know a hawk
from a handsaw.

Enter POLONIUS.

POL.   Well be with you, gentlemen!   329

HAM.   Hark you, Guildenstern; and you too: at each ear a hearer: that great baby you
see there is not yet out of his swaddling-clouts.

ROS.   Happily he is the second time come to them; for they say an old man is twice
a child.

HAM.   I will prophesy he comes to tell me of the players; mark it.—You say right,
sir: o' Monday morning; 'twas then indeed.

POL.   My lord, I have news to tell you.

HAM.   My lord, I have news to tell you. When Roscius was an actor in Rome,—

POL.   The actors are come hither, my lord.

HAM.   Buz, buz!

POL.   Upon my honour,—   340

HAM.   Then came each actor on his ass,—

POL.   The best actors in the world, either for tragedy, comedy, history, pastoral,
pastoral-comical, historical-pastoral, tragical-historical, tragical-comical-
historical-pastoral, scene individable, or poem unlimited: Seneca cannot be
too heavy, nor Plautus too light. For the law of writ and the liberty, these are
the only men.

HAM.   O Jephthah, judge of Israel, what a treasure hadst thou!

POL.   What a treasure had he, my lord?   348

HAM.   Why,
> 'One fair daughter, and no more,
> The which he loved passing well.'

POL.   [*Aside*] Still on my daughter.

HAM.   Am I not i' the right, old Jephthah?

POL.   If you call me Jephthah, my lord, I have a daughter that I love passing
well.

HAM.   Nay, that follows not.

POL.   What follows, then, my lord?

HAM.   Why,
'As by lot, God wot,'
and then, you know,
'It came to pass, as most like it was,'—   360
the first row of the pious chanson will show you more; for look, where my
abridgement comes.

Enter the PLAYERS.

You are welcome, masters; welcome, all. I am glad to see thee well. Welcome, good
friends. O, old friend! why, thy face is valanced since I saw thee last: comest
thou to beard me in Denmark? What, my young lady and mistress! By'r lady,
your ladyship is nearer to heaven than when I saw you last, by the altitude of a
chopine. Pray God, your voice, like a piece of uncurrent gold, be not cracked
within the ring. Masters, you are all welcome. We'll e'en to 't like French fal-
coners, fly at any thing we see: we'll have a speech straight: come, give us a
taste of your quality; come, a passionate speech.   370

FIRST PLAY.   What speech, my good lord?

HAM.   I heard thee speak me a speech once, but it was never acted; or, if it was, not
above once; for the play, I remember, pleased not the million; 'twas caviary to
the general: but it was—as I received it, and others, whose judgements in such
matters cried in the top of mine—an excellent play, well digested in the scenes,
set down with as much modesty as cunning. I remember, one said there were
no sallets in the lines to make the matter savoury, nor no matter in the phrase
that might indict the author of affectation; but called it an honest method, as
wholesome as sweet, and by very much more handsome than fine. One speech
in 't I chiefly loved: 'twas Æneas' tale to Dido; and thereabout of it especially,
where he speaks of Priam's slaughter: if it live in your memory, begin at this
line: let me see, let me see—   382
'The rugged Pyrrhus, like th' Hyrcanian beast,'—
'tis not so:—it begins with Pyrrhus:—
'The rugged Pyrrhus, he whose sable arms,
Black as his purpose, did the night resemble
When he lay couched in the ominous horse,
Hath now this dread and black complexion smear'd
With heraldry more dismal; head to foot
Now is he total gules; horridly trick'd   390
With blood of fathers, mothers, daughters, sons,
Bak'd and impasted with the parching streets,
That lend a tyrannous and a damned light
To their lord's murder: roasted in wrath and fire,
And thus o'er-sized with coagulate gore,
With eyes like carbuncles, the hellish Pyrrhus
Old grandsire Priam seeks.'

So, proceed you.

POL. 'Fore God, my lord, well spoken, with good accent and good discretion.   400

FIRST PLAY.   Anon he finds him
Striking too short at Greeks; his antique sword,
Rebellious to his arm, lies where it falls,
Repugnant to command: unequal match'd,
Pyrrhus at Priam drives; in rage strikes wide;
But with the whiff and wind of his fell sword
Th' unnerved father falls. Then senseless Ilium,
Seeming to feel this blow, with flaming top
Stoops to his base, and with a hideous crash
Takes prisoner Pyrrhus' ear: for, lo! his sword,   410
Which was declining on the milky head
Of reverend Priam, seem'd i' th' air to stick:
So, as a painted tyrant, Pyrrhus stood,
And like a neutral to his will and matter,
Did nothing.
But, as we often see, against some storm,
A silence in the heavens, the rack stand still,
The bold winds speechless and the orb below
As hush as death, anon the dreadful thunder
Doth rend the region, so, after Pyrrhus' pause,   420
Aroused vengeance sets him new a-work;
And never did the Cyclops' hammers fall
On Mars's armour forg'd for proof eterne
With less remorse than Pyrrhus' bleeding sword
Now falls on Priam.
Out, out, thou strumpet, Fortune! All you gods,
In general synod, take away her power;
Break all the spokes and fellies from her wheel,
And bowl the round nave down the hill of heaven.   430
As low as to the fiends!'

POL.   This is too long.

HAM.   It shall to the barber's, with your beard. Prithee, say on: he's for a jig or a tale
of bawdry, or he sleeps: say on: come to Hecuba.

FIRST PLAY.   'But who, ah woe! had seen the mobled queen—'

HAM.   'The mobled queen?'

POL.   That's good; 'mobled queen' is good.

FIRST PLAY.   'Run barefoot up and down, threat'ning the flames
With bisson rheum; a clout upon that head
Where late the diadem stood, and for a robe,   440
About her lank and all o'er-teemed loins,

A blanket, in the alarm of fear caught up;
Who this had seen, with tongue in venom steep'd,
'Gainst Fortune's state would treason have pronounc'd:
But if the gods themselves did see her then
When she saw Pyrrhus make malicious sport
In mincing with his sword her husband's limbs,
The instant burst of clamour that she made,
Unless things mortal move them not at all,
Would have made milch the burning eyes of heaven,   450
And passion in the gods.'

POL.   Look, whe'r he has not turned his colour and has tears in 's eyes. Prithee, no more.

HAM.   'Tis well; I'll have thee speak out the rest soon. Good my lord, will you see the players well bestowed? Do you hear, let them be well used; for they are the abstract and brief chronicles of the time: after your death you were better have a bad epitaph than their ill report while you live.

POL.   My lord, I will use them according to their desert.

HAM.   God's bodykins, man, much better: use every man after his desert, and who shall 'scape whipping? Use them after your own honour and dignity: the less they deserve, the more merit is in your bounty. Take them in.   461

POL.   Come, sirs.

HAM.   Follow him, friends: we'll hear a play tomorrow. [*Aside to* FIRST PLAYER.] Dost thou hear me, old friend; can you play the Murder of Gonzago?

FIRST PLAY.   Ay, my lord.

HAM.   We'll ha 't to-morrow night. You could, for a need, study a speech of some dozen or sixteen lines, which I would set down and insert in 't, could you not?

FIRST PLAY.   Ay, my lord.

HAM.   Very well. Follow that lord; and look you mock him not.—My good friends, I'll leave you till night: you are welcome to Elsinore.   470

Exeunt POL. *and* PLAYERS.

ROS.   Good my lord!   *Exeunt* [ROS. *and* GUIL].

HAM.   Ay, so, God bye to you.—Now I am alone.
O, what a rogue and peasant slave am I!
Is it not monstrous that this player here,
But in a fiction, in a dream of passion,
Could force his soul so to his own conceit
That from her working all his visage wann'd,
Tears in his eyes, distraction in 's aspect,
A broken voice, and his whole function suiting
With forms to his conceit? and all for nothing!   480
For Hecuba!

What's Hecuba to him, or he to Hecuba,
That he should weep for her? What would he do,
Had he the motive and the cue for passion
That I have? He would drown the stage with tears
And cleave the general ear with horrid speech,
Make mad the guilty and appal the free,
Confound the ignorant, and amaze indeed
The very faculties of eyes and ears.
Yet I,   490
A dull and muddy-mettled rascal, peak,
Like John-a-dreams, unpregnant of my cause,
And can say nothing; no, not for a king,
Upon whose property and most dear life
A damn'd defeat was made. Am I a coward?
Who calls me villain? breaks my pate across?
Plucks off my beard, and blows it in my face?
Tweaks me by the nose? gives me the lie i' th' throat,
As deep as to the lungs? who does me this?
Ha!   500
'Swounds, I should take it: for it cannot be
But I am pigeon-liver'd and lack gall
To make oppression bitter, or ere this
I should have fatted all the region kites
With this slave's offal: bloody, bawdy villain!
Remorseless, treacherous, lecherous, kindless villain!
O, vengeance!
Why, what an ass am I! This is most brave,
That I, the son of a dear father murder'd,
Prompted to my revenge by heaven and hell,   510
Must, like a whore, unpack my heart with words,
And fall a-cursing, like a very drab,
A stallion!
Fie upon 't! foh! About, my brains! Hum, I have heard
That guilty creatures sitting at a play
Have by the very cunning of the scene
Been struck so to the soul that presently
They have proclaim'd their malefactions;
For murder, though it have no tongue, will speak
With most miraculous organ. I'll have these players   520
Play something like the murder of my father
Before mine uncle: I'll observe his looks;
I'll tent him to the quick: if 'a do blench,
I know my course. The spirit that I have seen
May be the devil: and the devil hath power

T' assume a pleasing shape; yea, and perhaps
Out of my weakness and my melancholy,
As he is very potent with such spirits,
Abuses me to damn me: I'll have grounds
More relative than this: the play's the thing   530
Wherein I'll catch the conscience of the king.   *Exit.*

[ACT III.

SCENE I. *A room in the castle.*]

Enter KING, QUEEN, POLONIUS, OPHELIA, ROSENCRANTZ, GUILDENSTERN, LORDS.

KING.   And can you, by no drift of conference,
  Get from him why he puts on this confusion,
  Grating so harshly all his days of quiet
  With turbulent and dangerous lunacy?

ROS.   He does confess he feels himself distracted;
  But from what cause 'a will by no means speak.

GUIL.   Nor do we find him forward to be sounded,
  But, with a crafty madness, keeps aloof,
  When we would bring him on to some confession
  Of his true state.

QUEEN.   Did he receive you well?   10

ROS.   Most like a gentleman.

GUIL.   But with much forcing of his disposition.

ROS.   Niggard of question; but, of our demands,
  Most free in his reply.

QUEEN.   Did you assay him
  To any pastime?

ROS.   Madam, it so fell out, that certain players
  We o'er-raught on the way: of these we told him;
  And there did seem in him a kind of joy
  To hear of it: they are here about the court,   20
  And, as I think, they have already order
  This night to play before him.

POL.   'Tis most true:
  And he beseech'd me to entreat your majesties
  To hear and see the matter.

KING.   With all my heart; and it doth much content me
  To hear him so inclin'd.
  Good gentlemen, give him a further edge,
  And drive his purpose into these delights.

ROS.   We shall, my lord.   *Exeunt* ROSENCRANTZ *and* GUILDENSTERN.

KING.   Sweet Gertrude, leave us too;
     For we have closely sent for Hamlet hither,
     That he, as 'twere by accident, may here
     Affront Ophelia: 30
     Her father and myself, lawful espials,
     Will so bestow ourselves that, seeing, unseen,
     We may of their encounter frankly judge,
     And gather by him, as he is behav'd,
     If 't be th' affliction of his love or no
     That thus he suffers for.

QUEEN.   I shall obey you.
     And for your part, Ophelia, I do wish
     That your good beauties be the happy cause
     Of Hamlet's wildness: so shall I hope your virtues
     Will bring him to his wonted way again,   40
     To both your honours.

OPH.   Madam, I wish it may.   [*Exit* QUEEN.]

POL.   Ophelia, walk you here. Gracious, so please you,
     We will bestow ourselves. [*To* OPHELIA] Read on this book;
     That show of such an exercise may colour
     Your loneliness. We are oft to blame in this,—
     'Tis too much prov'd—that with devotion's visage
     And pious action we do sugar o'er
     The devil himself.

KING.   [*Aside*] O, 'tis too true!
     How smart a lash that speech doth give my conscience!
     The harlot's cheek, beautied with plast'ring art,   50
     Is not more ugly to the thing that helps it
     Than is my deed to my most painted word:
     O heavy burthen!

POL.   I hear him coming: let's withdraw, my lord.

                          [*Exeunt* KING *and* POLONIUS.]

Enter HAMLET.

HAM.   To be, or not to be: that is the question:
     Whether 'tis nobler in the mind to suffer
     The slings and arrows of outrageous fortune,
     Or to take arms against a sea of troubles,
     And by opposing end them? To die: to sleep;
     No more; and by a sleep to say we end   60
     The heartache and the thousand natural shocks
     That flesh is heir to, 'tis a consummation
     Devoutly to be wish'd. To die, to sleep;

To sleep: perchance to dream: ay, there's the rub;
For in that sleep of death what dreams may come
When we have shuffled off this mortal coil,
Must give us pause: there's the respect
That makes calamity of so long life;
For who would bear the whips and scorns of time,
Th' oppressor's wrong, the proud man's contumely,   70
The pangs of despis'd love, the law's delay,
The insolence of office and the spurns
That patient merit of th' unworthy takes,
When he himself might his quietus make
With a bare bodkin? who would fardels bear,
To grunt and sweat under a weary life,
But that the dread of something after death,
The undiscover'd country from whose bourn
No traveller returns, puzzles the will   80
And makes us rather bear those ills we have
Than fly to others that we know not of?
Thus conscience does make cowards of us all;
And thus the native hue of resolution
Is sicklied o'er with the pale cast of thought,
And enterprises of great pitch and moment
With this regard their currents turn awry,
And lose the name of action.—Soft you now!
The fair Ophelia! Nymph, in thy orisons
Be all my sins rememb'red.

OPH.   Good my lord,   90
How does your honour for this many a day?

HAM.   I humbly thank you; well, well, well.

OPH.   My lord, I have remembrances of yours,
That I have longed long to re-deliver;
I pray you, now receive them.

HAM.   No, not I;
I never gave you aught.

OPH.   My honour'd lord, you know right well you did;
And, with them, words of so sweet breath compos'd
As made the things more rich: their perfume lost,
Take these again; for to the noble mind   100
Rich gifts wax poor when givers prove unkind.
There, my lord.

HAM.   Ha, ha! are you honest?

OPH.   My lord?

HAM.   Are you fair?

OPH. What means your lordship?

HAM. That if you be honest and fair, your honesty should admit no discourse to your beauty.

OPH. Could beauty, my lord, have better commerce than with honesty? 109

HAM. Ay, truly; for the power of beauty will sooner transform honesty from what it is to a bawd than the force of honesty can translate beauty into his likeness: this was sometime a paradox, but now the time gives it proof. I did love you once.

OPH. Indeed, my lord, you made me believe so.

HAM. You should not have believed me; for virtue cannot so inoculate our old stock but we shall relish of it: I loved you not.

OPH. I was the more deceived.

HAM. Get thee to a nunnery: why wouldst thou be a breeder of sinners? I am my-self indifferent honest; but yet I could accuse me of such things that it were bet-ter my mother had not borne me: I am very proud, revengeful, ambitious, with more offences at my beck than I have thoughts to put them in, imagination to give them shape, or time to act them in. What should such fellows as I do crawl-ing between earth and heaven? We are arrant knaves, all; believe none of us. Go thy ways to a nunnery. Where's your father? 123

OPH. At home, my lord.

HAM. Let the doors be shut upon him, that he may play the fool no where but in 's own house. Farewell.

OPH. O, help him, you sweet heavens!

HAM. If thou dost marry, I'll give thee this plague for thy dowry: be thou as chaste as ice, as pure as snow, thou shalt not escape calumny. Get thee to a nunnery, go: farewell. Or, if thou wilt needs marry, marry a fool; for wise men know well enough what monsters you make of them. To a nunnery, go, and quickly too. Farewell.

OPH. O heavenly powers, restore him! 132

HAM. I have heard of your paintings too, well enough; God hath given you one face, and you make yourselves another: you jig, you amble, and you lisp; you nick-name God's creatures, and make your wantonness your ignorance. Go to, I'll no more on 't; it hath made me mad. I say, we will have no moe marriage: those that are married already, all but one, shall live; the rest shall keep as they are. To a nunnery, go. *Exit.*

OPH. O, what a noble mind is here o'er-thrown!
The courtier's, soldier's, scholar's, eye, tongue, sword; 140
Th' expectancy and rose of the fair state,
The glass of fashion and the mould of form,
Th' observ'd of all observers, quite, quite down!
And I, of ladies most deject and wretched,

That suck'd the honey of his music vows,
Now see that noble and most sovereign reason,
Like sweet bells jangled, out of time and harsh;
That unmatch'd form and feature of blown youth
Blasted with ecstasy: O, woe is me,
T' have seen what I have seen, see what I see!   150

Enter KING *and* POLONIUS.

KING.   Love! his affections do not that way tend;
Nor what he spake, though it lack'd form a little,
Was not like madness. There's something in his soul,
O'er which his melancholy sits on brood;
And I do doubt the hatch and the disclose
Will be some danger: which for to prevent,
I have in quick determination
Thus set it down: he shall with speed to England,
For the demand of our neglected tribute:
Haply the seas and countries different   160
With variable objects shall expel
This something-settled matter in his heart,
Whereon his brains still beating puts him thus
From fashion of himself. What think you on 't?

POL.   It shall do well: but yet do I believe
The origin and commencement of his grief
Sprung from neglected love. How now, Ophelia!
You need not tell us what Lord Hamlet said;
We heard it all. My lord, do as you please;
But, if you hold it fit, after the play   170
Let his queen mother all alone entreat him
To show his grief: let her be round with him;
And I'll be plac'd, so please you, in the ear
Of all their conference. If she find him not,
To England send him, or confine him where
Your wisdom best shall think.

KING.   It shall be so:
Madness in great ones must not unwatch'd go.   *Exeunt.*

[SCENE II. *A hall in the castle.*]

Enter HAMLET *and three of the* PLAYERS.

HAM.   Speak the speech, I pray you, as I pronounced it to you, trippingly on the
tongue: but if you mouth it, as many of your players do, I had as lief the town-
crier spoke my lines. Nor do not saw the air too much with your hand, thus, but
use all gently; for in the very torrent, tempest, and, as I may say, whirlwind of

your passion, you must acquire and beget a temperance that may give it smoothness. O, it offends me to the soul to hear a robustious periwig-pated fellow tear a passion to tatters, to very rags, to split the ears of the groundlings, who for the most part are capable of nothing but inexplicable dumb-shows and noise: I would have such a fellow whipped for o'er-doing Termagant; it out-herods Herod: pray you, avoid it.   10

FIRST PLAY.   I warrant your honour.

HAM.   Be not too tame neither, but let your own discretion be your tutor: suit the action to the word, the word to the action; with this special observance, that you o'er-step not the modesty of nature: for any thing so overdone is from the purpose of playing, whose end, both at the first and now, was and is, to hold, as 't were, the mirror up to nature; to show virtue her own feature, scorn her own image, and the very age and body of the time his form and pressure. Now this overdone, or come tardy off, though it make the unskillful laugh, cannot but make the judicious grieve; the censure of the which one must in your allowance o'erweigh a whole theatre of others. O, there be players that I have seen play,   20 and heard others praise, and that highly, not to speak it profanely, that, neither having the accent of Christians nor the gait of Christian, pagan, nor man, have so strutted and bellowed that I have thought some of nature's journeymen had made men and not made them well, they imitated humanity so abominably.

FIRST PLAY.   I hope we have reformed that indifferently with us, sir.

HAM.   O, reform it altogether. And let those that play your clowns speak no more than is set down for them; for there be of them that will themselves laugh, to set on some quantity of barren spectators to laugh too; though, in the mean time, some necessary question of the play be then to be considered: that 's villanous, and shows a most pitiful ambition in the fool that uses it. Go, make you ready.

[*Exeunt* PLAYERS.]

Enter POLONIUS, GUILDENSTERN, *and* ROSENCRANTZ.

How now, my lord! will the king hear this piece of work?   31

POL.   And the queen too, and that presently.

HAM.   Bid the players make haste.   [*Exit* POLONIUS.]
Will you two help to hasten them?

ROS. ⎫
           ⎬   We will, my lord.
GUIL. ⎭

Exeunt they two.

HAM.   What ho! Horatio!

Enter HORATIO.

HOR.   Here, sweet lord, at your service.

HAM.   Horatio, thou art e'en as just a man
As e'er my conversation cop'd withal.

HOR.   O, my dear lord,—

HAM.   Nay, do not think I flatter;   40
    For what advancement may I hope from thee
    That no revenue hast but thy good spirits,
    To feed and clothe thee? Why should the poor be flatter'd?
    No, let the candied tongue lick absurd pomp,
    And crook the pregnant hinges of the knee
    Where thrift may follow fawning. Dost thou hear?
    Since my dear soul was mistress of her choice
    And could of men distinguish her election,
    S' hath seal'd thee for herself; for thou hast been
    As one, in suff'ring all, that suffers nothing,
    A man that fortune's buffets and rewards   50
    Hast ta'en with equal thanks: and blest are those
    Whose blood and judgement are so well commeddled,
    That they are not a pipe for fortune's finger
    To sound what stop she please. Give me that man
    That is not passion's slave, and I will wear him
    In my heart's core, ay, in my heart of heart,
    As I do thee.—Something too much of this.—
    There is a play to-night before the king;
    One scene of it comes near the circumstance
    Which I have told thee of my father's death: 60
    I prithee, when thou seest that act afoot,
    Even with the very comment of thy soul
    Observe my uncle: if his occulted guilt
    Do not itself unkennel in one speech,
    It is a damned ghost that we have seen,
    And my imaginations are as foul
    As Vulcan's stithy. Give him heedful note;
    For I mine eyes will rivet to his face,
    And after we will both our judgements join
    In censure of his seeming.   70
HOR.   Well, my lord:
    If 'a steal aught the whilst this play is playing,
    And 'scape detecting, I will pay the theft.

Enter trumpets and kettledrums, KING, QUEEN, POLONIUS, OPHELIA
    [, ROSENCRANTZ, GUILDENSTERN, *and others*].

HAM.   They are coming to the play; I must be idle:
    Get you a place.
KING.   How fares our cousin Hamlet?
HAM.   Excellent, i' faith; of the chameleon's dish: I eat the air, promise-crammed:
    you cannot feed capons so.
KING.   I have nothing with this answer, Hamlet; these words are not mine.
HAM.   No, nor mine now. [*To* POLONIUS] My lord, you played once i' the university,

you say?   80

POL.   That did I, my lord; and was accounted a good actor.

HAM.   What did you enact?

POL.   I did enact Julius Cæsar: I was killed i' the Capitol; Brutus killed me.

HAM.   It was a brute part of him to kill so capital a calf there. Be the players ready?

ROS.   Ay, my lord; they stay upon your patience.

QUEEN.   Come hither, my dear Hamlet, sit by me.

HAM.   No, good mother, here's metal more attractive.

POL.   [*To the* KING] O, ho! do you mark that?

HAM.   Lady, shall I lie in your lap?

[Lying down at OPHELIA'S feet.]   90

OPH.   No, my lord.

HAM.   I mean, my head upon your lap?

OPH.   Ay, my lord.

HAM.   Do you think I meant country matters?

OPH.   I think nothing, my lord.

HAM.   That 's a fair thought to lie between maids' legs.

OPH.   What is, my lord?

HAM.   Nothing.

OPH.   You are merry, my lord.

HAM.   Who, I?

OPH.   Ay, my lord.   100

HAM.   O God, your only jig-maker. What should a man do but be merry? for, look
you, how cheerfully my mother looks, and my father died within's two hours.

OPH.   Nay, 'tis twice two months, my lord.

HAM.   So long? Nay then, let the devil wear black, for I'll have a suit of sables. O
heavens! die two months ago, and not forgotten yet? Then there's hope a great
man's memory may outlive his life half a year: but, by 'r lady, 'a must build
churches, then; or else shall 'a suffer not thinking on, with the hobby-horse,
whose epitaph is 'For, O, for, O, the hobby-horse is forgot.'

109

The trumpets sound. Dumb show follows.

Enter a KING *and a* QUEEN [*very lovingly*]; *the* Queen *embracing him, and he her.*
[*She kneels, and makes show of protestation unto him.*] *He takes her up, and
declines his head upon her neck: he lies him down upon a bank of flowers:
she, seeing him asleep, leaves him. Anon comes in another man, takes off his
crown, kisses it, pours poison in the sleeper's ears, and leaves him. The*
QUEEN *returns; finds the* KING *dead, makes passionate action. The* POISONER,
*with some three or four come in again, seem to condole with her. The dead
body is carried away. The* POISONER *wooes the* QUEEN *with gifts: she seems*

harsh awhile, but in the end accepts love.   [*Exeunt.*]

OPH. What means this, my lord?

HAM. Marry, this is miching mallecho; it means mischief.

OPH. Belike this show imports the argument of the play.

Enter PROLOGUE.

HAM. We shall know by this fellow: the players cannot keep counsel; they'll tell all.

OPH. Will 'a tell us what this show meant?

HAM. Ay, or any show that you'll show him: be not you ashamed to show, he'll not shame to tell you what it means.

OPH. You are naught, you are naught: I'll mark the play.

PRO. For us, and for our tragedy,
      Here stooping to your clemency,
      We beg your hearing patiently.   [*Exit.*]

HAM. Is this a prologue, or the posy of a ring?   121

OPH. 'Tis brief, my lord.

HAM. As woman's love.

Enter [*two* PLAYERS *as*] KING *and* QUEEN.

P. KING.   Full thirty times hath Phœbus' cart gone round
           Neptune's salt wash and Tellus' orbed ground,
           And thirty dozen moons with borrowed sheen
           About the world have times twelve thirties been,
           Since love our hearts and Hymen did our hands
           Unite commutual in most sacred bands.

P. QUEEN.   So many journeys may the sun and moon
            Make us again count o'er ere love be done!   130
            But, woe is me, you are so sick of late,
            So far from cheer and from your former state,
            That I distrust you. Yet, though I distrust,
            Discomfort you, my lord, it nothing must:
            For women's fear and love holds quantity;
            In neither aught, or in extremity.
            Now, what my love is, proof hath made you know;
            And as my love is siz'd, my fear is so:
            Where love is great, the littlest doubts are fear;
            Where little fears grow great, great love grows there.   140

P. KING.   'Faith, I must leave thee, love, and shortly too;
           My operant powers their functions leave to do:
           And thou shalt live in this fair world behind,
           Honour'd, belov'd; and haply one as kind

For husband shalt thou—

P. QUEEN.   O, confound the rest!
Such love must needs be treason in my breast:
In second husband let me be accurst!
None wed the second but who kill'd the first.

HAM.   [*Aside*] Wormwood, wormwood.   150

P. QUEEN.   The instances that second marriage move
Are base respects of thrift, but none of love:
A second time I kill my husband dead,
When second husband kisses me in bed.

P. KING.   I do believe you think what now you speak;
But what we do determine oft we break.
Purpose is but the slave to memory,
Of violent birth, but poor validity:
Which now, like fruit unripe, sticks on the tree;
But fall, unshaken, when they mellow be.   160
Most necessary 'tis that we forget
To pay ourselves what to ourselves is debt:
What to ourselves in passion we propose,
The passion ending, doth the purpose lose.
The violence of either grief or joy
Their own enactures with themselves destroy:
Where joy most revels, grief doth most lament;
Grief joys, joy grieves, on slender accident.
This world is not for aye, nor 'tis not strange
That even our loves should with our fortunes change;   170
For 'tis a question left us yet to prove,
Whether love lead fortune, or else fortune love.
The great man down, you mark his favourite flies;
The poor advanc'd makes friends of enemies.
And hitherto doth love on fortune tend;
For who not needs shall never lack a friend,
And who in want a hollow friend doth try,
Directly seasons him his enemy.
But, orderly to end where I begun,
Our wills and fates do so contrary run   180
That our devices still are overthrown;
Our thoughts are ours, their ends none of our own:
So think thou wilt no second husband wed;
But die thy thoughts when thy first lord is dead.

P. QUEEN.   Nor earth to me give food, nor heaven light!
Sport and repose lock from me day and night!
To desperation turn my trust and hope!

An anchor's cheer in prison be my scope!
Each opposite that blanks the face of joy
Meet what I would have well and it destroy!   190
Both here and hence pursue me lasting strife,
If, once a widow, ever I be wife!

HAM.   If she should break it now!

P. KING.   'Tis deeply sworn. Sweet, leave me here awhile;
My spirits grow dull, and fain I would beguile
The tedious day with sleep.   [*Sleeps.*]

P. QUEEN.   Sleep rock thy brain;
And never come mischance between us twain!   *Exit.*

HAM.   Madam, how like you this play?

QUEEN.   The lady doth protest too much, methinks.   200

HAM.   O, but she'll keep her word.

KING.   Have you heard the argument? Is there no offence in 't?

HAM.   No, no, they do but jest, poison in jest; no offence i' the world.

KING.   What do you call the play?

HAM.   The Mouse-trap. Marry, how? Tropically. This play is the image of a murder
done in Vienna: Gonzago is the duke's name; his wife, Baptista: you shall see
anon; 't is a knavish piece of work: but what o' that? your majesty and we that
have free souls, it touches us not: let the galled jade winch, our withers are un-
wrung.

Enter LUCIANUS.

This is one Lucianus, nephew to the king.   210

OPH.   You are as good as a chorus, my lord.

HAM.   I could interpret between you and your love, if I could see the puppets dally-
ing.

OPH.   You are keen, my lord, you are keen.

HAM.   It would cost you a groaning to take off my edge.

OPH.   Still better, and worse.

HAM.   So you mistake your husbands. Begin, murderer; pox, leave thy damnable
faces, and begin. Come: the croaking raven doth bellow for revenge.

LUC.   Thoughts black, hands apt, drugs fit, and time agreeing;
Confederate season, else no creature seeing;
Thou mixture rank, of midnight weeds collected,
With Hecate's ban thrice blasted, thrice infected,
Thy natural magic and dire property,   220
On wholesome life usurp immediately.
                    [*Pours the poison into the sleeper's ears.*]

HAM.   'A poisons him i' the garden for his estate. His name 's Gonzago: the story is extant, and written in very choice Italian: you shall see anon how the murderer gets the love of Gonzago's wife.

OPH.   The king rises.

HAM.   What, frighted with false fire!

QUEEN.   How fares my lord?

POL.   Give o'er the play.

KING.   Give me some light: away!

POL.   Lights, lights, lights!   *Exeunt all but* HAMLET *and* HORATIO.   230

HAM.   Why, let the strucken deer go weep,
            The hart ungalled play;
        For some must watch, while some must sleep
            Thus runs the world away.
        Would not this, sir, and a forest of feathers—if the rest of my fortunes turn Turk
        with me—with two Provincial roses on my razed shoes, get me a fellowship in   240
        a cry of players, sir?

HOR.   Half a share.

HAM.   A whole one, I.
        For thou dost know, O Damon dear,
            This realm dismantled was
        Of Jove himself; and now reigns here
            A very, very—pajock.

HOR.   You might have rhymed.

HAM.   O good Horatio, I'll take the ghost's word for a thousand pound. Didst perceive?

HOR.   Very well, my lord.

HAM.   Upon the talk of the poisoning?

HOR.   I did very well note him.

HAM.   Ah, ha! Come, some music! come, the recorders!
        For if the king like not the comedy,   250
        Why then, belike, he likes it not, perdy.
        Come, some music!

Enter ROSENCRANTZ *and* GUILDENSTERN.

GUIL.   Good my lord, vouchsafe me a word with you.

HAM.   Sir, a whole history.

GUIL.   The king, sir,—

HAM.   Ay, sir, what of him?

GUIL.   Is in his retirement marvellous distempered.

HAM.   With drink, sir?

GUIL.   No, my lord, rather with choler.

HAM.   Your wisdom should show itself more richer to signify this to his doctor; for,   260 for me to put him to his purgation would perhaps plunge him into far more choler.

GUIL.   Good my lord, put your discourse into some frame and start not so wildly from my affair.

HAM.   I am tame, sir: pronounce.

GUIL.   The queen, your mother, in most great affliction of spirit, hath sent me to you.

HAM.   You are welcome.

GUIL.   Nay, good my lord, this courtesy is not of the right breed. If it shall please you to make me a wholesome answer, I will do your mother's commandment: if not, your pardon and my return shall be the end of my business.

HAM.   Sir, I cannot.   271

GUIL.   What, my lord?

HAM.   Make you a wholesome answer; my wit 's diseased: but, sir, such answer as I can make, you shall command; or, rather, as you say, my mother: therefore no more, but to the matter: my mother, you say,—

ROS.   Then thus she says; your behaviour hath struck her into amazement and admiration.

HAM.   O wonderful son, that can so 'stonish a mother! But is there no sequel at the heels of this mother's admiration? Impart.

ROS.   She desires to speak with you in her closet, ere you go to bed.   280

HAM.   We shall obey, were she ten times our mother. Have you any further trade with us?

ROS.   My lord, you once did love me.

HAM.   And do still, by these pickers and stealers.

ROS.   Good my lord, what is your cause of distemper? you do, surely, bar the door upon your own liberty, if you deny your griefs to your friend.

HAM.   Sir, I lack advancement.

ROS.   How can that be, when you have the voice of the king himself for your succession in Denmark?

HAM.   Ay, sir, but 'While the grass grows,'—the proverb is something musty.   289

Enter the PLAYERS *with recorders.*

O, the recorders! let me see one. To withdraw with you:—why do you go about to recover the wind of me, as if you would drive me into a toil?

GUIL.   O, my lord, if my duty be too bold, my love is too unmannerly.

HAM.   I do not well understand that. Will you play upon this pipe?

GUIL.   My lord, I cannot.

HAM.   I pray you.

GUIL.   Believe me, I cannot.

HAM.   I do beseech you.

GUIL.   I know no touch of it, my lord.

HAM.   'Tis as easy as lying: govern these ventages with your fingers and thumb, give
it breath with your mouth, and it will discourse most eloquent music. Look you,   300
these are the stops.

GUIL.   But these cannot I command to any utterance of harmony; I have not the skill.

HAM.   Why, look you now, how unworthy a thing you make of me! You would play
upon me; you would seem to know my stops; you would pluck out the heart of
my mystery; you would sound me from my lowest note to the top of my com-
pass: and there is much music, excellent voice, in this little organ; yet cannot
you make it speak. 'Sblood, do you think I am easier to be played on than a
pipe? Call me what instrument you will, though you can fret me, you cannot
play upon me.   310

Enter POLONIUS.

God bless you, sir!

POL.   My lord, the queen would speak with you, and presently.

HAM.   Do you see yonder cloud that 's almost in shape of a camel?

POL.   By the mass, and 'tis like a camel, indeed.

HAM.   Methinks it is like a weasel.

POL.   It is backed like a weasel.

HAM.   Or like a whale?

POL.   Very like a whale.

HAM.   Then I will come to my mother by and by.
[*Aside*] They fool me to the top of my bent.—I will come by and by.   320

POL.   I will say so.   [*Exit.*]

HAM.   By and by is easily said.
Leave me, friends.   [*Exeunt all but* HAMLET.]
'Tis now the very witching time of night,
When churchyards yawn and hell itself breathes out
Contagion to this world: now could I drink hot blood,
And do such bitter business as the day
Would quake to look on. Soft! now to my mother.
O heart, lose not thy nature; let not ever
The soul of Nero enter this firm bosom: 330
Let me be cruel, not unnatural:
I will speak daggers to her, but use none;
My tongue and soul in this be hypocrites;
How in my words somever she be shent,
To give them seals never, my soul, consent!   *Exit.*

[SCENE III. *A room in the castle.*]

Enter KING, ROSENCRANTZ, *and* GUILDENSTERN.

KING.   I like him not, nor stands it safe with us
    To let his madness range. Therefore prepare you;
    I your commission will forthwith dispatch,
    And he to England shall along with you:
    The terms of our estate may not endure
    Hazard so near us as doth hourly grow
    Out of his brows.
GUIL.   We will ourselves provide:
    Most holy and religious fear it is
    To keep those many many bodies safe
    That live and feed upon your majesty.
ROS.   The single and peculiar life is bound,
    With all the strength and armour of the mind,   10
    To keep itself from noyance; but much more
    That spirit upon whose weal depend and rest
    The lives of many. The cess of majesty
    Dies not alone; but, like a gulf, doth draw
    What's near it with it: it is a massy wheel,
    Fix'd on the summit of the highest mount,
    To whose huge spokes ten thousand lesser things
    Are mortis'd and adjoin'd; which, when it falls,
    Each small annexment, petty consequence,
    Attends the boist'rous ruin. Never alone   20
    Did the king sigh, but with a general groan.
KING.   Arm you, I pray you, to this speedy voyage;
    For we will fetters put about this fear,
    Which now goes too free-footed.
ROS.   We will haste us.   *Exeunt* GENTLEMEN.

Enter POLONIUS.

POL.   My lord, he's going to his mother's closet:
    Behind the arras I'll convey myself,
    To hear the process; I'll warrant she'll tax him home:
    And, as you said, and wisely was it said,
    'Tis meet that some more audience than a mother,
    Since nature makes them partial, should o'erhear   30
    The speech, of vantage. Fare you well, my liege:
    I'll call upon you ere you go to bed,
    And tell you what I know.
KING.   Thanks, dear my lord.   *Exit* [POLONIUS].
    O, my offence is rank, it smells to heaven;

It hath the primal eldest curse upon 't,
A brother's murder. Pray can I not,
Though inclination be as sharp as will:
My stronger guilt defeats my strong intent;
And, like a man to double business bound,   40
I stand in pause where I shall first begin,
And both neglect. What if this cursed hand
Were thicker than itself with brother's blood,
Is there not rain enough in the sweet heavens
To wash it white as snow? Whereto serves mercy
But to confront the visage of offence?
A forestalled ere we come to fall,
Or pardon'd being down? Then I'll look up;
My fault is past. But, O, what form of prayer   50
Can serve my turn? 'Forgive me my foul murder'?
That cannot be: since I am still possess'd
Of those effects for which I did the murder,
My crown, mine own ambition and my queen.
May one be pardon'd and retain th' offence?
In the corrupted currents of this world
Offence's gilded hand may shove by justice,
And oft 'tis seen the wicked prize itself
Buys out the law: but 'tis not so above;
There is no shuffling, there the action lies   60
In his true nature; and we ourselves compell'd,
Even to the teeth and forehead of our faults,
To give in evidence. What then? what rests?
Try what repentance can: what can it not?
Yet what can it when one can not repent?
O wretched state! O bosom black as death!
O limed soul, that, struggling to be free,
Art more engag'd! Help, angels! Make assay!
Bow, stubborn knees; and, heart with strings of steel,
Be soft as sinews of the new-born babe!
All may be well.   [*He kneels.*]   71

Enter HAMLET.

HAM.   Now might I do it pat, now he is praying;
And now I'll do 't. And so 'a goes to heaven;
And so am I reveng'd. That would be scann'd:
A villain kills my father; and for that,
I, his sole son, do this same villain send
To heaven.
Why, this is hire and salary, not revenge.

'A took my father grossly, full of bread;
With all his crimes broad blown, as flush as May; 80
And how his audit stands who knows save heaven?
But in our circumstance and course of thought,
'Tis heavy with him: and am I then reveng'd,
To take him in the purging of his soul,
When he is fit and season'd for his passage?
No!
Up, sword; and know thou a more horrid hent:
When he is drunk asleep, or in his rage,
Or in th' incestuous pleasure of his bed;
At game, a-swearing, or about some act 90
That has no relish of salvation in 't;
Then trip him, that his heels may kick at heaven,
And that his soul may be as damn'd and black
As hell, whereto it goes. My mother stays:
This physic but prolongs thy sickly days. *Exit.*

KING. [*Rising*] My words fly up, my thoughts remain below:
Words without thoughts never to heaven go. *Exit.*

[SCENE IV. *The Queen's closet.*]

Enter [QUEEN] GERTRUDE *and* POLONIUS.

POL. 'A will come straight. Look you lay home to him:
Tell him his pranks have been too broad to bear with,
And that your grace hath screen'd and stood between
Much heat and him. I'll sconce me even here.
Pray you, be round with him.

HAM. *(Within)* Mother, mother, mother!

QUEEN. I'll warrant you,
Fear me not: withdraw, I hear him coming.

[POLONIUS *hides behind the arras.*]

Enter HAMLET.

HAM. Now, mother, what's the matter?

QUEEN. Hamlet, thou hast thy father much offended.

HAM. Mother, you have my father much offended.

QUEEN. Come, come, you answer with an idle tongue. 10

HAM. Go, go, you question with a wicked tongue.

QUEEN. Why, how now, Hamlet!

HAM. What's the matter now?

QUEEN. Have you forgot me?

HAM.   No, by the rood, not so:
You are the queen, your husband's brother's wife;
And—would it were not so!—you are my mother.

QUEEN.   Nay, then, I'll set those to you that can speak.

HAM.   Come, come, and sit you down; you shall not budge;
You go not till I set you up a glass
Where you may see the inmost part of you.

QUEEN.   What wilt thou do? thou wilt not murder me?   20
Help, help, ho!

POL.   [*Behind*] What, ho! help, help, help!

HAM.   [*Drawing*] How now! a rat? Dead, for a ducat, dead!
                                   [*Makes a pass through the
arras.*]

POL.   [*Behind*] O, I am slain!   [*Falls and dies.*]

QUEEN.   O me, what hast thou done?

HAM.   Nay, I know not:
Is it the king?

QUEEN.   O, what a rash and bloody deed is this!

HAM.   A bloody deed! almost as bad, good mother,
As kill a king, and marry with his brother.

QUEEN.   As kill a king!

HAM.   Ay, lady, it was my word.   30
                    [*Lifts up the arras and discovers* POLONIUS.]
Thou wretched, rash, intruding fool, farewell!
I took thee for thy better: take thy fortune;
Thou find'st to be too busy is some danger.
Leave wringing of your hands: peace! sit you down,
And let me wring your heart; for so I shall,
If it be made of penetrable stuff,
If damned custom have not braz'd it so
That it be proof and bulwark against sense.

QUEEN.   What have I done, that thou dar'st wag thy tongue
In noise so rude against me?

HAM.   Such an act
That blurs the grace and blush of modesty,   40
Calls virtue hypocrite, takes off the rose
From the fair forehead of an innocent love
And sets a blister there, makes marriage-vows
As false as dicers' oaths: O, such a deed
As from the body of contraction plucks
The very soul, and sweet religion makes
A rhapsody of words: heaven's face does glow

O'er this solidity and compound mass
With heated visage, as against the doom
Is thought-sick at the act.   50

QUEEN.   Ay me, what act,
That roars so loud, and thunders in the index?

HAM.   Look here, upon this picture, and on this.
The counterfeit presentment of two brothers.
See, what a grace was seated on this brow;
Hyperion's curls; the front of Jove himself;
An eye like Mars, to threaten and command;
A station like the herald Mercury
New-lighted on a heaven-kissing hill;
A combination and a form indeed,
Where every god did seem to set his seal,   60
To give the world assurance of a man:
This was your husband. Look you now, what follows:
Here is your husband; like a mildew'd ear,
Blasting his wholesome brother. Have you eyes?
Could you on this fair mountain leave to feed,
And batten on this moor? Ha! have you eyes?
You cannot call it love; for at your age
The hey-day in the blood is tame, it's humble,
And waits upon the judgement: and what judgement   69
Would step from this to this? Sense, sure, you have,
Else could you not have motion; but sure, that sense
Is apoplex'd; for madness would not err,
Nor sense to ecstasy was ne'er so thrall'd
But it reserv'd some quantity of choice,
To serve in such a difference. What devil was 't
That thus hath cozen'd you at hoodman-blind?
Eyes without feeling, feeling without sight,
Ears without hands or eyes, smelling sans all,
Or but a sickly part of one true sense
Could not so mope.   80
O shame! where is thy blush? Rebellious hell,
If thou canst mutine in a matron's bones,
To flaming youth let virtue be as wax,
And melt in her own fire: proclaim no shame
When the compulsive ardour gives the charge,
Since frost itself as actively doth burn
And reason pandars will.

QUEEN.   O Hamlet, speak no more:
Thou turn'st mine eyes into my very soul;
And there I see such black and grained spots

As will not leave their tinct.   90

HAM.   Nay, but to live
In the rank sweat of an enseamed bed,
Stew'd in corruption, honeying and making love
Over the nasty sty,—

QUEEN.   O, speak to me no more;
These words, like daggers, enter in mine ears;
No more, sweet Hamlet!

HAM.   A murderer and a villain;
A slave that is not twentieth part the tithe
Of your precedent lord; a vice of kings;
A cutpurse of the empire and the rule,
That from a shelf the precious diadem stole,
And put it in his pocket!   100

QUEEN.   No more!

Enter GHOST.

HAM.   A king of shreds and patches,—
Save me, and hover o'er me with your wings,
You heavenly guards! What would your gracious figure?

QUEEN.   Alas, he's mad!

HAM.   Do you not come your tardy son to chide,
That, laps'd in time and passion, lets go by
Th' important acting of your dread command?
O, say!

GHOST.   Do not forget: this visitation
Is but to whet thy almost blunted purpose.   110
But, look, amazement on thy mother sits:
O, step between her and her fighting soul:
Conceit in weakest bodies strongest works:
Speak to her, Hamlet.

HAM.   How is it with you, lady?

QUEEN.   Alas, how is 't with you,
That you do bend your eye on vacancy
And with th' incorporal air do hold discourse?
Forth at your eyes your spirits wildly peep;
And, as the sleeping soldiers in th' alarm,
Your bedded hair, like life in excrements,   120
Start up, and stand an end. O gentle son,
Upon the heat and flame of thy distemper
Sprinkle cool patience. Whereon do you look?

HAM.   On him, on him! Look you, how pale he glares!
His form and cause conjoin'd, preaching to stones,

Would make them capable.—Do not look upon me;
Lest with this piteous action you convert
My stern effects: then what I have to do
Will want true colour; tears perchance for blood.

QUEEN.   To whom do you speak this?   130

HAM.   Do you see nothing there?

QUEEN.   Nothing at all; yet all that is I see.

HAM.   Nor did you nothing hear?

QUEEN.   No, nothing but ourselves.

HAM.   Why, look you there! look, how it steals away!
My father, in his habit as he liv'd!
Look, where he goes, even now, out at the portal!

                                                        Exit GHOST.

QUEEN.   This is the very coinage of your brain:
This bodiless creation ecstasy
Is very cunning in.

HAM.   Ecstasy!
My pulse, as yours, doth temperately keep time,
And makes as healthful music: it is not madness   140
That I have utt'red: bring me to the test,
And I the matter will re-word, which madness
Would gambol from. Mother, for love of grace,
Lay not that flattering unction to your soul,
That not your trespass, but my madness speaks:
It will but skin and film the ulcerous place,
Whiles rank corruption, mining all within,
Infects unseen. Confess yourself to heaven;
Repent what's past; avoid what is to come;
And do not spread the compost on the weeds,   150
To make them ranker. Forgive me this my virtue;
For in the fatness of these pursy times
Virtue itself of vice must pardon beg,
Yea, curb and woo for leave to do him good.

QUEEN.   O Hamlet, thou hast cleft my heart in twain.

HAM.   O, throw away the worser part of it,
And live the purer with the other half.
Good night: but go not to my uncle's bed;
Assume a virtue, if you have it not.
That monster, custom, who all sense doth eat,   160
Of habits devil, is angel yet in this,
That to the use of actions fair and good
He likewise gives a frock or livery,

That aptly is put on. Refrain to-night,
And that shall lend a kind of easiness
To the next abstinence: the next more easy;
For use almost can change the stamp of nature,
And either [. . .] the devil, or throw him out
With wondrous potency. Once more, good night:
And when you are desirous to be bless'd,   170
I'll blessing beg of you. For this same lord,   [*Pointing to* POLONIUS.]
I do repent: but heaven hath pleas'd it so,
To punish me with this and this with me,
That I must be their scourge and minister.
I will bestow him, and will answer well
The death I gave him. So, again, good night.
I must be cruel, only to be kind:
Thus bad begins and worse remains behind.
One word more, good lady.

QUEEN.   What shall I do?

HAM.   Not this, by no means, that I bid you do:
Let the bloat king tempt you again to bed;   180
Pinch wanton on your cheek; call you his mouse;
And let him, for a pair of reechy kisses,
Or paddling in your neck with his damn'd fingers,
Make you to ravel all this matter out,
That I essentially am not in madness,
But mad in craft. 'Twere good you let him know;
For who, that's but a queen, fair, sober, wise,
Would from a paddock, from a bat, a gib,
Such dear concernings hide? who would do so?
No, in despite of sense and secrecy,   190
Unpeg the basket on the house's top,
Let the birds fly, and, like the famous ape,
To try conclusions, in the basket creep,
And break your own neck down.

QUEEN.   Be thou assur'd, if words be made of breath,
And breath of life, I have no life to breathe
What thou hast said to me.

HAM.   I must to England; you know that?

QUEEN.   Alack,
I had forgot: 'tis so concluded on.   200

HAM.   There's letters seal'd: and my two schoolfellows,
Whom I will trust as I will adders fang'd,
They bear the mandate; they must sweep my way,
And marshal me to knavery. Let it work;

For 'tis the sport to have the enginer
Hoist with his own petar: and 't shall go hard
But I will delve one yard below their mines,
And blow them at the moon: O, 'tis most sweet,
When in one line two crafts directly meet.
This man shall set me packing: 210
I'll lug the guts into the neighbour room.
Mother, good night. Indeed this counsellor
Is now most still, most secret and most grave,
Who was in life a foolish prating knave.
Come, sir, to draw toward an end with you.
Good night, mother.   *Exeunt* [*severally;* HAMLET *dragging in* POLO-
NIUS.]

[ACT IV.

SCENE I. *A room in the castle.*]

Enter KING *and* QUEEN, *with* ROSENCRANTZ *and* GUILDENSTERN.

KING.   There's matter in these sighs, these profound heaves:
          You must translate: 'tis fit we understand them.
          Where is your son?

QUEEN.   Bestow this place on us a little while.
                              [*Exeunt* ROSENCRANTZ *and* GUILDENSTERN.]
          Ah, mine own lord, what have I seen to-night!

KING.   What, Gertrude? How does Hamlet?

QUEEN.   Mad as the sea and wind, when both contend
          Which is the mightier: in his lawless fit,
          Behind the arras hearing something stir,
          Whips out his rapier, cries, 'A rat, a rat!'   10
          And, in this brainish apprehension, kills
          The unseen good old man.

KING.   O heavy deed!
          It had been so with us, had we been there:
          His liberty is full of threats to all;
          To you yourself, to us, to every one.
          Alas, how shall this bloody deed be answer'd?
          It will be laid to us, whose providence
          Should have kept short, restrain'd and out of haunt,
          This mad young man: but so much was our love,   20
          We would not understand what was most fit;
          But, like the owner of a foul disease,
          To keep it from divulging, let it feed
          Even on the pith of life. Where is he gone?

QUEEN.   To draw apart the body he hath kill'd:
        O'er whom his very madness, like some ore
        Among a mineral of metals base,
        Shows itself pure; 'a weeps for what is done.

KING.   O Gertrude, come away!
        The sun no sooner shall the mountains touch,
        But we will ship him hence: and this vile deed
        We must, with all our majesty and skill,   30
        Both countenance and excuse. Ho, Guildenstern!

Enter ROSENCRANTZ *and* GUILDENSTERN.

        Friends both, go join you with some further aid:
        Hamlet in madness hath Polonius slain,
        And from his mother's closet hath he dragg'd him:
        Go seek him out; speak fair, and bring the body
        Into the chapel. I pray you, haste in this.
                       [*Exeunt* ROSENCRANTZ *and* GUILDENSTERN.]
        Come, Gertrude, we'll call up our wisest friends;
        And let them know, both what we mean to do,
        And what's untimely done. [. . .]
        Whose whisper o'er the world's diameter,   40
        As level as the cannon to his blank,
        Transports his pois'ned shot, may miss our name,
        And hit the woundless air. O, come away!
        My soul is full of discord and dismay.   *Exeunt.*

                  [SCENE II. *Another room in the castle.*]

Enter HAMLET.

HAM.   Safely stowed.

ROS.
GUIL.   } (*Within*) Hamlet! Lord Hamlet!

HAM.   But soft, what noise? who calls on Hamlet?
        O, here they come.

Enter ROSENCRANTZ *and* GUILDENSTERN.

ROS.   What have you done, my lord, with the dead body?

HAM.   Compounded it with dust, whereto 'tis kin.

ROS.   Tell us where 'tis, that we may take it thence
        And bear it to the chapel.

HAM.   Do not believe it.

ROS.   Believe what?   10

HAM.   That I can keep your counsel and not mine own. Besides, to be demanded of a sponge! what replication should be made by the son of a king?

ROS.   Take you me for a sponge, my lord?

HAM.   Ay, sir, that soaks up the king's countenance, his rewards, his authorities. But such officers do the king best service in the end: he keeps them, like an ape an apple, in the corner of his jaw; first mouthed, to be last swallowed: when he needs what you have gleaned, it is but squeezing you, and, sponge, you shall be dry again.

ROS.   I understand you not, my lord.

HAM.   I am glad of it: a knavish speech sleeps in a foolish ear.

ROS.   My lord, you must tell us where the body is, and go with us to the king.   20

HAM.   The body is with the king, but the king is not with the body. The king is a thing—

GUIL.   A thing, my lord!

HAM.   Of nothing: bring me to him. Hide fox, and all after.   *Exeunt.*   31

[SCENE III. *Another room in the castle.*]

Enter KING, *and two or three.*

KING.   I have sent to seek him, and to find the body.
How dangerous is it that this man goes loose!
Yet must not we put the strong law on him:
He's lov'd of the distracted multitude,
Who like not in their judgement, but their eyes;
And where 'tis so, th' offender's scourge is weigh'd,
But never the offence. To bear all smooth and even,
This sudden sending him away must seem
Deliberate pause: diseases desperate grown
By desperate appliance are reliev'd,
Or not at all.   10

Enter ROSENCRANTZ, [GUILDENSTERN,] *and all the rest.*

How now! what hath befall'n?

ROS.   Where the dead body is bestow'd, my lord,
We cannot get from him.

KING.   But where is he?

ROS.   Without, my lord; guarded, to know your pleasure.

KING.   Bring him before us.

ROS.   Ho! bring in the lord.

They enter [*with* HAMLET].

KING.   Now, Hamlet, where's Polonius?

HAM.   At supper.

KING.   At supper! where?

HAM.   Not where he eats, but where 'a is eaten: a certain convocation of politic   19
worms are e'en at him. Your worm is your only emperor for diet: we fat all creatures else to fat us, and we fat ourselves for maggots: your fat king and your
lean beggar is but variable service, two dishes, but to one table: that's the end.

KING.   Alas, alas!

HAM.   A man may fish with the worm that hath eat of a king, and eat of the fish that
hath fed of that worm.

KING.   What dost thou mean by this?

HAM.   Nothing but to show you how a king may go a progress through the guts of
a beggar.

KING.   Where is Polonius?

HAM.   In heaven; send thither to see: if your messenger find him not there, seek him   30
i' the other place yourself. But if indeed you find him not within this month,
you shall nose him as you go up the stairs into the lobby.

KING.   Go seek him there,   [*To some* ATTENDANTS.]

HAM.   'A will stay till you come.   [*Exeunt* ATTENDANTS.]

KING.   Hamlet, this deed, for thine especial safety,—
Which we do tender, as we dearly grieve
For that which thou hast done,—must send thee hence
With fiery quickness: therefore prepare thyself;
The bark is ready, and the wind at help,
Th' associates tend, and everything is bent   40
For England.

HAM.   For England!

KING.   Ay, Hamlet.

HAM.   Good.

KING.   So is it, if thou knew'st our purposes.

HAM.   I see a cherub that sees them. But, come; for England! Farewell, dear mother.

KING.   Thy loving father, Hamlet.

HAM.   My mother: father and mother is man and wife; man and wife is one flesh;
and so, my mother.
Come, for England!   *Exit.*

KING.   Follow him at foot; tempt him with speed aboard;
Delay it not; I'll have him hence to-night:
Away! for every thing is seal'd and done   50
That else leans on th' affair: pray you, make haste. [*Exeunt all but the* KING.]
And, England, if my love thou hold'st at aught—
As my great power thereof may give thee sense,
Since yet thy cicatrice looks raw and red
After the Danish sword, and thy free awe

Pays homage to us—thou mayst not coldly set
Our sovereign process; which imports at full,
By letters congruing to that effect,
The present death of Hamlet. Do it, England;
For like the hectic in my blood he rages,   60
And thou must cure me: till I know 'tis done,
Howe'er my haps, my joys were ne'er begun.   *Exit.*

[SCENE IV. *A plain in Denmark.*]

Enter FORTINBRAS *with his Army over the stage.*

FOR.   Go, captain, from me greet the Danish king;
Tell him that, by his license, Fortinbras
Craves the conveyance of a promis'd march
Over his kingdom. You know the rendezvous.
If that his majesty would aught with us,
We shall express our duty in his eye;
And let him know so.

CAP.   I will do 't, my lord.

FOR.   Go softly on.   [*Exeunt all but* CAPTAIN.]

Enter HAMLET, ROSENCRANTZ, [GUILDENSTERN,] *and others.*

HAM.   Good sir, whose powers are these?

CAP.   They are of Norway, sir.   10

HAM.   How purpos'd, sir, I pray you?

CAP.   Against some part of Poland.

HAM.   Who commands them, sir?

CAP.   The nephew to old Norway, Fortinbras.

HAM.   Goes it against the main of Poland, sir,
Or for some frontier?

CAP.   Truly to speak, and with no addition,
We go to gain a little patch of ground
That hath in it no profit but the name.
To pay five ducats, five, I would not farm it;   20
Nor will it yield to Norway or the Pole
A ranker rate, should it be sold in fee.

HAM.   Why, then the Polack never will defend it.

CAP.   Yes, it is already garrison'd.

HAM.   Two thousand souls and twenty thousand ducats
Will not debate the question of this straw:
This is th' imposthume of much wealth and peace,

       That inward breaks, and shows no cause without
       Why the man dies. I humbly thank you, sir.
CAP.   God be wi' you, sir.   [*Exit.*]
ROS.   Will 't please you go, my lord?
HAM.   I'll be with you straight. Go a little before.   [*Exeunt all except* HAMLET.]   30
       How all occasions do inform against me,
       And spur my dull revenge! What is a man,
       If his chief good and market of his time
       Be but to sleep and feed? a beast, no more.
       Sure, he that made us with such large discourse,
       Looking before and after, gave us not
       That capability and god-like reason
       To fust in us unus'd. Now, whether it be
       Bestial oblivion, or some craven scruple
       Of thinking too precisely on th' event,   40
       A thought which, quarter'd, hath but one part wisdom
       And ever three parts coward, I do not know
       Why yet I live to say 'This thing's to do;'
       Sith I have cause and will and strength and means
       To do 't. Examples gross as earth exhort me:
       Witness this army of such mass and charge
       Led by a delicate and tender prince,
       Whose spirit with divine ambition puff'd
       Makes mouths at the invisible event,
       Exposing what is mortal and unsure   50
       To all that fortune, death and danger dare,
       Even for an egg-shell. Rightly to be great
       Is not to stir without great argument,
       But greatly to find quarrel in a straw
       When honour's at the stake. How stand I then,
       That have a father kill'd, a mother stain'd,
       Excitements of my reason and my blood,
       And let all sleep? while, to my shame, I see
       The imminent death of twenty thousand men,
       That, for a fantasy and trick of fame,   60
       Go to their graves like beds, fight for a plot
       Whereon the numbers cannot try the cause,
       Which is not tomb enough and continent
       To hide the slain? O, from this time forth,
       My thoughts be bloody, or be nothing worth!   *Exit.*

      [SCENE V. *Elsinore. A room in the castle.*]

Enter HORATIO, [QUEEN] GERTRUDE, *and a* GENTLEMAN.

QUEEN.   I will not speak with her.

GENT.   She is importunate, indeed distract:
   Her mood will needs be pitied.

QUEEN.   What would she have?

GENT.   She speaks much of her father; says she hears
   There's tricks i' th' world; and hems, and beats her heart;
   Spurns enviously at straws; speaks things in doubt,
   That carry but half sense: her speech is nothing,
   Yet the unshaped use of it doth move
   The hearers to collection; they yawn at it,
   And botch the words up fit to their own thoughts;
   Which, as her winks, and nods, and gestures yield them,   10
   Indeed would make one think there might be thought,
   Though nothing sure, yet much unhappily.

HOR.   'Twere good she were spoken with: for she may strew
   Dangerous conjectures in ill-breeding minds.

QUEEN.   Let her come in.   [*Exit* GENTLEMAN.]
   [*Aside*] To my sick soul, as sin's true nature is,
   Each toy seems prologue to some great amiss:
   So full of artless jealousy is guilt,
   It spills itself in fearing to be split.

Enter OPHELIA [*distracted*].   20

OPH.   Where is the beauteous majesty of Denmark?

QUEEN.   How now, Ophelia!

OPH.   (*She sings*) How should I your true love know
     From another one?
   By his cockle hat and staff,
     And his sandal shoon.

QUEEN.   Alas, sweet lady, what imports this song?

OPH.   Say you? nay, pray you, mark.
   He is dead and gone, lady,   (*Song*)
     He is dead and gone;
   At his head a grass-green turf,
     At his heels a stone.   30
   O, ho!

QUEEN.   Nay, but, Ophelia,—

OPH.   Pray you, mark
   [*Sings*] White his shroud as the mountain snow,—

Enter KING.

QUEEN.   Alas, look here, my lord.

OPH.   Larded all with flowers;   (*Song*)
            Which bewept to the grave did not go
                With true-love showers.

KING.   How do you, pretty lady?

OPH.   Well, God 'ild you! They say the owl was a baker's daughter. Lord, we know   40
        what we are, but know not what we may be. God be at your table!

KING.   Conceit upon her father.

OPH.   Pray let 's have no words of this; but when they ask you what it means, say
        you this:
            To-morrow is Saint Valentine's day,   (*Song*)
                All in the morning betime,
            And I a maid at your window,
                To be your Valentine.
            Then up he rose, and donn'd his clothes,
                And dupp'd the chamber-door;
            Let in the maid, that out a maid   50
                Never departed more.

KING.   Pretty Ophelia!

OPH.   Indeed, la, without an oath, I'll make an end on 't:
        [*Sings*] By Gis and by Saint Charity,
                Alack, and fie for shame!
            Young men will do 't, if they come to 't;
                By cock, they are to blame.
            Quoth she, before you tumbled me,
                You promis'd me to wed.
            So would I ha' done, by yonder sun,   60
                An thou hadst not come to my bed.

KING.   How long hath she been thus?

OPH.   I hope all will be well. We must be patient: but I cannot choose but weep, to
        think they would lay him i' the cold ground. My brother shall know of it: and
        so I thank you for your good counsel. Come, my coach! Good night, ladies;
        good night, sweet ladies; good night, good night.   [*Exit.*]

KING.   Follow her close; give her good watch, I pray you.   [*Exit* HORATIO.]
            O, this is the poison of deep grief; it springs
            All from her father's death. O Gertrude, Gertrude,
            When sorrows come, they come not single spies,   70
            But in battalions. First, her father slain:
            Next, your son gone; and he most violent author
            Of his own just remove: the people muddied,
            Thick and unwholesome in their thoughts and whispers,
            For good Polonius' death; and we have done but greenly,

In hugger-mugger to inter him: poor Ophelia
Divided from herself and her fair judgement,
Without the which we are pictures, or mere beasts:
Last, and as much containing as all these,   80
Her brother is in secret come from France;
Feeds on his wonder, keeps himself in clouds,
And wants not buzzers to infect his ear
With pestilent speeches of his father's death;
Wherein necessity, of matter beggar'd,
Will nothing stick our person to arraign
In ear and ear. O my dear Gertrude, this,
Like to a murd'ring-piece, in many places
Gives me superfluous death.   *A noise within.*

QUEEN.   Alack, what noise is this?

KING.   Where are my Switzers? Let them guard the door.   91

Enter a MESSENGER.

What is the matter?

MESS.   Save yourself, my lord:
The ocean, overpeering of his list,
Eats not the flats with more impiteous haste
Than young Laertes, in a riotous head,
O'erbears your officers. The rabble call him lord;
And, as the world were now but to begin,
Antiquity forgot, custom not known,
The ratifiers and props of every word,
They cry 'Choose we: Laertes shall be king:'   100
Caps, hands, and tongues, applaud it to the clouds:
'Laertes shall be king, Laertes king!'   *A noise within.*

QUEEN.   How cheerfully on the false trail they cry!
O, this is counter, you false Danish dogs!

KING.   The doors are broke.

Enter LAERTES *with others.*

LAER.   Where is this king? Sirs, stand you all without.
Danes. No, let's come in.

LAER.   I pray you, give me leave.
Danes. We will, we will.   [*They retire without the door.*]

LAER.   I thank you: keep the door. O thou vile king,
Give me my father!   110

QUEEN.   Calmly, good Laertes.

LAER.   That drop of blood that's calm proclaims me bastard,

> Cries cuckold to my father, brands the harlot
> Even here, between the chaste unsmirched brow
> Of my true mother.

KING.   What is the cause, Laertes,
> That thy rebellion looks so giant-like?
> Let him go, Gertrude; do not fear our person:
> There 's such divinity doth hedge a king,
> That treason can but peep to what it would,
> Acts little of his will. Tell me, Laertes,
> Why thou art thus incens'd. Let him go, Gertrude.   120
> Speak, man.

LAER.   Where is my father?

KING.   Dead.

QUEEN.   But not by him.

KING.   Let him demand his fill.

LAER.   How came he dead? I'll not be juggled with:
> To hell, allegiance! vows, to the blackest devil!
> Conscience and grace, to the profoundest pit!
> I dare damnation. To this point I stand,
> That both the worlds I give to negligence,
> Let come what comes; only I'll be reveng'd
> Most throughly for my father.   130

KING.   Who shall stay you?

LAER.   My will, not all the world's:
> And for my means, I'll husband them so well,
> They shall go far with little.

KING.   Good Laertes,
> If you desire to know the certainty
> Of your dear father, is 't writ in your revenge,
> That, swoopstake, you will draw both friend and foe,
> Winner and loser?

LAER.   None but his enemies.

KING.   Will you know them then?

LAER.   To his good friends thus wide I'll ope my arms;
> And like the kind life-rend'ring pelican,   140
> Repast them with my blood.

KING.   Why, now you speak
> Like a good child and a true gentleman.
> That I am guiltless of your father's death,
> And am most sensibly in grief for it,
> It shall as level to your judgment 'pear
> As day does to your eye.

A noise within: 'Let her come in.'

LAER.   How now! what noise is that?

Enter OPHELIA.

O heat, dry up my brains! tears seven times salt,
Burn out the sense and virtue of mine eye!
By heaven, thy madness shall be paid with weight,   150
Till our scale turn the beam. O rose of May!
Dear maid, kind sister, sweet Ophelia!
O heavens! is 't possible, a young maid's wits
Should be as mortal as an old man's life?
Nature is fine in love, and where 'tis fine,
It sends some precious instance of itself
After the thing it loves.

OPH.   *(Song)*
            They bore him barefac'd on the bier;
            Hey non nonny, nonny, hey nonny;
            And in his grave rain'd many a tear:—   160
Fare you well, my dove!

LAER.   Hadst thou thy wits, and didst persuade revenge,
It could not move thus.

OPH.   [*Sings*] You must sing a-down a-down,
                An you call him a-down-a.
O, how the wheel becomes it! It is the false steward, that stole his master's daughter.

LAER.   This nothing's more than matter.

OPH.   There's rosemary, that's for remembrance; pray you, love, remember: and there
is pansies, that's for thoughts.

LAER.   A document in madness, thoughts and remembrance fitted.   170

OPH.   There's fennel for you, and columbines: there's rue for you; and here's some
for me: we may call it herb of grace o' Sundays: O, you must wear your rue
with a difference. There's a daisy: I would give you some violets, but they withered all when my father died: they say 'a made a good end,—
[*Sings*] For bonny sweet Robin is all my joy.

LAER.   Thought and affliction, passion, hell itself,
She turns to favour and to prettiness.

OPH.   *(Song)*
            And will 'a not come again?
            And will 'a not come again?
                No, no, he is dead: 180
            Go to thy death-bed:
                He never will come again.

His beard was as white as snow,
All flaxen was his poll:
He is gone, he is gone,
And we cast away moan:
God ha' mercy on his soul!
And of all Christian souls, I pray God. God be wi' you.   [*Exit.*]

LAER.   Do you see this, O God?

KING.   Laertes, I must commune with your grief,   190
Or you deny me right. Go but apart,
Make choice of whom your wisest friends you will,
And they shall hear and judge 'twixt you and me:
If by direct or by collateral hand
They find us touch'd, we will our kingdom give,
Our crown, our life, and all that we call ours,
To you in satisfaction; but if not,
Be you content to lend your patience to us,
And we shall jointly labour with your soul
To give it due content.   200

LAER.   Let this be so;
His means of death, his obscure funeral—
No trophy, sword, nor hatchment o'er his bones,
No noble rite nor formal ostentation—
Cry to be heard, as 'twere from heaven to earth,
That I must call 't in question.

KING.   So you shall;
And where th' offence is let the great axe fall.
I pray you, go with me.   *Exeunt.*

[SCENE VI. *Another room in the castle.*]

Enter HORATIO *and others.*

HOR.   What are they that would speak with me?

GENT.   Sea-faring men, sir: they say they have letters for you.

HOR.   Let them come in.   [*Exit* GENT.]
I do not know from what part of the world
I should be greeted, if not from lord Hamlet.

Enter SAILORS.

FIRST SAIL.   God bless you, sir.

HOR.   Let him bless thee too.

FIRST SAIL.   'A shall, sir, an 't please him. There 's a letter for you, sir; it comes from
the ambassador that was bound for England; if your name be Horatio, as I am
let to know it is.

HOR.   [*Reads*] 'Horatio, when thou shalt have overlooked this, give these fellows

some means to the king: they have letters for him. Ere we were two days old at
sea, a pirate of very warlike appointment gave us chase. Finding ourselves too
slow of sail, we put on a compelled valour, and in the grapple I boarded them:
on the instant they got clear of our ship; so I alone became their prisoner. They
have dealt with me like thieves of mercy: but they knew what they did; I am to
do a good turn for them. Let the king have the letters I have sent; and repair
thou to me with as much speed as thou wouldest fly death. I have words to speak
in thine ear will make thee dumb; yet are they much too light for the bore of
the matter. These good fellows will bring thee where I am. Rosencrantz and
Guildenstern hold their course for England: of them I have much to tell thee.   20
Farewell.

'He that thou knowest thine, HAMLET.'

Come, I will give you way for these your letters;
And do 't the speedier, that you may direct me
To him from whom you brought them.   *Exeunt.*

[SCENE VII. Another room in the castle.]

Enter KING *and* LAERTES.

KING.   Now must your conscience my acquittance seal,
         And you must put me in your heart for friend,
         Sith you have heard, and with a knowing ear,
         That he which hath your noble father slain
         Pursued my life.

LAER.   It well appears: but tell me
         Why you proceeded not against these feats,
         So criminal and so capital in nature,
         As by your safety, wisdom, all things else,
         You mainly were stirr'd up.

KING.   O, for two special reasons;
         Which may to you, perhaps, seem much unsinew'd,
         But yet to me th' are strong. The queen his mother   10
         Lives almost by his looks; and for myself—
         My virtue or my plague, be it either which—
         She's so conjunctive to my life and soul,
         That, as the star moves not but in his sphere,
         I could not but by her. The other motive,
         Why to a public count I might not go,
         Is the great love the general gender bear him;
         Who, dipping all his faults in their affection,
         Would, like the spring that turneth wood to stone,
         Convert his gyves to graces; so that my arrows,   20
         Too slightly timber'd for so loud a wind,

> Would have reverted to my bow again,
> And not where I had aim'd them.

LAER.   And so have I a noble father lost;
> A sister driven into desp'rate terms,
> Whose worth, if praises may go back again,
> Stood challenger on mount of all the age
> For her perfections: but my revenge will come.

KING.   Break not your sleeps for that: you must not think
> That we are made of stuff so flat and dull   30
> That we can let our beard be shook with danger
> And think it pastime. You shortly shall hear more:
> I lov'd your father, and we love ourself;
> And that, I hope, will teach you to imagine—

Enter MESSENGER *with letters.*

> How now! what news?

MESS.   Letters, my lord, from Hamlet:
> These to your majesty; this to the queen.

KING.   From Hamlet! who brought them?

MESS.   Sailors, my lord, they say; I saw them not:
> They were given me by Claudio; he receiv'd them
> Of him that brought them.   40

KING.   Laertes, you shall hear them.
> Leave us.   [*Exit* MESSENGER.]
> [*Reads*] 'High and mighty, You shall know I am set naked on your kingdom.
> To-morrow shall I beg leave to see your kingly eyes: when I shall, first asking
> your pardon thereunto, recount the occasion of my sudden and more strange re-
> turn.   'HAMLET.'
> What should this mean? Are all the rest come back?
> Or is it some abuse, and no such thing?

LAER.   Know you the hand?

KING.   'Tis Hamlet's character. 'Naked!'
> And in a postscript here, he says 'alone.'
> Can you devise me?   50

LAER.   I'm lost in it, my lord. But let him come;
> It warms the very sickness in my heart,
> That I shall live and tell him to his teeth,
> 'Thus didst thou.'

KING.   If it be so, Laertes—
> As how should it be so? how otherwise?—
> Will you be rul'd by me?

LAER.   Ay, my lord;

So you will not o'errule me to a peace.

KING.   To thine own peace. If he be now return'd,
As checking at his voyage, and that he means
No more to undertake it, I will work him   60
To an exploit, now ripe in my device,
Under the which he shall not choose but fall:
And for his death no wind of blame shall breathe,
But even his mother shall uncharge the practice
And call it accident.

LAER.   My lord, I will be rul'd;
The rather, if you could devise it so
That I might be the organ.

KING.   It falls right.
You have been talk'd of since your travel much,
And that in Hamlet's hearing, for a quality
Wherein, they say, you shine: your sum of parts   70
Did not together pluck such envy from him
As did that one, and that, in my regard,
Of the unworthiest siege.

LAER.   What part is that, my lord?

KING.   A very riband in the cap of youth,
Yet needful too; for youth no less becomes
The light and careless livery that it wears
Than settled age his sables and his weeds,
Importing health and graveness. Two months since,
Here was a gentleman of Normandy:—
I have seen myself, and serv'd against, the French,   80
And they can well on horseback: but this gallant
Had witchcraft in 't; he grew unto his seat;
And to such wondrous doing brought his horse,
As had he been incorps'd and demi-natur'd
With the brave beast: so far he topp'd my thought,
That I, in forgery of shapes and tricks,
Come short of what he did.

LAER.   A Norman was 't?

KING.   A Norman.

LAER.   Upon my life, Lamord.   90

KING.   The very same.

LAER.   I know him well: he is the brooch indeed
And gem of all the nation.

KING.   He made confession of you,
And gave you such a masterly report

For art and exercise in your defence
And for your rapier most especial,
That he cried out, 'twould be a sight indeed,
If one could match you: the scrimers of their nation,
He swore, had neither motion, guard, nor eye,
If you oppos'd them. Sir, this report of his   100
Did Hamlet so envenom with his envy
That he could nothing do but wish and beg
Your sudden coming o'er, to play with you.
Now, out of this,—

LAER.   What out of this, my lord?

KING. Laertes, was your father dear to you?
Or are you like the painting of a sorrow,
A face without a heart?

LAER.   Why ask you this?

KING. Not that I think you did not love your father;
But that I know love is begun by time;
And that I see, in passages of proof,   110
Time qualifies the spark and fire of it.
There lives within the very flame of love
A kind of wick or snuff that will abate it;
And nothing is at a like goodness still;
For goodness, growing to a plurisy,
Dies in his own too much: that we would do,
We should do when we would; for this 'would' changes
And hath abatements and delays as many
As there are tongues, are hands, are accidents;
And then this 'should' is like a spendthrift sigh,   120
That hurts by easing. But, to the quick o' th' ulcer:—
Hamlet comes back: what would you undertake,
To show yourself your father's son in deed
More than in words?

LAER.   To cut his throat i' th' church.

KING. No place, indeed, should murder sanctuarize;
Revenge should have no bounds. But, good Laertes,
Will you do this, keep close within your chamber.
Hamlet return'd shall know you are come home:
We'll put on those shall praise your excellence   130
And set a double varnish on the fame
The Frenchman gave you, bring you in fine together
And wager on your heads: he, being remiss,
Most generous and free from all contriving,
Will not peruse the foils; so that, with ease,

Or with a little shuffling, you may choose
A sword unbated, and in a pass of practice
Requite him for your father.

LAER.   I will do 't:
And, for that purpose, I'll anoint my sword.
I bought an unction of a mountebank,
So mortal that, but dip a knife in it,   140
Where it draws blood no cataplasm so rare,
Collected from all simples that have virtue
Under the moon, can save the thing from death
That is but scratch'd withal: I'll touch my point
With this contagion, that, if I gall him slightly,
It may be death.

KING.   Let's further think of this;
Weigh what convenience both of time and means
May fit us to our shape: if this should fail,
And that our drift look through our bad performance,
'Twere better not assay'd: therefore this project   150
Should have a back or second, that might hold,
If this should blast in proof. Soft! let me see:
We'll make a solemn wager on your cunnings:
I ha 't:
When in your motion you are hot and dry—
As make your bouts more violent to that end—
And that he calls for drink, I'll have prepar'd him
A chalice for the nonce, whereon but sipping,
If he by chance escape your venom'd stuck,
Our purpose may hold there. But stay, what noise?   160

Enter QUEEN.

QUEEN.   One woe doth tread upon another's heel,
          So fast they follow: your sister 's drown'd, Laertes.

LAER.   Drown'd! O, where?

QUEEN.   There is a willow grows askant the brook,
          That shows his hoar leaves in the glassy stream;
          There with fantastic garlands did she make
          Of crow-flowers, nettles, daisies, and long purples
          That liberal shepherds give a grosser name,
          But our cold maids do dead men's fingers call them:
          There, on the pendent boughs her crownet weeds   170
          Clamb'ring to hang, an envious sliver broke;
          When down her weedy trophies and herself
          Fell in the weeping brook. Her clothes spread wide;

And, mermaid-like, awhile they bore her up:
Which time she chanted snatches of old lauds;
As one incapable of her own distress,
Or like a creature native and indued
Unto that element: but long it could not be
Till that her garments, heavy with their drink,
Pull'd the poor wretch from her melodious lay   180
To muddy death.

LAER.   Alas then, she is drown'd?

QUEEN.   Drown'd, drown'd.

LAER.   Too much of water hast thou, poor Ophelia,
And therefore I forbid my tears: but yet
It is our trick; nature her custom holds,
Let shame say what it will: when these are gone,
The woman will be out. Adieu, my lord:
I have a speech of fire, that fain would blaze,
But that this folly drowns it.   *Exit.* 190

KING.   Let's follow, Gertrude:
How much I had to do to calm his rage!
Now fear I this will give it start again;
Therefore let's follow.   *Exeunt.*

[ACT V.

SCENE I. *A churchyard.*]

Enter two CLOWNS [*with spades, etc.*].

FIRST CLO.   Is she to be buried in Christian burial when she wilfully seeks her own
salvation?

SEC. CLO.   I tell thee she is; therefore make her grave straight: the crowner hath sat
on her, and finds it Christian burial.

FIRST CLO.   How can that be, unless she drowned herself in her own defence?

SEC. CLO.   Why, 'tis found so.

FIRST CLO.   It must be 'se offendendo;' it cannot be else. For here lies the point: if I
drown myself wittingly, it argues an act: and an act hath three branches; it is,
to act, to do, and to perform: argal, she drowned herself wittingly.

SEC. CLO.   Nay, but hear you, goodman delver,—

FIRST CLO.   Give me leave. Here lies the water; good: here stands the man; good: if   10
the man go to this water, and drown himself, it is, will he, nill he, he goes,—
mark you that; but if the water come to him and drown him, he drowns not himself: argal, he that is not guilty of his own death shortens not his own life.

SEC. CLO.   But is this law?

FIRST CLO.   Ay, marry, is 't; crowner's quest law.

SEC. CLO.   Will you ha' the truth on 't? If this had not been a gentlewoman, she should have been buried out o' Christian burial.

FIRST CLO.   Why, there thou say'st: and the more pity that great folk should have countenance in this world to drown or hang themselves, more than their even Christian. Come, my spade. There is no ancient gentlemen but gardeners, ditchers, and grave-makers: they hold up Adam's profession.

SEC. CLO.   Was he a gentleman?   22

FIRST CLO.   'A was the first that ever bore arms.

SEC. CLO.   Why, he had none.

FIRST CLO.   What, art a heathen? How dost thou understand the Scripture? The Scripture says 'Adam digged:' could he dig without arms? I'll put another question to thee: if thou answerest me not to the purpose, confess thyself—

SEC. CLO.   Go to.

FIRST CLO.   What is he that builds stronger than either the mason, the shipwright, or the carpenter?

SEC. CLO.   The gallows-maker; for that frame outlives a thousand tenants.   31

FIRST CLO.   I like thy wit well, in good faith: the gallows does well; but how does it well? it does well to those that do ill: now thou dost ill to say the gallows is built stronger than the church: argal, the gallows may do well to thee. To 't again, come.

SEC. CLO.   'Who builds stronger than a mason, a shipwright, or a carpenter?'

FIRST CLO.   Ay, tell me that, and unyoke.

SEC. CLO.   Marry, now I can tell.

FIRST CLO.   To 't.

SEC. CLO.   Mass, I cannot tell.

                                                                          40

Enter HAMLET *and* HORATIO [*at a distance.*]

FIRST CLO.   Cudgel thy brains no more about it, for your dull ass will not mend his pace with beating; and, when you are asked this question next, say 'a grave-maker:' the houses he makes lasts till dooms-day. Go, get thee in, and fetch me a stoup of liquor.   [*Exit* SEC. CLOWN.]
                                                                 Song. [*He digs.*]

In youth, when I did love, did love,
Methought it was very sweet,
To contract—O—the time, for—a—my behove,
O, methought, there—a—was nothing—a—meet.

HAM.   Has this fellow no feeling of his business, that 'a sings at grave-making?

HOR.   Custom hath made it in him a property of easiness.

HAM.   'Tis e'en so: the hand of little employment hath the daintier sense.

FIRST CLO.   *Song.*   50
  But age, with his stealing steps,
    Hath claw'd me in his clutch,
  And hath shipped me into the land,
    As if I had never been such.   [*Throws up a skull.*]

HAM.   That skull had a tongue in it, and could sing once: how the knave jowls it to
the ground, as if 'twere Cain's jaw-bone, that did the first murder! This might
be the pate of a politician, which this ass now o'er-reaches; one that would cir-
cumvent God, might it not?

HOR.   It might, my lord.

HAM.   Or of a courtier; which could say 'Good morrow, sweet lord! How dost thou,   59
sweet lord?' This might be my lord such-a-one, that praised my lord such-a-
one's horse, when he meant to beg it; might it not?

HOR.   Ay, my lord.

HAM.   Why, e'en so: and now my Lady Worm's; chapless, and knocked about the
mazzard with a sexton's spade: here 's fine revolution, an we had the trick to
see 't. Did these bones cost no more the breeding, but to play at loggats with
'em? mine ache to think on 't.

FIRST CLO.   *Song.*
  A pick-axe, and a spade, a spade,
    For and a shrouding sheet:
  O, a pit of clay for to be made
    For such a guest is meet.   [*Throws up another skull.*]   70

HAM.   There's another: why may not that be the skull of a lawyer? Where be his
quiddities now, his quillities, his cases, his tenures, and his tricks? why does he
suffer this mad knave now to knock him about the sconce with a dirty shovel,
and will not tell him of his action of battery? Hum! This fellow might be in 's
time a great buyer of land, with his statutes, his recognizances, his fines, his
double vouchers, his recoveries: is this the fine of his fines, and the recovery of
his recoveries, to have his fine pate full of fine dirt? will his vouchers vouch
him no more of his purchases, and double ones too, than the length and breadth
of a pair of indentures? The very conveyances of his lands will scarcely lie in
this box; and must the inheritor himself have no more, ha?

HOR.   Not a jot more, my lord.   81

HAM.   Is not parchment made of sheep-skins?

HOR.   Ay, my lord, and of calf-skins too.

HAM.   They are sheep and calves which seek out assurance in that. I will speak to
this fellow. Whose grave 's this, sirrah?

FIRST CLO.   Mine, sir.
  [*Sings*] O, a pit of clay for to be made
      For such a guest is meet.

HAM.   I think it be thine, indeed; for thou liest in 't.

FIRST CLO.   You lie out on 't, sir, and therefore 't is not yours: for my part, I do not   90
lie in 't, yet it is mine.

HAM.   Thou dost lie in 't, to be in 't and say it is thine: 'tis for the dead, not for the
quick; therefore thou liest.

FIRST CLO.   'Tis a quick lie, sir; 'twill away again, from me to you.

HAM.   What man dost thou dig it for?

FIRST CLO.   For no man, sir.

HAM.   What woman, then?

FIRST CLO.   For none, neither.

HAM.   Who is to be buried in 't?

FIRST CLO.   One that was a woman, sir; but, rest her soul, she's dead.   100

HAM.   How absolute the knave is! we must speak by the card, or equivocation will
undo us. By the Lord, Horatio, these three years I have taken note of it; the age
is grown so picked that the toe of the peasant comes so near the heel of the
courtier, he galls his kibe. How long hast thou been a grave-maker?

FIRST CLO.   Of all the days i' the year, I came to 't that day that our last king Hamlet
overcame Fortinbras.

HAM.   How long is that since?

FIRST CLO.   Cannot you tell that? every fool can tell that; it was the very day that
young Hamlet was born; he that is mad, and sent into England.

HAM.   Ay, marry, why was he sent into England?   110

FIRST CLO.   Why, because 'a was mad: 'a shall recover his wits there; or, if 'a do not,
'tis no great matter there.

HAM.   Why?

FIRST CLO.   'Twill not be seen in him there; there the men are as mad as he.

HAM.   How came he mad?

FIRST CLO.   Very strangely, they say.

HAM.   How strangely?

FIRST CLO.   Faith, e'en with losing his wits.

HAM.   Upon what ground?

FIRST CLO.   Why, here in Denmark: I have been sexton here, man and boy, thirty   120
years.

HAM.   How long will a man lie i' the earth ere he rot?

FIRST CLO.   Faith, if 'a be not rotten before 'a die—as we have many pocky corses
now-a-days, that will scarce hold the laying in—'a will last you some eight year
or nine year: a tanner will last you nine year.

HAM.   Why he more than another?

FIRST CLO.   Why, sir, his hide is so tanned with his trade, that 'a will keep out water
a great while; and your water is a sore decayer of your whoreson dead body.

Here's a skull now hath lain you i' th' earth three and twenty years.

HAM.   Whose was it?

FIRST CLO.   A whoreson mad fellow's it was: whose do you think it was?   130

HAM.   Nay, I know not.

FIRST CLO.   A pestilence on him for a mad rogue! 'a poured a flagon of Rhenish on my head once. This same skull, sir, was Yorick's skull, the king's jester.

HAM.   This?

FIRST CLO.   E'en that.

HAM.   Let me see. [*Takes the skull.*] Alas, poor Yorick! I knew him, Horatio: a fellow of infinite jest, of most excellent fancy: he hath borne me on his back a thousand times; and now, how abhorred in my imagination it is! my gorge rises at it. Here hung those lips that I have kissed I know not how oft. Where be your gibes now? your gambols? your songs? your flashes of merriment, that were wont to set the table on a roar? Not one now, to mock your own grinning? quite chap-fallen? Now get you to my lady's chamber, and tell her, let her paint an inch thick, to this favour she must come; make her laugh at that. Prithee, Horatio, tell me one thing.

HOR.   What's that, my lord?   144

HAM.   Dost thou think Alexander looked o' this fashion i' the earth?

HOR.   E'en so.

HAM.   And smelt so? pah!   [*Puts down the skull.*]

HOR.   E'en so, my lord.

HAM.   To what base uses we may return, Horatio! Why may not imagination trace the noble dust of Alexander, till 'a find it stopping a bung-hole?

HOR.   'Twere to consider too curiously, to consider so.   151

HAM.   No, faith, not a jot; but to follow him thither with modesty enough, and likelihood to lead it: as thus: Alexander died, Alexander was buried, Alexander returneth into dust; the dust is earth; of earth we make loam; and why of that loam, whereto he was converted, might they not stop a beer-barrel?
Imperious Caesar, dead and turn'd to clay,
Might stop a hole to keep the wind away:
O, that that earth, which kept the world in awe,
Should patch a wall t' expel the winter's flaw!
But soft! but soft awhile! here comes the king,   160

Enter KING, QUEEN, LAERTES, *and the* Corse [*of* OPHELIA, *in procession, with* PRIEST, LORDS, *etc.*].

The queen, the courtiers: who is this they follow?
And with such maimed rites? This doth betoken
The corse they follow did with desp'rate hand
Fordo it own life: 'twas of some estate.

Couch we awhile, and mark.   *[Retiring with* HORATIO.]

LAER.   What ceremony else?

HAM.   That is Laertes,
    A very noble youth: mark.

LAER.   What ceremony else?

FIRST PRIEST.   Her obsequies have been as far enlarg'd
    As we have warranty: her death was doubtful;   170
    And, but that great command o'ersways the order,
    She should in ground unsanctified have lodg'd
    Till the last trumpet; for charitable prayers,
    Shards, flints and pebbles should be thrown on her:
    Yet here she is allow'd her virgin crants,
    Her maiden strewments and the bringing home
    Of bell and burial.

LAER.   Must there no more be done?

FIRST PRIEST.   No more be done:
    We should profane the service of the dead
    To sing a requiem and such rest to her   180
    As to peace-parted souls.

LAER.   Lay her i' th' earth:
    And from her fair and unpolluted flesh
    May violets spring! I tell thee, churlish priest,
    A minist'ring angel shall my sister be,
    When thou liest howling.

HAM.   What, the fair Ophelia!

QUEEN.   Sweets to the sweet: farewell!   *[Scattering flowers.]*
    I hop'd thou shouldst have been my Hamlet's wife;
    I thought thy bride-bed to have deck'd, sweet maid,
    And not have strew'd thy grave.

LAER.   O, treble woe
    Fall ten times treble on that cursed head,   190
    Whose wicked deed thy most ingenious sense
    Depriv'd thee of! Hold off the earth awhile,
    Till I have caught her once more in mine arms: *[Leaps into the grave.]*
    Now pile your dust upon the quick and dead,
    Till of this flat a mountain you have made,
    T' o'ertop old Pelion, or the skyish head
    Of blue Olympus.

HAM.   *[Advancing]* What is he whose grief
    Bears such an emphasis? whose phrase of sorrow
    Conjures the wand'ring stars, and makes them stand
    Like wonder-wounded hearers? This is I,   200

Hamlet the Dane.   [*Leaps into the grave.*]

LAER.   The devil take thy soul!

[*Grappling with him.*]

HAM.   Thou pray'st not well.
I prithee, take thy fingers from my throat;
For, though I am not splenitive and rash,
Yet have I in me something dangerous,
Which let thy wisdom fear: hold off thy hand.

KING.   Pluck them asunder.

QUEEN.   Hamlet, Hamlet!

ALL.   Gentlemen,—

HOR.   Good my lord, be quiet.
                    [*The* ATTENDANTS *part them, and they come out of the grave.*]   210

HAM.   Why, I will fight with him upon this theme
Until my eyelids will no longer wag.

QUEEN.   O my son, what theme?

HAM.   I lov'd Ophelia: forty thousand brothers
Could not, with all their quantity of love,
Make up my sum. What wilt thou do for her?

KING.   O, he is mad, Laertes.

QUEEN.   For love of God, forbear him.

HAM.   'Swounds, show me what thou 'lt do:
Woo 't weep? woo 't fight? woo 't fast? woo 't tear thyself?
Woo 't drink up eisel? eat a crocodile?   220
I'll do 't. Dost thou come here to whine?
To outface me with leaping in her grave?
Be buried quick with her, and so will I:
And, if thou prate of mountains, let them throw
Millions of acres on us, till our ground,
Singeing his pate against the burning zone,
Make Ossa like a wart! Nay, an thou 'lt mouth,
I'll rant as well as thou.

QUEEN.   This is mere madness:
And thus awhile the fit will work on him;
Anon, as patient as the female dove,   230
When that her golden couplets are disclos'd,
His silence will sit drooping.

HAM.   Hear you, sir;
What is the reason that you use me thus?
I lov'd you ever: but it is no matter;
Let Hercules himself do what he may,
The cat will mew and dog will have his day.

KING. I pray thee, good Horatio, wait upon him.   *Exit* HAMLET *and* HORATIO.
          [*To* LAERTES] Strengthen your patience in our last night's speech;
          We'll put the matter to the present push.
          Good Gertrude, set some watch over your son.   240
          This grave shall have a living monument:
          An hour of quiet shortly shall we see;
          Till then, in patience our proceeding be.   *Exeunt.*

[SCENE II. *A hall in the castle.*]

Enter HAMLET *and* HORATIO.

HAM.   So much for this, sir: now shall you see the other;
          You do remember all the circumstance?

HOR.   Remember it, my lord!

HAM.   Sir, in my heart there was a kind of fighting,
          That would not let me sleep: methought I lay
          Worse than the mutines in the bilboes. Rashly,
          And prais'd be rashness for it, let us know,
          Our indiscretion sometime serves us well,
          When our deep plots do pall: and that should learn us
          There's a divinity that shapes our ends,
          Rough-hew them how we will,—   10

HOR.   That is most certain.

HAM.   Up from my cabin,
          My sea-gown scarf'd about me, in the dark
          Grop'd I to find out them; had my desire,
          Finger'd their packet, and in fine withdrew
          To mine own room again; making so bold,
          My fears forgetting manners, to unseal
          Their grand commission; where I found, Horatio,—
          O royal knavery!—an exact command,
          Larded with many several sorts of reasons
          Importing Denmark's health and England's too,   20
          With, ho! such bugs and goblins in my life,
          That, on the supervise, no leisure bated,
          No, not to stay the grinding of the axe,
          My head should be struck off.

HOR.   Is 't possible?

HAM.   Here's the commission: read it at more leisure.
          But wilt thou hear me how I did proceed?

HOR.   I beseech you.

HAM.   Being thus be-netted round with villanies,—

Ere I could make a prologue to my brains,
They had begun the play—I sat me down, 30
Devis'd a new commission, wrote it fair:
I once did hold it, as our statists do,
A baseness to write fair and labour'd much
How to forget that learning, but, sir, now
It did me yeoman's service: wilt thou know
Th' effect of what I wrote?

HOR.   Ay, good my lord.

HAM.   An earnest conjuration from the king,
As England was his faithful tributary,
As love between them like the palm might flourish,
As peace should still her wheaten garland wear 40
And stand a comma 'tween their amities,
And many such-like 'As'es of great charge,
That, on the view and knowing of these contents,
Without debatement further, more or less,
He should the bearers put to sudden death,
Not shriving-time allow'd.

HOR.   How was this seal'd?

HAM.   Why, even in that was heaven ordinant.
I had my father's signet in my purse,
Which was the model of that Danish seal;
Folded the writ up in the form of th' other, 50
Subscrib'd it, gave 't th' impression, plac'd it safely,
The changeling never known. Now, the next day
Was our sea-fight; and what to this was sequent
Thou know'st already.

HOR.   So Guildenstern and Rosencrantz go to 't.

HAM.   Why, man, they did make love to this employment;
They are not near my conscience; their defeat
Does by their own insinuation grow:
'Tis dangerous when the baser nature comes
Between the pass and fell incensed points 60
Of mighty opposites.

HOR.   Why, what a king is this!

HAM.   Does it not, think thee, stand me now upon—
He that hath kill'd my king and whor'd my mother,
Popp'd in between th' election and my hopes,
Thrown out his angle for my proper life,
And with such coz'nage—is't not perfect conscience,
To quit him with this arm? and is't not to be damn'd,
To let this canker of our nature come

In further evil?

HOR.   It must be shortly known to him from England   70
What is the issue of the business there.

HAM.   It will be short: the interim is mine;
And a man's life's no more than to say 'One.'
But I am very sorry, good Horatio,
That to Laertes I forgot myself;
For, by the image of my cause, I see
The portraiture of his: I'll court his favours:
But, sure, the bravery of his grief did put me
Into a tow'ring passion.

HOR.   Peace! who comes here?

                                                  80

Enter a COURTIER [OSRIC].

OSR.   Your lordship is right welcome back to Denmark.

HAM.   I humbly thank you, sir. [To HOR.] Dost know this water-fly?

HOR.   No, my good lord.

HAM.   Thy state is the more gracious; for 'tis a vice to know him. He hath much land, and fertile: let a beast be lord of beasts, and his crib shall stand at the king's mess: 'tis a chough; but, as I say, spacious in the possession of dirt.

OSR.   Sweet lord, if your lordship were at leisure, I should impart a thing to you from his majesty.

HAM.   I will receive it, sir, with all diligence of spirit.
Put your bonnet to his right use; 'tis for the head.

OSR.   I thank your lordship, it is very hot.   90

HAM.   No, believe me, 'tis very cold; the wind is northerly.

OSR.   It is indifferent cold, my lord, indeed.

HAM.   But yet methinks it is very sultry and hot for my complexion.

OSR.   Exceedingly, my lord; it is very sultry,—as 'twere,—I cannot tell how. But, my lord, his majesty bade me signify to you that 'a has laid a great wager on your head: sir, this is the matter,—

HAM.   I beseech you, remember—   [HAMLET *moves him to put on his hat.*]

OSR.   Nay, good my lord; for mine ease, in good faith. Sir, here is newly come to court Laertes; believe me, an absolute gentleman, full of most excellent differences, of very soft society and great showing: indeed, to speak feelingly of him, he is the card or calendar of gentry, for you shall find in him the continent of what part a gentleman would see.

HAM.   Sir, his definement suffers no perdition in you; though, I know, to divide him 103
inventorially would dozy the arithmetic of memory, and yet but yaw neither, in respect of his quick sail. But, in the verity of extolment, I take him to be a soul of great article; and his infusion of such dearth and rareness, as, to make true

diction of him, his semblable is his mirror; and who else would trace him, his umbrage, nothing more.

OSR.   Your lordship speaks most infallibly of him.

HAM.   The concernancy, sir? why do we wrap the gentleman in our more rawer   110 breath?

OSR.   Sir?

HOR.   [*Aside to* HAM.] Is 't not possible to understand in another tongue? You will do 't, sir, really.

HAM.   What imports the nomination of this gentleman?

OSR.   Of Laertes?

HOR.   [*Aside to* HAM.] His purse is empty already; all 's golden words are spent.

HAM.   Of him, sir.

OSR.   I know you are not ignorant—

HAM.   I would you did, sir; yet, in faith, if you did, it would not much approve me. Well, sir?

OSR.   You are not ignorant of what excellence Laertes is—   121

HAM.   I dare not confess that, lest I should compare with him in excellence; but, to know a man well, were to know himself.

OSR.   I mean, sir, for his weapon; but in the imputation laid on him by them, in his meed he 's unfellowed.

HAM.   What's his weapon?

OSR.   Rapier and dagger.

HAM.   That's two of his weapons: but, well.

OSR.   The king, sir, hath wagered with him six Barbary horses: against the which he   129 has impawned, as I take it, six French rapiers and poniards, with their assigns, as girdle, hangers, and so: three of the carriages, in faith, are very dear to fancy, very responsive to the hilts, most delicate carriages, and of very liberal conceit.

HAM.   What call you the carriages?

HOR.   [*Aside to* HAM.] I knew you must be edified by the margent ere you had done.

OSR.   The carriages, sir, are the hangers.

HAM.   The phrase would be more german to the matter, if we could carry cannon by our sides: I would it might be hangers till then. But, on: six Barbary horses against six French swords, their assigns, and three liberal-conceited carriages; that 's the French bet against the Danish. Why is this 'impawned,' as you call it?

OSR.   The king, sir, hath laid, that in a dozen passes between yourself and him, he   140 shall not exceed you three hits: he hath laid on twelve for nine; and it would come to immediate trial, if your lordship would vouchsafe the answer.

HAM.   How if I answer 'no'?

OSR.   I mean, my lord, the opposition of your person in trial.

HAM.   Sir, I will walk here in the hall: if it please his majesty, it is the breathing time of day with me; let the foils be brought, the gentleman willing, and the king hold his purpose, I will win for him an I can; if not, I will gain nothing but my shame and the odd hits.

OSR.   Shall I re-deliver you e'en so?

HAM.   To this effect, sir; after what flourish your nature will.   150

OSR.   I commend my duty to your lordship.

HAM.   Yours, yours. [*Exit* OSRIC.] He does well to commend it himself; there are no tongues else for 's turn.

HOR.   This lapwing runs away with the shell on his head.

HAM.   'A did comply, sir, with his dug, before 'a sucked it. Thus has he—and many more of the same breed that I know the drossy age dotes on—only got the tune of the time and out of an habit of encounter; a kind of yesty collection, which carries them through and through the most fann'd and winnowed opinions; and do but blow them to their trial, the bubbles are out.

Enter a LORD.   160

LORD.   My lord, his majesty commended him to you by young Osric, who brings back to him, that you attend him in the hall: he sends to know if your pleasure hold to play with Laertes, or that you will take longer time.

HAM.   I am constant to my purposes; they follow the king's pleasure: if his fitness speaks, mine is ready; now or whensoever, provided I be so able as now.

LORD.   The king and queen and all are coming down.

HAM.   In happy time.

LORD.   The queen desires you to use some gentle entertainment to Laertes before you fall to play.

HAM.   She well instructs me.   [*Exit* LORD.]

HOR.   You will lose this wager, my lord.

HAM.   I do not think so; since he went into France, I have been in continual prac- 171 tice; I shall win at the odds. But thou wouldst not think how ill all 's here about my heart: but it is no matter.

HOR.   Nay, good my lord,—

HAM.   It is but foolery; but it is such a kind of gain-giving, as would perhaps trouble a woman.

HOR.   If your mind dislike any thing, obey it: I will forestal their repair hither, and say you are not fit.

HAM.   Not a whit, we defy augury: there's a special providence in the fall of a spar- 179 row. If it be now, 'tis not to come; if it be not to come, it will be now; if it be not now, yet it will come: the readiness is all: since no man of aught he leaves knows, what is 't to leave betimes? Let be.

A table prepared. [*Enter*] *Trumpets, Drums, and* OFFICERS *with cushions*; KING,

QUEEN, [OSRIC,] *and all the State; foils, daggers,* [*and wine borne in;*] *and* LAERTES.

KING.   Come, Hamlet, come, and take this hand from me. [*The* KING *puts* LAERTES' *hand into* HAMLET'S.]

HAM.   Give me your pardon, sir: I have done you wrong;
But pardon 't, as you are a gentleman.
This presence knows,
And you must needs have heard, how I am punish'd
With a sore distraction. What I have done,
That might your nature, honour and exception
Roughly awake, I here proclaim was madness.   190
Was 't Hamlet wrong'd Laertes? Never Hamlet:
If Hamlet from himself be ta'en away,
And when he 's not himself does wrong Laertes,
Then Hamlet does it not, Hamlet denies it.
Who does it, then? His madness: if 't be so,
Hamlet is of the faction that is wrong'd;
His madness is poor Hamlet's enemy.
Sir, in this audience,
Let my disclaiming from a purpos'd evil
Free me so far in your most generous thoughts,   200
That I have shot mine arrow o'er the house,
And hurt my brother.

LAER.   I am satisfied in nature,
Whose motive, in this case, should stir me most
To my revenge: but in my terms of honour
I stand aloof; and will no reconcilement,
Till by some elder masters, of known honour,
I have a voice and precedent of peace,
To keep my name ungor'd. But till that time,
I do receive your offer'd love like love,
And will not wrong it.   210

HAM.   I embrace it freely;
And will this brother's wager frankly play.
Give us the foils. Come on.

LAER.   Come, one for me.

HAM.   I'll be your foil, Laertes: in mine ignorance
Your skill shall, like a star i' th' darkest night,
Stick fiery off indeed.

LAER.   You mock me, sir.

HAM.   No, by this hand.

KING.   Give them the foils, young Osric. Cousin Hamlet,

You know the wager?

HAM.   Very well, my lord;
Your grace has laid the odds o' th' weaker side.

KING.   I do not fear it; I have seen you both: 220
But since he is better'd, we have therefore odds.

LAER.   This is too heavy, let me see another.

HAM.   This likes me well. These foils have all a length?   *[They prepare to play.]*

OSR.   Ay, my good lord.

KING.   Set me the stoups of wine upon that table.
If Hamlet give the first or second hit,
Or quit in answer of the third exchange,
Let all the battlements their ordnance fire;
The king shall drink to Hamlet's better breath;
And in the cup an union shall he throw,   230
Richer than that which four successive kings
In Denmark's crown have worn. Give me the cups;
And let the kettle to the trumpet speak,
The trumpet to the cannoneer without,
The cannons to the heavens, the heavens to earth,
'Now the king drinks to Hamlet.' Come, begin: *Trumpets the while.*
And you, the judges, bear a wary eye.

HAM.   Come on, sir.

LAER.   Come, my lord.   *[They play.]* 239

HAM.   One.

LAER.   No.

HAM.   Judgement.

OSR.   A hit, a very palpable hit.
                    Drum, trumpets, and shot. Flourish. A piece goes off.

LAER.   Well; again.

KING.   Stay; give me drink. Hamlet, this pearl is thine;
Here's to thy health. Give him the cup.

HAM.   I'll play this bout first; set it by awhile.
Come. *[They play.]* Another hit; what say you?

LAER.   A touch, a touch, I do confess 't.

KING.   Our son shall win.

QUEEN.   He's fat, and scant of breath.
Here, Hamlet, take my napkin, rub thy brows:
The queen carouses to thy fortune, Hamlet.

HAM.   Good madam!

KING.   Gertrude, do not drink.   250

QUEEN.   I will, my lord; I pray you, pardon me.   *[Drinks.]*

KING.   [*Aside*] It is the poison'd cup: it is too late.

HAM.   I dare not drink yet, madam; by and by.

QUEEN.   Come, let me wipe thy face.

LAER.   My lord, I'll hit him now.

KING.   I do not think 't.

LAER.   [*Aside*] And yet 'tis almost 'gainst my conscience.

HAM.   Come, for the third, Laertes: you but dally;
I pray you, pass with your best violence;
I am afeard you make a wanton of me.

LAER.   Say you so? come on.   [*They play.*] 260

OSR.   Nothing, neither way.

LAER.   Have at you now!

     [LAERTES *wounds* HAMLET; *then, in scuffling, they change rapiers, and* HAMLET
                                  wounds LAERTES.]

KING.   Part them; they are incens'd.

HAM.   Nay, come, again.   [*The* QUEEN *falls.*]

OSR.   Look to the queen there, ho!

HOR.   They bleed on both sides. How is it, my lord?

OSR.   How is 't, Laertes?

LAER.   Why, as a woodcock to mine own springe, Osric;
I am justly kill'd with mine own treachery.

HAM.   How does the queen?

KING.   She swounds to see them bleed.

QUEEN.   No, no, the drink, the drink,—O my dear Hamlet,—
The drink, the drink! I am poison'd.   [*Dies.*] 270

HAM.   O villany! Ho! let the door be lock'd:
Treachery! Seek it out.   [LAERTES *falls.*]

LAER.   It is here, Hamlet: Hamlet, thou art slain;
No medicine in the world can do thee good;
In thee there is not half an hour of life;
The treacherous instrument is in thy hand,
Unbated and envenom'd: the foul practice
Hath turn'd itself on me; lo, here I lie,
Never to rise again: thy mother's poison'd:
I can no more: the king, the king's to blame.   280

HAM.   The point envenom'd too!
Then, venom, to thy work.   [*Stabs the* KING.]

ALL.   Treason! treason!

KING.   O, yet defend me, friends; I am but hurt.

HAM.   Here, thou incestuous, murd'rous, damned Dane,

Drink off this potion. Is thy union here?
Follow my mother. [KING *dies.*]

LAER. He is justly serv'd;
It is a poison temper'd by himself.
Exchange forgiveness with me, noble Hamlet:
Mine and my father's death come not upon thee, 290
Nor thine on me! [*Dies.*]

HAM. Heaven make thee free of it! I follow thee.
I am dead, Horatio. Wretched queen, adieu!
You that look pale and tremble at this chance,
That are but mutes or audience to this act,
Had I but time—as this fell sergeant, Death,
Is strict in his arrest—O, I could tell you—
But let it be. Horatio, I am dead;
Thou livest; report me and my cause aright
To the unsatisfied. 300

HOR. Never believe it:
I am more an antique Roman than a Dane:
Here's yet some liquor left.

HAM. As th' art a man,
Give me the cup: let go; by heaven, I'll ha 't.
O God! Horatio, what a wounded name,
Things standing thus unknown, shall live behind me!
If thou didst ever hold me in thy heart,
Absent thee from felicity awhile,
And in this harsh world draw thy breath in pain,
To tell my story. *A march afar off.*
What warlike noise is this? 310

OSR. Young Fortinbras, with conquest come from Poland,
To the ambassadors of England gives
This warlike volley.

HAM. O, I die, Horatio;
The potent poison quite o'er-crows my spirit:
I cannot live to hear the news from England;
But I do prophesy th' election lights
On Fortinbras: he has my dying voice;
So tell him, with th' occurrents, more and less,
Which have solicited. The rest is silence. [*Dies.*]

HOR. Now cracks a noble heart. Good night, sweet prince;
And flights of angels sing thee to thy rest! 320
Why does the drum come hither? [*March within.*]

Enter FORTINBRAS, *with the* [ENGLISH] AMBASSADORS [*and others*].

FORT.   Where is this sight?

HOR.   What is it you would see?
If aught of woe or wonder, cease your search.

FORT.   This quarry cries on havoc. O proud Death,
What feast is toward in thine eternal cell,
That thou so many princes at a shot
So bloodily hast struck?

FIRST AMB.   The sight is dismal;
And our affairs from England come too late:
The ears are senseless that should give us hearing,   330
To tell him his commandment is fulfill'd,
That Rosencrantz and Guildenstern are dead:
Where should we have our thanks?

HOR.   Not from his mouth,
Had it th' ability of life to thank you:
He never gave commandment for their death.
But since, so jump upon this bloody question,
You from the Polack wars, and you from England,
Are here arriv'd, give order that these bodies
High on a stage be placed to the view;
And let me speak to th' yet unknowing world   340
How these things came about: so shall you hear
Of carnal, bloody, and unnatural acts,
Of accidental judgements, casual slaughters,
Of deaths put on by cunning and forc'd cause,
And, in this upshot, purposes mistook
Fall'n on th' inventors' heads: all this can I
Truly deliver.

FORT.   Let us haste to hear it,
And call the noblest to the audience.
For me, with sorrow I embrace my fortune:
I have some rights of memory in this kingdom,   350
Which now to claim my vantage doth invite me.

HOR.   Of that I shall have also cause to speak,
And from his mouth whose voice will draw on more:
But let this same be presently perform'd,
Even while men's minds are wild; lest more mischance,
On plots and errors, happen.

FORT.   Let four captains
Bear Hamlet, like a soldier, to the stage;
For he was likely, had he been put on,

To have prov'd most royal: and, for his passage,
The soldiers' music and the rites of war   360
Speak loudly for him.
Take up the bodies: such a sight as this
Becomes the field, but here shows much amiss.
Go, bid the soldiers shoot.

Exeunt [marching, bearing off the dead bodies;
after which a peal of ordnance is shot off].

MICHEL DE MONTAIGNE

Michel de Montaigne (1533–1592) appears at the end of the Renaissance, a correc-
tive voice of skepticism to moderate the age's speculative humanist confidence. After
a humanist education and a brief career in politics, Montaigne retired to his chateau
and there composed essays—highly individual concoctions of observation and opinion—that commented on the issues. Like the humanists, Montaigne sprinkled his essays with quotations from classical authors, often citing Lucretius, the Roman
materialist poet. Montaigne's essays were unique in their air of deliberative detach-
ment, the voice of a highly individual intelligence conversing with itself.

The *Apology for Raymond Sebond* engages a question familiar to Renaissance
philosophy: the position of humanity within creation and the distinguishing qualities
of human nature. Montaigne addresses the same questions as classical Greek humanists and the Renaissance scholar Pico. His concern with language as a feature of
civilization makes his speculations especially modern.

For analysis and interpretation:

1. Compare Montaigne's dictum that "presumption is our natural and original
malady" to Christian belief that disobedience and sinfulness are the original human
woes. How much of human error and suffering might be explained by the error of
vain presumptuousness?

2. What might Montaigne have said about modern views on animal rights and
the ethical treatment of animals? Cite specific passages to support your hypothesis.

3. Agree or disagree with Montaigne's assertion that a child reared in solitude
would develop the capacity of speech. What human faculties do you believe can only
develop through exposure to human society?

4. Evaluate Montaigne's opinion that humans are distinguished by an "unruliness of thought" that is the main source of human unhappiness.

From *Apology for Raymond Sebond*

[Man is no better than the animals]

Presumption is our natural and original malady. The most vulnerable and frail of all creatures is man, and at the same time the most arrogant. He feels and sees himself lodged here, amid the mire and dung of the world, nailed and riveted to the worst, the deadest, and the most stagnant part of the universe, on the lowest story of the house and the farthest from the vault of heaven, with the animals of the worst condition of the three; and in his imagination he goes planting himself above the circle of the moon, and bringing the sky down beneath his feet. It is by the vanity of this same imagination that he equals himself to God, attributes to himself divine characteristics, picks himself out and separates himself from the horde of other creatures, carves out their shares to his fellows and companions the animals, and distributes among them such portions of faculties and powers as he sees fit. How does he know, by the force of his intelligence, the secret internal stirrings of animals? By what comparison between them and us does he infer the stupidity that he attributes to them?

When I play with my cat, who knows if I am not a pastime to her more than she is to me? Plato, in his picture of the golden age under Saturn, counts among the principal advantages of the man of that time the communication he had with the beasts; inquiring of them and learning from them, he knew the true qualities and differences of each one of them; whereby he acquired a very perfect intelligence and prudence, and conducted his life far more happily than we could possibly do. Do we need a better proof to judge man's impudence with regard to the beasts? That great author opined that in most of the bodily form that Nature gave them, she considered solely the use of prognostications that were derived from them in his time.

This defect that hinders communication between them and us, why is it not just as much ours as theirs? It is a matter of guesswork whose fault it is that we do not understand one another; for we do not understand them any more than they do us. By this same reasoning they may consider us beasts, as we consider them. It is no great wonder if we do not understand them; neither do we understand the Basques and the Troglodytes. However, some have boasted of understanding them, like Apollonius of Tyana, Melampus, Tiresias, Thales, and others. And since it is a fact, as the cosmographers say, that there are nations that accept a dog as their king, they must give a definite interpretation to his voice and motions. We must notice the parity there is between us. We have some mediocre understanding of their meaning; so do they of ours, in about the same degree. They flatter us, threaten us, and implore us, and we them.

Furthermore, we discover very evidently that there is full and complete communication between them and that they understand each other, not only those of the same species, but also those of different species.

> Even dumb cattle and the savage beasts
> Varied and different noises do employ
> When they feel fear or pain, or thrill with joy.
> Lucretius

In a certain bark of the dog the horse knows there is anger; at a certain other sound of his he is not frightened. Even in the beasts that have no voice, from the mutual services we see between them we easily infer some other means of communication; their motions converse and discuss:

> Likewise in children, the tongue's speechlessness
> Leads them to gesture what they would express.
>   Lucretius

Why not; just as well as our mutes dispute, argue, and tell stories by signs? I have seen some so supple and versed in this, that in truth they lacked nothing of perfection in being able to make themselves understood. Lovers grow angry, are reconciled, entreat, thank, make assignations, and in fine say everything, with their eyes:

> And silence too records
> Our prayers and our words.
>   Tasso

What of the hands? We beg, we promise, call, dismiss, threaten, pray, entreat, deny, refuse, question, admire, count, confess, repent, fear, blush, doubt, instruct, command, incite, encourage, swear, testify, accuse, condemn, absolve, insult, despise, defy, vex, flatter, applaud, bless, humiliate, mock, reconcile, commend, exalt, entertain, rejoice, complain, grieve, mope, despair, wonder, exclaim, are silent, and what not, with a variation and multiplication that vie with the tongue. With the head: we invite, send away, avow, disavow, give the lie, welcome, honor, venerate, disdain, demand, show out, cheer, lament, caress, scold, submit, brave, exhort, menace, assure, inquire. What of the eyebrows? What of the shoulders? There is no movement that does not speak both a language intelligible without instruction, and a public language; which means, seeing the variety and particular use of other languages, that this one must rather be judged the one proper to human nature. I omit what necessity teaches privately and promptly to those who need it, and the finger alphabets, and the grammars in gestures, and the sciences which are practiced and expressed only by gestures, and the nations which Pliny says have no other language.

An ambassador of the city of Abdera, after speaking at length to King Agis of Sparta, asked him: "Well, Sire, what answer do you wish me to take back to our citizens?" "That I allowed you to say all you wanted, and as much as you wanted, without ever saying a word." Wasn't that an eloquent and thoroughly intelligible silence?

Moreover, what sort of faculty of ours do we not recognize in the actions of the animals? Is there a society regulated with more order, diversified into more charges and functions, and more consistently maintained, than that of the honeybees? Can we imagine so orderly an arrangement of actions and occupations as this to be conducted without reason and foresight?

Some, by these signs and instances inclined,
Have said that bees share in the divine mind
And the ethereal spirit.

Virgil

Do the swallows that we see on the return of spring ferreting in all the corners of our houses search without judgment, and choose without discrimination, out of a thousand places, the one which is most suitable for them to dwell in? And in that beautiful and admirable texture of their buildings, can birds use a square rather than a round figure, an obtuse rather than a right angle, without knowing their properties and their effects? Do they take now water, now clay, without judging that hardness is softened by moistening? Do they floor their palace with moss or with down, without foreseeing that the tender limbs of their little ones will lie softer and more comfortably on it? Do they shelter themselves from the rainy wind and face their dwelling toward the orient without knowing the different conditions of these winds and considering that one is more salutary to them than the other? Why does the spider thicken her web in one place and slacken it in another, use now this sort of knot, now that one, unless she has the power of reflection, and thought, and inference?

We recognize easily enough, in most of their works, how much superiority the animals have over us and how feeble is our skill to imitate them. We see, however, in our cruder works, the faculties that we use, and that our soul applies itself with all its power; why do we not think the same thing of them? Why do we attribute to some sort of natural and servile inclination these works which surpass all that we can do by nature and by art? Wherein, without realizing it, we grant them a very great advantage over us, by making Nature, with maternal tenderness, accompany them and guide them as by the hand in all the actions and comforts of their life; while us she abandons to chance and to fortune, and to seek by art the things necessary for our preservation, and denies us at the same time the power to attain, by any education and mental straining, the natural resourcefulness of the animals: so that their brutish stupidity surpasses in all conveniences all that our divine intelligence can do.

Truly, by this reckoning, we should be quite right to call her a very unjust stepmother. But this is not so; our organization is not so deformed and disorderly. Nature has universally embraced all her creatures; and there is none that she has not very amply furnished with all powers necessary for the preservation of its being. For these vulgar complaints that I hear men make (as the license of their opinions now raises them above the clouds, and then sinks them to the antipodes) that we are the only animal abandoned naked on the naked earth, tied, bound, having nothing to arm and cover ourselves with except the spoils of others; whereas all other creatures Nature has clothed with shells, husks, bark, hair, wool, spikes, hide, down, feathers, scales, fleece, and silk, according to the need of their being; has armed them with claws, teeth, or horns for attack and defense; and has herself instructed them in what is fit for them—to swim, to run, to fly, to sing—whereas man can neither walk, nor speak, nor eat, nor do anything but cry, without apprenticeship—

The infant, like a sailor tossed ashore
By raging seas, lies naked on the earth,
Speechless, helpless for life, when at his birth
Nature from out the womb brings him to light.
He fills the place with wailing, as is right
For one who through so many woes must pass.
Yet flocks, herds, savage beasts of every class
Grow up without the need for any rattle,
Or for a gentle nurse's soothing prattle;
They seek no varied clothes against the sky;
Lastly they need no arms, no ramparts high
To guard their own—since earth itself and nature
Amply bring forth all things for every creature
                                        Lucretius

—those complaints are false, there is a greater equality and a more uniform relationship in the organization of the world. Our skin is provided as adequately as theirs with endurance against the assaults of the weather: witness so many nations who have not yet tried the use of any clothes. Our ancient Gauls wore hardly any clothes; nor do the Irish, our neighbors, under so cold a sky. But we may judge this better by ourselves; for all the parts of the body that we see fit to expose to the wind and air are found fit to endure it: face, feet, hands, legs, shoulders, head, according as custom invites us. For if there is a part of us that is tender and that seems as though it should fear the cold, it should be the stomach, where digestion takes place; our fathers left it uncovered, and our ladies, soft and delicate as they are, sometimes go half bare down to the navel. Nor are the bindings and swaddlings of infants necessary either; and the Lacedaemonian mothers raised their children in complete freedom to move their limbs, without wrapping or binding them. Our weeping is common to most of the other animals; and there are scarcely any who are not observed to complain and wail long after their birth, since it is a demeanor most appropriate to the helplessness that they feel. As for the habit of eating, it is, in us as in them, natural and needing no instruction:

For each one feels his powers and his needs.
                                        Lucretius

Who doubts that a child, having attained the strength to feed himself, would be able to seek his food? And the earth produces and offers him enough of it for his need, with no other cultivation or artifice; and if not in all weather, neither does she for the beasts: witness the provisions we see the ants and others make for the sterile seasons of the year. These nations that we have just discovered to be so abundantly furnished with food and natural drink, without care or preparation, have now taught us that bread is not our only food, and that without plowing, our mother Nature had provided us in plenty with all we needed; indeed, as seems likely, more amply and richly than she does now that we have interpolated our artifice:

> At first and of her own accord the earth
> Brought forth sleek fruits and vintages of worth,
> Herself gave harvests sweet and pastures fair,
> Which now scarce grow, despite our toil and care,
> And we exhaust our oxen and our men;
>
> Lucretius

the excess and unruliness of our appetite outstripping all the inventions with which we seek to satisfy it. [. . .]

I have said all this to maintain this resemblance that exists to human things, and to bring us back and join us to the majority. We are neither above nor below the rest: all that is under heaven, says the sage, incurs the same law and the same fortune,

> All things are bound by their own chains of fate.
>
> Lucretius

There is some difference, there are orders and degrees; but it is under the aspect of one and the same nature:

> And all things go their own way, nor forget
> Distinctions by the law of nature set.
>
> Lucretius

Man must be constrained and forced into line inside the barriers of this order. The poor wretch is in no position really to step outside them; he is fettered and bound, he is subjected to the same obligation as the other creatures of his class, and in a very ordinary condition, without any real and essential prerogative or preeminence. That which he accords himself in his mind and in his fancy has neither body nor taste. And if it is true that he alone of all the animals has this freedom of imagination and this unruliness in thought that represents to him what is, what is not, what he wants, the false and the true, it is an advantage that is sold him very dear, and in which he has little cause to glory, for from it springs the principal source of the ills that oppress him: sin, disease, irresolution, confusion, despair.

So I say, to return to my subject, that there is no apparent reason to judge that the beasts do by natural and obligatory instinct the same things that we do by our choice and cleverness. We must infer from like results like faculties and consequently confess that this same reason, this same method that we have for working, is also that of the animals. Why do we imagine in them this compulsion of nature, we who feel no similar effect? Besides, it is more honorable, and closer to divinity, to be guided and obliged to act lawfully by a natural and inevitable condition, than to act lawfully by accidental and fortuitous liberty; and safer to leave the reins of our conduct to nature than to ourselves. The vanity of our presumption makes us prefer to owe our ability to our powers than to nature's liberality; and we enrich the other animals with natural goods and renounce them in their favor, in order to honor and ennoble ourselves with goods acquired: a very simple notion, it seems to me, for I should prize just as highly graces that were all mine and inborn as those I had gone begging and seeking from education. It is not in our power to acquire a fairer recommendation than to be favored by God and nature.

—Translated by Donald Frame

2

The Baroque and Enlightenment

The turmoil of seventeenth-century European society is evident in the currents of the age's literature and philosophy. Torn by religious war and astounded by new discoveries in science and exploration, the seventeenth century persistently sought truth and order but often found uncertainty and conflict. Even before René Descartes pursued the methodical skepticism of his *Discourse on Method*, Miguel de Cervantes was exploring the unreliability of human perception and knowledge in his novel *Don Quixote*. Some poets responded to these doubts by fervently reaffirming religious belief, in the form of both Catholic and Protestant faiths. Often perplexed by quandary, the baroque era was the first truly modern age, its problems much in sympathy with the contemporary age.

Inspired by the optimistic wish to apply human reason in improving human existence, the Enlightenment believed determinedly in the possibility of human progress. Yet, progress could come only through a clear-eyed analysis of human prejudice and social injustice. Both Jonathan Swift and Voltaire turned their satirical eye on eighteenth-century society, cataloging its barbarous excesses in the mocking tones of satirical exaggeration. Voltaire's urbane vision of a "garden" where humans tend to their own affairs, eschewing idle speculation, summarizes the practical bent of Enlightenment thinking.

In its rationalism, its excesses, its doubts, the age of baroque and the Enlightenment anticipated the outlines of modern thought. It was a time in which traditional verities dissolved, knowledge was reborn, and thinkers clung passionately to reason as the surest foundation of human progress.

MIGUEL DE CERVANTES

Although Miguel de Cervantes (1547–1616) wrote only one masterpiece, the greatness of *Don Quixote* assures Cervantes's place in any pantheon of literary genius. *Don Quixote* is at once a hilarious parody of human folly and a profound philosophical speculation on the tension between perception and reality.

In Part One of the novel, the hero Don Quixote imposes his feverish medieval fantasies on the world, attempting to recast the ordinary settings and characters of rural Spain as a chivalric drama. Despite the wry counsel of his "squire," Sancho Panza, Quixote often suffers defeat and humiliation. Quixote's imaginative vision is so powerful, however, that it compels others to engage the hero on his own terms. Quixote's friend Sansón Carrasco disguises himself as the Knight of the Wood, complying with and thus confirming Quixote's fantasy. Although they regard Quixote as a madman, the novel's other characters cannot resist the charm of his quaint and idealized view of the world. By the end of Part Two, however, a disheartened Quixote sheds his disguise and returns to his village; at Quixote's deathbed, Sancho vainly urges his master to continue their romance.

For analysis and interpretation:

1. What analogy can be drawn between Quixote's book-inspired fantasies and others who impose literary, religious, or political ideas upon a resistant reality (economic and political theories, literary or cinematic fantasies, and so on)?

2. In the episodes presented here, how does Sancho Panza respond to Quixote's bookish madness? What changes are apparent in Sancho's attitude, given his response to Quixote's deathbed disavowal of his knightly mission?

3. In your opinion, can a deluded vision or fantasy like Quixote's actually improve the lives of those who hold it? If you were Quixote's friend, would you seek (like the bachelor) to disillusion your friend?

From *Don Quixote*

CHAPTER I. *Which treats of the station in life and the pursuits of the famous gentleman, Don Quixote de la Mancha.*

In a village of La Mancha the name of which I have no desire to recall, there lived not so long ago one of those gentlemen who always have a lance in the rack, an ancient buckler, a skinny nag, and a greyhound for the chase. A stew with more beef than mutton in it, chopped meat for his evening meal, scraps for a Saturday, lentils on Friday, and a young pigeon as a special delicacy for Sunday, went to account for three-quarters of his income. The rest of it he laid out on a broadcloth greatcoat and velvet stockings for feast days, with slippers to match, while the other days of the week he cut a figure in a suit of the finest homespun. Living with him were a housekeeper in her forties, a niece who was not yet twenty, and a lad of the field and market place who saddled his horse for him and wielded the pruning knife.

This gentleman of ours was close on to fifty, of a robust constitution but with little flesh on his bones and a face that was lean and gaunt. He was noted for his early rising, being very fond of the hunt. They will try to tell you that his surname was Quijada or Quesada—there is some difference of opinion among those who have written on the subject—but according to the most likely conjectures we are to understand that it was really Quejana. But all this means very little so far as our story is concerned, providing that in the telling of it we do not depart one iota from the truth.

You may know, then, that the aforesaid gentleman, on those occasions when he was at leisure, which was most of the year around, was in the habit of reading books of chivalry with such pleasure and devotion as to lead him almost wholly to forget the life of a hunter and even the administration of his estate. So great was his curiosity and infatuation in this regard that he even sold many acres of tillable land in order to be able to buy and read the books that he loved, and he would carry home with him as many of them as he could obtain.

Of all those that he thus devoured none pleased him so well as the ones that had been composed by the famous Feliciano de Silva, whose lucid prose style and involved conceits were as precious to him as pearls; especially when he came to read those tales of love and amorous challenges that are to be met with in many places, such a passage as the following, for example: "The reason of the unreason that afflicts my reason, in such a manner weakens my reason that I with reason lament me of your comeliness." And he was similarly affected when his eyes fell upon such lines as these: ". . . the high Heaven of your divinity divinely fortifies you with the stars and renders you deserving of that desert your greatness doth deserve."

The poor fellow used to lie awake nights in an effort to disentangle the meaning and make sense out of passages such as these, although Aristotle himself would not have been able to understand them, even if he had been resurrected for that sole purpose. He was not at ease in his mind over those wounds that Don Belianís gave and received; for no matter how great the surgeons who treated him, the poor fellow must have been left with his face and his entire body covered with marks and scars. Nevertheless, he was grateful to the author for closing the book with the promise of an interminable adventure to come; many a time he was tempted to take up his pen and literally finish the tale as had been promised, and he undoubtedly would have done so, and would have succeeded at it very well, if his thoughts had not been constantly occupied with other things of greater moment.

He often talked it over with the village curate, who was a learned man, a graduate of Sigüenza, and they would hold long discussions as to who had been the better knight, Palmerin of England or Amadis of Gaul; but Master Nicholas, the barber of the same village, was in the habit of saying that no one could come up to the Knight of Phoebus, and that if anyone *could* compare with him it was Don Galaor, brother of Amadis of Gaul, for Galaor was ready for anything—he was none of your finical knights, who went around whimpering as his brother did, and in point of valor he did not lag behind him.

In short, our gentleman became so immersed in his reading that he spent whole nights from sundown to sunup and his days from dawn to dusk in poring over his books, until, finally, from so little sleeping and so much reading, his brain dried up and he went completely out of his mind. He had filled his imagination with everything that he had read, with enchantments, knightly encounters, battles, challenges, wounds, with tales of love and its torments, and all sorts of impossible things, and as a result had come to believe that all these fictitious happenings were true; they were more real to him than anything else in the world. He would remark that the Cid Ruy Díaz had been a very good knight, but there was no comparison between him and the

Knight of the Flaming Sword, who with a single backward stroke had cut in half two fierce and monstrous giants. He preferred Bernardo del Carpio, who at Roncesvalles had slain Roland despite the charm the latter bore, availing himself of the stratagem which Hercules employed when he strangled Antaeus, the son of Earth, in his arms.

He had much good to say for Morgante who, though he belonged to the haughty, overbearing race of giants, was of an affable disposition and well brought up. But, above all, he cherished an admiration for Rinaldo of Montalbán, especially as he beheld him sallying forth from his castle to rob all those that crossed his path, or when he thought of him overseas stealing the image of Mohammed which, so the story has it, was all of gold. And he would have liked very well to have had his fill of kicking that traitor Galalón, a privilege for which he would have given his housekeeper with his niece thrown into the bargain.

At last, when his wits were gone beyond repair, he came to conceive the strangest idea that ever occurred to any madman in this world. It now appeared to him fitting and necessary, in order to win a greater amount of honor for himself and serve his country at the same time, to become a knight-errant and roam the world on horseback, in a suit of armor; he would go in quest of adventures, by way of putting into practice all that he had read in his books; he would right every manner of wrong, placing himself in situations of the greatest peril such as would redound to the eternal glory of his name. As a reward for his valor and the might of his arm, the poor fellow could already see himself crowned Emperor of Trebizond at the very least; and so, carried away by the strange pleasure that he found in such thoughts as these, he at once set about putting his plan into effect.

The first thing he did was to burnish up some old pieces of armor, left him by his great-grandfather, which for ages had lain in a corner, moldering and forgotten. He polished and adjusted them as best he could, and then he noticed that one very important thing was lacking: there was no closed helmet, but only a morion, or visorless headpiece, with turned up brim of the kind foot soldiers wore. His ingenuity, however, enabled him to remedy this, and he proceeded to fashion out of cardboard a kind of half-helmet, which, when attached to the morion, gave the appearance of a whole one. True, when he went to see if it was strong enough to withstand a good slashing blow, he was somewhat disappointed; for when he drew his sword and gave it a couple of thrusts, he succeeded only in undoing a whole week's labor. The ease with which he had hewed it to bits disturbed him no little, and he decided to make it over. This time he placed a few strips of iron on the inside, and then, convinced that it was strong enough, refrained from putting it to any further test; instead, he adopted it then and there as the finest helmet ever made.

After this, he went out to have a look at his nag; and although the animal had more *cuartos*, or cracks, in its hoof than there are quarters in a real, and more blemishes than Gonela's steed which *tantum pellis et ossa fuit*, it nonetheless looked to its master like a far better horse than Alexander's Bucephalus or the Babieca of the Cid. He spent all of four days in trying to think up a name for his mount; for—so he told himself—seeing that it belonged to so famous and worthy a knight, there was no reason why it should not have a name of equal renown. The kind of name he wanted was one that would at once indicate what the nag had been before it came to belong to a knight-errant and what its present status was; for it stood to reason that, when the master's wordly condition changed, his horse also ought to have a famous, high-sounding appellation, one suited to the new order of things and the new profession that it was to follow.

After he in his memory and imagination had made up, struck out, and discarded many names, now adding to and now subtracting from the list, he finally hit upon "Rocinante," a name that impressed him as being sonorous and at the same time indicative of what the steed had been when it was but a hack, whereas now it was nothing other than the first and foremost of all the hacks in the world.

Having found a name for his horse that pleased his fancy, he then desired to do as much for himself, and this required another week, and by the end of that period he had made up his mind that he was henceforth to be known as Don Quixote, which, as has been stated, has led the authors of this veracious history to assume that his real name must undoubtedly have been Quijada, and not Quesada as others would have it. But remembering that the valiant Amadis was not content to call himself that and nothing more, but added the name of his kingdom and fatherland that he might make it famous also, and thus came to take the name Amadis of Gaul, so our good knight chose to add his place of origin and become "Don Quixote de la Mancha"; for by this means, as he saw it, he was making very plain his lineage and was conferring honor upon his country by taking its name as his own.

And so, having polished up his armor and made the morion over into a closed helmet, and having given himself and his horse a name, he naturally found but one thing lacking still: he must seek out a lady of whom he could become enamored; for a knight-errant without a ladylove was like a tree without leaves or fruit, a body without a soul.

"If," he said to himself, "as a punishment for my sins or by a stroke of fortune I should come upon some giant hereabouts, a thing that very commonly happens to knights-errant, and if I should slay him in a hand-to-hand encounter or perhaps cut him in two, or, finally, if I should vanquish and subdue him, would it not be well to have someone to whom I may send him as a present, in order that he, if he is living, may come in, fall upon his knees in front of my sweet lady, and say in a humble and submissive tone of voice, 'I, lady, am the giant Caraculiambro, lord of the island Malindrania, who has been overcome in single combat by that knight who never can be praised enough, Don Quixote de la Mancha, the same who sent me to present myself before your Grace that your Highness may dispose of me as you see fit'?"

Oh, how our good knight reveled in this speech, and more than ever when he came to think of the name that he should give his lady! As the story goes, there was a very good-looking farm girl who lived near by, with whom he had once been smitten, although it is generally believed that she never knew or suspected it. Her name was Aldonza Lorenzo, and it seemed to him that she was the one upon whom he should bestow the title of mistress of his thoughts. For her he wished a name that should not be incongruous with his own and that would convey the suggestion of a princess or a great lady; and, accordingly, he resolved to call her "Dulcinea del Toboso," she being a native of that place. A musical name to his ears, out of the ordinary and significant, like the others he had chosen for himself and his appurtenances. . . .

[*Quixote's first sally takes him to a tavern where he mistakes the establishment for a medieval castle and its inhabitants as noble ladies and gentlemen.*]

CHAPTER VII. *Of the second sally of our good knight, Don Quixote de la Mancha.*

. . . In the meanwhile Don Quixote was bringing his powers of persuasion to bear upon a farmer who lived near by, a good man—if this title may be applied to one who is poor—but with very few wits in his head. The short of it is, by pleas and promises, he got the hapless rustic to agree to ride forth with him and serve him as his squire. Among other things, Don Quixote told him that he ought to be more than willing to go, because no telling what adventure might occur which would win them an island, and then he (the farmer) would be left to be the governor of it. As a result of these and other similar assurances, Sancho Panza forsook his wife and children and consented to take upon himself the duties of squire to his neighbor.

Next, Don Quixote set out to raise some money, and by selling this thing and pawning that and getting the worst of the bargain always, he finally scraped together a reasonable amount. He also asked a friend of his for the loan of a buckler and patched up his broken helmet as well as he could. He advised his squire, Sancho, of the day and hour when they were to take the road and told him to see to laying in a supply of those things that were most necessary, and, above all, not to forget the saddlebags. Sancho replied that he would see to all this and added that he was also thinking of taking along with him a very good ass that he had, as he was not much used to going on foot.

With regard to the ass, Don Quixote had to do a little thinking, trying to recall if any knight-errant had ever had a squire thus asininely mounted. He could not think of any, but nevertheless he decided to take Sancho with the intention of providing him with a nobler steed as soon as occasion offered; he had but to appropriate the horse of the first discourteous knight he met. Having furnished himself with shirts and all the other things that the innkeeper had recommended, he and Panza rode forth one night unseen by anyone and without taking leave of wife and children, housekeeper or niece. They went so far that by the time morning came they were safe from discovery had a hunt been started for them.

Mounted on his ass, Sancho Panza rode along like a patriarch, with saddlebags and flask, his mind set upon becoming governor of that island that his master had promised him. Don Quixote determined to take the same route and road over the Campo de Montiel that he had followed on his first journey; but he was not so uncomfortable this time, for it was early morning and the sun's rays fell upon them slantingly and accordingly did not tire them too much.

"Look, Sir Knight-errant," said Sancho, "your Grace should not forget that island you promised me; for no matter how big it is, I'll be able to govern it right enough."

"I would have you know, friend Sancho Panza," replied Don Quixote, "that among the knights-errant of old it was a very common custom to make their squires governors of the islands or the kingdoms that they won, and I am resolved that in my case so pleasing a usage shall not fall into desuetude. I even mean to go them one better; for they very often, perhaps most of the time, waited until their squires were old men who had had their fill of serving their masters during bad days and worse nights, whereupon they would give them the title of count, or marquis at most, of some valley or province more or less. But if you live and I live, it well may be that within a week I shall win some kingdom with others dependent upon it, and it will be the easiest thing in the world to crown you king of one of them. You need not marvel at this, for all sorts of unforeseen things happen to knights like me, and I may readily be able to give you even more than I have promised."

"In that case," said Sancho Panza, "if by one of those miracles of which your Grace was speaking I should become king, I would certainly send for Juana Gutiérrez, my old lady, to come and be my queen, and the young ones could be infantes."

"There is no doubt about it," Don Quixote assured him.

"Well, I doubt it," said Sancho, "for I think that even if God were to rain kingdoms upon the earth, no crown would sit well on the head of Mari Gutiérrez,[4] for I am telling you, sir, as a queen she is not worth two maravedis. She would do better as a countess, God help her."

"Leave everything to God, Sancho," said Don Quixote, "and he will give you whatever is most fitting; but I trust you will not be so pusillanimous as to be content with anything less than the title of viceroy."

"That I will not," said Sancho Panza, "especially seeing that I have in your Grace so illustrious a master who can give me all that is suitable to me and all that I can manage."

CHAPTER VIII. *Of the good fortune which the valorous Don Quixote had in the terrifying and never-before-imagined adventure of the windmills, along with other events that deserve to be suitably recorded.*

At this point they caught sight of thirty or forty windmills which were standing on the plain there, and no sooner had Don Quixote laid eyes upon them than he turned to his squire and said, "Fortune is guiding our affairs better than we could have wished; for you see there before you, friend Sancho Panza, some thirty or more lawless giants with whom I mean to do battle. I shall deprive them of their lives, and with the spoils from this encounter we shall begin to enrich ourselves; for this is righteous warfare, and it is a great service to God to remove so accursed a breed from the face of the earth."

"What giants?" said Sancho Panza.

"Those that you see there," replied his master, "those with the long arms some of which are as much as two leagues in length."

"But look, your Grace, those are not giants but windmills, and what appear to be arms are their wings which, when whirled in the breeze, cause the millstone to go."

"It is plain to be seen," said Don Quixote, "that you have had little experience in this matter of adventures. If you are afraid, go off to one side and say your prayers while I am engaging them in fierce, unequal combat."

Saying this, he gave spurs to his steed Rocinante, without paying any heed to Sancho's warning that these were truly windmills and not giants that he was riding forth to attack. Nor even when he was close upon them did he perceive what they really were, but shouted at the top of his lungs, "Do not seek to flee, cowards and vile creatures that you are, for it is but a single knight with whom you have to deal!"

At that moment a little wind came up and the big wings began turning.

"Though you flourish as many arms as did the giant Briareus," said Don Quixote when he perceived this, "you still shall have to answer to me."

He thereupon commended himself with all his heart to his lady Dulcinea, be-seeching her to succor him in this peril; and, being well covered with his shield and with his lance at rest, he bore down upon them at a full gallop and fell upon the first mill that stood in his way, giving a thrust at the wing, which was whirling at such a speed that his lance was broken into bits and both horse and horseman went rolling over the plain, very much battered indeed. Sancho upon his donkey came hurrying to his master's assistance as fast as he could, but when he reached the spot, the knight was unable to move, so great was the shock with which he and Rocinante had hit the ground.

"God help us!" exclaimed Sancho, "did I not tell your Grace to look well, that those were nothing but windmills, a fact which no one could fail to see unless he had other mills of the same sort in his head?"

"Be quiet, friend Sancho," said Don Quixote. "Such are the fortunes of war, which more than any other are subject to constant change. What is more, when I come to think of it, I am sure that this must be the work of that magician Frestón, the one who robbed me of my study and my books, and who has thus changed the giants into windmills in order to deprive me of the glory of overcoming them, so great is the en-mity that he bears me; but in the end his evil arts shall not prevail against this trusty sword of mine."

"May God's will be done," was Sancho Panza's response. And with the aid of his squire the knight was once more mounted on Rocinante, who stood there with one shoulder half out of joint. And so, speaking of the adventure that had just befallen them, they continued along the Puerto Lápice highway; for there, Don Quixote said, they could not fail to find many and varied adventures, this being a much traveled thoroughfare. . . .

FROM CHAPTER XIV. [*Don Quixote's duel with the Knight of the Wood, also called the Knight of Mirrors.*]

. . . Don Quixote in the meanwhile was surveying his opponent, who had al-ready adjusted and closed his helmet so that it was impossible to make out what he looked like. It was apparent, however, that he was not very tall and was stockily built. Over his armor he wore a coat of some kind or other made of what appeared to be the finest cloth of gold, all bespangled with glittering mirrors that resembled little moons and that gave him a most gallant and festive air, while above his helmet were a large number of waving plumes, green, white, and yellow in color. His lance, which was leaning against a tree, was very long and stout and had a steel point of more than a palm in length. Don Quixote took all this in, and from what he observed concluded that his opponent must be of tremendous strength, but he was not for this reason filled with fear as Sancho Panza was. Rather, he proceeded to address the Knight of the Mirrors, quite boldly and in a highbred manner.

"Sir Knight," he said, "if in your eagerness to fight you have not lost your courtesy, I would beg you to be so good as to raise your visor a little in order that I may see if your face is as handsome as your trappings."

"Whether you come out of this emprise the victor or the vanquished, Sir Knight," he of the Mirrors replied, "there will be ample time and opportunity for you to have a sight of me. If I do not now gratify your desire, it is because it seems to me that I should be doing a very great wrong to the beauteous Casildea de Vandalia by wasting the time it would take me to raise my visor before having forced you to confess that I am right in my contention, with which you are well acquainted."

"Well, then," said Don Quixote, "while we are mounting our steeds you might at least inform me if I am that knight of La Mancha whom you say you conquered."

"To that our answer," said he of the Mirrors, "is that you are as like the knight I overcame as one egg is like another; but since you assert that you are persecuted by enchanters, I should not venture to state positively that you are the one in question."

"All of which," said Don Quixote, "is sufficient to convince me that you are laboring under a misapprehension; but in order to relieve you of it once and for all, let them bring our steeds, and in less time than you would spend in lifting your visor, if God, my lady, and my arm give me strength, I will see your face and you shall see that I am not the vanquished knight you take me to be."

With this, they cut short their conversation and mounted, and, turning Rocinante around, Don Quixote began measuring off the proper length of field for a run against his opponent as he of the Mirrors did the same. But the Knight of La Mancha had not gone twenty paces when he heard his adversary calling to him, whereupon each of them turned halfway and he of the Mirrors spoke.

"I must remind you, Sir Knight," he said, "of the condition under which we fight, which is that the vanquished, as I have said before, shall place himself wholly at the disposition of the victor."

"I am aware of that," replied Don Quixote, "not forgetting the provision that the behest laid upon the vanquished shall not exceed the bounds of chivalry."

"Agreed," said the Knight of the Mirrors.

At that moment Don Quixote caught sight of the other squire's weird nose and was as greatly astonished by it as Sancho had been. Indeed, he took the fellow for some monster, or some new kind of human being wholly unlike those that people this world. As he saw his master riding away down the field preparatory to the tilt, Sancho was alarmed; for he did not like to be left alone with the big-nosed individual, fearing that one powerful swipe of that protuberance against his own nose would end the battle so far as he was concerned and he would be lying stretched out on the ground, from fear if not from the force of the blow.

He accordingly ran after the knight, clinging to one of Rocinante's stirrup straps, and when he thought it was time for Don Quixote to whirl about and bear down upon his opponent, he called to him and said, "*Señor mio*, I beg your Grace, before you turn for the charge, to help me up into that cork tree yonder where I can watch the encounter which your Grace is going to have with this knight better than I can from the ground and in a way that is much more to my liking."

"I rather think, Sancho," said Don Quixote, "that what you wish to do is to mount a platform where you can see the bulls without any danger to yourself."

"The truth of the matter is," Sancho admitted, "the monstrous nose on that squire has given me such a fright that I don't dare stay near him."

"It is indeed of such a sort," his master assured him, "that if I were not the person I am, I myself should be frightened. And so, come, I will help you up."

While Don Quixote tarried to see Sancho ensconced in the cork tree, the Knight of the Mirrors measured as much ground as seemed to him necessary and then, assuming that his adversary had done the same, without waiting for sound of trumpet or any other signal, he wheeled his horse, which was no swifter nor any more impressive-looking than Rocinante, and bore down upon his enemy at a mild trot; but when he saw that the Manchegan was busy helping his squire, he reined in his mount and came to a stop midway in his course, for which his horse was extremely grateful, being no longer able to stir a single step. To Don Quixote, on the other hand, it seemed as if his enemy was flying, and digging his spurs with all his might into Rocinante's lean flanks he caused that animal to run a bit for the first and only time, according to the history, for on all other occasions a simple trot had represented his utmost speed. And so it was that, with an unheard-of fury, the Knight of the Mournful Countenance came down upon the Knight of the Mirrors as the latter sat there sinking his spurs all the way up to the buttons without being able to persuade his horse to budge a single inch from the spot where he had come to a sudden standstill.

It was at this fortunate moment, while his adversary was in such a predicament, that Don Quixote fell upon him, quite unmindful of the fact that the other knight was having trouble with his mount and either was unable or did not have time to put his lance at rest. The upshot of it was, he encountered him with such force that, much against his will, the Knight of the Mirrors went rolling over his horse's flanks and tumbled to the ground, where as a result of his terrific fall he lay as if dead, without moving hand or foot.

No sooner did Sancho perceive what had happened than he slipped down from the cork tree and ran up as fast as he could to where his master was. Dismounting from Rocinante, Don Quixote now stood over the Knight of the Mirrors, and undoing the helmet straps to see if the man was dead, or to give him air in case he was alive, he beheld—who can say what he beheld without creating astonishment, wonder, and amazement in those who hear the tale? The history tells us that it was the very countenance, form, aspect, physiognomy, effigy, and image of the bachelor Sansón Carrasco!

"Come, Sancho," he cried in a loud voice, "and see what is to be seen but is not to be believed. Hasten, my son, and learn what magic can do and how great is the power of wizards and enchanters.". . .

FROM CHAPTER LXXIV. *Of how Don Quixote fell sick, of the will that he made, and of the manner of his death.*

. . . "I have good news for you, kind sirs," said Don Quixote the moment he saw them. "I am no longer Don Quixote de la Mancha but Alonso Quijano, whose mode of life won for him the name of 'Good.' I am the enemy of Amadis of Gaul and all his innumerable progeny; for those profane stories dealing with knight-errantry are odious to me, and I realize how foolish I was and the danger I courted in reading them; but I am in my right senses now and I abominate them."

Hearing this, they all three were convinced that some new kind of madness must have laid hold of him.

"Why, Señor Don Quixote!" exclaimed Sansón. "What makes you talk like that, just when we have received news that my lady Dulcinea is disenchanted? And just when we are on the verge of becoming shepherds so that we may spend the rest of our lives in singing like a lot of princes, why does your Grace choose to turn hermit? Say no more, in Heaven's name, but be sensible and forget these idle tales."

"Tales of that kind," said Don Quixote, "have been the truth for me in the past, and to my detriment, but with Heaven's aid I trust to turn them to my profit now that I am dying. For I feel, gentlemen, that death is very near; so, leave all jesting aside and bring me a confessor for my sins and a notary to draw up my will. In such straits as these a man cannot trifle with his soul. Accordingly, while the Señor Curate is hearing my confession, let the notary be summoned."

Amazed at his words, they gazed at one another in some perplexity, yet they could not but believe him. One of the signs that led them to think he was dying was this quick return from madness to sanity and all the additional things he had to say, so well reasoned and well put and so becoming in a Christian that none of them could any longer doubt that he was in full possession of his faculties. Sending the others out of the room, the curate stayed behind to confess him, and before long the bachelor returned with the notary and Sancho Panza, who had been informed of his master's condition, and who, finding the housekeeper and the niece in tears, began weeping with them. When the confession was over, the curate came out.

"It is true enough," he said, "that Alonso Quijano the Good is dying, and it is also true that he is a sane man. It would be well for us to go in now while he makes his will."

At this news the housekeeper, niece, and the good squire Sancho Panza were so overcome with emotion that the tears burst forth from their eyes and their bosoms heaved with sobs; for, as has been stated more than once, whether Don Quixote was plain Alonso Quijano the Good or Don Quixote de la Mancha, he was always of a kindly and pleasant disposition and for this reason was beloved not only by the members of his household but by all who knew him.

The notary had entered along with the others, and as soon as the preamble had been attended to and the dying man had commended his soul to his Maker with all those Christian formalities that are called for in such a case, they came to the matter of bequests, with Don Quixote dictating as follows:

"ITEM. With regard to Sancho Panza, whom, in my madness, I appointed to be my squire, and who has in his possession a certain sum of money belonging to me: inasmuch as there has been a standing account between us, of debits and credits, it is my will that he shall not be asked to give any accounting whatsoever of this sum, but if any be left over after he has had payment for what I owe him, the balance, which will amount to very little, shall be his, and much good may it do him. If when I was mad I was responsible for his being given the governorship of an island, now that I am of sound mind I would present him with a kingdom if it were in my power, for his simplicity of mind and loyal conduct merit no less."

At this point he turned to Sancho. "Forgive me, my friend," he said, "for having caused you to appear as mad as I by leading you to fall into the same error, that of believing that there are still knights-errant in the world."

"Ah, master," cried Sancho through his tears, "don't die, your Grace, but take my advice and go on living for many years to come; for the greatest madness that a man can be guilty of in this life is to die without good reason, without anyone's killing him, slain only by the hands of melancholy. Look you, don't be lazy but get up from this bed and let us go out into the fields clad as shepherds as we agreed to do. Who knows but behind some bush we may come upon the lady Dulcinea, as disenchanted as you could wish. If it is because of worry over your defeat that you are dying, put the blame on me by saying that the reason for your being overthrown was that I had not properly fastened Rocinante's girth. For the matter of that, your Grace knows from reading your books of chivalry that it is a common thing for certain knights to overthrow others, and he who is vanquished today will be the victor tomorrow."

"That is right," said Sansón, "the worthy Sancho speaks the truth."

"Not so fast, gentlemen," said Don Quixote. "In last year's nests there are no birds this year. I was mad and now I am sane; I was Don Quixote de la Mancha, and now I am, as I have said, Alonso Quijano the Good. May my repentance and the truth I now speak restore to me the place I once held in your esteem. . . ."

—Translated by Samuel Putnam

RENÉ DESCARTES

René Descartes (1596–1650) developed the philosophical foundations of modern science, describing a method of scientific inquiry that freed science from its theological underpinnings. In his *Discourse on Method*, Descartes sought to apply a mathematical clarity of reasoning to all knowledge, concluding that certain truths can be known with certainty.

In the famous section of the *Discourse* excerpted here, Descartes determines to doubt everything that he has ever learned and to accept nothing as true except "clear and distinct ideas." This systematic doubt can affect every belief except the knowledge that he is a thinking being. Hence, the starting point of Descartes's certainty—"I think, therefore I am"—is the individual, knowing mind. From this certainty, Descartes establishes the existence of God and the foundation of all deductive knowledge. This thoroughly rational explanation of human knowledge became the basis of the modern scientific attitude, which Descartes defended and propagated in the intellectual circles of the seventeenth century.

For analysis and interpretation:

1. Apply a Cartesian-style skepticism to your most certain belief or knowledge. How would you explain the certainty with which you hold these beliefs?

2. Compare Descartes's faith in human understanding with the skepticism of Erasmus or Montaigne, for whom human knowledge inevitably involves folly and presumption.

3. With what philosophical argument might you cast doubt on Descartes's certainty? Might his clear and distinct ideas be as much a fantasm as Don Quixote's windmill giants?

From the *Discourse on Method*

When I was younger, I had studied a little logic in philosophy, and geometrical analysis and algebra in mathematics, three arts or sciences which would appear apt to contribute something towards my plan. But on examining them, I saw that, regarding logic, its syllogisms and most of its other precepts serve more to explain to others what one already knows, or even, like the art of Lully, to speak without judgement of those things one does not know, than to learn anything new. And although logic indeed contains many very true and sound precepts, there are, at the same time, so many others mixed up with them, which are either harmful or superfluous, that it is almost as difficult to separate them as to extract a Diana or a Minerva from a block of unprepared marble. Then, as for the geometrical analysis of the ancients and the algebra of the moderns, besides the fact that they extend only to very abstract matters which seem to be of no practical use, the former is always so tied to the inspection of figures that it cannot exercise the understanding without greatly tiring the imagination, while, in the latter, one is so subjected to certain rules and numbers that it has become a confused and obscure art which oppresses the mind instead of being a science which cultivates it. This was why I thought I must seek some other method which, while continuing the advantages of these three, was free from their defects. And as a multiplicity of laws often furnishes excuses for vice, so that a State is much better ordered when, having only very few laws, they are very strictly observed, so, instead of this great number of precepts of which logic is composed, I believed I would have sufficient in the four following rules, so long as I took a firm and constant resolve never once to fail to observe them.

The first was never to accept anything as true that I did not know to be evidently so: that is to say, carefully to avoid precipitancy and prejudice, and to include in my judgements nothing more than what presented itself so clearly and so distinctly to my mind that I might have no occasion to place it in doubt.

The second, to divide each of the difficulties that I was examining into as many parts as might be possible and necessary in order best to solve it.

The third, to conduct my thoughts in an orderly way, beginning with the simplest objects and the easiest to know, in order to climb gradually, as by degrees, as far as the knowledge of the most complex, and even supposing some order among those objects which do not precede each other naturally.

And the last, everywhere to make such complete enumerations and such general reviews that I would be sure to have omitted nothing.

These long chains of reasonings, quite simple and easy, which geometers are accustomed to using to teach their most difficult demonstrations, had given me cause to imagine that everything which can be encompassed by man's knowledge is linked in the same way, and that, provided only that one abstains from accepting any for true which is not true, and that one always keeps the right order for one thing to be deduced from that which precedes it, there can be nothing so distant that one does not reach it eventually, or so hidden that one cannot discover it. And I was in no great difficulty in seeking which to begin with because I knew already that it was with the simplest and easiest to know; and considering that, among all those who have already sought truth in the sciences, only the mathematicians have been able to arrive at any proofs, that is to say, certain and evident reasons, I had no doubt that it was by the same things which they had examined that I should begin, although I did not expect any other usefulness from this than to accustom my mind to nourish itself on truths and not to be content with false reasons. . . .

* * * *

I do not know if I ought to tell you about the first meditations I pursued there, for they are so abstract and unusual that they will probably not be to the taste of everyone; and yet, so that one may judge if the foundations I have laid are firm enough, I find myself to some extent forced to speak of them. I had long ago noticed that, in matters relating to conduct, one needs sometimes to follow, just as if they were absolutely indubitable, opinions one knows to be very unsure, as has been said above; but as I wanted to concentrate solely on the search for truth, I thought I ought to do just the opposite, and reject as being absolutely false everything in which I could suppose the slightest reason for doubt, in order to see if there did not remain after that anything in my belief which was entirely indubitable. So, because our senses sometimes play us false, I decided to suppose that there was nothing at all which was such as they cause us to imagine it; and because there are men who make mistakes in reasoning, even with the simplest geometrical matters, and make paralogisms, judging that I was as liable to error as anyone else, I rejected as being false all the reasonings I had hitherto accepted as proofs. And finally, considering that all the same thoughts that we have when we are awake can also come to us when we are asleep, without any one of them then being true, I resolved to pretend that nothing which had ever entered my mind was any more true than the illusions of my dreams. But immediately afterwards I became aware that, while I decided thus to think that everything was false, it followed necessarily that I who thought thus must be something; and observing that this truth: *I think, therefore I am,* was so certain and so evident that all the most extravagant suppositions of the sceptics were not capable of shaking it, I judged that I could accept it without scruple as the first principle of the philosophy I was seeking.

Then, examining attentively what I was, and seeing that I could pretend that I had no body and that there was no world or place that I was in, but that I could not, for all that, pretend that I did not exist, and that, on the contrary, from the very fact that I thought of doubting the truth of other things, it followed very evidently and very certainly that I existed; while, on the other hand, if I had only ceased to think, although all the rest of what I had ever imagined had been true, I would have had no reason to believe that I existed; I thereby concluded that I was a substance, of which the whole essence or nature consists in thinking, and which, in order to exist, needs no place and depends on no material thing; so that this 'I', that is to say, the mind, by which I am what I am, is entirely distinct from the body, and even that it is easier to know than the body, and moreover, that even if the body were not, it would not cease to be all that it is.

After this, I considered in general what is needed for a proposition to be true and certain; for, since I had just found one which I knew to be so, I thought that I ought also to know what this certainty consisted of. And having noticed that there is nothing at all in this, *I think, therefore I am*, which assures me that I am speaking the truth, except that I see very clearly that in order to think one must exist, I judged that I could take it to be a general rule that the things we conceive very clearly and very distinctly are all true, but that there is nevertheless some difficulty in being able to recognize for certain which are the things we see distinctly.

Following this, reflecting on the fact that I had doubts, and that consequently my being was not completely perfect, for I saw clearly that it was a greater perfection to know than to doubt, I decided to inquire whence I had learned to think of some thing more perfect than myself; and I clearly recognized that this must have been from some nature which was in fact more perfect. As for the notions I had of several other things outside myself, such as the sky, the earth, light, heat and a thousand others, I had not the same concern to know their source, because, seeing nothing in them which seemed to make them superior to myself, I could believe that, if they were true, they were dependencies of my nature, in as much as it had some perfection; and, if they were not, that I held them from nothing, that is to say that they were in me because of an imperfection in my nature. But I could not make the same judgement concerning the idea of a being more perfect than myself; for to hold it from nothing was something manifestly impossible; and because it is no less contradictory that the more perfect should proceed from and depend on the less perfect, than it is that something should emerge out of nothing, I could not hold it from myself; with the result that it remained that it must have been put into me by a being whose nature was truly more perfect than mine and which even had in itself all the perfections of which I could have any idea, that is to say, in a single word, which was God. To which I added that, since I knew some perfections that I did not have, I was not the only being which existed (I shall freely use here, with your permission, the terms of the School) but that there must of necessity be another more perfect, upon whom I depended, and from whom I had acquired all I had; for, if I had been alone and independent of all other, so as to have had from myself this small portion of perfection that I had by participation in the perfection of God, I could have given myself, by the same reason, all the remainder of perfection that I knew myself to lack, and thus to be myself infinite, eternal, immutable, omniscient, all-powerful, and finally to have all the perfections that I could observe to be in God. For, consequentially upon the reasonings by which I had proved the existence of God, in order to understand the nature of God as far as my own nature was capable of doing, I had only to consider, concerning all the things of which I found in myself some idea, whether it was a perfection or not to have them: and I was assured that none of those which indicated some imperfection was in him, but that all the others were. So I saw that doubt, inconstancy, sadness and similar things could not be in him, seeing that I myself would have been very pleased to be free from them. Then, further, I had ideas of many sensible and bodily things; for even supposing that I was dreaming, and that everything I saw or imagined was false, I could not, nevertheless, deny that the ideas were really in my thoughts. But, because I had already recognized in myself very clearly that intelligent nature is distinct from the corporeal, considering that all composition is evidence of dependency, and that dependency is manifestly a defect, I thence judged that it could not be a perfection in God to be composed of these two natures, and that, consequently, he was not so composed; but that, if there were any bodies in the world or any intelligences or other natures which were not wholly perfect, their existence must depend on his power, in such a way that they could not subsist without him for a single instant.

I set out after that to seek other truths; and turning to the object of the geometers, which I conceived as a continuous body, or a space extended indefinitely in length, width and height or depth, divisible into various parts, which could have various figures and sizes and be moved or transposed in all sorts of ways—for the geometers take all that to be in the object of their study—I went through some of their simplest proofs. And having observed that the great certainty that everyone attributes to them is based only on the fact that they are clearly conceived according to the rule I spoke of earlier, I noticed also that they had nothing at all in them which might assure me of the existence of their object. Thus, for example, I very well perceived that, supposing a triangle to be given, its three angles must be equal to two right angles, but I saw nothing, for all that, which assured me that any such triangle existed in the world; whereas, reverting to the examination of the idea I had of a perfect Being, I found that existence was comprised in the idea in the same way that the equality of the three angles of a triangle to two right angles is comprised in the idea of a triangle or, as in the idea of a sphere, the fact that all its parts are equidistant from its centre, or even more obviously so; and that consequently it is at least as certain that God, who is this perfect Being, is, or exists, as any geometric demonstration can be.

—Translated by F. E. Sutcliffe

THOMAS HOBBES

Thomas Hobbes (1588–1679), often considered the father of modern philosophy in England, was a pioneering thinker in psychology, ethics, and political philosophy. Born in the year of England's triumph over the Spanish Armada, Hobbes witnessed the bitter political conflicts that seized England in the mid-seventeenth century. While a refugee from the Puritans' rule, Hobbes wrote *Leviathan* (1651), an analysis of the origins of absolute political authority.

Hobbes's defense of monarchy differed from customary apologies for absolutism, which referred to divine right and traditional privilege. Hobbes argued from a modern and secular point of view, devising his own theory of the social contract, the idea that government originated in an agreement among the first members of society. According to Hobbes, humans were by nature so greedy and violent that peace could be achieved only by an all-powerful political authority. In the state of nature, humans are constantly at war and live a life that is "poor, nasty, brutish, and short. " In submitting to the sovereignty of a monarch, humans are able to improve their lives and build civilization through industry and science.

For analysis and interpretation:

1. Summarize Hobbes's view of humans in a state of nature, prior to the establishment of authoritarian government.

2. Compare Hobbes's description of warring humanity with historical examples of the breakdown of law and government (for example, war, revolution, or natural catastrophe). By what means have humans been able to restore social order in such circumstances?

3. Agree or disagree with Hobbes's assertion that humans willingly submit to authoritarian government in order to pursue personal gain.

From *Leviathan*

Of the Natural Condition of Mankind as Concerning Their Felicity, and Misery

Nature hath made men so equal, in the faculties of the body and mind; as that, though there be found one man sometimes manifestly stronger in body or of quicker mind than another, yet when all is reckoned together, the difference between man and man is not so considerable, as that one man can thereupon claim to himself any benefit, to which another may not pretend as well as he. For as to the strength of body, the weakest has strength enough to kill the strongest, either by secret machination, or by confederacy with others that are in the same danger with himself.

And as to the faculties of the mind—setting aside the arts grounded upon words, and especially that skill of proceeding upon general and infallible rules, called science; which very few have, and but in few things; as being not a native faculty, born with us; nor attained, as prudence, while we look after somewhat else—I find yet a greater equality amongst men, than that of strength. For prudence is but experience, which equal time equally bestows on all men, in those things they equally apply themselves unto. That which may perhaps make such equality incredible, is but a vain conceit of one's own wisdom, which almost all men think they have in a greater degree than the vulgar; that is, than all men but themselves, and a few others, whom by fame, or for concurring with themselves, they approve. For such is the nature of men, that howsoever they may acknowledge many others to be more witty, or more eloquent, or more learned, yet they will hardly believe there be many so wise as themselves; for they see their own wit at hand, and other men's at a distance. But this proveth rather that men are in that point equal, than unequal. For there is not ordinarily a greater sign of the equal distribution of anything, than that every man is contented with his share.

From this equality of ability, ariseth equality of hope in the attaining of our ends. And therefore if any two men desire the same thing, which nevertheless they cannot both enjoy, they become enemies; and in the way to their end, which is principally their own conservation, and sometimes their delectation only, endeavor to destroy, or subdue one another. And from hence it comes to pass that where an invader hath no more to fear than another man's single power; if one plant, sow, build, or possess a convenient seat, others may probably be expected to come prepared with forces united, to dispossess and deprive him, not only of the fruit of his labor, but also of his life or liberty. And the invader again is in the like danger of another.

And from this diffidence of one another, there is no way for any man to secure himself so reasonable an anticipation; that is, by force or wiles to master the persons of all men he can, so long, till he see no other power great enough to endanger him: and this is no more than his own conservation requireth, and is generally allowed. Also because there be some, that taking pleasure in contemplating their own power in the acts of conquest, which they pursue farther than their security requires; if others, that otherwise would be glad to be at ease within modest bounds, should not by invasion increase their power, they would not be able long time, by standing only on their defense, to subsist. And by consequence, such augmentation of dominion over men being necessary to a man's conservation, it ought to be allowed him.

Again, men have no pleasure, but on the contrary a great deal of grief, in keeping company, where there is no power able to overawe them all. For every man looketh that his companion should value him at the same rate he sets upon himself; and upon all signs of contempt, or undervaluing, naturally endeavors, as far as he dares (which amongst them that have no common power to keep them in quiet, is far enough to make them destroy each other), to extort a greater value from his contemners by damage, and from others by the example.

So that in the nature of man, we find three principal causes of quarrel. First, competition; second, diffidence; thirdly, glory.

The first maketh men invade for gain; the second, for safety; and the third, for reputation. The first use violence to make themselves masters of other men's persons, wives, children, and cattle; the second, to defend them; the third, for trifles, as a word, a smile, a different opinion, and any other sign of undervalue, either direct in their persons, or by reflection in their kindred, their friends, their nation, their profession, or their name.

Hereby it is manifest that during the time men live without a common power to keep them all in awe, they are in that condition which is called war; and such a war as is of every man against every man. For war consisteth not in battle only, or the act of fighting, but in a tract of time wherein the will to contend by battle is sufficiently known, and therefore the notion of time is to be considered in the nature of war, as it is in the nature of weather. For as the nature of foul weather lieth not in a shower or two of rain, but in an inclination thereto of many days together; so the nature of war consisteth not in actual fighting, but in the known disposition thereto, during all the time there is no assurance to the contrary. All other time is peace.

Whatsoever therefore is consequent to a time of war, where every man is enemy to every man; the same is consequent to the time, wherein men live without other security than what their own strength and their own invention shall furnish them withal. In such condition there is no place for industry, because the fruit thereof is uncertain: and consequently no culture of the earth; no navigation, nor use of the commodities that may be imported by sea; no commodious building; no instruments of moving, and removing, such things as require much force; no knowledge of the face of the earth; no account of time; no arts; no letters; no society; and which is worst of all, continual fear, and danger of violent death; and the life of man, solitary, poor, nasty, brutish, and short.

It may seem strange to some man that has not well weighed these things, that nature should thus dissociate, and render men apt to invade and destroy one another; and he may therefore, not trusting to this inference, made from the passions, desire perhaps to have the same confirmed by experience. Let him therefore consider with himself, when taking a journey, he arms himself and seeks to go well accompanied; when going to sleep, he locks his doors; when even in his house he locks his chests; and this when he knows there be laws, and public officers, armed, to revenge all injuries shall be done him: what opinion he has of his fellow-subjects, when he rides armed; of his fellow-citizens, when he locks his doors; and of his children, and servants, when he locks his chests. Does he not there as much accuse mankind by his actions, as I do by my words? But neither of us accuse man's nature in it. The desires, and other passions of man, are in themselves no sin. No more are the actions that proceed from those passions, till they know a law that forbids them: which till laws be made they cannot know; nor can any law be made, till they have agreed upon the person that shall make it.

It may peradventure be thought, there was never such a time nor condition of war as this; and I believe it was never generally so, over all the world: but there are many places where they live so now. For the savage people in many places of America, except the government of small families, the concord whereof dependeth on natural lust, have no government at all; and live at this day in that brutish manner, as I said before. Howsoever, it may be perceived what manner of life there would be, where there were no common power to fear; by the manner of life which men that have formerly lived under a peaceful government, use to degenerate into in a civil war.

But though there had never been any time wherein particular men were in a condition of war one against another; yet in all times, kings, and persons of sovereign authority, because of their independency, are in continual jealousies, and in the state and posture of gladiators; having their weapons pointing, and their eyes fixed on one another; that is, their forts, garrisons, and guns upon the frontiers of their kingdoms; and continual spies upon their neighbors; which is a posture of war. But because they uphold thereby the industry of their subjects, there does not follow from it that misery which accompanies the liberty of particular men.

To this war of every man against every man, this also is consequent: *that nothing can be unjust.* The notions of right and wrong, justice and injustice, have there no place. Where there is no common power, there is no law; where no law, no injustice. Force and fraud are in war the two cardinal virtues. Justice and injustice are none of the faculties neither of the body nor mind. If they were, they might be in a man that were alone in the world, as well as his senses and passions. They are qualities that relate to men in society, not in solitude. It is consequent also to the same condition, that there be no propriety, no dominion, no *mine* and *thine* distinct; but only that to be every man's, that he can get; and for so long as he can keep it. And thus much for the ill condition which man by mere nature is actually placed in; though with a possibility to come out of it, consisting partly in the passions, partly in his reason.

The passions that incline men to peace are fear of death, desire of such things as are necessary to commodious living, and a hope by their industry to obtain them. And reason suggesteth convenient articles of peace, upon which men may be drawn to agreement. These articles are they which otherwise are called the Laws of Nature. . . .

JONATHAN SWIFT

Jonathan Swift (1667–1745) was a master of eighteenth-century satire, bitterly mocking the age's injustice and pleading for social reform. One of his bitterest works is *A Modest Proposal* (1729), the shortened title of *A Modest Proposal for Preventing the Children of the Poor People from being a Burden to their Parents or Country; and for making them beneficial to their Publick.* Swift's pamphlet responded to the oppression and poverty of his native Ireland, where poor farmers suffered exploitation by absentee English landlords. Taking literally the political slogan that "people are the wealth of the nation," Swift proposes that Irish children be raised like beef and roasted for English dinner tables. He calculates with sardonic precision the monetary advantages to families and the general economy, with the kind of cynical practicality that can sometimes still be heard in the testimony of economic experts.

For analysis and interpretation:

1. What language does Swift use intentionally to confuse the differences between human children and domestic beasts?

2. What social problems does Swift claim to remedy with his proposal? What analogous problems can be found in the contemporary world?

3. Compare Swift's financial calculations to the cost-benefit analysis of modern economists, especially as they apply to safety standards, the provision of health care, and other life-related social measures. By what process of reasoning might one calculate the monetary value of a person's life, versus the social costs of saving that life?

A Modest Proposal

It is a melancholy object to those who walk through this great town, or travel in the country, when they see the streets, the roads and cabin-doors crowded with beggars of the female sex, followed by three, four, or six children, all in rags, and importuning every passenger for an alms. These mothers, instead of being able to work for their honest livelihood, are forced to employ all their time in strolling, to beg sustenance for their helpless infants, who, as they grow up, either turn thieves for want of work, or leave their dear native country to fight for the Pretender in Spain, or sell themselves to the Barbadoes.

I think it is agreed by all parties that this prodigious number of children, in the arms, or on the backs, or at the heels of their mothers, and frequently of their fathers, is in the present deplorable state of the kingdom a very great additional grievance; and therefore whoever could find out a fair, cheap, and easy method of making these children sound and useful members of the commonwealth would serve so well of the public as to have his statue set up for a preserver of the nation.

But my intention is very far from being confined to provide only for the children of professed beggars; it is of a much greater extent, and shall take in the whole number of infants at a certain age who are born of parents in effect as little able to support them as those who demand our charity in the streets.

As to my own part, having turned my thoughts for many years upon this important subject, and maturely weighed the several schemes of other projectors, I have always found them grossly mistaken in their computation. It is true a child just dropped from its dam may be supported by her milk for a solar year with little other nourishment, at most not above the value of two shillings, which the mother may certainly get, or the value in scraps, by her lawful occupation of begging, and it is exactly at one year old that I propose to provide for them, in such a manner as, instead of being a charge upon their parents, or the parish, or wanting food and raiment for the rest of their lives, they shall, on the contrary, contribute to the feeding and partly to the clothing of many thousands.

There is likewise another great advantage in my scheme, that it will prevent those voluntary abortions, and that horrid practice of women murdering their bastard children, alas, too frequent among us, sacrificing the poor innocent babes, I doubt, more to avoid the expense than the shame, which would move tears and pity in the most savage and inhuman breast.

The number of souls in Ireland being usually reckoned one million and a half, of these I calculate there may be about two hundred thousand couples whose wives are breeders, from which number I subtract thirty thousand couples who are able to maintain their own children, although I apprehend there cannot be so many under the present distresses of the kingdom, but this being granted, there will remain an hundred and seventy thousand breeders. I again subtract fifty thousand for those women who miscarry, or whose children die by accident or disease within the year. There only remain an hundred and twenty thousand children of poor parents annually born: the question therefore is, how this number shall be reared, and provided for, which, as I have already said, under the present situation of affairs is utterly impossible by all the methods hitherto proposed, for we can neither employ them in handicraft or agriculture; we neither build houses (I mean in the country), nor cultivate land: they can very seldom pick up a livelihood by stealing until they arrive at six years old, except where they are of towardly parts although I confess they learn the rudiments much earlier, during which time they can however be properly looked upon only as probationers, as I have been informed by a principal gentleman in the County of Cavan, who protested to me that he never knew above one or two instances under the age of six, even in a part of the kingdom so renowned for the quickest proficiency in that art.

I am assured by our merchants that a boy or a girl before twelve years old, is no saleable commodity, and even when they come to this age, they will not yield above three pounds, or three pounds and half-a-crown at most on the Exchange, which cannot turn to account either to the parents or the kingdom, the charge of nutriment and rags having been at least four times that value.

I shall now therefore humbly propose my own thoughts, which I hope will not be liable to the least objection.

I have been assured by a very knowing American of my acquaintance in London, that a young healthy child well nursed is at a year old a most delicious, nourishing and wholesome food, whether stewed, roasted, baked, or boiled, and I make no doubt that it will equally serve in a fricassee, or a ragout.

I do therefore humbly offer it to public consideration, that of the hundred and twenty thousand children, already computed, twenty thousand may be reserved for breed, whereof only one fourth part to be males, which is more than we allow to sheep, black-cattle, or swine, and my reason is that these children are seldom the fruits of marriage, a circumstance not much regarded by our savages, therefore one male will be sufficient to serve four females. That the remaining hundred thousand may at a year old be offered in sale to the persons of quality and fortune, through the kingdom, always advising the mother to let them suck plentifully in the last month, so as to render them plump, and fat for a good table. A child will make two dishes at an entertainment for friends, and when the family dines alone, the fore or hind quarter will make a reasonable dish, and seasoned with a little pepper or salt will be very good boiled on the fourth day, especially in winter.

I have reckoned upon a medium, that a child just born will weigh twelve pounds, and in a solar year if tolerably nursed increaseth to twenty-eight pounds.

I grant this food will be somewhat dear, and therefore very proper for landlords, who, as they have already devoured most of the parents, seem to have the best title to the children.

Infant's flesh will be in season throughout the year, but more plenful in March, and a little before and after, for we are told by a grave author, an eminent French physician, that fish being a prolific diet, there are more children born in Roman Catholic countries about nine months after Lent than at any other season; therefore reckoning a year after Lent, the markets will be more glutted than usual, because the number of Popish infants is at least three to one in this kingdom, and therefore it will have one other collateral advantage by lessening the number of Papists among us.

I have already computed the charge of nursing a begger's child (in which list I reckon all cottagers, labourers, and four-fifths of the farmers) to be about two shillings *per annum,* rags included, and I believe no gentleman would repine to give ten shillings for the carcass of a good fat child,which, as I have said, will make four dishes of excellent nutritive meat, when he hath only some particular friend of his own family to dine with him. Thus the Squire will learn to be a good landlord and grow popular among his tenants, the mother will have eight shillings net profit, and be fit for work until she produces another child.

Those who are more thrifty (as I must confess the times require) may flay the carcass; the skin of which artificially dressed, will make admirable gloves for ladies, and summer boots for fine gentleman.

As to our city of Dublin, shambles may be appointed for this purpose, in the most convenient parts of it, and butchers we may be assured will not be wanting, although I rather recommend buying the children alive, and dressing them hot from the knife, as we do roasting pigs.

A very worthy person, a true lover of his country, and whose virtues I highly esteem, was lately pleased, in discoursing on this matter to offer a refinement upon my scheme. He said that many gentleman of this kingdom, having of late destroyed their deer, he conceived that the want of venison might be well supplied by the bodies of young lads and maidens, not exceeding fourteen years of age, nor under twelve, so great a number of both sexes in every country being now ready to starve, for want of work and service: and these to be disposed of by their parents if alive, or otherwise by their nearest relations. But with due deference to so excellent a friend, and so deserving a patriot, I cannot be altogether in his sentiments. For as to the males, my American acquaintance assured me from frequent experience that their flesh was generally tough and lean, like that of our schoolboys, by continual exercise, and their taste disagreeable, and to fatten them would not answer the charge. Then as to the females,it would, I think with humble submission, be a loss to the public, because they soon would become breeders themselves: and besides, it is not improbable that some scrupulous people might be apt to censure such a practice (although indeed very unjustly) as a little bordering upon cruelty, which I confess, hath always been with me the strongest objection against any project, howsoever well intended.

But in order to justify my friend, he confessed that this expedient was put into his head by the famous Psalmanazar, a native of the island Formosa, who came from thence to London, above twenty years ago, and in conversation told my friend that in his country when any young person happened to be put to death, the executioner sold the carcass to persons of quality, as a prime dainty, and that, in his time, the body of a plump girl of fifteen, who was crucified for an attempt to poison the emperor, was sold to his Imperial Majesty's Prime Minister of State, and other great Mandarins of the Court, in joints from the gibbet, at four hundred crowns. Neither indeed can I deny that if the same use were made of several plump young girls in this town who, without one single groat to their fortunes, cannot stir abroad without a chair, and appear at the playhouse and assemblies in foreign fineries, which they never will pay for, the kingdom would not be the worse.

Some persons of a desponding spirit are in great concern about that vast number of poor people, who are aged, diseased, or maimed, and I have been desired to
employ my thoughts what course may be taken to ease the nation of so grievous an
encumbrance. But I am not in the least pain upon that matter, because it is very well
known that they are every day dying, and rotting, by cold, and famine, and filth, and
vermin, as fast as can be reasonably expected. And as to the younger labourers they
are now in almost as hopeful a condition. They cannot get work, and consequently
pine away from want of nourishment, to a degree that if at any time they are accidentally hired to common labour, they have not strength to perform it; and thus the
country and themselves are in a fair way of being soon delivered from the evils to
come.

I have too long digressed, and therefore shall return to my subject. I think the
advantages by the proposal which I have made are obvious and many, as well as of
the highest importance.

For first, as I have already observed, it would greatly lessen the number of
Papists, with whom we are yearly over-run, being the principal breeders of the nation,
as well as our most dangerous enemies, and who stay at home on purpose with a design to deliver the kingdom to the Pretender, hoping to take their advantage by the absence of so many good Protestants, who have chosen rather to leave their country than
stay at home and pay tithes against their conscience to an idolatrous Episcopal curate.

Secondly, the poorer tenants will have something valuable of their own, which
by law may be made liable to distress and help to pay their landlord's rent, their corn
and cattle being already seized, and money a thing unknown.

Thirdly, whereas the maintenance of an hundred thousand children, from two
years old, and upwards, cannot be computed at less than ten shillings a piece *per
annum*, the nation's stock will be thereby increased fifty thousand pounds *per annum*,
besides the profit of a new dish, introduced to the tables of all gentlemen of fortune
in the kingdom, who have any refinement in taste, and the money will circulate among
ourselves, the goods being entirely of our own growth and manufacture.

Fourthly, the constant breeders, besides the gain of eight shillings sterling *per
annum*, by the sale of their children, will be rid of the charge of maintaining them
after the first year.

Fifthly, this food would likewise bring great custom to taverns, where the vint-
ners will certainly be so prudent as to procure the best receipts for dressing it to perfection, and consequently have their houses frequented by all the fine gentlemen, who
justly value themselves upon their knowledge in good eating; and a skilful cook, who
understands how to oblige his guests, will contrive to make it as expensive as they
please.

Sixthly, this would be a great inducement to marriage, which all wise nations
have either encouraged by rewards, or enforced by laws and penalties. It would increase the care and tenderness of mothers towards their children, when they were sure
of a settlement for life, to the poor babes, provided in some sort by the public to their
annual profit instead of expense. We should soon see an honest emulation among the
married women, which of them could bring the fattest child to the market. Men would

become as fond of their wives, during the time of their pregnancy, as they are now of their mares in foal, their cows in calf, or sows when they are ready to farrow, nor offer to beat or trick them (as it is too frequent a practice) for fear of a miscarriage.

Many other advantages might be enumerated. For instance, the addition of some thousand carcasses in our exportation of barrelled beef; the propagation of swine's flesh, and improvement in the art of making good bacon, so much wanted among us by the great destruction of pigs, too frequent at our tables, are no way comparable in taste or magnificence to a well-grown, fat yearling child, which roasted whole will make a considerable figure at a Lord Mayor's feast, or any other public entertainment. But this and many others I omit, being studious of brevity.

Supposing that one thousand families in this city would be constant customers for infants flesh, besides others who might have it at merry meetings, particularly weddings and christenings; I compute that Dublin would take off annually about twenty thousand carcasses, and the rest of the kingdom (where probably they will be sold somewhat cheaper) the remaining eighty thousand.

I can think of no one objection that will possibly be raised against this proposal, unless it should be urged that the number of people will be thereby much lessened in the kingdom. This I freely own, and it was indeed one principal design in offering it to the world. I desire the reader will observe, that I calculate my remedy *for this one individual Kingdom* of Ireland, *and for no other that ever was, is, or, I think, ever can be upon earth.* Therefore let no man talk to me of other expedients: *Of taxing our absentees at five shillings a pound: Of using neither clothes, nor household furniture, except what is of our own growth and manufacture: Of utterly rejecting the materials and instruments that promote foreign luxury: Of curing the expensiveness of pride, vanity, idleness, and gaming in our women: Of introducing a vein of parsimony, prudence, and temperance: Of learning to love our country, wherein we differ even from* Laplanders, *and the inhabitants of* Topinamboo: *Of quitting our animosities and factions, nor act any longer like the* Jews, *who were murdering one another at the very moment their city was taken: Of being a little cautious not to sell our country and consciences for nothing: Of teaching landlords to have at least one degree of mercy towards their tenants.* Lastly, *of putting a spirit of honesty, industry, and skill into our shopkeepers, who, if a resolution could now be taken to buy only our native goods, would immediately unite to cheat and exact upon us in the price, the measure and the goodness, nor could ever yet be brought to make one fair proposal of just dealing, though often and earnestly invited to it.*

Therefore I repeat, let no man talk to me of these and the like expedients, till he hath at least a glimpse of hope that there will ever be some hearty and sincere attempt to put them in practice.

But as to myself, having been wearied out for many years with offering vain, idle, visionary thoughts, and at length utterly despairing of success, I fortunately fell upon this proposal, which as it is wholly new, so it hath something solid and real, of no expense and little trouble, full in our own power, and whereby we can incur no danger in disobliging England. For this kind of commodity will not bear exportation, the flesh being of too tender a consistence to admit a long continuance in salt, *although perhaps I could name a country which would be glad to eat up our whole nation without it.*

After all I am not so violently bent upon my own opinion as to reject any offer, proposed by wise men, which shall be found equally innocent, cheap, easy and effectual. But before some thing of that kind shall be advanced in contradiction to my scheme, and offering a better, I desire the author, or authors, will be pleased maturely to consider two points. First, as things now stand, how they will be able to find food and raiment for a hundred thousand useless mouths and backs? And secondly, there being a round million of creatures in human figure, throughout this kingdom, whose whole subsistence put into a common stock would leave them in debt two millions of pounds sterling; adding those who are beggars by profession, to the bulk of farmers, cottagers, and labourers with their wives and children, who are beggars in effect; I desire those politicians who dislike my overture, and may perhaps be so bold to attempt an answer, that they will first ask the parents of these mortals whether they would not at this day think it a great happiness to have been sold for food at a year old, in the manner I prescribed, and thereby have avoided such a perpetual scene of misfortunes as they have since gone through, by the oppression of landlords, the impossibility of paying rent without money or trade, the want of common sustenance, with neither house nor clothes to cover them from the inclemencies of weather, and the most inevitable prospect of entailing the like, or greater miseries upon their breed for ever.

I profess in the sincerity of my heart that I have not the least personal interest in endeavouring to promote this necessary work, having no other motive than the *public good of my country, by advancing our trade, providing for infants, relieving the poor, and giving some pleasure to the rich.* I have no children by which I can propose to get a single penny; the youngest being nine years old, and my wife past child-bearing.

VOLTAIRE

François Marie Arouet, known as Voltaire (1694–1778), was the most brilliant figure of the Enlightenment in France, a wide-ranging literary talent and stalwart critic of injustice and prejudice. Voltaire is best known for his satiric tale *Candide*, the story of a naive young man whose adventures illustrate the absurdity and horror of human prejudice.

Candide begins his career in the kingdom of Baron Thunder-ten-tronckh, where he is taught by Pangloss, a caricature of Enlightenment optimism. Expelled for courting the baron's daughter Cunegonde, Candide embarks on a journey around the world. Each new calamity causes him to muse naively on the reasonableness of God's universe. In a pivotal episode, not excerpted here, Candide reaches the utopia of El Dorado, a land free from poverty, injustice, and religious intolerance. However, Candide yearns for Cunegonde and leaves El Dorado, taking a pack train of sheep laden with precious jewels. Candide's wealth makes him the target of swindlers, while a new companion, the pessimist Martin, comments on the ubiquity of human greed and corruption. All of Candide's companions are reunited in the final episodes and speculate on the meaning of their misfortunes.

For analysis and interpretation:

1. Analyze Chapter 1 of *Candide* as Voltaire's satiric replay of the fall of Adam and Eve. What does this episode imply about the nature of human desire and folly?

2. Speculate on the reasons that a convinced rationalist like Voltaire would mock such Enlightenment principles as liberty, reason, and science. How might *Candide* be interpreted as Voltaire's *self*-criticism?

3. How might a rationalist explain the cruel and arbitrary death of Jacques the Anabaptist, perhaps the only thoroughly good character in the entire story? What is our response today to similar examples of random violence and death?

4. Evaluate the story's final prescription for a happy life, to "work without theorizing." How does Voltaire's prescription for happiness compare to other voices in the philosophical tradition? (Compare, for example, Confucius, Aristotle, Montaigne, and Freud.)

From *Candide, or Optimism*

CHAPTER I. *How Candide was Brought Up in a Noble Castle and How He was Expelled from the Same.*

In the castle of Baron Thunder-ten-tronckh in Westphalia there lived a youth, endowed by Nature with the most gentle character. His face was the expression of his soul. His judgment was quite honest and he was extremely simpleminded; and this was the reason, I think, that he was named Candide. Old servants in the house suspected that he was the son of the Baron's sister and a decent honest gentleman of the neighborhood, whom this young lady would never marry because he could only prove seventy-one quarterings, and the rest of his genealogical tree was lost, owing to the injuries of time.

The Baron was one of the most powerful lords in Westphalia, for his castle possessed a door and windows. His Great Hall was even decorated with a piece of tapestry. The dogs in his stable-yards formed a pack of hounds when necessary; his grooms were his huntsmen; the village curate was his Grand Almoner. They all called him "My Lord," and laughed heartily at his stories.

The Baroness weighed about three hundred and fifty pounds, was therefore greatly respected, and did the honors of the house with a dignity which rendered her still more respectable. Her daughter Cunegonde, aged seventeen, was rosy-cheeked, fresh, plump and tempting. The Baron's son appeared in every respect worthy of his father. The tutor Pangloss was the oracle of the house, and little Candide followed his lessons with all the candor of his age and character.

Pangloss taught metaphysico-theologo-cosmolonigology. He proved admirably that there is no effect without a cause and that in this best of all possible worlds, My

Lord the Baron's castle was the best of castles and his wife the best of all possible Baronesses.

"'Tis demonstrated," said he, "that things cannot be otherwise; for, since everything is made for an end, everything is necessarily for the best end. Observe that noses were made to wear spectacles; and so we have spectacles. Legs were visibly instituted to be breeched, and we have breeches. Stones were formed to be quarried and to build castles; and My Lord has a very noble castle; the greatest Baron in the province should have the best house; and as pigs were made to be eaten, we eat pork all the year round; consequently, those who have asserted that all is well talk nonsense; they ought to have said that all is for the best."

Candide listened attentively and believed innocently; for he thought Mademoiselle Cunegonde extremely beautiful, although he was never bold enough to tell her so. He decided that after the happiness of being born Baron of Thunder-ten-tronckh, the second degree of happiness was to be Mademoiselle Cunegonde; the third, to see her every day; and the fourth to listen to Doctor Pangloss, the greatest philosopher of the province and therefore of the whole world.

One day when Cunegonde was walking near the castle, in a little wood which was called The Park, she observed Doctor Pangloss in the bushes, giving a lesson in experimental physics to her mother's waiting maid, a very pretty and docile brunette. Mademoiselle Cunegonde had a great inclination for science and watched breathlessly the reiterated experiments she witnessed; she observed clearly the Doctor's sufficient reason, the effects and the causes, and returned home very much excited, pensive, filled with the desire of learning, reflecting that she might be the sufficient reason of young Candide and that he might be hers.

On her way back to the castle she met Candide and blushed; Candide also blushed. She bade him good-morning in a hesitating voice; Candide replied without knowing what he was saying. Next day, when they left the table after dinner, Cunegonde and Candide found themselves behind a screen; Cunegonde dropped her handkerchief, Candide picked it up; she innocently held his hand; the young man innocently kissed the young lady's hand with remarkable vivacity, tenderness and grace; their lips met, their eyes sparkled, their knees trembled, their hands wandered. Baron Thunder-ten-tronckh passed near the screen, and, observing this cause and effect, expelled Candide from the castle by kicking him in the backside frequently and hard. Cunegonde swooned; when she recovered her senses, the Baroness slapped her in the face; and all was in consternation in the noblest and most agreeable of all possible castles.

CHAPTER II. *What Happened to Candide Among the Bulgarians.*

Candide, expelled from the earthly paradise, wandered for a long time without knowing where he was going, weeping, turning up his eyes to Heaven, gazing back frequently at the noblest of castles which held the most beautiful of young Baronesses; he lay down to sleep supperless between two furrows in the open fields; it snowed heavily in large flakes. The next morning the shivering Candide, penniless, dying of cold and exhaustion, dragged himself towards the neighboring town, which was called Waldberghoff-trarbk-dikdorff. He halted sadly at the door of an inn. Two men dressed in blue noticed him.

"Comrade," said one, "there's a well-built young man of the right height." They went up to Candide and very civilly invited him to dinner.

"Gentlemen," said Candide with charming modesty, "you do me a great honor, but I have no money to pay my share."

"Ah, sir," said one of the men in blue, "persons of your figure and merit never pay anything; are you not five feet five tall?"

"Yes, gentlemen," said he, bowing, "that is my height."

"Ah, sir, come to table; we will not only pay your expenses, we will never allow a man like you to be short of money; men were only made to help each other."

"You are in the right," said Candide, "that is what Doctor Pangloss was always telling me, and I see that everything is for the best."

They begged him to accept a few crowns, he took them and wished to give them an IOU; they refused to take it and all sat down to table. "Do you not love tenderly . . ."

"Oh, yes," said he. "I love Mademoiselle Cunegonde tenderly."

"No," said one of the gentlemen. "We were asking if you do not tenderly love the King of the Bulgarians."

"Not a bit," said he, "for I have never seen him."

"What! He is the most charming of Kings, and you must drink his health."

"Oh, gladly, gentlemen." And he drank.

"That is sufficient," he was told. "You are now the support, the aid, the defender, the hero of the Bulgarians; your fortune is made and your glory assured."

They immediately put irons on his legs and took him to a regiment. He was made to turn to the right and left, to raise the ramrod and return the ramrod, to take aim, to fire, to double up, and he was given thirty strokes with a stick; the next day he drilled not quite so badly, and received only twenty strokes; the day after, he only had ten, and was looked on as a prodigy by his comrades.

Candide was completely mystified and could not make out how he was a hero. One fine spring day he thought he would take a walk, going straight ahead, in the belief that to use his legs as he pleased was a privilege of the human species as well as of animals. He had not gone two leagues when four other heroes, each six feet tall, fell upon him, bound him and dragged him back to a cell. He was asked by his judges whether he would rather be thrashed thirty-six times by the whole regiment or receive a dozen lead bullets at once in his brain. Although he protested that men's wills are free and that he wanted neither one nor the other, he had to make a choice; by virtue of that gift of God which is called *liberty*, he determined to run the gauntlet thirty-six times and actually did so twice. There were two thousand men in the regiment. That made four thousand strokes which laid bare the muscles and nerves from his neck to his backside. As they were about to proceed to a third turn, Candide, utterly exhausted, begged as a favor that they would be so kind as to smash his head; he obtained this favor; they bound his eyes and he was made to kneel down. At that moment the King of the Bulgarians came by and inquired the victim's crime; and as this King was possessed of a vast genius, he perceived from what he learned about Candide that he was a young metaphysician very ignorant in worldly matters, and therefore pardoned him with a clemency which will be praised in all newspapers and all ages. An honest surgeon healed Candide in three weeks with the ointments recommended by Dioscorides. He had already regained a little skin and could walk when the King of the Bulgarians went to war with the King of the Abares.

CHAPTER III. *How Candide Escaped from the Bulgarians and What Became of Him.*

Nothing could be smarter, more splendid, more brilliant, better drawn up than the two armies. Trumpets, fifes, hautboys, drums, cannons, formed a harmony such as has never been heard even in hell. The cannons first of all laid flat about six thousand men on each side; then the musketry removed from the best of worlds some nine or ten thousand blackguards who infested its surface. The bayonet also was the sufficient reason for the death of some thousands of men. The whole might amount to thirty thousand souls. Candide, who trembled like a philosopher, hid himself as well as he could during this heroic butchery.

At last, while the two Kings each commanded a *Te Deum* in his camp, Candide decided to go elsewhere to reason about effects and causes. He clambered over heaps of dead and dying men and reached a neighboring village, which was in ashes; it was an Abare village which the Bulgarians had burned in accordance with international law. Here, old men dazed with blows watched the dying agonies of their murdered wives who clutched their children to their bleeding breasts; there, disembowelled girls who had been made to satisfy the natural appetites of heroes gasped their last sighs; others, half-burned, begged to be put to death. Brains were scattered on the ground among dismembered arms and legs.

Candide fled to another village as fast as he could; it belonged to the Bulgarians, and Abarian heroes had treated it in the same way. Candide, stumbling over quivering limbs or across ruins, at last escaped from the theatre of war, carrying a little food in his knapsack, and never forgetting Mademoiselle Cunegonde. His provisions were all gone when he reached Holland; but, having heard that everyone in that country was rich and a Christian, he had no doubt at all but that he would be as well treated as he had been in the Baron's castle before he had been expelled on account of Mademoiselle Cunegonde's pretty eyes.

He asked an alms of several grave persons, who all replied that if he continued in that way he would be shut up in a house of correction to teach him how to live. He then addressed himself to a man who had been discoursing on charity in a large assembly for an hour on end. This orator, glancing at him askance, said: "What are you doing here? Are you for the good cause?"

"There is no effect without a cause," said Candide modestly. "Everything is necessarily linked up and arranged for the best. It was necessary that I should be expelled from the company of Mademoiselle Cunegonde, that I ran the gauntlet, and that I beg my bread until I can earn it; all this could not have happened differently."

"My friend," said the orator, "do you believe that the Pope is Anti-Christ?"

"I had never heard so before," said Candide, "but whether he is or isn't, I am starving."

"You don't deserve to eat," said the other. "Hence, rascal; hence, you wretch; and never come near me again."

The orator's wife thrust her head out of the window and seeing a man who did not believe that the Pope was Anti-Christ, she poured on his head a full . . . O Heavens! To what excess religious zeal is carried by ladies!

A man who had not been baptized, an honest Anabaptist named Jacques, saw the cruel and ignominious treatment of one of his brothers, a featherless two-legged creature with a soul; he took him home, cleaned him up, gave him bread and beer, presented him with two florins, and even offered to teach him to work at the manufacture of Persian stuffs which are made in Holland. Candide threw himself at the man's feet, exclaiming: "Doctor Pangloss was right in telling me that all is for the best in this world, for I am vastly more touched by your extreme generosity than by the harshness of the gentleman in the black cloak and his good lady."

The next day when he walked out he met a beggar covered with sores, dull-eyed, with the end of his nose fallen away, his mouth awry, his teeth black, who talked huskily, was tormented with a violent cough and spat out a tooth at every cough.

CHAPTER IV. *How Candide Met His Old Master in Philosophy, Doctor Pangloss, and What Happened.*

Candide, moved even more by compassion than by horror, gave this horrible beggar the two florins he had received from the honest Anabaptist, Jacques. The phantom gazed fixedly at him, shed tears and threw its arms round his neck. Candide recoiled in terror.

"Alas!" said the wretch to the other wretch, "don't you recognise your dear Pangloss?"

"What do I hear? You, my dear master! You, in this horrible state! What misfortune has happened to you? Why are you no longer in the noblest of castles? What has become of Mademoiselle Cunegonde, the pearl of young ladies, the masterpiece of Nature?"

"I am exhausted," said Pangloss. Candide immediately took him to the Anabaptist's stable where he gave him a little bread to eat; and when Pangloss had recovered: "Well!" said he, "Cunegonde?"

"Dead," replied the other.

At this word Candide swooned; his friend restored him to his senses with a little bad vinegar which happened to be in the stable. Candide opened his eyes. "Cunegonde dead! Ah! best of worlds, where are you? But what illness did she die of? Was it because she saw me kicked out of her father's noble castle?"

"No," said Pangloss. "She was disembowelled by Bulgarian soldiers, after having been raped to the limit of possibility; they broke the Baron's head when he tried to defend her; the Baroness was cut to pieces; my poor pupil was treated exactly like his sister; and as to the castle, there is not one stone standing on another, not a barn, not a sheep, not a duck, not a tree; but we were well avenged, for the Abares did exactly the same to a neighboring barony which belonged to a Bulgarian Lord." At this, Candide swooned again; but, having recovered and having said all that he ought to say, he inquired the cause and effect, the sufficient reason which had reduced Pangloss to so piteous a state.

"Alas!" said Pangloss, "'tis love; love, the consoler of the human race, the preserver of the universe, the soul of all tender creatures, gentle love."

"Alas!" said Candide, "I am acquainted with this love, this sovereign of hearts, this soul of our soul; it has never brought me anything but one kiss and twenty kicks in the backside. How could this beautiful cause produce in you so abominable an effect?"

Pangloss replied as follows: "My dear Candide! You remember Paquette, the maidservant of our august Baroness; in her arms I enjoyed the delights of Paradise which have produced the tortures of Hell by which you see I am devoured; she was infected and perhaps is dead. Paquette received this present from a most learned monk, who had it from the source; for he received it from an old countess, who had it from a cavalry captain, who owed it to a marchioness, who derived it from a page, who had received it from a Jesuit, who, when a novice, had it in a direct line from one of the companions of Christopher Columbus. For my part, I shall not give it to anyone, for I am dying."

"O Pangloss!" exclaimed Candide, "this is a strange genealogy! Wasn't the devil at the root of it?"

"Not at all," replied that great man. "It was something indispensable in this best of worlds, a necessary ingredient; for, if Columbus in an island of America had not caught this disease, which poisons the source of generation, and often indeed prevents generation, we should not have chocolate and cochineal; it must also be noticed that hitherto in our continent this disease is peculiar to us, like theological disputes. The Turks, the Indians, the Persians, the Chinese, the Siamese and the Japanese are not yet familiar with it; but there is a sufficient reason why they in their turn should become familiar with it in a few centuries. Meanwhile, it has made marvellous progress among us, and especially in those large armies composed of honest, well-bred stipendiaries who decide the destiny of States; it may be asserted that when thirty thousand men fight a pitched battle against an equal number of troops, there are about twenty thousand with the pox on either side."

"Admirable!" said Candide. "But you must get cured."

"How can I?" said Pangloss. "I haven't a sou, my friend, and in the whole extent of this globe, you cannot be bled or receive an enema without paying or without someone paying for you."

This last speech determined Candide; he went and threw himself at the feet of his charitable Anabaptist, Jacques, and drew so touching a picture of the state to which his friend was reduced that the good easy man did not hesitate to succor Pangloss; he had him cured at his own expense. In this cure Pangloss only lost one eye and one ear. He could write well and knew arithmetic perfectly. The Anabaptist made him his bookkeeper. At the end of two months he was compelled to go to Lisbon on business and took his two philosophers on the boat with him. Pangloss explained to him how everything was for the best. Jacques was not of this opinion.

"Men," said he, "must have corrupted nature a little, for they were not born wolves, and they have become wolves. God did not give them twenty-four-pounder cannons or bayonets, and they have made bayonets and cannons to destroy each other. I might bring bankruptcies into the account and Justice which seizes the goods of bankrupts in order to deprive the creditors of them."

"It was all indispensable," replied the one-eyed doctor, "and private misfortunes make the public good, so that the more private misfortunes there are, the more everything is well."

While he was reasoning, the air grew dark, the winds blew from the four quarters of the globe and the ship was attacked by the most horrible tempest in sight of the port of Lisbon.

CHAPTER V. *Storm, Shipwreck, Earthquake, and What Happened to Dr. Pangloss, to Candide and the Anabaptist Jacques.*

Half the enfeebled passengers, suffering from that inconceivable anguish which the rolling of a ship causes in the nerves and in all the humors of bodies shaken in contrary directions, did not retain strength enough even to trouble about the danger. The other half screamed and prayed; the sails were torn, the masts broken, the vessel leaking. Those worked who could, no one cooperated, no one commanded. The Anabaptist tried to help the crew a little; he was on the main deck; a furious sailor struck him violently and stretched him on the deck; but the blow he delivered gave him so violent a shock that he fell head-first out of the ship. He remained hanging and clinging to part of the broken mast. The good Jacques ran to his aid, helped him to climb back, and from the effort he made was flung into the sea in full view of the sailor, who allowed him to drown without condescending even to look at him. Candide came up, saw his benefactor reappear for a moment and then be engulfed for ever. He tried to throw himself after him into the sea; he was prevented by the philosopher Pangloss, who proved to him that the Lisbon roads had been expressly created for the Anabaptist to be drowned in them. While he was proving this *a priori*, the vessel sank, and every one perished except Pangloss,

Candide and the brutal sailor who had drowned the virtuous Anabaptist; the black-guard swam successfully to the shore and Pangloss and Candide were carried there on a plank.

When they had recovered a little, they walked toward Lisbon; they had a little money by the help of which they hoped to be saved from hunger after having escaped the storm. Weeping the death of their benefactor, they had scarcely set foot in the town when they felt the earth tremble under their feet; the sea rose in foaming masses in the port and smashed the ships which rode at anchor. Whirlwinds of flame and ashes covered the streets and squares; the houses collapsed, the roofs were thrown upon the foundations, and the foundations were scattered; thirty thousand inhabitants of every age and both sexes were crushed under the ruins. Whistling and swearing, the sailor said: "There'll be something to pick up here."

"What can be the sufficient reason for this phenomenon?" said Pangloss.

"It is the last day!" cried Candide.

The sailor immediately ran among the debris, dared death to find money, found it, seized it, got drunk, and having slept off his wine, purchased the favors of the first woman of good will he met on the ruins of the houses and among the dead and dying. Pangloss, however, pulled him by the sleeve. "My friend," said he, "this is not well, you are disregarding universal reason, you choose the wrong time."

"Blood and 'ounds!" he retorted, "I am a sailor and I was born in Batavia; four times have I stamped on the crucifix during four voyages to Japan; you have found the right man for your universal reason!"

Candide had been hurt by some falling stones; he lay in the street covered with debris. He said to Pangloss: "Alas! Get me a little wine and oil; I am dying."

"This earthquake is not a new thing," replied Pangloss. "The town of Lima felt the same shocks in America last year; similar causes produce similar effects; there must certainly be a train of sulphur underground from Lima to Lisbon."

"Nothing is more probable," replied Candide; "but, for God's sake, a little oil and wine."

"What do you mean, probable?" replied the philosopher; "I maintain that it is proved."

Candide lost consciousness, and Pangloss brought him a little water from a neighboring fountain.

Next day they found a little food as they wandered among the ruins and regained a little strength. Afterwards they worked like others to help the inhabitants who had escaped death. Some citizens they had assisted gave them as good a dinner as could be expected in such a disaster; true, it was a dreary meal; the hosts watered their bread with their tears, but Pangloss consoled them by assuring them that things could not be otherwise. "For," said he, "all this is for the best; for, if there is a volcano at Lisbon, it cannot be anywhere else; for it is impossible that things should not be where they are; for all is well."

A little, dark man, a familiar of the Inquisition, who sat beside him, politely took up the conversation, and said: "Apparently, you do not believe in original sin; for, if everything is for the best, there was neither fall nor punishment."

"I most humbly beg your excellency's pardon," replied Pangloss still more politely, "for the fall of man and the curse necessarily entered into the best of all possible worlds."

"Then you do not believe in free will?" said the familiar.

"Your excellency will pardon me," said Pangloss; "free will can exist with absolute necessity; for it was necessary that we should be free; for in short, limited will . . ."

Pangloss was in the middle of his phrase when the familiar nodded to his armed attendant who was pouring out port or Oporto wine for him.

CHAPTER VI. *How a Splendid Auto-da-fé was Held to Prevent Earthquakes, and How Candide was Flogged.*

After the earthquake which destroyed three-quarters of Lisbon, the wise men of that country could discover no more efficacious way of preventing a total ruin than by giving the people a splendid *auto-da-fé*. It was decided by the university of Coimbre that the sight of several persons being slowly burned in great ceremony is an infallible secret for preventing earthquakes. Consequently they had arrested a Biscayan convicted of having married his fellow-godmother, and two Portuguese who, when eating a chicken, had thrown away the bacon; after dinner they came and bound Dr. Pangloss and his disciple Candide, one because he had spoken and the other because he had listened with an air of approbation; they were both carried separately to extremely cool apartments where there was never any discomfort from the sun; a week afterwards each was dressed in a sanbenito and their heads were ornamented with paper mitres; Candide's mitre and sanbenito were painted with flames upside down and with devils who had neither tails nor claws; but Pangloss's devils had claws and tails, and his flames were upright.

Dressed in this manner they marched in procession and listened to a most pathetic sermon, followed by lovely plain song music. Candide was flogged in time to the music, while the singing went on; the Biscayan and the two men who had not wanted to eat the bacon were burned, and Pangloss was hanged, although this is not the custom. The very same day, the earth shook again with a terrible clamor.

Candide, terrified, dumbfounded, bewildered, covered with blood, quivering from head to foot, said to himself: "If this is the best of all possible worlds, what are the others? Let it pass that I was flogged, for I was flogged by the Bulgarians, but, O my dear Pangloss! The greatest of philosophers! Must I see you hanged without knowing why! O my dear Anabaptist! The best of men! Was it necessary that you should be drowned in port! O Mademoiselle Cunegonde! The pearl of women! Was it necessary that your belly should be slit!"

He was returning, scarcely able to support himself, preached at, flogged, absolved and blessed, when an old woman accosted him and said: "Courage, my son, follow me."

* * * *

[The hero's outlandish adventures continue until all the tale's main characters are miraculously reunited in Chapter 29.]

CHAPTER XXIX. *How Candide Found Cunegonde and the Old Woman Again*

While Candide, the Baron, Pangloss, Martin and Cacambo were relating their adventures, reasoning upon contingent or non-contingent events of the universe, arguing about effects and causes, moral and physical evil, free will and necessity, and the consolation to be found in the Turkish galleys, they came to the house of the Transylvanian prince on the shores of Propontis.

The first objects which met their sight were Cunegonde and the old woman hanging out towels to dry on the line. At this sight the Baron grew pale. Candide, that tender lover, seeing his fair Cunegonde sunburned, blear-eyed, flat-breasted, with wrinkles round her eyes and red, chapped arms, recoiled three paces in horror, and then advanced from mere politeness. She embraced Candide and her brother. They embraced the old woman; Candide bought them both.

In the neighborhood was a little farm; the old woman suggested that Candide should buy it, until some better fate befell the group. Cunegonde did not know that she had become ugly, for nobody had told her so; she reminded Candide of his promises in so peremptory a tone that the good Candide dared not refuse her. He therefore informed the Baron that he was about to marry his sister.

"Never," said the Baron, "will I endure such baseness on her part and such insolence on yours; nobody shall ever reproach me with this infamy; my sister's children could never enter the chapters of Germany. No, my sister shall never marry anyone but a Baron of the Empire."

Cunegonde threw herself at his feet and bathed them in tears; but he was inflexible.

"Madman," said Candide, "I rescued you from the galleys, I paid your ransom and your sister's; she was washing dishes here, she is ugly, I am so kind as to make her my wife, and you pretend to oppose me! I should re-kill you if I listened to my anger."

"You may kill me again," said the Baron, "but you shall never marry my sister while I am alive."

CHAPTER XXX. *Conclusion.*

At the bottom of his heart Candide had not the least wish to marry Cunegonde. But the Baron's extreme impertinence determined him to complete the marriage, and Cunegonde urged it so warmly that he could not retract. He consulted Pangloss, Martin and the faithful Cacambo. Pangloss wrote an excellent memorandum by which he proved that the Baron had no rights over his sister and that by all the laws of the empire she could make a left-handed marriage with Candide. Martin advised that the

Baron should be thrown into the sea; Cacambo decided that he should be returned to the Levantine captain and sent back to the galleys, after which he would be returned by the first ship to the Vicar-General at Rome. This was thought to be very good advice; the old woman approved it; they said nothing to the sister; the plan was carried out with the aid of a little money and they had the pleasure of duping a Jesuit and punishing the pride of a German Baron.

It would be natural to suppose that when, after so many disasters, Candide was married to his mistress, and living with the philosopher Pangloss, the philosopher Martin, the prudent Cacambo and the old woman, having brought back so many diamonds from the country of the ancient Incas, he would lead the most pleasant life imaginable. But he was so cheated by the Jews that he had nothing left but his little farm; his wife, growing uglier every day, became shrewish and unendurable; the old woman was ailing and even more bad tempered than Cunegonde. Cacambo, who worked in the garden and then went to Constantinople to sell vegetables, was overworked and cursed his fate. Pangloss was in despair because he did not shine in some German university.

As for Martin, he was firmly convinced that people are equally uncomfortable everywhere; he accepted things patiently. Candide, Martin and Pangloss sometimes argued about metaphysics and morals. From the windows of the farm they often watched the ships going by, filled with effendis, pashas, and cadis, who were being exiled to Lemnos, to Mitylene and Erzerum. They saw other cadis, other pashas and other effendis coming back to take the place of the exiles and to be exiled in their turn. They saw the neatly impaled heads which were taken to the Sublime Porte. These sights redoubled their discussions; and when they were not arguing, the boredom was so excessive that one day the old woman dared to say to them: "I should like to know which is worse, to be raped a hundred times by negro pirates, to have a buttock cut off, to run the gauntlet among the Bulgarians, to be whipped and flogged in an *auto-da-fé*, to be dissected, to row in a galley, in short, to endure all the miseries through which we have passed, or to remain here doing nothing?"

"'Tis a great question," said Candide.

These remarks led to new reflections, and Martin especially concluded that man was born to live in the convulsions of distress or in the lethargy of boredom. Candide did not agree, but he asserted nothing. Pangloss confessed that he had always suffered horribly; but, having once maintained that everything was for the best, he had continued to maintain it without believing it.

One thing confirmed Martin in his destestable principles, made Candide hesitate more than ever, and embarrassed Pangloss. And it was this. One day there came to their farm Paquette and Friar Giroflée, who were in the most extreme misery; they had soon wasted their three thousand piastres, had left each other, made it up, quarrelled again, been put in prison, escaped, and finally Friar Giroflée had turned Turk. Paquette continued her occupation everywhere and now earned nothing by it.

"I foresaw," said Martin to Candide, "that your gifts would soon be wasted and would only make them the more miserable. You and Cacambo were once bloated with millions of piastres and you are no happier than Friar Giroflée and Paquette."

"Ah! Ha!" said Pangloss to Paquette, "so Heaven brings you back to us, my dear child? Do you know that you cost me the end of my nose, an eye and an ear! What a plight you are in! Ah! What a world this is!"

This new occurrence caused them to philosophise more than ever. In the neighborhood there lived a very famous Dervish, who was supposed to be the best philosopher in Turkey; they went to consult him; Pangloss was the spokesman and said: "Master, we have come to beg you to tell us why so strange an animal as man was ever created."

"What has it to do with you?" said the Dervish. "Is it your business?"

"But, reverend father," said Candide, "there is a horrible amount of evil in the world."

"What does it matter," said the Dervish, "whether there is evil or good? When his highness sends a ship to Egypt, does he worry about the comfort or discomfort of the rats in the ship?"

"Then what should we do?" said Pangloss.

"Hold your tongue," said the Dervish.

"I flattered myself," said Pangloss, "that I should discuss with you effects and causes, this best of all possible worlds, the origin of evil, the nature of the soul and pre-established harmony."

At these words the Dervish slammed the door in their faces.

During this conversation the news went round that at Constantinople two viziers and the mufti had been strangled and several of their friends impaled. This catastrophe made a prodigious noise everywhere for several hours. As Pangloss, Candide and Martin were returning to their little farm, they came upon an old man who was taking the air under a bower of orange trees at his door. Pangloss, who was as curious as he was argumentative, asked him what was the name of the mufti who had just been strangled.

"I do not know," replied the old man. "I have never known the name of any mufti or of any vizier. I am entirely ignorant of the occurrence you mention; I presume that in general those who meddle with public affairs sometimes perish miserably and that they deserve it; but I never inquire what is going on in Constantinople; I content myself with sending there for sale the produce of the garden I cultivate."

Having spoken thus, he took the strangers into his house. His two daughters and his two sons presented them with several kinds of sherbert which they made themselves, caymac flavored with candied citron peel, oranges, lemons, limes, pineapples, dates, pistachios and Mocha coffee which had not been mixed with the bad coffee of Batavia and the Isles. After which this good Mussulman's two daughters perfumed the beards of Candide, Pangloss and Martin.

"You must have a vast and magnificent estate?" said Candide to the Turk.

"I have only twenty acres," replied the Turk. "I cultivate them with my children; and work keeps at bay three great evils: boredom, vice and need."

As Candide returned to his farm he reflected deeply on the Turk's remarks. He said to Pangloss and Martin: "That good old man seems to me to have chosen an existence preferable by far to that of the six kings with whom we had the honor to sup."

"Exalted rank," said Pangloss, "is very dangerous, according to the testimony of all philosophers; for Eglon, King of the Moabites, was murdered by Ehud; Absalom was hanged by the hair and pierced by three darts; King Nadab, son of Jeroboam, was killed by Baasha; King Elah by Zimri; Ahaziah by Jehu; Athaliah by Jehoiada; the Kings Jehoiakim, Jeconiah and Zedekiah were made slaves. You know in what manner died Croesus, Astyages, Darius, Denys of Syracuse, Pyrrhus, Perseus, Hannibal, Jugurtha, Ariovistus, Caesar, Pompey, Nero, Otho, Vitellius, Domitian, Richard II of England, Edward II, Henry VI, Richard III, Mary Stuart, Charles I, the three Henrys of France, the Emperor Henry IV. You know . . ."

"I also know," said Candide, "that we should cultivate our gardens."

"You are right," said Pangloss, "for, when man was placed in the Garden of Eden, he was placed there *ut operaretur eum*, to dress it and to keep it; which proves that man was not born for idleness."

"Let us work without theorizing," said Martin; "'tis the only way to make life endurable."

The whole small fraternity entered into this praiseworthy plan, and each started to make use of his talents. The little farm yielded well. Cunegonde was indeed very ugly, but she became an excellent pastry cook; Paquette embroidered; the old woman took care of the linen. Even Friar Giroflée performed some service; he was a very good carpenter and even became a man of honor; and Pangloss sometimes said to Candide: "All events are linked up in this best of all possible worlds; for, if you had not been expelled from the noble castle, by hard kicks in your backside for love of Mademoiselle Cunegonde, if you had not been clapped into the Inquisition, if you had not wandered about America on foot, if you had not stuck your sword in the Baron, if you had not lost all your sheep from the land of Eldorado, you would not be eating candied citrons and pistachios here."

"'Tis well said," replied Candide, "but we must cultivate our gardens."

—Translated by Richard Aldington

BAROQUE AND ENLIGHTENMENT POETRY

St. Teresa of Avila (1515–1582) was a religious mystic who inspired fervent devotion in the baroque era. Teresa recounted her feats of spiritual courage in two autobiographies and composed a mystical guide book for spiritual self-education. The poem included here describes her ecstatic union with God, later depicted in sculpture by the Italian baroque master Gianlorenzo Bernini.

The seventeenth-century English poets John Donne (1572?–1631) and Andrew Marvell (1621–1678) typify the complex sensibility of the so-called "metaphysical poets," known for their learned and unorthodox imagery. Donne enjoyed the company of elegant women and wrote sensual love poetry based on witty and complicated images; but he was also a cleric famed for his eloquent preaching and religious poetry.

"Death, be not proud" and "Batter My Heart" are from a series entitled *Holy Sonnets*. Andrew Marvell frequently examined the tension between contradictory states of mind. In the famed poem of seduction "To His Coy Mistress," he wavers between the languor of eternity and the lustful urgency of approaching death.

Rather than the overwrought passion of the baroque, Alexander Pope (1688–1744) practiced the reasoned and restrained style of the eighteenth century. He typically wrote in rhymed couplets, a particularly constraining verse form in English. His long philosophical poem *An Essay on Man* (1733–34) declared that "whatever is, is right," expressing the rationalist view of deism.

For analysis and interpretation:

1. Compare the sensual language of Teresa's ecstatic vision with other descriptions of human encounters with God. Why might religious believers be more attracted to Teresa's imagery of hunting and seduction than more intellectualized or spiritualized descriptions of God?

2. Explain Donne's assertion that death is "slave to fate." Connect this phrase to other images of mastery and slavery in the poem. How does Donne's tone of triumph compare to Marvell's attitude toward aging and death?

3. What philosophical reasons does the Marvell's speaker give for his advice to "seize the day" and enjoy oneself? What would be the wisest and truest reply that Marvell's mistress might give to his eloquent blandishments?

4. Analyze the "middle state" in which humans find themselves, according to the brief excerpt from Pope's *Essay on Man*.

Teresa of Avila

I gave myself to Love Divine

I gave myself to Love Divine,
And lo! my lot so changèd is
That my Beloved One is mine
And I at last am surely His.

When that sweet Huntsman from above   5
First wounded me and left me prone,
Into the very arms of Love
My stricken soul forthwith was thrown.
Since then my life's no more my own
And all my lot so changèd is   10
That my Beloved One is mine
And I at last am surely His.

The dart wherewith He wounded me
Was all embarbèd round with love,

And thus my spirit came to be   15
One with its Maker, God above.
No love but this I need to prove:
My life to God surrender'd is
And my Beloved One is mine
And I at last am surely His.   20

John Donne

Death, be not proud

Death, be not proud, though some have calléd thee
Mighty and dreadful, for thou are not so;
For those whom thou think'st thou dost overthrow
Die not, poor Death, nor yet canst thou kill me.
From rest and sleep, which but thy pictures be,
Much pleasure; then from thee much more must flow,
And soonest our best men with thee do go,
Rest of their bones, and soul's delivery.
Thou'art slave to fate, chance, kings, and desperate men,
And dost with poison, war, and sickness dwell,   10
And poppy'or charms can make us sleep as well
And better than thy stroke; why swell'st thou then?
One short sleep past, we wake eternally
And death shall be no more; Death, thou shalt die.

Andrew Marvell

To His Coy Mistress

Had we but world enough, and time,
This coyness, lady, were no crime.
We would sit down, and think which way
To walk, and pass our long love's day.
Thou by the Indian Ganges' side   5
Shoudst rubies find; I by the tide
Of Humber would complain. I would
Love you ten years before the flood,
And you should, if you please, refuse
Till the conversion of the Jews.   10
My vegetable love should grow
Vaster than empires and more slow;
An hundred years should go to praise

Thine eyes, and on thy forehead gaze;
Two hundred to adore each breast,   15
But thirty thousand to the rest;
An age at least to every part,
And the last age should show your heart.
For, lady, you deserve this state,
Nor would I love at lower rate.   20
But at my back I always hear
Time's wingéd chariot hurrying near;
And yonder all before us lie
Deserts of vast eternity.
Thy beauty shall no more be found;   25
Nor, in thy marble vault, shall sound
My echoing song; then worms shall try
That long-preserved virginity,
And your quaint honor turn to dust,
And into ashes all my lust: 30
The grave's a fine and private place,
But none, I think, do there embrace.
Now therefore, while the youthful hue
Sits on thy skin like morning glow,
And while thy willing soul transpires   35
At every pore with instant fires,
Now let us sport us while we may,
And now, like amorous birds of prey,
Rather at once our time devour
Than languish in his slow-chapped power.   40
Let us roll all our strength and all
Our sweetness up into one ball,
And tear our pleasures with rough strife
Thorough the iron gates of life:
Thus, though we cannot make our sun   45
Stand still, yet we will make him run.

Alexander Pope

From *An Essay on Man*

Know then thyself, presume not God to scan;
The proper study of mankind is Man.
Placed on this isthmus of a middle state,
A being darkly wise, and rudely great:
With too much knowledge for the skeptic side,   5
With too much weakness for the Stoic's pride,

He hangs between; in doubt to act, or rest,
In doubt to deem himself a god, or beast;
In doubt his mind or body to prefer,
Born but to die, and reasoning but to err;   10
Alike in ignorance, his reason such,
Whether he thinks too little, or too much:
Chaos of thought and passion, all confused;
Still by himself abused, or disabused;
Created half to rise, and half to fall;   15
Great lord of all things, yet a prey to all;
Sole judge of truth, in endless error hurled:
The glory, jest, and riddle of the world!

3

Revolution, Romanticism, and Realism

The age of revolution brought bold action on behalf of truths that the revolutionaries, if not all men, held to be self-evident: the Enlightenment's truths of equality, freedom, and progress. The early nineteenth century saw a prevailing spirit of political liberalism and an expanding industrial society. The age fostered romantic heroes like Goethe's Faust and Whitman's rambling poet, creatures of unfettered ambition and vision. However, the expansive spirit of romanticism could not shake a haunting sense of loss, expressed in Wordsworth's yearning for fleeting youth and receding nature. The romantic ambition could also create demons and monsters. In his relentless pursuit of scientific knowledge, Mary Shelley's Doctor Frankenstein created a fearsome alter ego, a new "Adam" created by genius but ruined by humans' inhumanity.

By mid-nineteenth century, the logic of modernity had seized European civilization. For the symbolic poets, to be completely modern was to adopt the idling, mocking voice in Baudelaire's *Flowers of Evil* seeming to celebrate moral decadence. The sensitive perceptions of Emily Dickinson and Rainer Maria Rilke indicated that human experience resists the simple facts of industry or science. Repelled by modernity, Fyodor Dostoevsky's Inquisitor peered straight into the twentieth century, foreseeing a mass society of cannibalistic materialism and a spiritual desolation that could be redeemed only by false miracles and deceitful authority.

Paradoxically, the spiritual crisis of the end of the century would give rise to the great modernist renewal, in which literary and philosophical traditions were renewed by the most radical break with tradition ever.

THOMAS JEFFERSON

The American Declaration of Independence was a direct expression of the European Enlightenment and an application of the liberal political theory of John Locke. The Declaration's principal author was Thomas Jefferson, who, like his American revolutionary comrades, had been schooled in the writings of English and continental philosophy. Their rationale for revolution rested on Locke's concept of popular sovereignty, which supported the right of the people to dissolve their bond with an oppressive government and found a new state. The American rebels prevailed, of course, not by the righteousness of their ideas but by force of arms; their ideas, however, fueled a greater revolutionary upheaval in France in 1789.

For analysis and interpretation:

1. What sovereign "people" does the Declaration seem to speak for? In today's political circumstances, what groups might justifiably identify themselves as a "people" possessing the sovereign right to break away from one government and form another?

2. Compare the Declaration's political idealism to the realism of Machiavelli and Hobbes. How might a political realist analyze the motivations of the American colonists, apart from their eloquent philosophical rationale?

3. To what extent would people today affirm the revolutionary principles of Jefferson's Declaration? What checks or limitations might justifiably be placed on the right of citizens to oppose or withdraw from their government?

The Declaration of Independence

In Congress, July 4, 1776: The unanimous Declaration of the thirteen United States of America

When in the Course of human events, it becomes necessary for one people to dissolve the political bands which have connected them with another, and to assume among the Powers of the earth, the separate and equal station to which the Laws of Nature and of Nature's God entitle them, a decent respect to the opinions of mankind requires that they should declare the causes which impel them to the separation.

We hold these truths to be self-evident, that all men are created equal, that they are endowed by their Creator with certain unalienable Rights, that among these are Life, Liberty and the pursuit of Happiness. That to secure these rights, Governments are instituted among Men, deriving their just powers from the consent of the governed, That whenever any Form of Government becomes destructive of these ends, it is the Right of the People to alter or to abolish it, and to institute new Government, laying its foundation on such principles and organizing its powers in such form, as to them shall seem most likely to effect their Safety and Happiness. Prudence, indeed, will dictate that Governments long established should not be changed for light and transient causes; and accordingly all experience hath shown, that mankind are more disposed to suffer, while evils are sufferable, than to right themselves by abolishing the forms to which they are accustomed. But when a long train of abuses and usurpations, pursuing invariably the same Object evinces a design to reduce them under absolute Despotism, it is their right, it is their duty, to throw off such Government, and to provide new Guards for their future security.—Such has been the patient sufferance of these Colonies; and such is now the necessity which constrains them to alter their former Systems of Government. The history of the present King of Great Britain is a history of repeated injuries and usurpations, all having in direct object the establishment of an absolute Tyranny over these States. To prove this, let Facts be submitted to a candid world.

He has refused his Assent to Laws, the most wholesome and necessary for the public good.

He has forbidden his Governors to pass Laws of immediate and pressing importance, unless suspended in their operation till his Assent should be obtained; and when so suspended he has utterly neglected to attend to them.

He has refused to pass other Laws for the accommodation of large districts of people, unless those people would relinquish the right of Representation in the Legislature, a right inestimable to them and formidable to tyrants only.

He has called together legislative bodies at places unusual, uncomfortable, and distant from the depository of their Public Records, for the sole purpose of fatiguing them into compliance with his measures.

He has dissolved Representative Houses repeatedly, for opposing with manly firmness his invasions on the rights of the people.

He has refused for a long time, after such dissolutions, to cause others to be elected; whereby the Legislative Powers, incapable of Annihilation, have returned to the People at large for their exercise; the State remaining in the mean time exposed to all the dangers of invasion from without, and convulsions within.

He has endeavoured to prevent the population of these States; for that purpose obstructing the Laws for Naturalization of Foreigners; refusing to pass others to encourage their migration hither, and raising the conditions of new Appropriations of Lands.

He has obstructed the Administration of Justice, by refusing his Assent to Laws for establishing Judiciary Powers.

He has made Judges dependent on his Will alone, for the tenure of their offices, and the amount and payment of their salaries.

He has erected a multitude of New Offices, and sent hither swarms of Officers to harrass our People, and eat out their substance.

He has kept among us, in times of peace, Standing Armies without the Consent of our legislature.

He has affected to render the Military independent of and superior to the Civil Power.

He has combined with others to subject us to a jurisdiction foreign to our constitution, and unacknowledged by our laws; giving his Assent to their acts of pretended Legislation:

For quartering large bodies of armed troops among us:

For protecting them, by a mock Trial, from Punishment for any Murders which they should commit on the Inhabitants of these States:

For cutting off our Trade with all parts of the world:

For imposing taxes on us without our Consent:

For depriving us in many cases, of the benefits of Trial by Jury:

For transporting us beyond Seas to be tried for pretended offences:

For abolishing the free System of English Laws in a neighbouring Province, establishing therein an Arbitrary government, and enlarging its Boundaries so as to render it at once an example and fit instrument for introducing the same absolute rule into these Colonies:

For taking away our Charters, abolishing our most valuable Laws, and altering fundamentally the Forms of our Governments:

For suspending our own Legislatures, and declaring themselves invested with Powers to legislate for us in all cases whatsoever.

He has abdicated Government here, by declaring us out of his Protection and waging War against us.

He has plundered our seas, ravaged our Coasts, burnt our towns, and destroyed the lives of our people.

He is at this time transporting large armies of foreign mercenaries to complete the works of death, desolation and tyranny, already begun with circumstances of Cruelty & perfidy scarcely paralleled in the most barbarous ages, and totally unworthy the Head of a civilized nation.

He has constrained our fellow Citizens taken Captive on the high Seas to bear Arms against their Country, to become the executioners of their friends and Brethren, or to fall themselves by their Hands.

He has excited domestic insurrections amongst us, and has endeavoured to bring on the inhabitants of our frontiers, the merciless Indian Savages, whose known rule of warfare, is an undistinguished destruction of all ages, sexes and conditions.

In every stage of these Oppressions We have Petitioned for Redress in the most humble terms: Our repeated Petitions have been answered only by repeated injury. A Prince, whose character is thus marked by every act which may define a Tyrant, is unfit to be a ruler of a free People.

Nor have We been wanting in attention to our British brethren. We have warned them from time to time of attempts by their legislature to extend an unwarrantable jurisdiction over us. We have reminded them of the circumstances of our emigration and settlement here. We have appealed to their native justice and magnanimity, and we have conjured them by the ties of our common kindred to disavow these usurpations, which, would inevitably interrupt our connections and correspondence. They too have been deaf to the voice of justice and of consanguinity. We must, therefore, acquiesce in the necessity, which denounces our Separation, and hold them, as we hold the rest of mankind, Enemies in War, in Peace Friends.

We, therefore, the Representatives of the united States of America, in General Congress, Assembled, appealing to the Supreme Judge of the world for the rectitude of our intentions, do, in the Name, and by Authority of the good People of these Colonies, solemnly publish and declare, That these United Colonies are, and of Right ought to be Free and Independent States; that they are Absolved from all Allegiance to the British Crown, and that all political connection between them and the State of Great Britain, is and ought to be totally dissolved; and that as Free and Independent States, they have full Power to levy War, conclude Peace, contract Alliances, establish Commerce, and to do all other Acts and Things which Independent States may of right do. And for the support of this Declaration, with a firm reliance on the Protection of Divine Providence, we mutually pledge to each other our Lives, our Fortunes and our sacred Honor.

JOHANN WOLFGANG VON GOETHE

The career of Johann Wolfgang von Goethe (1749–1832) spanned the Enlightenment and romantic eras, encompassing achievements in literature, science, and public service. His master work, the two-part poetic drama *Faust* (1808, 1832), defined the archetypal romantic hero, a man whose quest for experience ultimately leads to a maturity of moral conscience.

Goethe's drama was based on the medieval legend of Dr. Faustus, a scholar who supposedly sold his soul to the devil in the pursuit of forbidden knowledge. In Goethe's version, the wager between Faust and the devil Mephistopheles has particularly romantic terms: Mephistopheles offers boundless sensual experience, while Faust promises to forfeit his soul only if his thirst for experience is quenched. In Part I, Faust pursues and ultimately destroys the innocent girl Margaret; in Part II, Faust broadens his quest to great public projects but confronts, in his encounter with Care, the moral limits on human achievement. At the tragedy's end, Faust is still unsatisfied and his soul is taken into heaven despite his destructive folly.

Goethe's expansive masterpiece, more poetry than drama, establishes the fictional type of such historical romantic personages as Napoleon and Lord Byron. Goethe's romantic enthusiasm, believing always in the human struggle to prevail, may be balanced against the reservations of such commentators as Montaigne and Alexander Pope regarding the presumptuousness of human ambition.

For analysis and interpretation:

1. Speculate on the reasons that Faust curses the pleasures of life in his conversation with the devil. How might you respond to someone so consumed with depression and despair?

2. Analyze the wager of Faust and Mephistopheles. How do the terms of the wager express a romantic conception of human nature?

3. Compare Faust's description of humanity—"*moving on*, to weal and woe assent—He, at each moment ever discontent"—to other philosophical descriptions of human happiness.

4. Do you agree with the tragedy's ending, which implies that so long as humans strive to achieve, their most harmful errors should be forgiven?

From *Faust*

[*From Part I: Mephistopheles returns to Faust's study, where the scholar is brooding.*]

FAUST.   Who's knocking? Come in! *Now* who wants to annoy me?

MEPHISTOPHELES. (*outside door*):   It's I.

FAUST.   Come in!

MEPHISTOPHELES (*outside door*):
　　You must say 'Come in' three times.

FAUST.   Come in then!

MEPHISTOPHELES (entering).   Thank you; you overjoy me.
　　We two, I hope, we shall be good friends;
　　To chase those megrims of yours away
　　I am here like a fine young squire to-day,
　　In a suit of scarlet trimmed with gold
　　And a little cape of stiff brocade,
　　With a cock's feather in my hat   10
　　And at my side a long sharp blade,
　　And the most succinct advice I can give
　　Is that you dress up just like me,
　　So that uninhibited and free
　　You may find out what it means to live.

FAUST.   The pain of earth's constricted life, I fancy,
　　Will pierce me still, whatever my attire;
　　I am too old for mere amusement,
　　Too young to be without desire.
　　How can the world dispel my doubt?   20
　　You must do without, you must do without!
　　That is the everlasting song
　　Which rings in every ear, which rings,
　　And which to us our whole life long
　　Every hour hoarsely sings.
　　I wake in the morning only to feel appalled,
　　My eyes with bitter tears could run
　　To see the day which in its course
　　Will not fulfil a wish for me, not one;
　　The day which whittles away with obstinate carping   30
　　All pleasures—even those of anticipation,
　　Which makes a thousand grimaces to obstruct
　　My heart when it is stirring in creation.
　　And again, when night comes down, in anguish
　　I must stretch out upon my bed

And again no rest is granted me,
For wild dreams fill my mind with dread.
The God who dwells within my bosom
Can make my inmost soul react;
The God who sways my every power   40
Is powerless with external fact.
And so existence weighs upon my breast
And I long for death and life—life I detest.

MEPHISTOPHELES.   Yet death is never a wholly welcome guest.

FAUST.   O happy is he whom death in the dazzle of victory
Crowns with the bloody laurel in the battling swirl!
Or he whom after the mad and breakneck dance
He comes upon in the arms of a girl!
O to have sunk away, delighted, deleted,
Before the Spirit of the Earth, before his might!   50

MEPHISTOPHELES.   Yet I know someone who failed to drink
A brown juice on a certain night.

FAUST.   Your hobby is espionage—is it not?

MEPHISTOPHELES.   Oh I'm not omniscient—but I know a lot.

FAUST.   Whereas that tumult in my soul
Was stilled by sweet familiar chimes
Which cozened the child that yet was in me
With echoes of more happy times,
I now curse all things that encompass
The soul with lures and jugglery   60
And bind it in this dungeon of grief
With trickery and flattery.
Cursed in advance be the high opinion
That serves our spirit for a cloak!
Cursed be the dazzle of appearance
Which bows our senses to its yoke!
Cursed be the lying dreams of glory,
The illusion that our name survives!
Cursed be the flattering things we own,
Servants and ploughs, children and wives!   70
Cursed be Mammon when with his treasures
He makes us play the adventurous man
Or when for our luxurious pleasures
He duly spreads the soft divan!
A curse on the balsam of the grape!
A curse on the love that rides for a fall!
A curse on hope! A curse on faith!
And a curse on patience most of all!

(*The invisible Spirits sing again*)

SPIRITS.   Woe! Woe!
        You have destroyed it,   80
        The beautiful world;
        By your violent hand
        'Tis downward hurled!
        A half-god has dashed it asunder!
        From under
        We bear off the rubble to nowhere
        And ponder
        Sadly the beauty departed.
        Magnipotent
        One among men,   90
        Magnificent
        Build it again,
        Build it again in your breast!
        Let a new course of life
        Begin
        With vision abounding
        And new songs resounding
        To welcome it in!

MEPHISTOPHELES.   These are the juniors
        Of my faction.   100
        Hear how precociously they counsel
        Pleasure and action.
        Out and away
        From your lonely day
        Which dries your senses and your juices
        Their melody seduces.

Stop playing with your grief which battens
Like a vulture on your life, your mind!
The worst of company would make you feel
That you are a man among mankind.   110
Not that it's really my proposition
To shove you among the common men;
Though I'm not one of the Upper Ten,
If you would like a coalition
With me for your career through life,
I am quite ready to fit in,
I'm yours before you can say knife.
I am your comrade;
If you so crave,
I am your servant, I am your slave.   120

FAUST.   And what have I to undertake in return?

MEPHISTOPHELES.   Oh it's early days to discuss what that is.

FAUST.   No, no, the devil is an egoist
And ready to do nothing gratis
Which is to benefit a stranger.
Tell me your terms and don't prevaricate!
A servant like you in the house is a danger.

MEPHISTOPHELES.   I will bind myself to your service in this world,
To be at your beck and never rest nor slack;
When we meet again on the other side,   130
In the same coin you shall pay me back.

FAUST.   The other side gives me little trouble;
First batter this present world to rubble,
Then the other may rise—if that's the plan.
This earth is where my springs of joy have started,
And this sun shines on me when broken-hearted;
If I can first from them be parted,
Then let happen what will and can!
I wish to hear no more about it—
Whether there too men hate and love   140
Or whether in those spheres too, in the future,
There is a Below or an Above.

MEPHISTOPHELES.   With such an outlook you can risk it.
Sign on the line! In these next days you will get
Ravishing samples of my arts;
I am giving you what never man saw yet.

FAUST.   Poor devil, can *you* give anything ever?
Was a human spirit in its high endeavour
Even once understood by one of your breed?
Have you got food which fails to feed?   150
Or red gold which, never at rest,
Like mercury runs away through the hand?
A game at which one never wins?
A girl who, even when on my breast,
Pledges herself to my neighbour with her eyes?
The divine and lovely delight of honour
Which falls like a falling star and dies?
Show me the fruits which, before they are plucked, decay
And the trees which day after day renew their green!

MEPHISTOPHELES.   Such a commission doesn't alarm me,   170
I have such treasures to purvey.

But, my good friend, the time draws on when we
Should be glad to feast at our ease on something good.

FAUST. If ever I stretch myself on a bed of ease.
Then I am finished! Is that understood?
If ever your flatteries can coax me
To be pleased with myself, if ever you cast
A spell of pleasure that can hoax me—
Then let *that* day be my last!
That's my wager! 180

MEPHISTOPHELES. Done!

FAUST. Let's shake!
If ever I say to the passing moment
'Linger a while! Thou art so fair!'
Then you may cast me into fetters,
I will gladly perish then and there!
Then you may set the death-bell tolling,
Then from my service you are free,
The clock may stop, its hand may fall,
And that be the end of time for me!

MEPHISTOPHELES. Think what you're saying, we shall not forget it.

FAUST. And you are fully within your rights; 190
I have made no mad or outrageous claim.
If I stay as I am, I am a slave—
Whether yours or another's, it's all the same.

MEPHISTOPHELES. I shall this very day at the College Banquet
Enter your service with no more ado,
But just one point—As a life-and-death insurance
I must trouble you for a line or two.

FAUST. So you, you pedant, you too like things in writing?
Have you never known a man? Or a man's word? Never?
Is it not enough that my word of mouth 200
Puts all my days in bond for ever?
Does not the world rage on in all its streams
And shall a promise hamper *me*?
Yet this illusion reigns within our hearts
And from it who would be gladly free?
Happy the man who can inwardly keep his word;
Whatever the cost, he will not be loath to pay!
But a parchment, duly inscribed and sealed,
Is a bogey from which all wince away.
The word dies on the tip of the pen 210
And wax and leather lord it then.
What do you, evil spirit, require?

Bronze, marble, parchment, paper?
Quill or chisel or pencil of slate?
You may choose whichever you desire.

MEPHISTOPHELES.   How can you so exaggerate
With such a hectic rhetoric?
Any little snippet is quite good—
And you sign it with one little drop of blood.

FAUST.   If that is enough and is some use,   220
One may as well pander to your fad.

MEPHISTOPHELES.   Blood is a very special juice.

FAUST.   Only do not fear that I shall break this contract.
What I promise is nothing more
Than what all my powers are striving for.
I have puffed myself up too much, it is only
Your sort that really fits my case.
The great Earth Spirit has despised me
And Nature shuts the door in my face.
The thread of thought is snapped asunder,   230
I have long loathed knowledge in all its fashions.
In the depths of sensuality
Let us now quench our glowing passions!
And at once make ready every wonder
Of unpenetrated sorcery!
Let us cast ourselves into the torrent of time,
Into the whirl of eventfulness,
Where disappointment and success,
Pleasure and pain may chop and change
As chop and change they will and can;   240
It is restless action makes the man.

MEPHISTOPHELES.   No limit is fixed for you, no bound;
If you'd like to nibble at everything
Or to seize upon something flying round—
Well, may you have a run for your money!
But seize your chance and don't be funny!

FAUST.   I've told you, it is no question of happiness.
The most painful joy, enamoured hate, enlivening
Disgust—I devote myself to all excess.
My breast, now cured of its appetite for knowledge,   250
From now is open to all and every smart,
And what is allotted to the whole of mankind
That will I sample in my inmost heart,
Grasping the highest and lowest with my spirit,
Piling men's weal and woe upon my neck,

To extend myself to embrace all human selves
And to founder in the end, like them, a wreck. . . .

*[From Part II: After a career of diplomatic service and soldiering, the aged Faust has
undertaken a huge public works project, the draining of a marsh. He pursues his plan
despite the hardship it brings to an innocent old couple. In this scene, the allegorical
figure of Care casts a spell of blindness on Faust, symbol of his moral blindness to
the victims of his ambition.]*

Midnight

(Four Grey Women approach)

WANT.   They call me Want.

DEBT.   They call me Debt.

CARE.   They call me Care.

NEED.   They call me Need.

DEBT.   The door is locked and we cannot get in.

NEED.   Nor do we want to, there's wealth within.

WANT.   That makes me a shadow.

DEBT.   That makes me naught.

NEED.   The pampered spare me never a thought.

CARE.   My sisters, you cannot and may not get in.   10
    But the keyhole there lets Care creep in.
                     (Care vanishes)

WANT.   Come, grey sisters, away from here!

DEBT.   Debt at your side as close as fear.

NEED.   And Need at your heels as close as breath.

THE THREE.   Drifting cloud and vanishing star!
    Look yonder, look yonder!
             From far, from far,
    He's coming, our brother, he's coming . . .
            Death.

FAUST *(in the palace).*   Where four came hither, but three go hence;
    I heard them speak, I could not catch the sense.
    An echoing word resembling 'breath'—   20
    And a dark rhyme-word followed: 'Death'.
    A hollow, muffled, spectral sound to hear.
    Not yet have I fought my way out to the air.
    All magic—from my path if I could spurn it,
    All incantation—once for all unlearn it,

To face you, Nature, as one man of men—
It would be worth it to be human then.
As I was once, before I probed the hidden,
And cursed my world and self with words forbidden.
But now such spectredom so throngs the air   30
That none knows how to dodge it, none knows where.
Though one day greet us with a rational gleam,
The night entangles us in webs of dream.
We come back happy from the fields of spring—
And a bird croaks. Croaks what? Some evil thing.
Enmeshed in superstition night and morn,
It forms and shows itself and comes to warn.
And we, so scared, stand without friend or kin,
And the door creaks—and nobody comes in.
Anyone here?

CARE.   The answer should be clear.   40

FAUST.   And you, who are you then?

CARE.   am just here.

FAUST.   Take yourself off!

CARE.   This is where I belong.
                    (Faust is first angry, then recovers himself)

FAUST *(to himself)*.   Take care, Faust, speak no magic spell, be strong.

CARE.   Though to me no ear would hearken,
            Echoes through the heart must darken;
            Changing shape from hour to hour
            I employ my savage power.
            On the road or on the sea,
            Constant fearful company,
            Never looked for, always found,   50
            Cursed—but flattered by the sound.
    Care? Have you never met with Care?

FAUST.   I have only galloped through the world
    And clutched each lust and longing by the hair;
    What did not please me, I let go,
    What flowed away, I let it flow.
    I have only felt, only fulfilled desire,
    And once again desired and thus with power
    Have stormed my way through life; first great and strong,
    Now moving sagely, prudently along.   60
    This earthly circle I know well enough.
    Towards the Beyond the view has been cut off;
    Fool—who directs that way his dazzled eye,

Contrives himself a double in the sky!
Let him look round him here, not stray beyond;
To a sound man this world must needs respond.
To roam into eternity is vain!
What he perceives, he can attain.
Thus let him walk along his earthlong day;
Though phantoms haunt him, let him go his way,   70
And, moving on, to weal and woe assent—
He, at each moment ever discontent!

CARE.   Whomsoever I possess,
Finds the world but nothingness;
Gloom descends on him for ever,
Seeing sunrise, sunset, never;
Though his senses are not wrong,
Darknesses within him throng,
Who—of all that he may own—
Never owns himself alone.   80
Luck, ill luck, become but fancy;
Starving in the midst of plenty,
Be it rapture, be it sorrow,
He postpones it till to-morrow,
Fixed upon futurity,
Can never really come to be.

FAUST.   Stop! You cannot touch me so!
Such nonsense I refuse to hear.
Away! Your evil tale of woe
Could fog a wise man's brain, however clear.   90

CARE.   Let him come or go—he'll find
That he can't make up his mind;
Half-way down his destined way
Starts to stumble, grope and sway,
Ever deeper lost and thwarted,
Seeing all things more distorted,
Burden to himself and others,
Who takes breath and, breathing, smothers;
If not smothered, yet not living,
Not revolted, not self-giving.   100
Endless round—he must pursue it:
Painful Leave-it, hateful Do-it,
Freedom now, now harsh constraint,
Broken sleep that leaves him faint,
Bind him to his one position
And prepare him for perdition.

FAUST.   You outcast phantoms! Thus a thousand times
    You lead the human race into illusion;
    Even indifferent days you thus transform
    To nets of torment, nightmares of confusion.
    Demons, I know, are hardly shaken off,
    Their ghostly gripping bonds man cannot sever;
    But you, O Care, your power that creeps and grows—
    I shall not recognize it ever.

CARE.   Then feel it now! As, leaving you,
      This final curse on you I cast.
    The human race are blind their whole life through;
    Now, Faust, let *you* be blind at last.
         (She breathes upon him)

FAUST *(blinded).*   The night seems pressing in more thickly, thickly,
    Yet in my inmost heart a light shines clear;   120
    What I have planned, I must complete it quickly;
    Only the master's word is weighty here.
    Up and to work, my men! Each man of you!
    And bring my bold conception to full view.
    Take up your tools and toil with pick and spade!
    What has been outlined must at once be made.
    Good order, active diligence,
    Ensure the fairest recompense;
    That this vast work completion find,
    A thousand hands need but one mind. . . .   130
          —Translated by Louis Mac Neice

ROMANTIC POETRY

William Blake (1757–1827) prefigured romanticism in his rejection of Enlightenment rationalism and its mockery of religious revelation. Blake's own mystical vision of truth was childlike in its moral principles, yet also metaphysical. In "The Lamb," from *Songs of Innocence* (1789), Blake speaks through the wondering voice of a child, who addresses the lamb as a symbol of Christian meekness and love. In "The Tyger," from *Songs of Experience* (1794), Blake acknowledges the mysterious power of nature, questioning how the same creator could fashion both the furious tiger and the tender lamb.

    William Wordsworth (1770–1850) expressed the romantic yearning for an elusive happiness in his "Tintern Abbey," first published in 1807. Amid the peaceful ruin, recalling his visit with his sister five years before, Wordsworth finds respite from his hectic city life. While nature has shaped the speaker's moral awareness, still the poet cannot avoid a haunting sense of loss, compounded by distance from his now-absent companion. As in many of Wordsworth's poems, this melancholy arises from the poet's realization that mature wisdom inevitably involves a loss in the immediacy of experience.

Walt Whitman (1819–1892) was himself a kind of romantic hero, his poetry celebrating the rich experience of himself. The record of Whitman's unfolding powers is found in his *Song of Myself*, first published as part of *Leaves of Grass* in 1855 and revised until the poet's death. Whitman employed a loose, unrhymed verse form which permitted him to adopt many voices; the poetic self becomes an all-inclusive metaphor for the poet and the human community. In the excerpt here, Whitman explores the symbolic possibilities of a blade of grass, the "uniform hieroglyphic" in which the speaker encounters all humanity.

For analysis and interpretation:

1. Analyze the tension in Blake's two poems between a gentle and peaceful nature and the nature of fury and destruction. Describe this tension as an expression of the "fearful symmetry" questioned in the last lines of "The Tyger."

2. In Wordsworth's "Tintern Abbey," what are the speaker's feelings as he recalls his earlier visit to this spot? Explain the speaker's "sense sublime" of "a motion and a spirit." Do you agree with Wordsworth that the contemplation of nature can protect us from evil thoughts and others' selfishness?

3. Draw up a catalog of the things that the blade of grass represents to Whitman in *Song of Myself*. In what ways do these images reinforce or contradict each other? How do you respond to Whitman's sense of the profound unity of humanity, as symbolized in the blade of grass?

William Blake

The Lamb

Little Lamb, who made thee?
Dost thou know who made thee?
Gave thee life & bid thee feed,
By the stream & o'er the mead;
Gave thee clothing of delight,   5
Softest clothing wooly bright;
Gave thee such a tender voice,
Making all the vales rejoice!
Little Lamb who made thee?
Dost thou know who made thee?   10

Little Lamb I'll tell thee,
Little Lamb I'll tell thee!
He is callèd by thy name,
For he calls himself a Lamb:
He is meek & he is mild,   15

He became a little child:
I a child & thou a lamb,
We are callèd by his name.
Little Lamb God bless thee.
Little Lamb God bless thee.   20

The Tyger

Tyger! Tyger! burning bright
In the forests of the night,
What immortal hand or eye
Could frame thy fearful symmetry?

In what distant deeps or skies   5
Burnt the fire of thine eyes?
On what wings dare he aspire?
What the hand dare seize the fire?

And what shoulder, & what art,
Could twist the sinews of thy heart?   10
And when thy heart began to beat,
What dread hand? & what dread feet?

What the hammer? what the chain?
In what furnace was thy brain?
What the anvil? what dread grasp   15
Dare its deadly terrors clasp?

When the stars threw down their spears,
And watered heaven with their tears,
Did he smile his work to see?
Did he who made the Lamb make thee?   20

Tyger! Tyger! burning bright
In the forests of the night,
What immortal hand or eye
Dare frame thy fearful symmetry?

William Wordsworth

Lines Composed a Few Miles Above Tintern Abbey
on Revisiting the Banks of the Wye during a Tour, July 13, 1798

Five years have past; five summers, with the length
Of five long winters! and again I hear

These waters, rolling from their mountain-springs
With a soft inland murmur.—Once again
Do I behold these steep and lofty cliffs,   5
That on a wild secluded scene impress
Thoughts of more deep seclusion; and connect
The landscape with the quiet of the sky.
The day is come when I again repose
Here, under this dark sycamore, and view   10
These plots of cottage-ground, these orchard-tufts,
Which at this season, with their unripe fruits,
Are clad in one green hue, and lose themselves
'Mid groves and copses. Once again I see
These hedge-rows, hardly hedge-rows, little lines   15
Of sportive wood run wild: these pastoral farms,
Green to the very door; and wreaths of smoke
Sent up, in silence, from among the trees!
With some uncertain notice, as might seem
Of vagrant dwellers in the houseless woods,   20
Or of some Hermit's cave, where by his fire
The Hermit sits alone.

                    These beauteous forms,
Through a long absence, have not been to me
As is a landscape to a blind man's eye:
But oft, in lonely rooms, and 'mid the din   25
Of towns and cities, I have owed to them,
In hours of weariness, sensations sweet,
Felt in the blood, and felt along the heart;
And passing even into my purer mind,
With tranquil restoration:—feelings too   30
Of unremembered pleasure: such, perhaps,
As have no slight or trivial influence
On that best portion of a good man's life,
His little, nameless, unremembered, acts
Of kindness and of love. Nor less, I trust,   35
To them I may have owed another gift,
Of aspect more sublime; that blessèd mood,
In which the burthen of the mystery,
In which the heavy and the weary weight
Of all this unintelligible world,   40
Is lightened:—that serene and blessèd mood,
In which the affections gently lead us on,—
Until, the breath of this corporeal frame
And even the motion of our human blood

Almost suspended, we are laid asleep   45
In body, and become a living soul:
While with an eye made quiet by the power
Of harmony, and the deep power of joy,
We see into the life of things.

                  If this
Be but a vain belief, yet, oh! how oft—   50
In darkness and amid the many shapes
Of joyless daylight; when the fretful stir
Unprofitable, and the fever of the world,
Have hung upon the beatings of my heart—
How oft, in spirit, have I turned to thee,   55
O sylvan Wye! thou wanderer thro' the woods,
How often has my spirit turned to thee!

   And now, with gleams of half-extinguished thought,
With many recognitions dim and faint,
And somewhat of a sad perplexity,   60
The picture of the mind revives again:
While here I stand, not only with the sense
Of present pleasure, but with pleasing thoughts
That in this moment there is life and food
For future years. And so I dare to hope,   65
Though changed, no doubt, from what I was when first
I came among these hills; when like a roe
I bounded o'er the mountains, by the sides
Of the deep rivers, and the lonely streams,
Wherever nature led: more like a man   70
Flying from something that he dreads, than one
Who sought the thing he loved. For nature then
(The coarser pleasures of my boyish days,
And their glad animal movements all gone by)
To me was all in all.—I cannot paint   75
What then I was. The sounding cataract
Haunted me like a passion: the tall rock,
The mountain, and the deep and gloomy wood,
Their colours and their forms, were then to me
An appetite; a feeling and a love,   80
That had no need of a remoter charm,
By thought supplied, nor any interest
Unborrowed from the eye.—That time is past,
And all its aching joys are now no more,
And all its dizzy raptures. Not for this   85
Faint I, nor mourn nor murmur; other gifts

Have followed; for such loss, I would believe,
Abundant recompense. For I have learned
To look on nature, not as in the hour
Of thoughtless youth; but hearing oftentimes   90
The still, sad music of humanity,
Nor harsh nor grating, though of ample power
To chasten and subdue. And I have felt
A presence that disturbs me with the joy
Of elevated thoughts; a sense sublime   95
Of something far more deeply interfused,
Whose dwelling is the light of setting suns,
And the round ocean and the living air,
And the blue sky, and in the mind of man:
A motion and a spirit, that impels   100
All thinking things, all objects of all thought,
And rolls through all things. Therefore am I still
A lover of the meadows and the woods,
And mountains; and of all that we behold
From this green earth; of all the mighty world   105
Of eye, and ear,—both what they half create,
And what perceive; well pleased to recognise
In nature and the language of the sense,
The anchor of my purest thoughts, the nurse,
The guide, the guardian of my heart, and soul   110
Of all my moral being.

                Nor perchance,
If I were not thus taught, should I the more
Suffer my genial spirits to decay:
For thou art with me here upon the banks
Of this fair river; thou my dearest Friend,   115
My dear, dear Friend; and in thy voice I catch
The language of my former heart, and read
My former pleasures in the shooting lights
Of thy wild eyes. Oh! yet a little while
May I behold in thee what I was once,   120
My dear, dear Sister! and this prayer I make,
Knowing that Nature never did betray
The heart that loved her; 'tis her privilege,
Through all the years of this our life, to lead
From joy to joy: for she can so inform   125
The mind that is within us, so impress
With quietness and beauty, and so feed
With lofty thoughts, that neither evil tongues,

Rash judgments, nor the sneers of selfish men,
Nor greetings where no kindness is, nor all   130
The dreary intercourse of daily life,
Shall e'er prevail against us, or disturb
Our cheerful faith, that all which we behold
Is full of blessings. Therefore let the moon
Shine on thee in thy solitary walk;   135
And let the misty mountain-winds be free
To blow against thee: and, in after years,
When these wild ecstasies shall be matured
Into a sober pleasure; when thy mind
Shall be a mansion for all lovely forms,   140
Thy memory be as a dwelling-place
For all sweet sounds and harmonies; oh! then,
If solitude, or fear, or pain, or grief
Should be thy portion, with what healing thoughts
Of tender joy wilt thou remember me,   145
And these my exhortations! Nor, perchance—
If I should be where I no more can hear
Thy voice, nor catch from thy wild eyes these gleams
Of past existence—wilt thou then forget
That on the banks of this delightful stream   150
We stood together; and that I, so long
A worshipper of Nature, hither came
Unwearied in that service; rather say
With warmer love—oh! with far deeper zeal
Of holier love. Nor wilt thou then forget   155
That after many wanderings, many years
Of absence, these steep woods and lofty cliffs,
And this green pastoral landscape, were to me
More dear, both for themselves and for thy sake!

Walt Whitman

From *Song of Myself* (1855 edition)

[1]

I celebrate myself,
And what I assume you shall assume,
For every atom belonging to me as good belongs to you.

I loafe and invite my soul,
I lean and loafe at my ease .... observing a spear of summer grass. ...

[6]

A child said, What is the grass? fetching it to me with full hands;
How could I answer the child? .... I do not know what it is any more than he.

I guess it must be the flag of my disposition, out of hopeful green stuff woven.

Or I guess it is the handkerchief of the Lord,
A scented gift and remembrancer designedly dropped,
Bearing the owner's name someway in the corners, that we may see and remark, and
    say Whose?

Or I guess the grass is itself a child . . . . the produced babe of the vegetation.

Or I guess it is a uniform hieroglyphic,
And it means, Sprouting alike in broad zones and narrow zones,
Growing among black folks as among white,
Kanuck, Tuckahoe, Congressman, Cuff, I give them the same, I receive them the same.
And now it seems to me the beautiful uncut hair of graves.

Tenderly will I use you curling grass,
It may be you transpire from the breasts of young men,
It may be if I had known them I would have loved them;
It may be you are from old people and from women, and from offspring taken soon
    out of their mothers' laps,
And here you are the mothers' laps.

This grass is very dark to be from the white heads of old mothers,
Darker than the colorless beards of old men,
Dark to come from under the faint red roofs of mouths.

O I perceive after all so many uttering tongues!
And I perceive they do not come from the roofs of mouths for nothing.
I wish I could translate the hints about the dead young men and women,
And the hints about old men and mothers, and the offspring taken soon out of their
    laps.

What do you think has become of the young and old men?
And what do you think has become of the women and children?

They are alive and well somewhere;
The smallest sprout shows there is really no death,
And if ever there was it led forward life, and does not wait at the end to arrest it,
And ceased the moment life appeared.

All goes onward and outward . . . . and nothing collapses,
And to die is different from what any one supposed, and luckier.

MARY SHELLEY

Amidst her own life of romantic passion and adventure, Mary Shelley (1797–1851)
composed the archetypal romantic novel, *Frankenstein.* Shelley's tale of the
Promethean Dr. Frankenstein and his ill-fated creation posed fundamental questions

about human achievement and moral responsibility. In its Gothic settings of laboratories and Alpine crags, the novel explores the darker side of that scientific impulse that Descartes had explained so clearly and distinctly two centuries earlier.

In the excerpts provided here, Victor Frankenstein confronts the creature that he has brought to life through his experimentation. In repulsion, Victor abandons the creature and succumbs to a long illness. Left to roam free, rejected by humanity at every turn, the monster pursues his creator, murdering Victor's young brother and finally confronting Victor again on a desolate glacier. Though first agreeing to the monster's appeal for a mate, Victor cannot carry through this act of humanity. The monster vows to make Victor as lonely and desolate as he himself, and the reader last glimpses the pair in obsessive pursuit of each other across the Arctic ice.

For analysis and interpretation:

1. What actual human inventions might reasonably inspire the same horror that Victor feels for the monster? About what human inventions might one say that humanity would be better off if they had never been created?

2. Is the monster's hatred of humanity a reasonable and morally defensible reaction to his treatment? To what extent does ill treatment—in a marriage or family, or in society at large—justify a violent response?

3. What analogy can be found between Frankenstein's monster and people who face social rejection or abandonment? To what extent should we be morally bound to embrace and care for all humans?

From *Frankenstein*

[*Chapter 5*]

It was on a dreary night of November that I beheld the accomplishment of my toils. With an anxiety that almost amounted to agony, I collected the instruments of life around me, that I might infuse a spark of being into the lifeless thing that lay at my feet. It was already one in the morning; the rain pattered dismally against the panes, and my candle was nearly burnt out, when, by the glimmer of the half-extinguished light, I saw the dull yellow eye of the creature open; it breathed hard, and a convulsive motion agitated its limbs.

How can I describe my emotions at this catastrophe, or how delineate the wretch whom with such infinite pains and care I had endeavoured to form? His limbs were in proportion, and I had selected his features as beautiful. Beautiful! Great God! His yellow skin scarcely covered the work of muscles and arteries beneath; his hair was of a lustrous black, and flowing; his teeth of pearly whiteness; but these luxuriances only formed a more horrid contrast with his watery eyes, that seemed almost of the same colour as the dun-white sockets in which they were set, his shrivelled complexion and straight black lips.

The different accidents of life are not so changeable as the feelings of human nature. I had worked hard for nearly two years, for the sole purpose of infusing life into an inanimate body. For this I had deprived myself of rest and health. I had desired it with an ardour that far exceeded moderation; but now that I had finished, the beauty of the dream vanished, and breathless horror and disgust filled my heart. Unable to endure the aspect of the being I had created, I rushed out of the room and continued a long time traversing my bedchamber, unable to compose my mind to sleep. At length lassitude succeeded to the tumult I had before endured, and I threw myself on the bed in my clothes, endeavouring to seek a few moments of forgetfulness. But it was in vain; I slept, indeed, but I was disturbed by the wildest dreams. I thought I saw Elizabeth, in the bloom of health, walking in the streets of Ingolstadt. Delighted and surprized, I embraced her, but as I imprinted the first kiss on her lips, they became livid with the hue of death; her features appeared to change, and I thought that I held the corpse of my dead mother in my arms; a shroud enveloped her form, and I saw the grave-worms crawling in the folds of the flannel. I started from my sleep with horror; a cold dew covered my forehead, my teeth chattered, and every limb became convulsed; when, by the dim and yellow light of the moon, as it forced its way through the window shutters, I beheld the wretch—the miserable monster whom I had created. He held up the curtain of the bed; and his eyes, if eyes they may be called, were fixed on me. His jaws opened, and he muttered some inarticulate sounds, while a grin wrinkled his cheeks. He might have spoken, but I did not hear; one hand was stretched out, seemingly to detain me, but I escaped and rushed downstairs. I took refuge in the courtyard belonging to the house which I inhabited, where I remained during the rest of the night, walking up and down in the greatest agitation, listening attentively, catching and fearing each sound as if it were to announce the approach of the daemoniacal corpse to which I had so miserably given life.

Oh! No mortal could support the horror of that countenance. A mummy again endued with animation could not be so hideous as that wretch. I had gazed on him while unfinished; he was ugly then, but when those muscles and joints were rendered capable of motion, it became a thing such as even Dante could not have conceived.

I passed the night wretchedly. Sometimes my pulse beat so quickly and hardly that I felt the palpitation of every artery; at others, I nearly sank to the ground through languor and extreme weakness. Mingled with this horror, I felt the bitterness of disappointment; dreams that had been my food and pleasant rest for so long a space were now become a hell to me; and the change was so rapid, the overthrow so complete!

Morning, dismal and wet, at length dawned and discovered to my sleepless and aching eyes the church of Ingolstadt, its white steeple and clock, which indicated the sixth hour. The porter opened the gates of the court, which had that night been my asylum, and I issued into the streets, pacing them with quick steps, as if I sought to avoid the wretch whom I feared every turning of the street would present to my view. I did not dare return to the apartment which I inhabited, but felt impelled to hurry on, although drenched by the rain which poured from a black and comfortless sky.

I continued walking in this manner for some time, endeavouring by bodily exercise to ease the load that weighed upon my mind. I traversed the streets without any clear conception of where I was or what I was doing. My heart palpitated in the sickness of fear, and I hurried on with irregular steps, not daring to look about me:

Like one, that on a lonesome road
Doth walk in fear and dread,
And having once turned round walks on,
And turns no more his head;
Because he knows, a frightful fiend
Doth close behind him tread.[1]

Continuing thus, I came at length opposite to the inn at which the various diligences and carriages usually stopped. Here I paused, I knew not why; but I remained some minutes with my eyes fixed on a coach that was coming towards me from the other end of the street. As it drew nearer I observed that it was the Swiss diligence; it stopped just where I was standing, and on the door being opened, I perceived Henry Clerval, who, on seeing me, instantly sprung out. "My dear Frankenstein," exclaimed he, "how glad I am to see you! How fortunate that you should be here at the very moment of my alighting!"

Nothing could equal my delight on seeing Clerval; his presence brought back to my thoughts my father, Elizabeth, and all those scenes of home so dear to my recollection. I grasped his hand, and in a moment forgot my horror and misfortune; I felt suddenly, and for the first time during many months, calm and serene joy. I welcomed my friend, therefore, in the most cordial manner, and we walked towards my college. Clerval continued talking for some time about our mutual friends and his own good fortune in being permitted to come to Ingolstadt. "You may easily believe," said he, "how great was the difficulty to persuade my father that all necessary knowledge was not comprised in the noble art of bookkeeping; and, indeed, I believe I left him incredulous to the last, for his constant answer to my unwearied intreaties was the same as that to the Dutch schoolmaster in *The Vicar of Wakefield*: 'I have ten thousand florins a year without Greek, I eat heartily without Greek.' But his affection for me at length overcame his dislike of learning, and he has permitted me to undertake a voyage of discovery to the land of knowledge."

"It gives me the greatest delight to see you; but tell me how you left my father, brothers, and Elizabeth."

"Very well, and very happy, only a little uneasy that they hear from you so seldom. By the bye, I mean to lecture you a little upon their account myself. But, my dear Frankenstein," continued he, stopping short and gazing full in my face, "I did not before remark how very ill you appear; so thin and pale; and look as if you had been watching for several nights."

"You have guessed right; I have lately been so deeply engaged in one occupation that I have not allowed myself sufficient rest, as you see; but I hope, I sincerely hope, that all these employments are now at an end and that I am at length free."

I trembled excessively; I could not endure to think of, and far less to allude to, the occurrences of the preceding night. I walked with a quick pace, and we soon arrived at my college. I then reflected, and the thought made me shiver, that the crea-

---

[1]Coleridge's *Ancient Mariner* [author's footnote].

ture whom I had left in my apartment might still be there, alive and walking about. I dreaded to behold this monster, but I feared still more that Henry should see him. Intreating him, therefore, to remain a few minutes at the bottom of the stairs, I darted up towards my own room. My hand was already on the lock of the door before I recollected myself. I then paused, and a cold shivering came over me. I threw the door forcibly open, as children are accustomed to do when they expect a spectre to stand in waiting for them on the other side; but nothing appeared. I stepped fearfully in: the apartment was empty, and my bedroom was also freed from its hideous guest. I could hardly believe that so great a good fortune could have befallen me, but when I became assured that my enemy had indeed fled, I clapped my hands for joy and ran down to Clerval.

We ascended into my room, and the servant presently brought breakfast; but I was unable to contain myself. It was not joy only that possessed me; I felt my flesh tingle with excess of sensitiveness, and my pulse beat rapidly. I was unable to remain for a single instant in the same place; I jumped over the chairs, clapped my hands, and laughed aloud. Clerval at first attributed my unusual spirits to joy on his arrival, but when he observed me more attentively, he saw a wildness in my eyes for which he could not account, and my loud, unrestrained, heartless laughter frightened and astonished him.

"My dear Victor," cried he, "what, for God's sake, is the matter? Do not laugh in that manner. How ill you are! What is the cause of all this?"

"Do not ask me," cried I, putting my hands before my eyes, for I thought I saw the dreaded spectre glide into the room; "*he* can tell. Oh, save me! Save me!" I imagined that the monster seized me; I struggled furiously and fell down in a fit.

Poor Clerval! What must have been his feelings? A meeting, which he anticipated with such joy, so strangely turned to bitterness. But I was not the witness of his grief, for I was lifeless and did not recover my senses for a long, long time.

This was the commencement of a nervous fever which confined me for several months. During all that time Henry was my only nurse. I afterwards learned that, knowing my father's advanced age and unfitness for so long a journey, and how wretched my sickness would make Elizabeth, he spared them this grief by concealing the extent of my disorder. He knew that I could not have a more kind and attentive nurse than himself; and, firm in the hope he felt of my recovery, he did not doubt that, instead of doing harm, he performed the kindest action that he could towards them.

But I was in reality very ill, and surely nothing but the unbounded and unremitting attentions of my friend could have restored me to life. The form of the monster on whom I had bestowed existence was forever before my eyes, and I raved incessantly concerning him. Doubtless my words surprized Henry; he at first believed them to be the wanderings of my disturbed imagination, but the pertinacity with which I continually recurred to the same subject persuaded him that my disorder indeed owed its origin to some uncommon and terrible event.

By very slow degrees, and with frequent relapses that alarmed and grieved my friend, I recovered. I remember the first time I became capable of observing outward objects with any kind of pleasure, I perceived that the fallen leaves had disappeared and that the young buds were shooting forth from the trees that shaded my window. It was a divine spring, and the season contributed greatly to my convalescence. I felt also sentiments of joy and affection revive in my bosom; my gloom disappeared, and in a short time I became as cheerful as before I was attacked by the fatal passion.

'Dearest Clerval,' exclaimed I, 'how kind, how very good you are to me. This whole winter, instead of being spent in study, as you promised yourself, has been consumed in my sick room. How shall I ever repay you? I feel the greatest remorse for the disappointment of which I have been the occasion, but you will forgive me.'

'You will repay me entirely if you do not discompose yourself, but get well as fast as you can; and since you appear in such good spirits, I may speak to you on one subject, may I not?'

I trembled. One subject! What could it be? Could he allude to an object on whom I dared not even think?

'Compose yourself,' said Clerval, who observed my change of colour, 'I will not mention it if it agitates you; but your father and cousin would be very happy if they received a letter from you in your own handwriting. They hardly know how ill you have been and are uneasy at your long silence.'

'Is that all, my dear Henry? How could you suppose that my first thought would not fly towards those dear, dear friends whom I love and who are so deserving of my love?'

'If this is your present temper, my friend, you will perhaps be glad to see a letter that has been lying here some days for you; it is from your cousin, I believe.'

[*Frankenstein learns that his young brother has been murdered; the doctor knows the monster is responsible but keeps silent while an innocent girl is convicted and executed for the crime.*]

[*Chapter 10*]

I spent the following day roaming through the valley. I stood beside the sources of the Arveiron, which take their rise in a glacier, that with slow pace is advancing down from the summit of the hills to barricade the valley. The abrupt sides of vast mountains were before me; the icy wall of the glacier overhung me; a few shattered pines were scattered around; and the solemn silence of this glorious presence-chamber of imperial nature was broken only by the brawling waves or the fall of some vast fragment, the thunder sound of the avalanche or the cracking, reverberated along the mountains, of the accumulated ice, which, through the silent working of immutable laws, was ever and anon rent and torn, as if it had been but a plaything in their hands. These sublime and magnificent scenes afforded me the greatest consolation that I was capable of receiving. They elevated me from all littleness of feeling, and although they did not remove my grief, they subdued and tranquillized it. In some degree, also, they diverted my mind from the thoughts over which it had brooded for the last month. I retired to rest at night; my slumbers, as it were, waited on and ministered to by the assemblage of grand shapes which I had contemplated during the day. They congregated round me; the unstained snowy mountain-top, the glittering pinnacle, the pine woods, and ragged bare ravine, the eagle, soaring amidst the clouds—they all gathered round me and bade me be at peace.

Where had they fled when the next morning I awoke? All of soul-inspiriting fled with sleep, and dark melancholy clouded every thought. The rain was pouring in torrents, and thick mists hid the summits of the mountains, so that I even saw not the faces of those mighty friends. Still I would penetrate their misty veil and seek them in their cloudy retreats. What were rain and storm to me? My mule was brought to the door, and I resolved to ascend to the summit of Montanvert. I remembered the effect that the view of the tremendous and ever-moving glacier had produced upon my mind when I first saw it. It had then filled me with a sublime ecstasy that gave wings to the soul and allowed it to soar from the obscure world to light and joy. The sight of the awful and majestic in nature had indeed always the effect of solemnizing my mind and causing me to forget the passing cares of life. I determined to go without a guide, for I was well acquainted with the path, and the presence of another would destroy the solitary grandeur of the scene.

The ascent is precipitous, but the path is cut into continual and short windings, which enable you to surmount the perpendicularity of the mountain. It is a scene terrifically desolate. In a thousand spots the traces of the winter avalanche may be perceived, where trees lie broken and strewed on the ground, some entirely destroyed, others bent, leaning upon the jutting rocks of the mountain or transversely upon other trees. The path, as you ascend higher, is intersected by ravines of snow, down which stones continually roll from above; one of them is particularly dangerous, as the slightest sound, such as even speaking in a loud voice, produces a concussion of air sufficient to draw destruction upon the head of the speaker. The pines are not tall or luxuriant, but they are sombre and add an air of severity to the scene. I looked on the valley beneath; vast mists were rising from the rivers which ran through it and curling in thick wreaths around the opposite mountains, whose summits were hid in the uniform clouds, while rain poured from the dark sky and added to the melancholy impression I received from the objects around me. Alas! Why does man boast of sensibilities superior to those apparent in the brute; it only renders them more necessary beings. If our impulses were confined to hunger, thirst, and desire, we might be nearly free; but now we are moved by every wind that blows and a chance word or scene that that word may convey to us.

> We rest; a dream has power to poison sleep.
> We rise; one wand'ring thought pollutes the day.
> We feel, conceive, or reason; laugh or weep,
> Embrace fond woe, or cast our cares away;
> It is the same: for, be it joy or sorrow,
> The path of its departure still is free.
> Man's yesterday may ne'er be like his morrow;
> Nought may endure but mutability!

It was nearly noon when I arrived at the top of the ascent. For some time I sat upon the rock that overlooks the sea of ice. A mist covered both that and the surrounding mountains. Presently a breeze dissipated the cloud, and I descended upon the glacier. The surface is very uneven, rising like the waves of a troubled sea, descending low, and interspersed by rifts that sink deep. The field of ice is almost a league in width, but I spent nearly two hours in crossing it. The opposite mountain is a bare perpendicular rock. From the side where I now stood Montanvert was exactly opposite, at the distance of a league; and above it rose Mont Blanc, in awful majesty. I remained in a recess of the rock, gazing on this wonderful and stupendous scene. The sea, or rather the vast river of ice, wound among its dependent mountains, whose aerial summits hung over its recesses. Their icy and glittering peaks shone in the sunlight over the clouds. My heart, which was before sorrowful, now swelled with something like joy; I exclaimed—"Wandering spirits, if indeed ye wander, and do not rest in your narrow beds, allow me this faint happiness, or take me, as your companion, away from the joys of life."

As I said this I suddenly beheld the figure of a man, at some distance, advancing towards me with superhuman speed. He bounded over the crevices in the ice, among which I had walked with caution; his stature, also, as he approached, seemed to exceed that of man. I was troubled; a mist came over my eyes, and I felt a faintness seize me; but I was quickly restored by the cold gale of the mountains. I perceived, as the shape came nearer (sight tremendous and abhorred!) that it was the wretch whom I had created. I trembled with rage and horror, resolving to wait his approach and then close with him in mortal combat. He approached; his countenance bespoke bitter anguish, combined with disdain and malignity, while its unearthly ugliness rendered it almost too horrible for human eyes. But I scarcely observed this; rage and hatred had at first deprived me of utterance, and I recovered only to overwhelm him with words expressive of furious detestation and contempt.

"Devil," I exclaimed, …"do you dare approach me? And do not you fear the fierce vengeance of my arm wreaked on your miserable head? Begone, vile insect! Or rather, stay, that I may trample you to dust! And, oh! That I could, with the extinction of your miserable existence, restore those victims whom you have so diabolically murdered!"

"I expected this reception," said the daemon. "All men hate the wretched; how, then, must I be hated, who am miserable beyond all living things! Yet you, my creator, detest and spurn me, thy creature, to whom thou art bound by ties only dissoluble by the annihilation of one of us. You purpose to kill me. How dare you sport thus with life? Do your duty towards me, and I will do mine towards you and the rest of mankind. If you will comply with my conditions, I will leave them and you at peace; but if you refuse, I will glut the maw of death, until it be satiated with the blood of your remaining friends."

"Abhorred monster! Fiend that thou art! The tortures of hell are too mild a vengeance for thy crimes. Wretched devil! You reproach me with your creation; come on, then, that I may extinguish the spark which I so negligently bestowed."

My rage was without bounds; I sprang on him, impelled by all the feelings which can arm one being against the existence of another.

He easily eluded me and said—"Be calm! I intreat you to hear me before you give vent to your hatred on my devoted head. Have I not suffered enough, that you seek to increase my misery? Life, although it may only be an accumulation of anguish, is dear to me, and I will defend it. Remember, thou hast made me more powerful than thyself; my height is superior to thine, my joints more supple. But I will not be tempted to set myself in opposition to thee. I am thy creature, and I will be even mild and docile to my natural lord and king if thou wilt also perform thy part, the which thou owest me. Oh, Frankenstein, be not equitable to every other and trample upon me alone, to whom thy justice, and even thy clemency and affection, is most due. Remember that I am thy creature; I ought to be thy Adam, but I am rather the fallen angel, whom thou drivest from joy for no misdeed. Everywhere I see bliss, from which I alone am irrevocably excluded. I was benevolent and good; misery made me a fiend. Make me happy, and I shall again be virtuous."

"Begone! I will not hear you. There can be no community between you and me; we are enemies. Begone, or let us try our strength in a fight, in which one must fall."

"How can I move thee? Will no intreaties cause thee to turn a favourable eye upon thy creature, who implores thy goodness and compassion? Believe me, Frankenstein, I was benevolent; my soul glowed with love and humanity; but am I not alone, miserably alone? You, my creator, abhor me; what hope can I gather from your fellow creatures, who owe me nothing? They spurn and hate me. The desert mountains and dreary glaciers are my refuge. I have wandered here many days; the caves of ice, which I only do not fear, are a dwelling to me, and the only one which man does not grudge. These bleak skies I hail, for they are kinder to me than your fellow beings. If the multitude of mankind knew of my existence, they would do as you do, and arm themselves for my destruction. Shall I not then hate them who abhor me? I will keep no terms with my enemies. I am miserable, and they shall share my wretchedness. Yet it is in your power to recompense me, and deliver them from an evil which it only remains for you to make so great, that not only you and your family, but thousands of others, shall be swallowed up in the whirlwinds of its rage. Let your compassion be moved, and do not disdain me. Listen to my tale; when you have heard that, abandon or commiserate me, as you shall judge that I deserve. But hear me. The guilty are allowed, by human laws, bloody as they are, to speak in their own defence before they are condemned. Listen to me, Frankenstein. You accuse me of murder, and yet you would, with a satisfied conscience, destroy your own creature. Oh, praise the eternal justice of man! Yet I ask you not to spare me; listen to me, and then, if you can, and if you will, destroy the work of your hands."

"Why do you call to my remembrance," I rejoined, "circumstances of which I shudder to reflect, that I have been the miserable origin and author? Cursed be the day, abhorred devil, in which you first saw light! Cursed (although I curse myself) be the hands that formed you! You have made me wretched beyond expression. You have left me no power to consider whether I am just to you or not. Begone! Relieve me from the sight of your detested form."

"Thus I relieve thee, my creator," he said, and placed his hated hands before my eyes, which I flung from me with violence; "thus I take from thee a sight which you abhor. Still thou canst listen to me and grant me thy compassion. By the virtues that

I once possessed, I demand this from you. Hear my tale; it is long and strange, and the temperature of this place is not fitting to your fine sensations; come to the hut upon the mountain. The sun is yet high in the heavens; before it descends to hide itself behind yon snowy precipices and illuminate another world, you will have heard my story and can decide. On you it rests, whether I quit forever the neighbourhood of man and lead a harmless life, or become the scourge of your fellow creatures and the author of your own speedy ruin. . . ."

[*Frankenstein hears the monster recount his miserable life and, in Chapter 17, make a poignant appeal.*]

The being finished speaking and fixed his looks upon me in the expectation of a reply. But I was bewildered, perplexed, and unable to arrange my ideas sufficiently to understand the full extent of his proposition. He continued, "You must create a female for me with whom I can live in the interchange of those sympathies necessary for my being. This you alone can do, and I demand it of you as a right which you must not refuse to concede."

The latter part of his tale had kindled anew in me the anger that had died away while he narrated his peaceful life among the cottagers, and as he said this I could no longer suppress the rage that burned within me.

"I do refuse it," I replied; "and no torture shall ever extort a consent from me. You may render me the most miserable of men, but you shall never make me base in my own eyes. Shall I create another like yourself, whose joint wickedness might desolate the world. Begone! I have answered you; you may torture me, but I will never consent."

"You are in the wrong," replied the fiend; "and instead of threatening, I am content to reason with you. I am malicious because I am miserable. Am I not shunned and hated by all mankind? You, my creator, would tear me to pieces and triumph; remember that, and tell me why I should pity man more than he pities me? You would not call it murder if you could precipitate me into one of those ice-rifts and destroy my frame, the work of your own hands. Shall I respect man when he contemns me? Let him live with me in the interchange of kindness, and instead of injury I would bestow every benefit upon him with tears of gratitude at his acceptance. But that cannot be; the human senses are insurmountable barriers to our union. Yet mine shall not be the submission of abject slavery. I will revenge my injuries; if I cannot inspire love, I will cause fear, and chiefly towards you my arch-enemy, because my creator, do I swear inextinguishable hatred. Have a care; I will work at your destruction, nor finish until I desolate your heart, so that you shall curse the hour of your birth."

A fiendish rage animated him as he said this; his face was wrinkled into contortions too horrible for human eyes to behold; but presently he calmed himself and proceeded, "I intended to reason. This passion is detrimental to me, for you do not reflect that *you* are the cause of its excess. If any being felt emotions of benevolence towards me, I should return them a hundred and a hundredfold; for that one creature's sake I would make peace with the whole kind! But I now indulge in dreams of bliss that cannot be realized. What I ask of you is reasonable and moderate; I demand a creature of another sex, but as hideous as myself; the gratification is small, but it is all that I can receive, and it shall content me. It is true, we shall be monsters, cut off from all the world; but on that account we shall be more attached to one another. Our lives will not be happy, but they will be harmless and free from the misery I now feel. Oh! My creator, make me happy; let me feel gratitude towards you for one benefit! Let me see that I excite the sympathy of some existing thing; do not deny me my request!"

I was moved. I shuddered when I thought of the possible consequences of my consent, but I felt that there was some justice in his argument. His tale and the feelings he now expressed proved him to be a creature of fine sensations, and did I not as his maker owe him all the portion of happiness that it was in my power to bestow? He saw my change of feeling and continued, "If you consent, neither you nor any other human being shall ever see us again; I will go to the vast wilds of South America. My food is not that of man; I do not destroy the lamb and the kid to glut my appetite; acorns and berries afford me sufficient nourishment. My companion will be of the same nature as myself and will be content with the same fare. We shall make our bed of dried leaves; the sun will shine on us as on man and will ripen our food. The picture I present to you is peaceful and human, and you must feel that you could deny it only in the wantonness of power and cruelty. Pitiless as you have been towards me, I now see compassion in your eyes; let me seize the favourable moment and persuade you to promise what I so ardently desire."

"You propose," replied I, "to fly from the habitations of man, to dwell in those wilds where the beasts of the field will be your only companions. How can you, who long for the love and sympathy of man, persevere in this exile? You will return and again seek their kindness, and you will meet with their detestation; your evil passions will be renewed, and you will then have a companion to aid you in the task of destruction. This may not be; cease to argue the point, for I cannot consent."

"How inconstant are your feelings! But a moment ago you were moved by my representations, and why do you again harden yourself to my complaints? I swear to you, by the earth which I inhabit, and by you that made me, that with the companion you bestow I will quit the neighbourhood of man and dwell, as it may chance, in the most savage of places. My evil passions will have fled, for I shall meet with sympathy! My life will flow quietly away, and in my dying moments I shall not curse my maker."

His words had a strange effect upon me. I compassionated him and sometimes felt a wish to console him, but when I looked upon him, when I saw the filthy mass that moved and talked, my heart sickened and my feelings were altered to those of horror and hatred. I tried to stifle these sensations; I thought that as I could not sympathize with him, I had no right to withhold from him the small portion of happiness which was yet in my power to bestow.

"You swear," I said, "to be harmless; but have you not already shown a degree of malice that should reasonably make me distrust you? May not even this be a feint that will increase your triumph by affording a wider scope for your revenge?"

"How is this? I must not be trifled with, and I demand an answer. If I have no ties and no affections, hatred and vice must be my portion; the love of another will destroy the cause of my crimes, and I shall become a thing of whose existence everyone will be ignorant. My vices are the children of a forced solitude that I abhor, and my virtues will necessarily arise when I live in communion with an equal. I shall feel the affections of a sensitive being and become linked to the chain of existence and events from which I am now excluded."

I paused some time to reflect on all he had related and the various arguments which he had employed. I thought of the promise of virtues which he had displayed on the opening of his existence and the subsequent blight of all kindly feeling by the loathing and scorn which his protectors had manifested towards him. His power and threats were not omitted in my calculations; a creature who could exist in the ice caves of the glaciers and hide himself from pursuit among the ridges of inaccessible precipices was a being possessing faculties it would be vain to cope with. After a long pause of reflection I concluded that the justice due both to him and my fellow creatures demanded of me that I should comply with his request. Turning to him, therefore, I said, "I consent to your demand, on your solemn oath to quit Europe forever, and every other place in the neighbourhood of man, as soon as I shall deliver into your hands a female who will accompany you in your exile."

"I swear," he cried, "by the sun, and by the blue sky of heaven, and by the fire of love that burns my heart, that if you grant my prayer, while they exist you shall never behold me again. Depart to your home and commence your labours; I shall watch their progress with unutterable anxiety; and fear not but that when you are ready I shall appear."

Saying this, he suddenly quitted me, fearful, perhaps, of any change in my sentiments. I saw him descend the mountain with greater speed than the flight of an eagle, and quickly lost among the undulations of the sea of ice . . .

SYMBOLIST POETRY

Charles Baudelaire (1821–1867) might well be considered the first "modern," with his celebration of the city, his decadent sensibility, and his dreamily erotic poetry. In "To the Reader," the introduction to his scandalous *Flowers of Evil* (1857), Baudelaire draws the reader into the putrid atmosphere of violence and decay, celebrating ironically the brotherhood of humanity in squalid boredom. The poet's *ennui*—pathological inactivity—is the psychic disease of modern city life, the punishment imposed in a modern equivalent of Dante's *Inferno*.

Emily Dickinson (1830–1886) led a reclusive life in Amherst, Massachusetts, publishing in her lifetime only a handful of the pithy lyric poems which now earn her acclaim as one of the greatest American poets. In contrast to the expansive romantic rambling of her contemporary Walt Whitman, Dickinson possessed a fine awareness of the paradoxical truths in ordinary objects and experience. In "Much Madness is Divinest Sense," the division between madness and reason is more the result of social convention; in "Tell All the Truth," Dickinson comments on the poet's task of deflecting truth so that humans can bear it. This latter poem might serve as an epitaph for Dostoevsky's Grand Inquisitor, who offers humanity deceptions because humans cannot suffer the truth.

Rainer Maria Rilke (1875–1926) lived as a Baudelairean voyager on the river of modern life, haunted by a sense of loneliness even though he dwelled in the capitals and befriended the leading figures of the end-of-the-century era. Rilke's poetry became explicitly symbolist through his friendship with the sculptor Auguste Rodin, who taught Rilke to seek the "concentrated reality" in simple objects. In the "Archaic Torso of Apollo" from *New Poems* (1907–08), Rilke contemplates the distilled brilliance of an ancient sculptural fragment, finding a moral imperative in its damaged classical beauty. Like Walt Whitman's blade of grass, Rilke finds in this work of art a "hieroglyphic" of human experience.

For analysis and interpretation:

1. Respond to the exaggerated self-contempt of the speaker in Baudelaire's "To the Reader." Compare Baudelaire's description of life as a steady slide into hell with Goethe's Faustian idea of life as a lustful gallop through experience. Which image is more appealing? Which is truer, in your estimation?

2. Agree or disagree with the point of Dickinson's "Much Madness;" ask yourself whether your response represents a majority or minority point of view.

3. What truths are, as Dickinson says, "too bright for our infirm delight"? In what artistically indirect ways do humans manage to express truths that are too blinding to confront directly?

4. What object in your daily world has the most power to command your attention and affect your awareness by its sheer presence? (Think of religious icons, souvenirs, photographs, or works of art.) Compare this object's force to the powerful aura of the sculpture described in Rilke's "Archaic Torso."

Charles Baudelaire

To the Reader

Stupidity, delusion, selfishness and lust
torment our bodies and possess our minds,
and we sustain our affable remorse
the way a beggar nourishes his lice.

Our sins are stubborn, our contrition lame;   5
we want our scruples to be worth our while—
how cheerfully we crawl back to the mire:
a few cheap tears will wash our stains away!

Satan Trismegistus subtly rocks
our ravished spirits on his wicked bed   10
until the precious metal of our will
is leached out by this cunning alchemist:

the Devil's hand directs our every move—
the things we loathed become the things we love;
day by day we drop through stinking shades   15
quite undeterred on our descent to Hell.

Like a poor profligate who sucks and bites
the withered breast of some well-seasoned trull,
we snatch in passing at clandestine joys
and squeeze the oldest orange harder yet.   20

Wriggling in our brains like a million worms,
a demon demos holds its revels there,
and when we breathe, the Lethe in our lungs
trickles sighing on its secret course.

If rape and arson, poison and the knife   25
have not yet stitched their ludicrous designs
onto the banal buckram of our fates,
it is because our souls lack enterprise!

But here among the scorpions and the hounds,
the jackals, apes and vultures, snakes and wolves,   30
monsters that howl and growl and squeal and crawl,
in all the squalid zoo of vices, one

is even uglier and fouler than the rest,
although the least flamboyant of the lot;
this beast would gladly undermine the earth   35
and swallow all creation in a yawn;
I speak of Boredom which with ready tears
dreams of hangings as it puffs its pipe.
Reader, you know this squeamish monster well,
—hypocrite reader,—my alias,—my twin!

—Translated by Richard Howard

Emily Dickinson

Much Madness is divinest Sense

Much Madness is divinest Sense—
To a discerning Eye—
Much Sense—the starkest Madness—
'Tis the Majority
In this, as All, prevail—   5
Assent—and you are sane—

Demur—you're straightway dangerous—
And handled with a Chain—

Tell All the Truth But Tell It Slant

Tell all the Truth but tell it slant—
Success in Circuit lies
Too bright for our infirm Delight
The Truth's superb surprise

As Lightning to the Children eased   5
With explanation kind
The Truth must dazzle gradually
Or every man be blind—

Rainer Maria Rilke

Torso of an Archaic Apollo[1]

We can't have known that fabulous head
with eyes like apples ripening. Yet
its torso glows still like a candelabra
in which the gaze, just turned back a bit,

holds steady and shining. Otherwise the breast's   5
curve could not blind you, and in the gentle turn
of the loins, a smile couldn't pass through
to that center which once bore its sex.

Otherwise this stone would seem deformed and broken
underneath the shoulders' transparent fall
and wouldn't glimmer like a lion's pelt;   10

And wouldn't break from all its borders
out like starlight: for there is no place there
that doesn't see you. You must change your life.

Archaïscher Torso Apollos

Wir kannten nicht sein unerhörtes Haupt,
darin die Augenäpfel reiften. Aber
sein Torso glüht noch wie ein Kandelaber,
in dem sein Schauen, nur zurückgeschraubt,

---

[1]Translated by the editor

sich hält und glänzt. Sonst könnte nicht der Bug
der Brust dich blenden, und im leisen Drehen
der Lenden könnte nicht ein Lächeln gehen
zu jener Mitte, die die Zeugung trug.

Sonst stünde dieser Stein entstellt und kurz
unter der Schultern durchsichtigem Sturz
und flimmerte nicht so wie Raubtierfelle;

und bräche nicht aus allen seinen Rändern
aus wie ein Stern: denn da ist keine Stelle,
die dich nicht sieht. Du musst dein Leben ändern.

FYODOR DOSTOEVSKY

Fyodor Dostoevsky (1821–1881) wrote novels of profound psychological insight whose rendering of philosophical and social truths influenced many thinkers of the twentieth century. In his last novel, *The Brothers Karamazov* (1880), a Dostoevsky character recounts the legend of the Grand Inquisitor, a parable intended to illustrate the modern situation.

Ivan Karamazov's story of the Grand Inquisitor, told in conversation with his saintly brother, Alyosha, is an attempt to illustrate the moral dilemmas of modern life. Rather than affirm the violent and corrupt nature of humanity, as does Baudelaire's bored speaker, the Inquisitor declares his wish to save humans from themselves. He foresees an age of frantic materialism and cannibalistic violence; peace will reign only if the priestly elect forsake the teachings of Christ and rescue humanity from self-destructiveness.

Like most of Dostoevsky's heroes, the Inquisitor is a profoundly ambivalent character. His ominous view of human nature, which echoes Hobbes and Montaigne, contradicts the material progress and glib optimism of industrialism. His view of human freedom and happiness contradicts a central tenet of Western philosophical values. For, in the Inquisitor's view, human freedom can bring only an anguished moral consciousness, while happiness is achieved only by those too ignorant or weak to understand the nature of human freedom.

For analysis and interpretation:

1. Read the gospel story of Christ's temptation (Matthew 4). How do the devil's three questions serve as the basis of the Inquisitor's argument against Christ?

2. In the Inquisitor's view, what makes the freedom Christ has brought so difficult for humans to bear? Explain why, in the Inquisitor's words, humans prefer "peace, and even death, to freedom of choice in the knowledge of good and evil."

3. Do you agree with the Inquisitor that a society based on science and material progress will bring humans to a rebellious cannibalism?

4. What is Christ saying to the Inquisitor when he kisses him on the lips? Why do you think does the kiss "burns" in the Inquisitor's heart?

From *The Brothers Karamazov*

The Legend of the Grand Inquisitor

". . . Do you know, Alyosha—don't laugh! I made a poem about a year ago. If you can—waste another ten minutes on me, I'll tell it to you."

"You wrote a poem?"

"Oh, no, I didn't write it," laughed Ivan, "and I've never written two lines of poetry in my life. But I made up this poem in prose and I remembered it. I was carried away when I made it up. You will be my first reader—that is, listener. Why should an author forego even one listener?" smiled Ivan. "Shall I tell it to you?"

"I am all attention," said Alyosha.

"My poem is called 'The Grand Inquisitor'; it's a ridiculous thing, but I want to tell it to you."

"Even this must have a preface—that is, a literary preface," laughed Ivan, "and I am a poor hand at making one. You see, my action takes place in the sixteenth century, and at that time, as you probably learnt at school, it was customary in poetry to bring down heavenly powers on earth. Not to speak of Dante, in France clerks, as well as the monks in the monasteries, used to give regular performances in which the Madonna, the saints, the angels, Christ, and God Himself were brought on the stage. In those days it was done in all simplicity. In Victor Hugo's 'Notre Dame de Paris' an edifying and gratuitous spectacle was provided for the people in the Hotel de Ville of Paris in the reign of Louis XI in honor of the birth of the dauphin. It was called *Le bon jugement de la très sainte et gracieuse Vierge Marie*, and she appears herself on the stage and pronounces her *bon jugement*. Similar plays, chiefly from the Old Testament, were occasionally performed in Moscow, too, up to the times of Peter the Great. But besides plays there were all sorts of legends and ballads scattered about the world, in which the saints and angels and all the powers of Heaven took part when required. In our monasteries the monks busied themselves in translating, copying, and even composing such poems—and even under the Tatars. There is, for instance, one such poem (of course, from the Greek), 'The Wanderings of Our Lady Through Hell,' with descriptions as bold as Dante's. Our Lady visits Hell, and the Archangel Michael leads her through the torments. She sees the sinners and their punishment. There she sees among others one noteworthy set of sinners in a burning lake; some of them sink to the bottom of the lake so that they can't swim out, and 'these God forgets'—an expression of extraordinary depth and force. And so Our Lady, shocked and weeping, falls before the throne of God and begs for mercy for all in Hell—for all she has seen there, and indiscriminately. Her conversation with God is immensely interesting. She beseeches Him, she will not desist, and when God points to the hands and feet of her Son, nailed to the Cross, and asks, 'How can I forgive His tormentors?' she bids all the saints, all the martyrs, all the angels and archangels to fall down with her and pray for mercy on all without distinction. It ends by her winning from God a respite of suffering every year from Good Friday till Trinity day, and the sinners at once raise a cry of thankfulness from Hell, chanting, 'Thou art just, O Lord, in this judgment.' Well, my poem would have been of that kind if it had appeared at that time. He comes on the scene in my poem, but He says nothing, only appears and passes on. Fifteen centuries have passed since He promised to come in His glory, fifteen centuries since His prophet wrote, 'Behold, I come quickly'; 'Of that day and that hour knoweth no man, neither the Son, but the Father,' as He Himself predicted on earth. But humanity awaits him with the same faith and with the same love. Oh, with greater faith, for it is fifteen centuries since man has ceased to see signs from Heaven.

> No signs from Heaven come today
> To add to what the heart doth say.

There was nothing left but faith in what the heart doth say. It is true there were many miracles in those days. There were saints who performed miraculous cures; some holy people, according to their biographies, were visited by the Queen of Heaven herself. But the devil did not slumber, and doubts were already arising among men of the truth of these miracles. And just then there appeared in the north of Germany a terrible new heresy. 'A huge star like to a torch' (that is, to a church) 'fell on the sources of the waters and they became bitter.' These heretics began blasphemously denying miracles. But those who remained faithful were all the more ardent in their faith. The tears of humanity rose up to Him as before, awaiting His coming, loved Him, hoped for Him, yearned to suffer and die for Him as before. And so many ages mankind had prayed with faith and fervor, 'O Lord our God, hasten Thy coming,' so many ages called upon Him, that in His infinite mercy He deigned to come down to His servants. Before that day He had come down, He had visited some holy men, martyrs, and hermits, as is written in their 'Lives.' Among us, Tyutchev, with absolute faith in the truth of his words, bore witness that

> Bearing the Cross, in slavish dress,
> Weary and worn, the Heavenly King
> Our mother, Russia, came to bless,
> And through our land went wandering.

And that certainly was so, I assure you.

"And behold, He deigned to appear for a moment to the people, to the tortured, suffering people, sunk in iniquity, but loving Him like children. My story is laid in Spain, in Seville, in the most terrible time of the Inquisition, when fires were lighted every day to the glory of God, and 'in the splendid *auto da fé* the wicked heretics were burnt.' Oh, of course, this was not the coming in which He will appear according to His promise at the end of time in all His heavenly glory, and which will be sudden 'as lightning flashing from east to west.' No, He visited His children only for a moment, and there where the flames were crackling round the heretics. In His infinite mercy He came once more among men in that human shape in which He walked among men for three years fifteen centuries ago. He came down to the 'hot pavement' of the southern town in which on the day before almost a hundred heretics had, *ad majorem glo-*

riam Dei, been burnt by the cardinal, the Grand Inquisitor, in a magnificent *auto da fé*, in the presence of the king, the court, the knights, the cardinals, the most charming ladies of the court, and the whole population of Seville.

"He came softly, unobserved, and yet, strange to say, every one recognized Him. That might be one of the best passages in the poem. I mean, why they recognized Him. The people are irresistibly drawn to Him, they surround Him, they flock about Him, follow Him. He moves silently in their midst with a gentle smile of infinite compassion. The sun of love burns in His heart, light and power shine from His eyes, and their radiance, shed on the people, stirs their hearts with responsive love. He holds out His hands to them, blesses them, and a healing virtue comes from contact with Him, even with His garments. An old man in the crowd, blind from childhood, cries out, 'O Lord, heal me and I shall see Thee!' and, as it were, scales fall from his eyes and the blind man sees Him. The crowd weeps and kisses the earth under His feet. Children throw flowers before Him, sing, and cry hosannah. 'It is He—it is He!' all repeat. 'It must be He, it can be no one but Him!' He stops at the steps of the Seville cathedral at the moment when the weeping mourners are bringing in a little open white coffin. In it lies a child of seven, the only daughter of a prominent citizen. The dead child lies hidden in flowers. 'He will raise your child,' the crowd shouts to the weeping mother. The priest, coming to meet the coffin, looks perplexed and frowns, but the mother of the dead child throws herself at His feet with a wail. 'If it is Thou, raise my child!' she cries, holding out her hands to Him. The procession halts, the coffin is laid on the steps at His feet. He looks with compassion, and His lips once more softly pronounce, 'Maiden, arise!' and the maiden arises. The little girl sits up in the coffin and looks round, smiling with wide-open wondering eyes, holding a bunch of white roses they had put in her hand.

"There are cries, sobs, confusion among the people, and at that moment the cardinal himself, the Grand Inquisitor, passes by the cathedral. He is an old man, almost ninety, tall and erect, with a withered face and sunken eyes, in which there is still a gleam of light. He is not dressed in his gorgeous cardinal's robes, as he was the day before, when he was burning the enemies of the Roman Church—at that moment he was wearing his coarse, old, monk's cassock. At a distance behind him come his gloomy assistants and slaves and the 'holy guard.' He stops at the sight of the crowd and watches it from a distance. He sees everything; he sees them set the coffin down at His feet, sees the child rise up, and his face darkens. He knits his thick grey brows and his eyes gleam with a sinister fire. He holds out his finger and bids the guards take Him. And such is his power, so completely are the people cowed into submission and trembling obedience to him, that the crowd immediately makes way for the guards, and in the midst of deathlike silence they lay hands on Him and lead Him away. The crowd instantly bows down to the earth, like one man, before the old inquisitor. He blesses the people in silence and passes on. The guards lead their prisoner to the close, gloomy, vaulted prison in the ancient palace of the Holy Inquisition and shut Him in it. The day passes and is followed by the dark, burning 'breathless' night of Seville. The air is 'fragrant with laurel and lemon.' In the pitch darkness the iron door of the prison is suddenly opened and the Grand Inquisitor himself comes in with a light in his hand. He is alone; the door is closed at once behind him. He stands in the doorway and for a minute or two gazes into His face. At last he goes up slowly, sets the light on the table and speaks.

" 'Is it Thou? Thou?' but receiving no answer, he adds at once, 'Don't answer, be silent. What canst Thou say, indeed? I know too well what Thou wouldst say. And Thou hast no right to add anything to what Thou hadst said of old. Why, then, art Thou come to hinder us? For Thou hast come to hinder us, and Thou knowest that. But dost Thou know what will be tomorrow? I know not who Thou art and care not to know whether it is Thou or only a semblance of Him, but tomorrow I shall condemn Thee and burn Thee at the stake as the worst of heretics. And the very people who have today kissed Thy feet, tomorrow at the faintest sign from me will rush to heap up the embers of Thy fire. Knowest Thou that? Yes, maybe Thou knowest it,' he added with thoughtful penetration, never for a moment taking his eyes off the Prisoner."

"I don't quite understand, Ivan. What does it mean?" Alyosha, who had been listening in silence, said with a smile. "Is it simply a wild fantasy, or a mistake on the part of the old man—some impossible *qui pro quo?*"

"Take it as the last," said Ivan, laughing, "if you are so corrupted by modern realism and can't stand anything fantastic. If you like it to be a case of mistaken identity, let it be so. It is true," he went on, laughing, "the old man was ninety, and he might well be crazy over his set idea. He might have been struck by the appearance of the Prisoner. It might, in fact, be simply his ravings, the delusion of an old man of ninety, over-excited by the *auto da fé* of a hundred heretics the day before. But does it matter to us after all whether it was a mistake of identity or a wild fantasy? All that matters is that the old man should speak out, should speak openly of what he has thought in silence for ninety years."

"And the Prisoner too is silent? Does He look at him and not say a word?"

"That's inevitable in any case," Ivan laughed again. "The old man has told Him He hasn't the right to add anything to what He has said of old. One may say it is the most fundamental feature of Roman Catholicism, in my opinion at least. 'All has been given by Thee to the Pope,' they say, 'and all, therefore, is still in the Pope's hands, and there is no need for Thee to come now at all. Thou must not meddle for the time, at least.' That's how they speak and write, too—the Jesuits, at any rate. I have read it myself in the works of their theologians. 'Hast Thou the right to reveal to us one of the mysteries of that world from which Thou hast come?' my old man asks Him, and answers the question for Him. 'No, Thou hast not; that Thou mayest not add to what has been said of old, and mayest not take from men the freedom which Thou didst exalt when Thou wast on earth. Whatsoever Thou revealest anew will encroach on men's freedom of faith; for it will be manifest as a miracle, and the freedom of their faith was dearer to Thee than anything in those days fifteen hundred years ago. Didst Thou not often say then, "I will make you free"? But now Thou hast seen these "free" men,' the old man adds suddenly, with a pensive smile. 'Yes, we've paid dearly for it,' he goes on, looking sternly at Him, 'but at last we have completed that work in Thy name. For fifteen centuries we have been wrestling with Thy freedom, but now it is ended and over for good. Dost Thou not believe that it's over for good? Thou lookest meekly at me and deignest not even to be wroth with me. But let me tell Thee that now, today, people are more persuaded than ever that they have perfect freedom, yet they have brought their freedom to us and laid it humbly at our feet. But that has been our doing. Was this what Thou didst? Was this Thy freedom?' "

"I don't understand again," Alyosha broke in. "Is he ironical, is he jesting?"

"Not a bit of it! He claims it as a merit for himself and his Church that at last they have vanquished freedom and have done so to make men happy. 'For now' (he is speaking of the Inquisition, of course) 'for the first time it has become possible to think of the happiness of men. Man was created a rebel; and how can rebels be happy? Thou wast warned,' he says to Him. 'Thou hast had no lack of admonitions, and warnings, but Thou didst not listen to those warnings; Thou didst reject the only way by which men might be made happy. But, fortunately, departing Thou didst hand on the work to us. Thou hast promised, Thou hast established by Thy word, Thou hast given to us the right to bind and to unbind, and now, of course, Thou canst not think of taking it away. Why, then, hast Thou come to hinder us?' "

"And what's the meaning of 'no lack of admonitions and warnings'?" asked Alyosha.

"Why, that's the chief part of what the old man must say.

"'The wise and dread Spirit, the spirit of self-destruction and nonexistence,' the old man goes on, 'the great spirit talked with Thee in the wilderness, and we are told in the books that he "tempted" Thee. Is that so? And could anything truer be said than what he revealed to Thee in three questions and what Thou didst reject, and what in the books is called "the temptation"? And yet if there has ever been on earth a real stupendous miracle, it took place on that day, on the day of the three temptations. The statement of those three questions was itself the miracle. If it were possible to imagine simply for the sake of argument that those three questions of the dread spirit had perished utterly from the books, and that we had to restore them and to invent them anew, and to do so had gathered together all the wise men of the earth—rulers, chief priests, learned men, philosophers, poets—and had set them the task to invent three questions, such as would not only fit the occasion, but express in three words, three human phrases, the whole future history of the world and of humanity—dost Thou believe that all the wisdom of the earth united could have invented anything in depth and force equal to the three questions which were actually put to Thee then by the wise and mighty spirit in the wilderness? From those questions alone, from the miracle of their statement, we can see that we have here to do not with the fleeting human intelligence, but with the absolute and eternal. For in those three questions the whole subsequent history of mankind is, as it were, brought together into one whole, and foretold, and in them are united all the unsolved historical contradictions of human nature. At the time it could not be so clear, since the future was unknown; but now that fifteen hundred years have passed, we see that everything in those three questions was so justly divined and foretold, and has been so truly fulfilled, that nothing can be added to them or taken from them.

" 'Judge Thyself who was right—Thou or he who questioned Thee then? Remember the first question; its meaning, in other words, was this: "Thou wouldst go into the world, and art going with empty hands, with some promise of freedom which men in their simplicity and their natural unruliness cannot even understand, which they fear and dread—for nothing has ever been more insupportable for a man and a human society than freedom. But seest Thou these stones in this parched and barren wilderness? Turn them into bread, and mankind will run after Thee like a flock of sheep, grateful and obedient, though forever trembling, lest Thou withdraw Thy hand and deny them Thy bread." But Thou wouldst not deprive man of freedom and didst reject the offer, thinking, what is that freedom worth, if obedience is bought with bread? Thou didst reply that man lives not by bread alone. But dost Thou know that for the sake of that earthly bread the spirit of the earth will rise up against Thee and will strive with Thee and overcome Thee, and all will follow him, crying, "Who can compare with this beast? He has given us fire from heaven!" Dost Thou know that the ages will pass, and humanity will proclaim by the lips of their sages that there is no crime, and therefore no sin; there is only hunger? "Feed men, and then ask of them virtue!" that's what they'll write on the banner which they will raise against Thee, and with which they will destroy Thy temple. Where Thy temple stood will rise a new building; the terrible tower of Babel will be built again, and though, like the one of old, it will not be finished, yet Thou mightest have prevented that new tower and have cut short the sufferings of men for a thousand years; for they will come back to us after a thousand years of agony with their tower. They will seek us again, hidden underground in the catacombs, for we shall be again persecuted and tortured. They will find us and cry to us, "Feed us, for those who have promised us fire from heaven haven't given it!" And then we shall finish building their tower, for he finishes the building who feeds them. And we alone shall feed them in Thy name, declaring falsely that it is in Thy name. Oh, never, never can they feed themselves without us! No science will give them bread so long as they remain free. In the end they will lay their freedom at our feet, and say to us, "Make us your slaves, but feed us." They will understand themselves, at last, that freedom and bread enough for all are inconceivable together, for never, never will they be able to share between them! They will be convinced, too, that they can never be free, for they are weak, vicious, worthless and rebellious. Thou didst promise them the bread of Heaven, but, I repeat again, can it compare with earthly bread in the eyes of the weak, ever-sinful and ignoble race of man? And if for the sake of the bread of Heaven thousands and tens of thousands shall follow Thee, what is to become of the millions and tens of thousands of millions of creatures who will not have the strength to forego the earthly bread for the sake of the heavenly? Or dost Thou care only for the tens of thousands of the great and strong, while the millions, numerous as the sands of the sea, who are weak but love Thee, must exist only for the sake of the great and strong? No, we care for the weak, too. They are sinful and rebellious, but in the end they too will become obedient. They will marvel at us and look on us as gods, because we are ready to endure the freedom which they have found so dreadful and to rule over them—so awful it will seem to them to be free. But we shall tell them that we are Thy servants and rule them in Thy name. We shall deceive them again, for we will not let Thee come to us again. That deception will be our suffering, for we shall be forced to lie.

"'This is the significance of the first question in the wilderness, and this is what Thou hast rejected for the sake of that freedom which Thou hast exalted above everything. Yet in this question lies hidden the great secret of this world. Choosing "bread," Thou wouldst have satisfied the universal and everlasting craving of humanity—to find someone to worship. So long as man remains free he strives for nothing so incessantly and so painfully as to find someone to worship. But man seeks to worship what is established beyond dispute, so that all men would agree at once to worship it. For these pitiful creatures are concerned not only to find what one or the other can worship, but to find something that all would believe in and worship; what is essential is that all may be *together* in it. This craving for *community* of worship is the chief misery of every man individually and of all humanity from the beginning of time. For the sake of common worship they've slain each other with the sword. They have set up gods and challenged one another, "Put away your gods and come and worship ours, or we will kill you and your gods!" And so it will be to the end of the world, even when gods disappear from the earth; they will fall down before idols just the same. Thou didst know, Thou couldst not but have known, this fundamental secret of human nature, but Thou didst reject the one infallible banner which was offered Thee to make all men bow down to Thee alone—the banner of earthly bread; and Thou hast rejected it for the sake of freedom and the bread of Heaven. Behold what Thou didst further. And all again in the name of freedom! I tell Thee that man is tormented by no greater anxiety than to find someone quickly to whom he can hand over the gift of freedom with which the ill-fated creature is born. But only one who can appease their conscience can take over their freedom. In bread there was offered Thee an invincible banner; give bread, and man will worship Thee, for nothing is more certain than bread. But if someone else gains possession of his conscience—oh! then he will cast away Thy bread and follow after him who has ensnared his conscience. In that Thou wast right. For the secret of man's being is not only to live but to have something to live for. Without a stable conception of the object of life, man would not consent to go on living, and would rather destroy himself than remain on earth, though he had bread in abundance. That is true. But what happened? Instead of taking men's freedom from them, Thou didst make it greater than ever! Didst Thou forget that man prefers peace, and even death, to freedom of choice in the knowledge of good and evil? Nothing is more seductive for man than his freedom of conscience, but nothing is a greater cause of suffering. And behold, instead of giving a firm foundation for setting the conscience of man at rest forever, Thou didst choose all that is exceptional, vague and enigmatic; Thou didst choose what was utterly beyond the strength of men, acting as though Thou didst not love them at all—Thou who didst come to give Thy life for them! Instead of taking possession of man's freedom, Thou didst increase it, and burdened the spiritual kingdom of mankind with its sufferings forever. Thou didst desire man's free love, that he should follow Thee freely, enticed and taken captive by Thee. In place of the rigid, ancient law, man must hereafter with free heart decide for himself what is good and what is evil, having only Thy image before him as his guide. But didst Thou not know he would at last reject even Thy image and Thy truth, if he is weighed down with the fearful burden of free choice? They will cry aloud at last that the truth is not in Thee, for they could not have been left in greater confusion and suffering than Thou hast caused, laying upon them so many cares and unanswerable problems.

"'So that, in truth, Thou didst Thyself lay the foundation for the destruction of Thy kingdom, and no one is more to blame for it. Yet what was offered Thee? There are three powers, three powers alone, able to conquer and to hold captive forever the conscience of these impotent rebels for their happiness—those forces are miracle, mystery and authority. Thou hast rejected all three and hast set the example for doing so. When the wise and dread spirit set Thee on the pinnacle of the temple and said to Thee, "If Thou wouldst know whether Thou art the Son of God then cast Thyself down, for it is written: the angels shall hold him up lest he fall and bruise himself, and Thou shalt know then whether Thou art the Son of God and shalt prove then how great is Thy faith in Thy Father." But Thou didst refuse and wouldst not cast Thyself down. Oh! of course, Thou didst proudly and well like God; but the weak, unruly race of men, are they gods? Oh, Thou didst know then that in taking one step, in making one movement to cast Thyself down, Thou wouldst be tempting God and have lost all Thy faith in Him, and wouldst have been dashed to pieces against that earth which Thou didst come to save. And the wise spirit that tempted Thee would have rejoiced. But I ask again, are there many like Thee? And couldst Thou believe for one moment that men, too, could face such a temptation? Is the nature of men such that they can reject miracle, and at the great moments of their life, the moments of their deepest, most agonizing spiritual difficulties, cling only to the free verdict of the heart? Oh, Thou didst know that Thy deed would be recorded in books, would be handed down to remote times and the utmost ends of the earth, and Thou didst hope that man, following Thee, would cling to God and not ask for a miracle. But Thou didst not know that when man rejects miracle he rejects God too; for man seeks not so much God as the miraculous. And as man cannot bear to be without the miraculous, he will create new miracles of his own for himself, and will worship deeds of sorcery and witchcraft, though he might be a hundred times over a rebel, heretic and infidel. Thou didst not come down from the Cross when they shouted to Thee, mocking and reviling Thee, "Come down from the Cross and we will believe that Thou art He." Thou didst not come down, for again Thou wouldst not enslave man by a miracle, and didst crave faith given freely, not based on miracle. Thou didst crave for free love and not the base raptures of the slave before the might that has overawed him forever. But Thou didst think too highly of men therein, for they are slaves, of course, though rebellious by nature. Look round and judge; fifteen centuries have passed; look upon them. Whom hast Thou raised up to Thyself? I swear, man is weaker and baser by nature than Thou hast believed him! Can he, can he do what Thou didst? By showing him so much respect, Thou didst, as it were, cease to feel for him, for Thou didst ask far too much from him—Thou who hast loved him more than Thyself! Respecting him less, Thou wouldst have asked less of him. That would have been more like love, for his burden would have been lighter. He is weak and vile. What though he is everywhere now rebelling against our power, and proud of his rebellion? It is the pride of a child and a schoolboy. They are little children rioting and barring out the teacher at school. But their childish delight will end; it will cost them dear. They will cast down temples and drench the earth with blood. But they will see at last, the foolish children, that, though they are rebels, they are impotent rebels, unable to keep up their own rebellion. Bathed in their foolish tears, they will recognize at last that He who created them rebels must have meant to mock at them. They will say this in despair, and their utterance will be a blasphemy which will make them more unhappy still, for man's nature cannot bear blasphemy, and in the end always avenges it on itself. And so unrest, confusion and unhappiness— that is the present lot of man after Thou didst bear so much for their freedom! Thy great prophet tells in vision and in image that he saw all those who took part in the first resurrection and that there were of each tribe twelve thousand. But if there were so many of them, they must have been not men but gods. They had borne Thy cross, they had endured scores of years in the barren, hungry wilderness, living upon locusts and roots—and Thou mayest indeed point with pride at those children of freedom, of free love, of free and splendid sacrifice for Thy name. But remember that they were only some thousands; and what of the rest? And how are the other weak ones to blame, because they could not endure what the strong have endured? How is the weak soul to blame that it is unable to receive such terrible gifts? Canst Thou have simply come to the elect and for the elect? But if so, it is a mystery and we cannot understand it. And if it is a mystery, we too have a right to preach a mystery, and to teach them that it's not the free judgment of their hearts, not love, that matters, but a mystery which they must follow blindly, even against their conscience. So we have done. We have corrected Thy work and have founded it upon *miracle, mystery* and *authority*. And men rejoiced that they were again led like sheep, and that the terrible gift that had brought them such suffering was, at last, lifted from their hearts. Were we right teaching them this? Speak! Did we not love mankind, so meekly acknowledging their feebleness, lovingly lightening their burden, and permitting their weak nature even sin with our sanction? Why hast Thou come now to hinder us? And why dost Thou look silently and searchingly at me with Thy mild eyes? Be angry. I don't want Thy love, for I love Thee not. And what use is it for me to hide anything from Thee? Don't I know to Whom I am speaking? All that I can say is known to Thee already. And is it for me to conceal from Thee our mystery? Perhaps it is Thy will to hear it from my lips. Listen, then. We are not working with Thee, but with *him*—that is our mystery. It's long—eight centuries—since we have been on *his* side and not on Thine. Just eight centuries ago, we took from him what Thou didst reject with scorn, that last gift he offered Thee, showing Thee all the kingdoms of the earth. We took from him Rome and the sword of Cæsar, and proclaimed ourselves sole rulers of the earth, though hitherto we have not been able to complete our work. But whose fault is that? Oh, the work is only beginning, but it has begun. It has long to await completion and the earth has yet much to suffer, but we shall triumph and shall be Cæsars, and then we shall plan the universal happiness of man. But Thou mightest have taken even the sword of Cæsar. Why didst Thou reject that last gift? Hadst Thou accepted that last counsel of the mighty spirit, Thou wouldst have accomplished all that man seeks on earth—that is, someone to worship, someone to keep his conscience, and some means of uniting all in one unanimous and harmonious ant heap, for the craving for universal unity is the third and last anguish of men. Mankind as a whole has always striven to organize a universal state. There have been many great nations with great histories, but the more highly they were developed the more unhappy they were, for they felt more acutely than other people the craving for world-wide union. The great conquerors, Timours and Genghis Khans, whirled like hurricanes over the face of the earth, striving to subdue its people, and they too were but the unconscious expression of the same craving for universal unity. Hadst Thou taken the world and Cæsar's purple, Thou wouldst have founded the universal state and have given universal peace. For who can rule men if not he who holds their conscience and their bread in his hands? We have taken the sword of Cæsar, and in taking it, of course, have rejected Thee and followed *him*. Oh, ages are yet to come of the confusion of free thought, of their science and cannibalism. For having begun to build their tower of Babel without us, they will end, of course, with cannibalism. But then the beast will crawl to us and lick our feet and spatter them with tears of blood. And we shall sit upon the beast and raise the cup, and on it will be written, "Mystery." But then, and only then, the reign of peace and happiness will come for men. Thou art proud of Thine elect, but Thou hast only the elect, while we give rest to all. And besides, how many of those elect, those mighty ones who could become elect, have grown weary waiting for Thee, and have transferred and will transfer the powers of their spirit and the warmth of their heart to the other camp, and end by raising their *free* banner against Thee. Thou didst Thyself lift up that banner. But with us all will be happy and will no more rebel, nor destroy one another as under Thy freedom. Oh, we shall persuade them that they will only become free when they renounce their freedom to us and submit to us. And shall we be right or shall we be lying? They will be convinced that we are right, for they will remember the horrors of slavery and confusion to which Thy freedom brought them. Freedom, free thought and science, will lead them into such straits and will bring them face to face with such marvels and insoluble mysteries that some of them, the fierce and rebellious, will destroy themselves; others, rebellious but weak, will destroy one another, while the rest, weak and unhappy, will crawl fawning to our feet and whine to us: "Yes, you were right, you alone possess His mystery, and we come back to you, save us from ourselves!"

"'Receiving bread from us, they will see clearly that we take the bread made by their hands from them, to give it to them, without any miracle. They will see that we do not change the stones to bread, but in truth they will be more thankful for taking it from our hands than for the bread itself! For they will remember only too well that in old days, without our help, even the bread they made turned to stones in their hands, while since they have come back to us, the very stones have turned to bread in their hands. Too, too well they know the value of complete submission! And until men know that, they will be unhappy. Who is most to blame for their not knowing it, speak? Who scattered the flock and sent it astray on unknown paths? But the flock will come together again and will submit once more, and then it will be once for all. Then we shall give them the quiet humble happiness of weak creatures such as they are by nature. Oh, we shall persuade them at last not to be proud, for Thou didst lift them up and thereby taught them to be proud. We shall show them that they are weak, that they are only pitiful children, but that child-like happiness is the sweetest of all. They will become timid and will look to us and huddle close to us in fear, as chicks to the hen.

They will marvel at us and will be awe-stricken before us, and will be proud at our being so powerful and clever, that we have been able to subdue such a turbulent flock of thousands of millions. They will tremble impotently before our wrath, their minds will grow fearful, they will be quick to shed tears like women and children, but they will be just as ready at a sign from us to pass to laughter and rejoicing, to happy mirth and childish song. Yes, we shall set them to work, but in their leisure hours we shall make their life like a child's game, with children's songs and innocent dance. Oh, we shall allow them even sin; they are weak and helpless, and they will love us like children because we allow them to sin. We shall tell them that every sin will be expiated, if it is done with our permission, that we allow them to sin because we love them, and the punishment for these sins we take upon ourselves. And we shall take it upon ourselves, and they will adore us as their saviors who have taken on themselves their sins before God. And they will have no secrets from us. We shall allow or forbid them to live with their wives and mistresses, to have or not to have children—according to whether they have been obedient or disobedient—and they will submit to us gladly and cheerfully. The most painful secrets of their conscience, all, all they will bring to us, and we shall have an answer for all. And they will be glad to believe our answer, for it will save them from the great anxiety and terrible agony they endure at present in making a free decision for themselves. And all will be happy, all the millions of creatures, except the hundred thousand who rule over them. For only we, we who guard the mystery, shall be unhappy. There will be thousands of millions of happy babes, and a hundred thousand sufferers who have taken upon themselves the curse of the knowledge of good and evil. Peacefully they will die, peacefully they will expire in Thy name, and beyond the grave they will find nothing but death. But we shall keep the secret, and for their happiness we shall allure them with the reward of heaven and eternity. Though if there were anything in the other world, it certainly would not be for such as they. It is prophesied that Thou wilt come again in victory, Thou wilt come with Thy chosen, the proud and strong, but we will say that they have only saved themselves, but we have saved all. We are told that the harlot who sits upon the beast, and holds in her hands the *mystery*, shall be put to shame, that the weak will rise up again, and will rend her royal purple and will strip naked her loathsome body. But then I will stand up and point out to Thee the thousand millions of happy children who have known no sin. And we who have taken their sins upon us for their happiness will stand up before Thee and say: "Judge us if Thou canst and darest." Know that I fear Thee not. Know that I too have been in the wilderness, I too have lived on roots and locusts, I too prized the freedom with which Thou hast blessed men, and I too was striving to stand among Thy elect, among the strong and powerful, thirsting "to make up the number." But I awakened and would not serve madness. I turned back and joined the ranks of those *who have corrected Thy work.* I left the proud and went back to the humble, for the happiness of the humble. What I say to Thee will come to pass, and our dominion will be built up. I repeat, tomorrow Thou shalt see that obedient flock who at a sign from me will hasten to heap up the hot cinders about the pile on which I shall burn Thee for coming to hinder us. For if anyone has ever deserved our fires, it is Thou. Tomorrow I shall burn Thee. *Dixi.*' "

Ivan stopped. He was carried away as he talked and spoke with excitement; when he had finished, he suddenly smiled.

Alyosha had listened in silence; toward the end he was greatly moved and seemed several times on the point of interrupting, but restrained himself. Now his words came with a rush.

"But . . . that's absurd!" he cried, flushing. "Your poem is in praise of Jesus, not in blame of Him—as you meant it to be. And who will believe you about freedom? Is that the way to understand it? That's not the idea of it in the Orthodox Church . . . That's Rome, and not even the whole of Rome, it's false—those are the worst of the Catholics, the Inquisitors, the Jesuits! . . . And there could not be such a fantastic creature as your Inquisitor. What are these sins of mankind they take on themselves? Who are these keepers of the mystery who have taken some curse upon themselves for the happiness of mankind? When have they been seen? We know the Jesuits, they are spoken ill of, but surely they are not what you describe? They are not that at all, not at all. . . . They are simply the Romish army for the earthly sovereignty of the world in the future, with the Pontiff of Rome for Emperor . . . that's their ideal, but there's no sort of mystery or lofty melancholy about it. . . . It's simple lust of power, of filthy earthly gain, of domination—something like a universal serfdom with them as masters—that's all they stand for. They don't even believe in God, perhaps. Your suffering inquisitor is a mere fantasy."

"Stay, stay," laughed Ivan, "how hot you are! A fantasy you say, let it be so! Of course it's a fantasy. But allow me to say: do you really think that the Roman Catholic movement of the last centuries is actually nothing but the lust of power, of filthy earthly gain? Is that Father Païssy's teaching?"

"No, no, on the contrary, Father Païssy did once say something the same as you . . . but of course it's not the same, not a bit the same," Alyosha hastily corrected himself.

"A precious admission, in spite of your 'not a bit the same.' I ask you why your Jesuits and inquisitors have united simply for vile material gain? Why can there not be among them one martyr oppressed by great sorrow and loving humanity? You see, only suppose that there was one such man among all those who desire nothing but filthy material gain—if there's only one like my old inquisitor, who had himself eaten roots in the desert and made frenzied efforts to subdue his flesh to make himself free and perfect. But yet all his life he loved humanity, and suddenly his eyes were opened, and he saw that it is no great moral blessedness to attain perfection and freedom, if at the same time one gains the conviction that billions of God's creatures have been created as a mockery, that they will never be capable of using their freedom, that these poor rebels can never turn into giants to complete the tower, that it was not for such geese that the great idealist dreamt his dream of harmony. Seeing all that, he turned back and joined—the clever people. Surely that could have happened?"

"Joined whom, what clever people?" cried Alyosha, completely carried away. "They have no such great cleverness and no mysteries and secrets. . . . Perhaps nothing but atheism, that's all their secret. Your inquisitor does not believe in God, that's his secret!"

"What if it is so! At last you have guessed it. It's perfectly true that that's the whole secret, but isn't that suffering, at least for a man like that, who has wasted his whole life in the desert and yet could not shake off his incurable love of humanity? In his old age he reached the clear conviction that nothing but the advice of the great dread spirit could build up any tolerable sort of life for the feeble, unruly, 'incomplete, empirical creatures created in jest.' And so, convinced of this, he sees that he must follow the council of the wise spirit, the dread spirit of death and destruction, and therefore accept lying and deception, and lead men consciously to death and destruction, and yet deceive them all the way so that they may not notice where they are being led, that the poor, blind creatures may at least on the way think themselves happy. And note, the deception is in the name of Him in Whose ideal the old man had so fervently believed all his life long. Is not that tragic? And if only one such stood at the head of the whole army 'filled with the lust of power only for the sake of filthy gain'—would not one such be enough to make a tragedy? More than that, one such standing at the head is enough to create the actual leading idea of the Roman Church with all its armies and Jesuits, its highest idea. I tell you frankly that I firmly believe that there has always been such a man among those who stood at the head of the movement. Who knows, there may have been some such even among the Roman Popes. Who knows, perhaps the spirit of that accursed old man who loves mankind so obstinately in his own way is to be found even now in a whole multitude of such old men, existing not by chance but by agreement, as a secret league formed long ago for the guarding of the mystery, to guard it from the weak and the unhappy, so as to make them happy. No doubt it is so, and so it must be indeed. I fancy that even among the Masons there's something of the same mystery at the bottom, and that that's why the Catholics so detest the Masons as their rivals breaking up the unity of the idea, while it is so essential that there should be one flock and one shepherd. . . . But from the way I defend my idea I might be an author impatient of your criticism. Enough of it."

"You are perhaps a Mason yourself!" broke suddenly from Alyosha. "You don't believe in God," he added, speaking this time very sorrowfully. He fancied besides that his brother was looking at him ironically. "How does your poem end?" he asked, suddenly looking down. "Or was it the end?"

"I meant it to end like this: When the Inquisitor ceased speaking, he waited some time for his Prisoner to answer him. His silence weighed down upon him. He saw the Prisoner had listened intently all the time, looking gently in his face and evidently not wishing to reply. The old man longed for Him to say something, however bitter and terrible. But He suddenly approached the old man in silence and softly kissed him on his bloodless, aged lips. That was all his answer. The old man shuddered. His lips moved. He went to the door, opened it, and said to him: 'Go, and come no more. . . . Come not at all, never, never!' And he let him out into the dark alleys of the town. The Prisoner went away."

"And the old man?"

"The kiss glows in his heart, but the old man adheres to his idea."

"And you with him, you too?" cried Alyosha, mournfully.

Ivan laughed.

"Why, it's all nonsense, Alyosha. It's only a senseless poem of a senseless student, who could never write two lines of verse. Why do you take it so seriously? Surely you don't suppose I am going straight off to the Jesuits, to join the men who are correcting His work? Good Lord, it's no business of mine. I told you, all I want is to live on to thirty, and then . . . dash the cup to the ground!"

"But the little sticky leaves, and the precious tombs, and the blue sky, and the woman you love! How will you live, how will you love them?" Alyosha cried sorrowfully. "With such a hell in your heart and your head, how can you? No, that's just what you are going away for, to join them . . . if not, you will kill yourself, you can't endure it!"

"There is a strength to endure everything," Ivan said with a cold smile.

"What strength?"

"The strength of the Karamazovs—the strength of the Karamazov baseness."

"To sink into debauchery, to stifle your soul with corruption, yes?"

"Possibly even that . . . only perhaps till I am thirty I shall escape it, and then—"

"How will you escape it? By what will you escape it? That's impossible with your ideas."

"In the Karamazov way, again."

" 'Everything is lawful,' you mean? Everything is lawful, is that it?"

Ivan scowled, and all at once turned strangely pale.

"Ah, you've caught up yesterday's phrase, which so offended Miüsov—and which Dmitri pounced upon so naïvely and paraphrased!" he smiled queerly. "Yes, if you like, 'everything is lawful' since the word has been said. I won't deny it. And Mitya's version isn't bad."

Alyosha looked at him in silence.

"I thought that going away from here I have you at least," Ivan said suddenly, with unexpected feeling; "but now I see that there is no place for me even in your heart, my dear hermit. The formula, 'all is lawful,' I won't renounce—will you renounce me for that, yes?"

Alyosha got up, went to him and softly kissed him on the lips.

"That's plagiarism," cried Ivan, highly delighted.

"You stole that from my poem. Thank you, though. Get up, Alyosha. it's time we were going, both of us. . . ."

—Translated by Constance Garnett

4

The Modern Mind

The shock of modern circumstances, felt even before the cataclysm of World War I, caused a decisive break with Western literary and philosophical traditions. Sigmund Freud turned a scientific eye on the workings of human rationality itself and found that human desire, not reason, was the root of all thought. Modernist authors like James Joyce, W. B. Yeats, and T. S. Eliot attuned their writings to the rhythms of primitive and unconscious thought, finding new insights in myth, dream, and the occult. While they discarded traditional literary forms, modernist authors often claimed, paradoxically, that their innovations had reinvigorated a tradition grown moribund and decadent.

In the 1910s and 1920s, the legitimacy of tradition was questioned from a different quarter, as new critical and poetic voices were heard from among women and American blacks. While undertaking her own influential innovations in the novel, Virginia Woolf founded modern feminist criticism with her forthright contention that women needed an income and a room of their own. The Harlem Renaissance planted a vigorous new strain of literary tradition in American soil, as African-American poets and dramatists gave literary shape to their racial experience.

In attacking Western civilization's exhausted forms of thought and expression, modernism established itself as a new kind of orthodoxy, a powerful and "antitraditional" tradition. The post-World War II generation would find the modernist giants towering over them and would seek still more radical forms for their own rebellious self-assertion.

SIGMUND FREUD

Sigmund Freud (1856–1939), the inventor of psychoanalysis, revolutionized the modern view of the human mind with his concepts of human desire and the unconscious. In his later career, Freud applied his theory of human psychodynamics to larger questions of philosophy, anthropology, and religion. In *Civilization and Its Discontents* (1930), Freud analyzed the inevitable conflict between humans' drive to satisfy their desires and the necessary restraints of civilization, which deflect sexual energy into the constructive activities of work, science, and art. In this excerpt, Freud analyzes the purpose of human life, the obstacles to human happiness, and the various means by which humans avoid these obstacles and achieve a measure of happiness. The Freudian idea of the pleasure principle is central to this discussion: The pleasure principle dictates that all human action is motivated ultimately by the seeking of pleasure or avoidance of pain. Thus, from his psychoanalytic point of view, Freud engaged fundamental questions of the Western philosophical tradition, questions that reached back to Voltaire and Aristotle.

For analysis and interpretation:

1. How does Freud define happiness? How does this definition compare with others from the philosophical tradition?

2. Analyze the scientific tone of Freud's analysis. In what way does he propose a psychological realism analogous to Machiavelli's political realism?

3. Based on what psychological principle does a "madman" protect himself from suffering? How might Freud's description apply to such literary characters as Don Quixote and Voltaire's Pangloss?

4. What is the role of art and beauty in human happiness, according to Freud? What makes these activities a suitable or desirable relief from suffering?

From *Civilization and Its Discontents*

. . . Life, as we find it, is too hard for us; it brings us too many pains, disappointments and impossible tasks. In order to bear it we cannot dispense with palliative measures. "We cannot do without auxiliary constructions", as Theodor Fontane tells us. There are perhaps three such measures: powerful deflections, which cause us to make light of our misery; substitutive satisfactions, which diminish it; and intoxicating substances, which make us insensitive to it. Something of the kind is indispensable. Voltaire has deflections in mind when he ends *Candide* with the advice to cultivate one's garden; and scientific activity is a deflection of this kind, too. The substitutive satisfactions, as offered by art, are illusions in contrast with reality, but they are none the less psychically effective, thanks to the role which phantasy has assumed in mental life. The intoxicating substances influence our body and alter its chemistry. It is no simple matter to see where religion has its place in this series. We must look further afield.

The question of the purpose of human life has been raised countless times; it has never yet received a satisfactory answer and perhaps does not admit of one. Some of those who have asked it have added that if it should turn out that life has *no* purpose, it would lose all value for them. But this threat alters nothing. It looks, on the contrary, as though one had a right to dismiss the question, for it seems to derive from the human presumptuousness, many other manifestations of which are already familiar to us. Nobody talks about the purpose of the life of animals, unless, perhaps, it may be supposed to lie in being of service to man. But this view is not tenable either, for there are many animals of which man can make nothing, except to describe, classify and study them; and innumerable species of animals have escaped even this use, since they existed and became extinct before man set eyes on them. Once again, only religion can answer the question of the purpose of life. One can hardly be wrong in concluding that the idea of life having a purpose stands and falls with the religious system.

We will therefore turn to the less ambitious question of what men themselves show by their behaviour to be the purpose and intention of their lives. What do they demand of life and wish to achieve in it? The answer to this can hardly be in doubt. They strive after happiness; they want to become happy and to remain so. This endeavour has two sides, a positive and a negative aim. It aims, on the one hand, at an absence of pain and unpleasure, and, on the other, at the experiencing of strong feelings of pleasure. In its narrower sense the word "happiness" only relates to the last. In conformity with this dichotomy in his aims, man's activity develops in two directions, according as it seeks to realize—in the main, or even exclusively—the one or the other of these aims.

As we see, what decides the purpose of life is simply the program of the pleasure principle. This principle dominates the operation of the mental apparatus from the start. There can be no doubt about its efficacy, and yet its program is at loggerheads with the whole world, with the macrocosm as much as with the microcosm. There is no possibility at all of its being carried through; all the regulations of the universe run counter to it. One feels inclined to say that the intention that man should be "happy" is not included in the plan of "Creation". What we call happiness in the strictest sense comes from the (preferably sudden) satisfaction of needs which have been dammed up to a high degree, and it is from its nature only possible as an episodic phenomenon. When any situation that is desired by the pleasure principle is prolonged, it only produces a feeling of mild contentment. We are so made that we can derive intense enjoyment only from a contrast and very little from a state of things.[1] Thus our possibilities of happiness are already restricted by our constitution. Unhappiness is much less difficult to experience. We are threatened with suffering from three directions: from our own body, which is doomed to decay and dissolution and which cannot even do without pain and anxiety as warning signals; from the external world, which may rage against us with overwhelming and merciless forces of destruction; and finally from our relations to other men. The suffering which comes from this last source is perhaps more painful to us than any other. We tend to regard it as a kind of gratuitous addition, although it cannot be any less fatefully inevitable than the suffering which comes from elsewhere.

It is no wonder if, under the pressure of these possibilities of suffering, men are accustomed to moderate their claims to happiness—just as the pleasure principle it-

[1] Goethe, indeed, warns us that "nothing is harder to bear than a succession of fair days." But this may be an exaggeration. [Freud's note]

self, indeed, under the influence of the external world, changed into the more modest reality principle—, if a man thinks himself happy merely to have escaped unhappiness or to have survived his suffering, and if in general the task of avoiding suffering pushes that of obtaining pleasure into the background. Reflection shows that the accomplishment of this task can be attempted along very different paths; and all these paths have been recommended by the various schools of worldly wisdom and put into practice by men. An unrestricted satisfaction of every need presents itself as the most enticing method of conducting one's life, but it means putting enjoyment before caution, and soon brings its own punishment. The other methods, in which avoidance of unpleasure is the main purpose, are differentiated according to the source of unpleasure to which their attention is chiefly turned. Some of these methods are extreme and some moderate; some are one-sided and some attack the problem simultaneously at several points. Against the suffering which may come upon one from human relationships the readiest safeguard is voluntary isolation, keeping oneself aloof from other people. The happiness which can be achieved along this path is, as we see, the happiness of quietness. Against the dreaded external world one can only defend oneself by some kind of turning away from it, if one intends to solve the task by oneself. There is, indeed, another and better path: that of becoming a member of the human community, and, with the help of a technique guided by science, going over to the attack against nature and subjecting her to the human will. Then one is working with all for the good of all. But the most interesting methods of averting suffering are those which seek to influence our own organism. In the last analysis, all suffering is nothing else than sensation; it only exists in so far as we feel it, and we only feel it in consequence of certain ways in which our organism is regulated.

The crudest, but also the most effective among these methods of influence is the chemical one—intoxication. I do not think that anyone completely understands its mechanism, but it is a fact that there are foreign substances which, when present in the blood or tissues, directly cause us pleasurable sensations; and they also so alter the conditions governing our sensibility that we become incapable of receiving unpleasurable impulses. The two effects not only occur simultaneously, but seem to be intimately bound up with each other. But there must be substances in the chemistry of our own bodies which have similar effects, for we know at least one pathological state, mania, in which a condition similar to intoxication arises without the administration of any intoxicating drug. Besides this, our normal mental life exhibits oscillations between a comparatively easy liberation of pleasure and a comparatively difficult one, parallel with which there goes a diminished or an increased receptivity to unpleasure. It is greatly to be regretted that this toxic side of mental processes has so far escaped scientific examination. The service rendered by intoxicating media in the struggle for happiness and in keeping misery at a distance is so highly prized as a benefit that individuals and peoples alike have given them an established place in the economics of their libido. We owe to such media not merely the immediate yield of pleasure, but also a greatly desired degree of independence from the external world. For one knows that, with the help of this "drowner of cares" one can at any time withdraw from the pressure of reality and find refuge in a world of one's own with better conditions of sensibility. As is well known, it is precisely this property of intoxicants which also determines their danger and their injuriousness. They are responsible, in certain circumstances, for the useless waste of a large quota of energy which might have been employed for the improvement of the human lot.

The complicated structure of our mental apparatus admits, however, of a whole number of other influences. Just as a satisfaction of instinct spells happiness for us, so severe suffering is caused us if the external world lets us starve, if it refuses to sate our needs. One may therefore hope to be freed from a part of one's sufferings by influencing the instinctual impulses. This type of defense against suffering is no longer brought to bear on the sensory apparatus; it seeks to master the internal sources of our needs. The extreme form of this is brought about by killing off the instincts, as is prescribed by the worldly wisdom of the East and practised by Yoga. If it succeeds, then the subject has, it is true, given up all other activities as well— he has sacrificed his life; and, by another path, he has once more only achieved the happiness of quietness. We follow the same path when our aims are less extreme and we merely attempt to control our instinctual life. In that case, the controlling elements are the higher psychical agencies, which have subjected themselves to the reality principle. Here the aim of satisfaction is not by any means relinquished; but a certain amount of protection against suffering is secured, in that non-satisfaction is not so painfully felt in the case of instincts kept in dependence as in the case of uninhibited ones. As against this, there is an undeniable diminution in the potentialities of enjoyment. The feeling of happiness derived from the satisfaction of a wild instinctual impulse untamed by the ego is incomparably more intense than that derived from sating an instinct that has been tamed. The irresistibility of perverse instincts, and perhaps the attraction in general of forbidden things finds an economic explanation here.

Another technique for fending off suffering is the employment of the displacements of libido which our mental apparatus permits of and through which its function gains so much in flexibility. The task here is that of shifting the instinctual aims in such a way that they cannot come up against frustration from the external world. In this, sublimation of the instincts lends its assistance. One gains the most if one can sufficiently heighten the yield of pleasure from the sources of psychical and intellectual work. When that is so, fate can do little against one. A satisfaction of this kind, such as an artist's joy in creating, in giving his phantasies body, or a scientist's in solving problems or discovering truths, has a special quality which we shall certainly one day be able to characterize in metapsychological terms. At present we can only say figuratively that such satisfactions seem "finer and higher". But their intensity is mild as compared with that derived from the sating of crude and primary instinctual impulses; it does not convulse our physical being. And the weak point of this method is that it is not applicable generally: it is accessible to only a few people. It presupposes the possession of special dispositions and gifts which are far from being common to any practical degree. And even to the few who do possess them, this method cannot give complete protection from suffering. It creates no impenetrable armour against the arrows of fortune, and it habitually fails when the source of suffering is a person's own body.[1]

While this procedure already clearly shows an intention of making oneself independent of the external world by seeking satisfaction in internal, psychical processes, the next procedure brings out those features yet more strongly. In it, the connection with reality is still further loosened; satisfaction is obtained from illusions, which are recognized as such without the discrepancy between them and reality being allowed to interfere with enjoyment. The region from which these illusions arise is the life of the imagination; at the time when the development of the sense of reality took place, this region was expressly exempted from the demands of reality-testing and was set apart for the purpose of fulfilling wishes which were difficult to carry out. At the head of these satisfactions through phantasy stands the enjoyment of works of art—an enjoyment which, by the agency of the artist, is made accessible even to those who are not themselves creative.[2] People who are receptive to the influence of art cannot set too high a value on it as a source of pleasure and consolation in life. Nevertheless the mild narcosis induced in us by art can do no more than bring about a transient withdrawal from the pressure of vital needs, and it is not strong enough to make us forget real misery.

Another procedure operates more energetically and more thoroughly. It regards reality as the sole enemy and as the source of all suffering, with which it is impossible to live, so that one must break off all relations with it if one is to be in any way happy. The hermit turns his back on the world and will have no truck with it. But one can do more than that; one can try to re-create the world, to build up in its stead another world in which its most unbearable features are eliminated and replaced by others that are in conformity with one's own wishes. But whoever, in desperate defiance, sets out upon this path to happiness will as a rule attain nothing. Reality is too strong for him. He becomes a madman, who for the most part finds no one to help him in carrying through his delusion. It is asserted, however, that each one of us behaves in some one respect like a paranoic, corrects some aspect of the world which is unbearable to him by the construction of a wish and introduces this delusion into reality. A

---

[1]When there is no special disposition in a person which imperatively prescribes what direction his interests in life shall take, the ordinary professional work that is open to everyone can play the part assigned to it by Voltaire's wise advice. It is not possible, within the limits of a short survey, to discuss adequately the significance of work for the economics of the libido. No other technique for the conduct of life attaches the individual so firmly to reality as laying emphasis on work; for his work at least gives him a secure place in a portion of reality, in the human community. The possibility it offers of displacing a large amount of libidinal components, whether narcissistic, aggressive or even erotic, on to professional work and on to the human relations connected with it lends it a value by no means second to what it enjoys as something indispensible to the preservation and justification of existence in society. Professional activity is a source of special satisfaction if it is a freely chosen one—if, that is to say, by means of sublimation, it makes possible the use of existing inclinations, of persisting or constitutionally reinforced instinctual impulses. And yet, as a path to happiness, work is not highly prized by men. They do not strive after it as they do after other possibilities of satisfaction. The great majority of people only work under the stress of necessity, and this natural human aversion to work raises most difficult social problems. [Freud's note]

[2]Cf. 'Formulations on the Two Principles of Mental Functioning' (1911*b*), and Lecture XXIII of my *Introductory Lectures* (1916–17). [Freud's note]

special importance attaches to the case in which this attempt to procure a certainty of happiness and a protection against suffering through a delusional remoulding of reality is made by a considerable number of people in common. The religions of mankind must be classed among the mass-delusions of this kind. No one, needless to say, who shares a delusion ever recognizes it as such.

I do not think that I have made a complete enumeration of the methods by which men strive to gain happiness and keep suffering away and I know, too, that the material might have been differently arranged. One procedure I have not yet mentioned—not because I have forgotten it but because it will concern us later in another connection. And how could one possibly forget, of all others, this technique in the art of living? It is conspicuous for a most remarkable combination of characteristic features. It, too, aims of course at making the subject independent of Fate (as it is best to call it), and to that end it locates satisfaction in internal mental processes, making use, in so doing, of the displaceability of the libido of which we have already spoken. But it does not turn away from the external world; on the contrary, it clings to the objects belonging to that world and obtains happiness from an emotional relationship to them. Nor is it content to aim at an avoidance of unpleasure—a goal, as we might call it, of weary resignation; it passes this by without heed and holds fast to the original, passionate striving for a positive fulfilment of happiness. And perhaps it does in fact come nearer to this goal than any other method. I am, of course, speaking of the way of life which makes love the centre of everything, which looks for all satisfaction in loving and being loved. A psychical attitude of this sort comes naturally enough to all of us; one of the forms in which love manifests itself—sexual love—has given us our most intense experience of an overwhelming sensation of pleasure and has thus furnished us with a pattern for our search for happiness. What is more natural than that we should persist in looking for happiness along the path on which we first encountered it? The weak side of this technique of living is easy to see; otherwise no human being would have thought of abandoning this path to happiness for any other. It is that we are never so defenceless against suffering as when we love, never so helplessly unhappy as when we have lost our loved object or its love. But this does not dispose of the technique of living based on the value of love as a means to happiness. There is much more to be said about it.

We may go on from here to consider the interesting case in which happiness in life is predominantly sought in the enjoyment of beauty, wherever beauty presents itself to our senses and our judgement—the beauty of human forms and gestures, of natural objects and landscapes and of artistic and even scientific creations. This aesthetic attitude to the goal of life offers little protection against the threat of suffering, but it can compensate for a great deal. The enjoyment of beauty has a peculiar, mildly intoxicating quality of feeling. Beauty has no obvious use; nor is there any clear cultural necessity for it. Yet civilization could not do without it. The science of aesthetics investigates the conditions under which things are felt as beautiful, but it has been unable to give any explanation of the nature and origin of beauty, and, as usually happens, lack of success is concealed beneath a flood of resounding and empty words. Psychoanalysis, unfortunately, has scarcely anything to say about beauty either. All that seems certain is its derivation from the field of sexual feeling. The love of beauty seems a perfect example of an impulse inhibited in its aim. 'Beauty' and 'attraction' are originally attributes of the sexual object. It is worth remarking that the genitals themselves, the sight of which is always exciting, are nevertheless hardly ever judged to be beautiful; the quality of beauty seems, instead, to attach to certain secondary sexual characters. . . .

—Translated by James Strachey

MODERN POETRY

William Butler Yeats (1865–1939) is a central figure in twentieth-century modernist literature, a dramatist and poet of deep political commitment and consummate literary skill. Yeats associated with such innovators of modern poetry as Ezra Pound and T. S. Eliot, though his own verse was technically less daring. "The Second Coming" shows Yeats's sensitivity to the historical crisis of Western civilization, however, and the ominous image of Yeats's rough beast has been seen as a portent of fascism and world war.

The poetry of T. S. Eliot (1888–1965) came to define modernism in English. His "Love Song of J. Alfred Prufrock" employed irregular lines, internal and half-rhymes, and other free-verse techniques that suited the poem's ironic tone. The neurotic anxiety of Prufrock typifies the modern hero; the character's climactic seashore fantasy is an escape from the futility of modern life.

Marianne Moore (1887–1972) helped to define modernism in poetry, not only through her own condensed and allusive poetic style, but also in her editorship of *The Dial*, the literary magazine that introduced such modernist pioneers as Ezra Pound and James Joyce to North American audiences. The graceful language of her "Paper Nautilus" illustrates the density of modern poetry, with its overlaid images and broken lines. The image of the paper nautilus, fragile but resolute, can be regarded as an indirect self-portrait of Moore.

Countee Cullen (1903–1946) and Langston Hughes (1902–1967) were both leading members of the Harlem Renaissance, the artistic movement of African-Americans centered in postwar Harlem. Cullen's verse was largely traditional in style, but dealt often with racial themes. "Scottsboro, Too" demands sympathy for a group of black youngsters unjustly accused of rape, comparing them to the case of Sacco and Vanzetti, a political *cause célèbre* among white liberals and leftists.

Langston Hughes was a central figure in the development of African-American letters in this century. Not only did Hughes write poetry in a simple, direct style that captured the rhythms of African-American speech; he also edited volumes of African-American poetry and prose, collaborated with other black writers, and energetically supported the growth of racial pride. "Theme for English B" illustrates his idiomatic style, which sheds the artificial poetic language of earlier black poets.

For analysis and interpretation:

1. In "The Second Coming," how does Yeats characterize the civilization that is passing away? What fear or anticipation is symbolized in the "rough beast"?

2. Trace the journey of Prufrock as depicted in the poem. How do the events in this journey represent the nature of modern life? What do Prufrock's responses indicate about the possibility of heroic action in this world?

3. In contrast to Prufrock, Moore's paper nautilus is pointedly compared to Hercules and other classical symbols. How does the nautilus's parental duty give its existence a purpose that Prufrock's lacks?

4. In light of Cullen's "Scottsboro, Too," what role do you think writers and poets should play in highlighting instances of social injustice? To whom might Cullen have appealed in today's world had he wished to gain support for such a cause?

5. What does Hughes's "Theme for English B" reveal about the racial divisions he felt in his English classroom? Describe the irony or tension residing in the succinct line, "That's American."

William Butler Yeats

The Second Coming

Turning and turning in the widening gyre
The falcon cannot hear the falconer;
Things fall apart; the centre cannot hold;
Mere anarchy is loosed upon the world,
The blood-dimmed tide is loosed, and everywhere
The ceremony of innocence is drowned;
The best lack all conviction, while the worst
Are full of passionate intensity.

Surely some revelation is at hand;
Surely the Second Coming is at hand.   10
The Second Coming! Hardly are those words out
When a vast image out of *Spiritus Mundi*
Troubles my sight: somewhere in sands of the desert
A shape with lion body and the head of a man
A gaze blank and pitiless as the sun,
Is moving its slow thighs, while all about it
Reel shadows of the indignant desert birds.
The darkness drops again; but now I know
That twenty centuries of stony sleep
Were vexed to nightmare by a rocking cradle,   20
And what rough beast, its hour come round at last,
Slouches towards Bethlehem to be born?

T. S. Eliot

The Love Song of J. Alfred Prufrock

S'io credesse che mia risposta fosse
A persona che mai tornasse al mondo,
Questa fiamma staria senza più scosse.
Ma perciocche giammai di questo fondo
Non tornò viva alcun, s'i'odo il vero,
Senza tema d'infamia ti rispondo.

Let us go then, you and I,
When the evening is spread out against the sky
Like a patient etherised upon a table;
Let us go, through certain half-deserted streets,
The muttering retreats
Of restless nights in one-night cheap hotels
And sawdust restaurants with oyster-shells:
Streets that follow like a tedious argument
Of insidious intent
To lead you to an overwhelming question . . .
Oh, do not ask, "What is it?"
Let us go and make our visit.

In the room the women come and go
Talking of Michelangelo.

The yellow fog that rubs its back upon the window-panes,
The yellow smoke that rubs its muzzle on the window-panes
Licked its tongue into the corners of the evening,
Lingered upon the pools that stand in drains,
Let fall upon its back the soot that falls from chimneys,
Slipped by the terrace, made a sudden leap,
And seeing that it was a soft October night,
Curled once about the house, and fell asleep.

And indeed there will be time
For the yellow smoke that slides along the street
Rubbing its back upon the window-panes;
There will be time, there will be time
To prepare a face to meet the faces that you meet;
There will be time to murder and create,
And time for all the works and days of hands
That lift and drop a question on your plate;
Time for you and time for me,
And time yet for a hundred indecisions,

And for a hundred visions and revisions,
Before the taking of a toast and tea.

In the room the women come and go
Talking of Michelangelo.

And indeed there will be time
To wonder, "Do I dare?" and, "Do I dare?"
Time to turn back and descend the stair,
With a bald spot in the middle of my hair—
[They will say: "How his hair is growing thin!"]
My morning coat, my collar mounting firmly to the chin,
My necktie rich and modest, but asserted by a simple pin—
[They will say: "But how his arms and legs are thin!"]
Do I dare
Disturb the universe?
In a minute there is time
For decisions and revisions which a minute will reverse.

For I have known them all already, known them all—
Have known the evenings, mornings, afternoons,
I have measured out my life with coffee spoons;
I know the voices dying with a dying fall
Beneath the music from a farther room.
      So how should I presume?

And I have known the eyes already, known them all—
The eyes that fix you in a formulated phrase,
And when I am formulated, sprawling on a pin,
When I am pinned and wriggling on the wall,
Then how should I begin
To spit out all the butt-ends of my days and ways?
      And how should I presume?

And I have known the arms already, known them all—
Arms that are braceleted and white and bare
[But in the lamplight, downed with light brown hair!]
Is it perfume from a dress
That makes me so digress?
Arms that lie along a table, or wrap about a shawl.
      And should I then presume?
      And how should I begin?

Shall I say, I have gone at dusk through narrow streets
And watched the smoke that rises from the pipes
Of lonely men in shirt-sleeves, leaning out of windows? . . .

I should have been a pair of ragged claws
Scuttling across the floors of silent seas.

. . . . .

And the afternoon, the evening, sleeps so peacefully!
Smoothed by long fingers,
Asleep . . . tired . . . or it malingers,
Stretched on the floor, here beside you and me.
Should I, after tea and cakes and ices,
Have the strength to force the moment to its crisis?
But though I have wept and fasted, wept and prayed,
Though I have seen my head [grown slightly bald]
    brought in upon a platter,
I am no prophet—and here's no great matter;
I have seen the moment of my greatness flicker,
And I have seen the eternal Footman hold my coat, and snicker,
And in short, I was afraid.

And would it have been worth it, after all,
After the cups, the marmalade, the tea,
Among the porcelain, among some talk of you and me,
Would it have been worth while,
To have bitten off the matter with a smile,
To have squeezed the universe into a ball
To roll it toward some overwhelming question,
To say: "I am Lazarus, come from the dead,
Come back to tell you all, I shall tell you all"—
If one, settling a pillow by her head,
    Should say: "That is not what I meant at all.
    That is not it, at all."

And would it have been worth it, after all,
Would it have been worth while,
After the sunsets and the dooryards and the sprinkled streets,
After the novels, after the teacups, after the skirts that trail along the
    floor—
And this, and so much more?—
It is impossible to say just what I mean!
But as if a magic lantern threw the nerves in patterns on a screen:
Would it have been worth while
If one, settling a pillow or throwing off a shawl,
And turning toward the window, should say:
    "That is not it at all,
    That is not what I meant, at all."

. . . . .

No! I am not Prince Hamlet, nor was meant to be;
Am an attendant lord, one that will do
To swell a progress, start a scene or two,
Advise the prince; no doubt, an easy tool,

Deferential, glad to be of use,
Politic, cautious, and meticulous;
Full of high sentence, but a bit obtuse;
At times, indeed, almost ridiculous—
Almost, at times, the Fool.

I grow old . . . I grow old . . .
I shall wear the bottoms of my trousers rolled.

Shall I part my hair behind? Do I dare to eat a peach?
I shall wear white flannel trousers, and walk upon the beach.
I have heard the mermaids singing, each to each.

I do not think that they will sing to me.

I have seen them riding seaward on the waves
Combing the white hair of the waves blown back
When the wind blows the water white and black.

We have lingered in the chambers of the sea
By sea-girls wreathed with seaweed red and brown
Till human voices wake us, and we drown.

Marianne Moore

The Paper Nautilus

For authorities whose hopes
are shaped by mercenaries?
Writers entrapped by
teatime fame and by
commuters' comforts? Not for these
the paper nautilus
constructs her thin glass shell.

Giving her perishable
souvenir of hope, a dull
white outside and smooth-
edged inner surface
glossy as the sea, the watchful
maker of it guards it
day and night; she scarcely

eats until the eggs are hatched.
Buried eightfold in her eight
arms, for she is in
a sense a devil-
fish, her glass ram's-horn-cradled freight

is hid but is not crushed;
as Hercules, bitten

by a crab loyal to the hydra,
was hindered to succeed,
the intensively
watched eggs coming from
the shell free it when they are freed—
leaving its wasp-nest flaws
of white on white, and close-

laid Ionic chiton-folds
like the lines in the mane of
a Parthenon horse,
round which the arms had
wound themselves as if they knew love
is the only fortress
strong enough to trust to.

Countee Cullen

Scottsboro, Too, Is Worth Its Song

(A poem to American poets)

I said:
Now will the poets sing,—
Their cries go thundering
Like blood and tears
Into the nation's ears,
Like lightning dart
Into the nation's heart.
Against disease and death and all things fell,
And war,
Their strophes rise and swell
To jar
The foe smug in his citadel.

Remembering their sharp and pretty
Tunes for Sacco and Vanzetti,
I said:
Here too's a cause divinely spun
For those whose eyes are on the sun,
Here in epitome

Is all disgrace
And epic wrong,
Like wine to brace
The minstrel heart, and blare it into song.

Surely, I said,
Now will the poets sing.
    But they have raised no cry.
    I wonder why

Langston Hughes

Theme for English B

The instructor said,

Go home and write
a page tonight.
And let that page come out of you—
Then, it will be true.

I wonder if it's that simple?

I am twenty-two, colored, born in Winston-Salem.
I went to school there, then Durham, then here
to this college on the hill above Harlem.
I am the only colored student in my class.
The steps from the hill lead down into Harlem,
through a park, then I cross St. Nicholas,
Eighth Avenue, Seventh, and I come to the Y,
the Harlem Branch Y, where I take the elevator
up to my room, sit down, and write this page:

It's not easy to know what is true for you or me
at twenty-two, my age. But I guess I'm what
I feel and see and hear. Harlem, I hear you:
hear you, hear me—we two—you, me, talk on this page.
(I hear New York, too.) Me—who?

Well, I like to eat, sleep, drink, and be in love.
I like to work, read, learn, and understand life.
I like a pipe for a Christmas present,
or records—Bessie, bop, or Bach.
I guess being colored doesn't make me *not* like
the same things other folks like who are other races.

So will my page be colored that I write?
Being me, it will not be white.

But it will be
a part of you, instructor.
You are white—
yet a part of me, as I am a part of you.
That's American.
Sometimes perhaps you don't want to be a part of me.
Nor do I often want to be a part of you.
But we are, that's true!
As I learn from you,
I guess you learn from me—
although you're older—and white—
and somewhat more free.

This is my page for English B.

VIRGINIA WOOLF

Virginia Woolf (1882–1941) was one of the inventors of the modern novel and the most eloquent literary voice of feminism in her day. She was a central figure in the "Bloomsbury group," an important London literary circle, and with her husband founded the Hogarth Press, publisher of the works of T. S. Eliot and Sigmund Freud. Woolf's own fictional works often employed a fragmented point of view, mixed literary genres, and—in *Orlando* (1929)—recast English history from a feminist point of view. In the famous chapter of her essay on "women and fiction," *A Room of One's Own* (1929), she pointedly details the obstacles to women's literary achievement in her own and past ages. Woolf's description of an imaginary sister to Shakespeare is a pivotal writing of modern feminism and a foundation of feminist literary criticism.

For analysis and interpretation:

1. Explain the contradiction that Woolf sees in the prominence of women in poetic works but their absence from history.

2. According to Woolf, what probably would have been the fate of a woman in Shakespeare's time born with a poetic gift? Would the same woman born today face no greater obstacles than a man?

3. Why might the history of men's opposition to women's emancipation be more interesting to Woolf than the history of that emancipation itself? Have women today achieved the freedom that Woolf envisioned?

From *A Room of One's Own:*

Shakespeare's Sister

It was disappointing not to have brought back in the evening some important statement, some authentic fact. Women are poorer than men because—this or that. Perhaps now it would be better to give up seeking for the truth, and receiving on one's head an avalanche of opinion hot as lava, discoloured as dish-water. It would be better to draw the curtains; to shut out distractions; to light the lamp; to narrow the enquiry and to ask the historian, who records not opinions but facts, to describe under what conditions women lived, not throughout the ages, but in England, say in the time of Elizabeth.

For it is a perennial puzzle why no woman wrote a word of that extraordinary literature when every other man, it seemed, was capable of song or sonnet. What were the conditions in which women lived, I asked myself; for fiction, imaginative work that is, is not dropped like a pebble upon the ground, as science may be; fiction is like a spider's web, attached ever so lightly perhaps, but still attached to life at all four corners. Often the attachment is scarcely perceptible; Shakespeare's plays, for instance, seem to hang there complete by themselves. But when the web is pulled askew, hooked up at the edge, torn in the middle, one remembers that these webs are not spun in midair by incorporeal creatures, but are the work of suffering human beings, and are attached to grossly material things, like health and money and the houses we live in.

I went, therefore, to the shelf where the histories stand and took down one of the latest, Professor Trevelyan's *History of England*. Once more I looked up Women, found "position of," and turned to the pages indicated. "Wife-beating," I read, "was a recognised right of man, and was practised without shame by high as well as low. . . . Similarly," the historian goes on, "the daughter who refused to marry the gentleman of her parents' choice was liable to be locked up, beaten and flung about the room, without any shock being inflicted on public opinion. Marriage was not an affair of personal affection, but of family avarice, particularly in the 'chivalrous' upper classes. . . . Betrothal often took place while one or both of the parties was in the cradle, and marriage when they were scarcely out of the nurses' charge." That was about 1470, soon after Chaucer's time. The next reference to the position of women is some two hundred years later, in the time of the Stuarts. "It was still the exception for women of the upper and middle class to choose their own husbands, and when the husband had been assigned, he was lord and master, so far at least as law and custom could make him. Yet even so," Professor Trevelyan concludes, "neither Shakespeare's women nor those of authentic seventeenth-century memoirs, like the Verneys and the Hutchinsons, seem wanting in personality and character." Certainly, if we consider it, Cleopatra must have had a way with her; Lady Macbeth, one would suppose, had a will of her own; Rosalind, one might conclude, was an attractive girl. Professor Trevelyan is speaking no more than the truth when he remarks that Shakespeare's women do not seem wanting in personality and character. Not being a historian, one might go even further and say that women have burnt like beacons in all the works of all the poets from the beginning of time—Clytemnestra, Antigone, Cleopatra, Lady Macbeth, Phèdre, Cressida, Rosalind, Desdemona, the Duchess of Malfi, among the dramatists; then among the prose writers: Millamant, Clarissa, Becky Sharp, Anna Karenina, Emma Bovary, Madame de Guermantes—the names flock to mind, nor do they recall women "lacking in personality and character." Indeed, if woman had no existence save in the fiction written by men, one would imagine her a person of the utmost importance; very various; heroic and mean; splendid and sordid; infinitely beautiful and hideous in the extreme; as great as a man, some think even greater.[1] But this is woman in fiction. In fact, as Professor Trevelyan points out, she was locked up, beaten and flung about the room.

A very queer, composite being thus emerges. Imaginatively she is of the highest importance; practically she is completely insignificant. She pervades poetry from cover to cover; she is all but absent from history. She dominates the lives of kings and conquerors in fiction; in fact she was the slave of any boy whose parents forced a ring upon her finger. Some of the most inspired words, some of the most profound thoughts in literature fall from her lips; in real life she could hardly read, could scarcely spell, and was the property of her husband.

It was certainly an odd monster that one made up by reading the historians first and the poets afterwards—a worm winged like an eagle; the spirit of life and beauty in a kitchen chopping up suet. But these monsters, however amusing to the imagination, have no existence in fact. What one must do to bring her to life was to think poetically and prosaically at one and the same moment, thus keeping in touch with fact—that she is Mrs. Martin, aged thirty-six, dressed in blue, wearing a black hat and brown shoes; but not losing sight of fiction either—that she is a vessel in which all sorts of spirits and forces are coursing and flashing perpetually. The moment, however, that one tries this method with the Elizabethan woman, one branch of illumination fails; one is held up by the scarcity of facts. One knows nothing detailed, nothing perfectly true and substantial about her. History scarcely mentions her. And I turned to Professor Trevelyan again to see what history meant to him. I found by looking at his chapter headings that it meant—

"The Manor Court and the Methods of Open-field Agriculture . . . The Cistercians and Sheep-farming . . . The Crusades . . . The University . . . The House of Commons . . . The Hundred Years' War . . . The Wars of the Roses . . . The Renaissance Scholars . . . The Dissolution of the Monasteries . . . Agrarian and Religious Strife . . . The Origin of English Sea-power . . . The Armada . . ." and so on. Occasionally an individual woman is mentioned, an Elizabeth, or a Mary; a queen or a great lady. But by no possible means could middle-class women with nothing but brains and character at their command have taken part in any one of the great movements which, brought together, constitute the historian's view of the past. Nor shall we find her in any collection of anecdotes. Aubrey hardly mentions her. She never writes her own life and scarcely keeps a diary; there are only a handful of her letters

---

[1]"It remains a strange and almost inexplicable fact that in Athena's city, where women were kept in almost Oriental suppression as odalisques or drudges, the stage should yet have produced figures like Clytemnestra and Cassandra, Atossa and Antigone, Phèdre and Medea, and all the other heroines who dominate play after play of the 'misogynist' Euripides. But the paradox of this world where in real life a respectable woman could hardly show her face alone in the street, and yet on the stage woman equals or surpasses man, has never been satisfactorily explained. In modern tragedy the same predominance exists. At all events, a very cursory survey of Shakespeare's work (similarly with Webster, though not with Marlowe or Jonson) suffices to reveal how this dominance, this initiative of women, persists from Rosalind to Lady Macbeth. So too in Racine; six of his tragedies bear their heroines' names; and what male characters of his shall we set against Hermione and Andromaque, Bérénice and Roxane, Phèdre and Athalie? So again with Ibsen; what men shall we match with Solveig and Nora, Hedda and Hilda Wangel and Rebecca West?"—F. L. Lucas, Tragedy, pp. 114–15. [Woolf's note]

in existence. She left no plays or poems by which we can judge her. What one wants, I thought—and why does not some brilliant student at Newnham or Girton supply it?—is a mass of information; at what age did she marry; how many children had she as a rule; what was her house like; had she a room to herself; did she do the cooking; would she be likely to have a servant? All these facts lie somewhere, presumably, in parish registers and account books; the life of the average Elizabethan woman must be scattered about somewhere, could one collect it and make a book of it. It would be ambitious beyond my daring, I thought, looking about the shelves for books that were not there, to suggest to the students of those famous colleges that they should re-write history, though I own that it often seems a little queer as it is, unreal, lop-sided; but why should they not add a supplement to history? calling it, of course, by some inconspicuous name so that women might figure there without impropriety? For one often catches a glimpse of them in the lives of the great, whisking away into the background, concealing, I sometimes think, a wink, a laugh, perhaps a tear. And, after all, we have lives enough of Jane Austen; it scarcely seems necessary to consider again the influence of the tragedies of Joanna Baillie upon the poetry of Edgar Allan Poe; as for myself, I should not mind if the homes and haunts of Mary Russell Mitford were closed to the public for a century at least. But what I find deplorable, I continued, looking about the bookshelves again, is that nothing is known about women before the eighteenth century. I have no model in my mind to turn about this way and that. Here am I asking why women did not write poetry in the Elizabethan age, and I am not sure how they were educated; whether they were taught to write; whether they had sitting-rooms to themselves; how many women had children before they were twenty-one; what, in short, they did from eight in the morning till eight at night. They had no money evidently; according to Professor Trevelyan they were married whether they liked it or not before they were out of the nursery, at fifteen or sixteen very likely. It would have been extremely odd, even upon this showing, had one of them suddenly written the plays of Shakespeare, I concluded, and I thought of that old gentleman, who is dead now, but was a bishop, I think, who declared that it was impossible for any woman, past, present, or to come, to have the genius of Shakespeare. He wrote to the papers about it. He also told a lady who applied to him for information that cats do not as a matter of fact go to heaven, though they have, he added, souls of a sort. How much thinking those old gentlemen used to save one! How the borders of ignorance shrank back at their approach! Cats do not go to heaven. Women cannot write the plays of Shakespeare.

Be that as it may, I could not help thinking, as I looked at the works of Shakespeare on the shelf, that the bishop was right at least in this; it would have been impossible, completely and entirely, for any woman to have written the plays of Shakespeare in the age of Shakespeare. Let me imagine, since facts are so hard to come by, what would have happened had Shakespeare had a wonderfully gifted sister, called Judith, let us say. Shakespeare himself went, very probably—his mother was an heiress—to the grammar school, where he may have learnt Latin—Ovid, Virgil and Horace—and the elements of grammar and logic.

He was, it is well known, a wild boy who poached rabbits, perhaps shot a deer,

and had, rather sooner than he should have done, to marry a woman in the neighbourhood, who bore him a child rather quicker than was right. That escapade sent him
to seek his fortune in London. He had, it seemed, a taste for the theatre; he began by
holding horses at the stage door. Very soon he got work in the theatre, became a successful actor, and lived at the hub of the universe, meeting everybody, knowing everybody, practising his art on the boards, exercising his wits in the streets, and even getting
access to the palace of the queen. Meanwhile his extraordinarily gifted sister, let us
suppose, remained at home. She was as adventurous, as imaginative, as agog to see
the world as he was. But she was not sent to school. She had no chance of learning
grammar and logic, let alone of reading Horace and Virgil. She picked up a book now
and then, one of her brother's perhaps, and read a few pages. But then her parents
came in and told her to mend the stockings or mind the stew and not moon about with
books and papers. They would have spoken sharply but kindly, for they were substantial people who knew the conditions of life for a woman and loved their daughter—indeed, more likely than not she was the apple of her father's eye. Perhaps she
scribbled some pages up in an apple loft on the sly, but was careful to hide them or
set fire to them. Soon, however, before she was out of her teens, she was to be be-
trothed to the son of a neighbouring wool-stapler. She cried out that marriage was
hateful to her, and for that she was severely beaten by her father. Then he ceased to
scold her. He begged her instead not to hurt him, not to shame him in this matter of
her marriage. He would give her a chain of beads or a fine petticoat, he said; and there
were tears in his eyes. How could she disobey him? How could she break his heart?
The force of her own gift alone drove her to it. She made up a small parcel of her be-
longings, let herself down by a rope one summer's night and took the road to London.
She was not seventeen. The birds that sang in the hedge were not more musical than
she was. She had the quickest fancy, a gift like her brother's, for the tune of words.
Like him, she had a taste for the theatre. She stood at the stage door; she wanted to
act, she said. Men laughed in her face. The manager—a fat, loose-lipped man—guf-
fawed. He bellowed something about poodles dancing and women acting—no woman,
he said, could possibly be an actress. He hinted—you can imagine what. She could
get no training in her craft. Could she even seek her dinner in a tavern or roam the
streets at midnight? Yet her genius was for fiction and lusted to feed abundantly upon
the lives of men and women and the study of their ways. At last—for she was very
young, oddly like Shakespeare the poet in her face, with the same grey eyes and
rounded brows—at last Nick Greene the actor-manager took pity on her; she found
herself with child by that gentleman and so—who shall measure the heat and violence
of the poet's heart when caught and tangled in a woman's body?—killed herself one
winter's night and lies buried at some cross-roads where the omnibuses now stop outside the Elephant and Castle.

    That, more or less, is how the story would run, I think, if a woman in
Shakespeare's day had had Shakespeare's genius. But for my part, I agree with the
deceased bishop, if such he was—it is unthinkable that any woman in Shakespeare's
day should have had Shakespeare's genius. For genius like Shakespeare's is not born

among labouring, uneducated, servile people. It was not born in England among the Saxons and the Britons. It is not born today among the working classes. How, then, could it have been born among women whose work began, according to Professor Trevelyan, almost before they were out of the nursery, who were forced to it by their parents and held to it by all the power of law and custom? Yet genius of a sort must have existed among women as it must have existed among the working classes. Now and again an Emily Brontë or a Robert Burns blazes out and proves its presence. But certainly it never got itself on to paper. When, however, one reads of a witch being ducked, of a woman possessed by devils, of a wise woman selling herbs, or even of a very remarkable man who had a mother, then I think we are on the track of a lost novelist, a suppressed poet, of some mute and inglorious Jane Austen, some Emily Brontë who dashed her brains out on the moor or mopped and mowed about the highways crazed with the torture that her gift had put her to. Indeed, I would venture to guess that Anon, who wrote so many poems without signing them, was often a woman. It was a woman Edward Fitzgerald, I think, suggested who made the ballads and the folk-songs, crooning them to her children, beguiling her spinning with them, or the length of the winter's night.

This may be true or it may be false—who can say?—but what is true in it, so it seemed to me, reviewing the story of Shakespeare's sister as I had made it, is that any woman born with a great gift in the sixteenth century would certainly have gone crazed, shot herself, or ended her days in some lonely cottage outside the village, half witch, half wizard, feared and mocked at. For it needs little skill in psychology to be sure that a highly gifted girl who had tried to use her gift for poetry would have been so thwarted and hindered by other people, so tortured and pulled asunder by her own contrary instincts, that she must have lost her health and sanity to a certainty. No girl could have walked to London and stood at a stage door and forced her way into the presence of actor-managers without doing herself a violence and suffering an anguish which may have been irrational—for chastity may be a fetish invented by certain societies for unknown reasons—but were none the less inevitable. Chastity had then, it has even now, a religious importance in a woman's life, and has so wrapped itself round with nerves and instincts that to cut it free and bring it to the light of day demands courage of the rarest. To have lived a free life in London in the sixteenth century would have meant for a woman who was poet and playwright a nervous stress and dilemma which might well have killed her. Had she survived, whatever she had written would have been twisted and deformed, issuing from a strained and morbid imagination. And undoubtedly, I thought, looking at the shelf where there are no plays by women, her work would have gone unsigned. That refuge she would have sought certainly. It was the relic of the sense of chastity that dictated anonymity to women even so late as the nineteenth century. Currer Bell, George Eliot, George Sand, all the victims of inner strife as their writings prove, sought ineffectively to veil themselves by using the name of a man. Thus they did homage to the convention, which if not implanted by the other sex was liberally encouraged by them (the chief glory of a woman is not to be talked of, said Pericles, himself a much-talked-of man), that publicity in women is detestable. Anonymity runs in their blood. The desire to be veiled still possesses them. They are not even now as concerned about the health of their fame as men are, and, speaking generally, will pass a tombstone or a signpost without feeling an irresistible desire to cut their names on it, as Alf, Bert or Chas. must do in obedience to their instinct, which murmurs if it sees a fine woman go by, or even a dog, Ce chien est à moi. And, of course, it may not be a dog, I thought, remembering Parliament Square, the Sieges Allee and other avenues; it may be a piece of land or a man with curly black hair. It is one of the great advantages of being a woman that one can pass even a very fine negress without wishing to make an Englishwoman of her.

That woman, then, who was born with a gift of poetry in the sixteenth century, was an unhappy woman, a woman at strife against herself. All the conditions of her life, all her own instincts, were hostile to the state of mind which is needed to set free whatever is in the brain. But what is the state of mind that is most propitious to the act of creation, I asked. Can one come by any notion of the state that furthers and makes possible that strange activity? Here I opened the volume containing the Tragedies of Shakespeare. What was Shakespeare's state of mind, for instance, when he wrote *Lear* and *Antony and Cleopatra*? It was certainly the state of mind most favourable to poetry that there has ever existed. But Shakespeare himself said nothing about it. We only know casually and by chance that he "never blotted a line." Nothing indeed was ever said by the artist himself about his state of mind until the eighteenth century perhaps. Rousseau perhaps began it. At any rate, by the nineteenth century self-consciousness had developed so far that it was the habit for men of letters to describe their minds in confessions and autobiographies. Their lives also were written, and their letters were printed after their deaths. Thus, though we do not know what Shakespeare went through when he wrote *Lear*, we do know what Carlyle went through when he wrote the *French Revolution*; what Flaubert went through when he wrote *Madame Bovary*; what Keats was going through when he tried to write poetry against the coming of death and the indifference of the world.

And one gathers from this enormous modern literature of confession and self-analysis that to write a work of genius is almost always a feat of prodigious difficulty. Everything is against the likelihood that it will come from the writer's mind whole and entire. Generally material circumstances are against it. Dogs will bark; people will interrupt; money must be made; health will break down. Further, accentuating all these difficulties and making them harder to bear is the world's notorious indifference. It does not ask people to write poems and novels and histories; it does not need them. It does not care whether Flaubert finds the right word or whether Carlyle scrupulously verifies this or that fact. Naturally, it will not pay for what it does not want. And so the writer, Keats, Flaubert, Carlyle, suffers, especially in the creative years of youth, every form of distraction and discouragement. A curse, a cry of agony, rises from those books of analysis and confession. "Mighty poets in their misery dead"— that is the burden of their song. If anything comes through in spite of all this, it is a miracle, and probably no book is born entire and uncrippled as it was conceived.

But for women, I thought, looking at the empty shelves, these difficulties were infinitely more formidable. In the first place, to have a room of her own, let alone a quiet room or a sound-proof room, was out of the question, unless her parents were exceptionally rich or very noble, even up to the beginning of the nineteenth century. Since her pin money, which depended on the good will of her father, was only enough to keep her clothed, she was debarred from such alleviations as came even to Keats or Tennyson or Carlyle, all poor men, from a walking tour, a little journey to France, from the separate lodging which, even if it were miserable enough, sheltered them from the claims and tyrannies of their families. Such material difficulties were formidable; but much worse were the immaterial. The indifference of the world which Keats and Flaubert and other men of genius have found so hard to bear was in her case not indifference but hostility. The world did not say to her as it said to them, Write if you choose; it makes no difference to me. The world said with a guffaw, Write? What's the good of your writing? Here the psychologists of Newnham and Girton might come to our help, I thought, looking again at the blank spaces on the shelves. For surely it is time that the effect of discouragement upon the mind of the artist should be measured, as I have seen a dairy company measure the effect of ordinary milk and Grade A milk upon the body of the rat. They set two rats in cages side by side, and of the two one was furtive, timid and small, and the other was glossy, bold and big. Now what food do we feed women as artists upon? I asked, remembering, I suppose, that dinner of prunes and custard. To answer that question I had only to open the evening paper and to read that Lord Birkenhead is of opinion—but really I am not going to trouble to copy out Lord Birkenhead's opinion upon the writing of women. What Dean Inge says I will leave in peace. The Harley Street specialist may be allowed to rouse the echoes of Harley Street with his vociferations without raising a hair on my head. I will quote, however, Mr. Oscar Browning, because Mr. Oscar Browning was a great figure in Cambridge at one time, and used to examine the students at Girton and Newnham. Mr. Oscar Browning was wont to declare "that the impression left on his mind, after looking over any set of examination papers, was that, irrespective of the marks he might give, the best woman was intellectually the inferior of the worst man." After saying that Mr. Browning went back to his rooms—and it is this sequel that endears him and makes him a human figure of some bulk and majesty—he went back to his rooms and found a stable-boy lying on the sofa—"a mere skeleton, his cheeks were cavernous and sallow, his teeth were black, and he did not appear to have the full use of his limbs. . . . 'That's Arthur' [said Mr. Browning]. 'He's a dear boy really and most high-minded.' " The two pictures always seem to me to complete each other. And happily in this age of biography the two pictures often do complete each other, so that we are able to interpret the opinions of great men not only by what they say, but by what they do.

But though this is possible now, such opinions coming from the lips of important people must have been formidable enough even fifty years ago. Let us suppose that a father from the highest motives did not wish his daughter to leave home and become writer, painter or scholar. "See what Mr. Oscar Browning says," he would say; and there was not only Mr. Oscar Browning; there was the *Saturday Review*; there was Mr. Greg—the "essentials of a woman's being," said Mr. Greg emphatically, "are

that *they are supported by, and they minister to, men*"—there was an enormous body
of masculine opinion to the effect that nothing could be expected of women intellectually. Even if her father did not read out loud these opinions, any girl could read them
for herself; and the reading, even in the nineteenth century, must have lowered her vitality, and told profoundly upon her work. There would always have been that assertion—you cannot do this, you are incapable of doing that—to protest against, to
overcome. Probably for a novelist this germ is no longer of much effect; for there have
been women novelists of merit. But for painters it must still have some sting in it; and
for musicians, I imagine, is even now active and poisonous in the extreme. The woman
composer stands where the actress stood in the time of Shakespeare. Nick Greene, I
thought, remembering the story I had made about Shakespeare's sister, said that a
woman acting put him in mind of a dog dancing. Johnson repeated the phrase two
hundred years later of women preaching. And here, I said, opening a book about music,
we have the very words used again in this year of grace, 1928, of women who try to
write music. "Of Mlle. Germaine Tailleferre one can only repeat Dr. Johnson's dictum concerning a woman preacher, transposed into terms of music. 'Sir, a woman's
composing is like a dog's walking on his hind legs. It is not done well, but you are
surprised to find it done at all.' "[2] So accurately does history repeat itself.

Thus, I concluded, shutting Mr. Oscar Browning's life and pushing away the
rest, it is fairly evident that even in the nineteenth century a woman was not encouraged to be an artist. On the contrary, she was snubbed, slapped, lectured and exhorted.
Her mind must have been strained and her vitality lowered by the need of opposing
this, of disproving that. For here again we come within range of that very interesting
and obscure masculine complex which has had so much influence upon the woman's
movement; that deep-seated desire, not so much that *she* shall be inferior as that *he*
shall be superior, which plants him wherever one looks, not only in front of the arts,
but barring the way to politics too, even when the risk to himself seems infinitesimal
and the suppliant humble and devoted. Even Lady Bessborough, I remembered, with
all her passion for politics, must humbly bow herself and write to Lord Granville
Leveson-Gower: ". . . notwithstanding all my violence in politics and talking so much
on that subject, I perfectly agree with you that no woman has any business to meddle
with that or any other serious business, farther than giving her opinion (if she is ask'd)."
And so she goes on to spend her enthusiasm where it meets with no obstacle whatsoever upon that immensely important subject, Lord Granville's maiden speech in the
House of Commons. The spectacle is certainly a strange one, I thought. The history
of men's opposition to women's emancipation is more interesting perhaps than the
story of that emancipation itself. An amusing book might be made of it if some young
student at Girton or Newnham would collect examples and deduce a theory—but she
would need thick gloves on her hands, and bars to protect her of solid gold.

But what is amusing now, I recollected, shutting Lady Bessborough, had to be
taken in desperate earnest once. Opinions that one now pastes in a book labelled cock-
a-doodle-dum and keeps for reading to select audiences on summer nights once drew

---

[2]*A Survey of Contemporary Music*, Cecil Gray, p. 246. [Woolf's note]

tears, I can assure you. Among your grandmothers and great-grandmothers there were many that wept their eyes out. Florence Nightingale shrieked aloud in her agony.[3] Moreover, it is all very well for you, who have got yourselves to college and enjoy sitting-rooms—or is it only bed-sitting-rooms?—of your own to say that genius should disregard such opinions; that genius should be above caring what is said of it. Unfortunately, it is precisely the men or women of genius who mind most what is said of them. Remember Keats. Remember the words he had cut on his tombstone. Think of Tennyson; think—but I need hardly multiply instances of the undeniable, if very unfortunate, fact that it is the nature of the artist to mind excessively what is said about him. Literature is strewn with the wreckage of men who have minded beyond reason the opinions of others.

And this susceptibility of theirs is doubly unfortunate, I thought, returning again to my original enquiry into what state of mind is most propitious for creative work, because the mind of an artist, in order to achieve the prodigious effort of freeing whole and entire the work that is in him, must be incandescent, like Shakespeare's mind, I conjectured, looking at the book which lay open at *Antony and Cleopatra*. There must be no obstacle in it, no foreign matter unconsumed.

For though we say that we know nothing about Shakespeare's state of mind, even as we say that, we are saying something about Shakespeare's state of mind. The reason perhaps why we know so little of Shakespeare—compared with Donne or Ben Jonson or Milton—is that his grudges and spites and antipathies are hidden from us. We are not held up by some "revelation" which reminds us of the writer. All desire to protest, to preach, to proclaim an injury, to pay off a score, to make the world the witness of some hardship or grievance was fired out of him and consumed. Therefore his poetry flows from him free and unimpeded. If ever a human being got his work expressed completely, it was Shakespeare. If ever a mind was incandescent, unimpeded, I thought, turning again to the bookcase, it was Shakespeare's mind.

FRANZ KAFKA

In the stories of Franz Kafka (1883–1924), the spiritual alienation of the modern era finds expression in the most grotesque of modernist heroes. The circumstances of Kafka's own life were the fertile ground of alienation: Born a German-speaking Jew in Prague, Kafka suffered an exaggerated fear of his father and never brought himself to complete a marriage to his long-suffering fiancée. Most of his writings were never published in his lifetime, and Kafka asked that his works be burned after his death.

"The Hunger Artist" is a typical Kafka story in its bizarre premise: a man dedicated to the art of fasting loses the public's interest and finally is cast aside in favor of a vigorous animal. The narrative's matter-of-fact tone heightens the sense of grotesque fascination. The hero's pointless devotion to his art can be seen as a metaphor for many pursuits, including perhaps Kafka's own career in an insurance office. In the

---

[3]See *Cassandra*, by Florence Nightingale, printed in *The Cause*, by R. Strachey. [Woolf's note]

largest sense, the hunger artist's career is Kafka's metaphor for life in the modern world, a self-defeating commitment to principle to which the world is indifferent.

For analysis and interpretation:

1. Compare the hunger artist's purist devotion to his art to the showmanship of his impresario. What criticism of modern life can you see in the artist's attitude?

2. What human pursuits make the best analogy to the "art" of hunger—that is, pursuits that inspire passionate devotion in some but that others find absurd?

3. Compare Kafka's hunger artist to T. S. Eliot's Prufrock. How do circumstances seem to mock and frustrate these characters? In what ways do people react as they do to modern circumstances?

A Hunger Artist

During these last decades the interest in professional fasting has markedly diminished. It used to pay very well to stage such great performances under one's own management, but today that is quite impossible. We live in a different world now. At one time the whole town took a lively interest in the hunger artist; from day to day of his fast the excitement mounted; everybody wanted to see him at least once a day; there were people who bought season tickets for the last few days and sat from morning till night in front of his small barred cage; even in the nighttime there were visiting hours, when the whole effect was heightened by torch flares; on fine days the cage was set out in the open air, and then it was the children's special treat to see the hunger artist; for their elders he was often just a joke that happened to be in fashion, but the children stood open-mouthed, holding each other's hands for greater security, marveling at him as he sat there pallid in black tights, with his ribs sticking out so prominently, not even on a seat but down among straw on the ground, sometimes giving a courteous nod, answering questions with a constrained smile, or perhaps stretching an arm through the bars so that one might feel how thin it was, and then again withdrawing deep into himself, paying no attention to anyone or anything, not even to the all-important striking of the clock that was the only piece of furniture in his cage, but merely staring into vacancy with half-shut eyes, now and then taking a sip from a tiny glass of water to moisten his lips.

Besides casual onlookers there were also relays of permanent watchers selected by the public, usually butchers, strangely enough, and it was their task to watch the hunger artist day and night, three of them at a time, in case he should have some secret recourse to nourishment. This was nothing but a formality, instituted to reassure the masses, for the initiates knew well enough that during his fast the artist would never in any circumstances, not even under forcible compulsion, swallow the smallest morsel of food; the honor of his profession forbade it. Not every watcher, of course, was capable of understanding this, there were often groups of night watchers who were very lax in carrying out their duties and deliberately huddled together in a retired corner to play cards with great absorption, obviously intending to give the hunger artist the chance of a little refreshment, which they supposed he could draw from some private hoard. Nothing annoyed the artist more than such watchers; they made him miserable; they made his fast seem unendurable; sometimes he mastered his feebleness sufficiently to sing during their watch for as long as he could keep going, to show them how unjust their suspicions were. But that was of little use; they only wondered at his cleverness in being able to fill his mouth even while singing. Much more to his taste were the watchers who sat close up to the bars, who were not content with the dim night lighting of the hall but focused him in the full glare of the electric pocket torch given them by the impresario. The harsh light did not trouble him at all. In any case he could never sleep properly, and he could always drowse a little, whatever the light, at any hour, even when the hall was thronged with noisy onlookers. He was quite happy at the prospect of spending a sleepless night with such watchers; he was ready to exchange jokes with them, to tell them stories out of his nomadic life, anything at all to keep them awake and demonstrate to them again that he had no eatables in his cage and that he was fasting as not one of them could fast. But his happiest moment was when the morning came and an enormous breakfast was brought them, at his expense, on which they flung themselves with the keen appetite of healthy men after a weary night of wakefulness. Of course there were people who argued that this breakfast was an unfair attempt to bribe the watchers, but that was going rather too far, and when they were invited to take on a night's vigil without a breakfast, merely for the sake of the cause, they made themselves scarce, although they stuck stubbornly to their suspicions.

Such suspicions, anyhow, were a necessary accompaniment to the profession of fasting. No one could possibly watch the hunger artist continuously, day and night, and so no one could produce first-hand evidence that the fast had really been rigorous and continuous; only the artist himself could know that; he was therefore bound to be the sole completely satisfied spectator of his own fast. Yet for other reasons he was never satisfied; it was not perhaps mere fasting that had brought him to such skeleton thinness that many people had regretfully to keep away from his exhibitions, because the sight of him was too much for them, perhaps it was dissatisfaction with himself that had worn him down. For he alone knew, what no other initiate knew, how easy it was to fast. It was the easiest thing in the world. He made no secret of this, yet people did not believe him; at the best they set him down as modest, most of them, however, thought he was out for publicity or else was some kind of cheat who found it easy to fast because he had discovered a way of making it easy, and then had the impudence to admit the fact, more or less. He had to put up with all that, and in the course of time had got used to it, but his inner dissatisfaction always rankled, and never yet, after any term of fasting—this must be granted to his credit—had he left the cage of his own free will. The longest period of fasting was fixed by his impresario at forty days, beyond that term he was not allowed to go, not even in great cities, and there was good reason for it, too. Experience had proved that for about forty days the interest of the public could be stimulated by a steadily increasing pressure of advertisement, but after that the town began to lose interest, sympathetic support began notably to fall off; there were of course local variations as between one town and another or one country and another, but as a general rule forty days marked the limit. So on the fortieth day the flower-bedecked cage was opened, enthusiastic spectators filled the hall, a military band played, two doctors entered the cage to measure the results of the fast, which were announced through a megaphone, and finally two young ladies appeared, blissful at having been selected for the honor, to help the hunger artist down the few steps leading to a small table on which was spread a carefully chosen invalid repast. And at this very moment the artist always turned stubborn. True, he would entrust his bony arms to the outstretched helping hands of the ladies bending over him, but stand up he would not. Why stop fasting at this particular moment, after forty days of it? He had held out for a long time, an illimitably long time; why stop now, when he was in his best fasting form, or rather, not yet quite in his best fasting form? Why should he be cheated of the fame he would get for fasting longer, for being not only the record hunger artist of all time, which presumably he was already, but for beating his own record by a performance beyond human imagination, since he felt that there were no limits to his capacity for fasting? His public pretended to admire him so much, why should it have so little patience with him; if he could endure fasting longer, why shouldn't the public endure it? Besides, he was tired, he was comfortable sitting in the straw, and now he was supposed to lift himself to his full height and go down to a meal the very thought of which gave him a nausea that only the presence of the ladies kept him from betraying, and even that with an effort. And he looked up into the eyes of the ladies who were apparently so friendly and in reality so cruel, and shook his head, which felt too heavy on its strengthless neck. But then there happened yet again what always happened. The impresario came forward, without a word—for the band made speech impossible—lifted his arms in the air above the artist, as if inviting Heaven to look down upon its creature here in the straw, this suffering martyr, which indeed he was, although in quite another sense; grasped him round the emaciated waist, with exaggerated caution, so that the frail condition he was in might be appreciated; and committed him to the care of the blenching ladies, not without secretly giving him a shaking so that his legs and body tottered and swayed. The artist now submitted completely; his head lolled on his breast as if it had landed there by chance; his body was hollowed out; his legs in a spasm of self-preservation clung close to each other at the knees, yet scraped on the ground as if it were not really solid ground, as if they were only trying to find solid ground; and the whole weight of his body, a featherweight after all, relapsed onto one of the ladies, who, looking round for help and panting a little—this post of honor was not at all what she had expected it to be—first stretched her neck as far as she could to keep her face at least free from contact with the artist, then finding this impossible, and her more fortunate companion not coming to her aid but merely holding extended on her own trembling hand the little bunch of knucklebones that was the artist's, to the great delight of the spectators burst into tears and had to be replaced by an attendant who had long been stationed in readiness. Then came the food, a little of which the impresario managed to get between the artist's lips, while he sat in a kind of half-fainting trance, to the accompaniment of cheerful patter designed to distract the public's attention from the artist's condition; after that, a toast was drunk to the public, supposedly prompted by a whisper from the artist in the impresario's ear; the band confirmed it with a mighty flourish, the spectators melted away, and no one had any cause to be dissatisfied with the proceedings, no one except the hunger artist himself, he only, as always.

So he lived for many years, with small regular intervals of recuperation, in visible glory, honored by the world, yet in spite of that troubled in spirit, and all the more troubled because no one would take his trouble seriously. What comfort could he possibly need? What more could he possibly wish for? And if some good-natured person, feeling sorry for him, tried to console him by pointing out that his melancholy was probably caused by fasting, it could happen, especially when he had been fasting for some time, that he reacted with an outburst of fury and to the general alarm began to shake the bars of his cage like a wild animal. Yet the impresario had a way of punishing these outbreaks which he rather enjoyed putting into operation. He would apologize publicly for the artist's behavior, which was only to be excused, he admitted, because of the irritability caused by fasting; a condition hardly to be understood by well-fed people; then by natural transition he went on to mention the artist's equally incomprehensible boast that he could fast for much longer than he was doing; he praised the high ambition, the good will, the great self-denial undoubtedly implicit in such a statement; and then quite simply countered it by bringing out photographs, which were also on sale to the public, showing the artist on the fortieth day of a fast lying in bed almost dead from exhaustion. This perversion of the truth, familiar to the artist though it was, always unnerved him afresh and proved too much for him. What was a consequence of the premature ending of his fast was here presented as the cause of it! To fight against this lack of understanding, against a whole world of non-understanding, was impossible. Time and again in good faith he stood by the bars listening to the impresario, but as soon as the photographs appeared he always let go and sank with a groan back on to his straw, and the reassured public could once more come close and gaze at him.

A few years later when the witnesses of such scenes called them to mind, they often failed to understand themselves at all. For meanwhile the aforementioned change in public interest had set in; it seemed to happen almost overnight; there may have been profound causes for it, but who was going to bother about that; at any rate the pampered hunger artist suddenly found himself deserted one fine day by the amusement seekers, who went streaming past him to other more favored attractions. For the last time the impresario hurried him over half Europe to discover whether the old interest might still survive here and there; all in vain; everywhere, as if by secret agreement, a positive revulsion from professional fasting was in evidence. Of course it could not really have sprung up so suddenly as all that, and many premonitory symptoms which had not been sufficiently remarked or suppressed during the rush and glitter of success now came retrospectively to mind, but it was now too late to take any countermeasures. Fasting would surely come into fashion again at some future date, yet that was no comfort for those living in the present. What, then, was the hunger artist to do? He had been applauded by thousands in his time and could hardly come down to showing himself in a street booth at village fairs, and as for adopting another profession, he was not only too old for that but too fanatically devoted to fasting. So he took leave of the impresario, his partner in an unparalleled career, and hired himself to a large circus; in order to spare his own feelings he avoided reading the conditions of his contract.

A large circus with its enormous traffic in replacing and recruiting men, animals and apparatus can always find a use for people at any time, even for a hunger artist, provided of course that he does not ask too much, and in this particular case anyhow it was not only the artist who was taken on but his famous and long-known name as well; indeed considering the peculiar nature of his performance, which was not impaired by advancing age, it could not be objected that here was an artist past his prime, no longer at the height of his professional skill, seeking a refuge in some quiet corner of a circus; on the contrary, the hunger artist averred that he could fast as well as ever, which was entirely credible; he even alleged that if he were allowed to fast as he liked, and this was at once promised him without more ado, he could astound the world by establishing a record never yet achieved, a statement which certainly provoked a smile among the other professionals, since it left out of account the change in public opinion, which the hunger artist in his zeal conveniently forgot.

He had not, however, actually lost his sense of the real situation and took it as a matter of course that he and his cage should be stationed, not in the middle of the ring as a main attraction, but outside, near the animal cages, on a site that was after all easily accessible. Large and gaily painted placards made a frame for the cage and announced what was to be seen inside it. When the public came thronging out in the intervals to see the animals, they could hardly avoid passing the hunger artist's cage and stopping there for a moment, perhaps they might even have stayed longer had not those pressing behind them in the narrow gangway, who did not understand why they should be held up on their way towards the excitements of the menagerie, made it impossible for anyone to stand gazing quietly for any length of time. And that was the reason why the hunger artist, who had of course been looking forward to these visiting hours as the main achievement of his life, began instead to shrink from them. At first he could hardly wait for the intervals; it was exhilarating to watch the crowds come streaming his way, until only too soon—not even the most obstinate self-deception, clung to almost consciously, could hold out against the fact—the conviction was borne in upon him that these people, most of them, to judge from their actions, again and again, without exception, were all on their way to the menagerie. And the first sight of them from the distance remained the best. For when they reached his cage he was at once deafened by the storm of shouting and abuse that arose from the two contending factions, which renewed themselves continuously, of those who wanted to stop and stare at him—he soon began to dislike them more than the others—not out of real interest but only out of obstinate self-assertiveness, and those who wanted to go straight on to the animals. When the first great rush was past, the stragglers came along, and these, whom nothing could have prevented from stopping to look at him as long as they had breath, raced past with long strides, hardly even glancing at him, in their haste to get to the menagerie in time. And all too rarely did it happen that he had a stroke of luck, when some father of a family fetched up before him with his children, pointed a finger at the hunger artist and explained at length what the phenomenon meant, telling stories of earlier years when he himself had watched similar but much more thrilling performances, and the children, still rather uncomprehending, since neither inside nor outside school had they been sufficiently prepared for this lesson—what did they care about fasting?—yet showed by the brightness of their intent eyes that new and better times might be coming. Perhaps, said the hunger artist to himself many a time, things would be a little better if his cage were set not quite so near the menagerie. That made it too easy for people to make their choice, to say nothing of what he suffered from the stench of the menagerie, the animals' restlessness by night, the carrying past of raw lumps of flesh for the beasts of prey, the roaring at feeding times, which depressed him continually. But he did not dare to lodge a complaint with the management; after all, he had the animals to thank for the troops of people who passed his cage, among whom there might always be one here and there to take an interest in him, and who could tell where they might seclude him if he called attention to his existence and thereby to the fact that, strictly speaking, he was only an impediment on the way to the menagerie.

A small impediment, to be sure, one that grew steadily less. People grew familiar with the strange idea that they could be expected, in times like these, to take an interest in a hunger artist, and with this familiarity the verdict went out against him. He might fast as much as he could, and he did so; but nothing could save him now, people passed him by. Just try to explain to anyone the art of fasting! Anyone who has no feeling for it cannot be made to understand it. The fine placards grew dirty and illegible, they were torn down; the little notice board telling the number of fast days achieved, which at first was changed carefully every day, had long stayed at the same figure, for after the first few weeks even this small task seemed pointless to the staff; and so the artist simply fasted on and on, as he had once dreamed of doing, and it was no trouble to him, just as he had always foretold, but no one counted the days, no one, not even the artist himself, knew what records he was already breaking, and his heart grew heavy. And when once in a time some leisurely passer-by stopped, made merry over the old figure on the board and spoke of swindling, that was in its way the stupidest lie ever invented by indifference and inborn malice, since it was not the hunger artist who was cheating; he was working honestly, but the world was cheating him of his reward.

Many more days went by, however, and that too came to an end. An overseer's eye fell on the cage one day and he asked the attendants why this perfectly good stage should be left standing there unused with dirty straw inside it; nobody knew, until one man, helped out by the notice board, remembered about the hunger artist. They poked into the straw with sticks and found him in it. "Are you still fasting?" asked the overseer. "When on earth do you mean to stop?" "Forgive me, everybody," whispered the hunger artist; only the overseer, who had his ear to the bars, understood him. "Of course," said the overseer, and tapped his forehead with a finger to let the attendants know what state the man was in, "we forgive you." "I always wanted you to admire my fasting," said the hunger artist. "We do admire it," said the overseer, affably. "But you shouldn't admire it," said the hunger artist. "Well, then we don't admire it," said the overseer, "but why shouldn't we admire it?" "Because I have to fast, I can't help it," said the hunger artist. "What a fellow you are," said the overseer, "and why can't you help it?" "Because," said the hunger artist, lifting his head a little and speaking, with his lips pursed, as if for a kiss, right into the overseer's ear, so that no syllable might be lost, "because I couldn't find the food I liked. If I had found it, believe me, I should have made no fuss and stuffed myself like you or anyone else." These were his last words, but in his dimming eyes remained the firm though no longer proud persuasion that he was still continuing to fast.

"Well, clear this out now!" said the overseer, and they buried the hunger artist, straw and all. Into the cage they put a young panther. Even the most insensitive felt it refreshing to see this wild creature leaping around the cage that had so long been dreary. The panther was all right. The food he liked was brought him without hesitation by the attendants; he seemed not even to miss his freedom; his noble body, furnished almost to the bursting point with all that it needed, seemed to carry freedom around with it too; somewhere in his jaws it seemed to lurk; and the joy of life streamed with such ardent passion from his throat that for the onlookers it was not easy to stand the shock of it. But they braced themselves, crowded round the cage, and did not want ever to move away.

—Translated by Willa and Edwin Muir

5

The Contemporary Era

In the decentered world of the contemporary era, perspectives shift, voices speak from the margins, cultures multiply and overlap. Since 1945, the stable configuration of Western civilization has been shaken by national and ethnic uprisings and global shifts of power. The age began with the anguished and intensely reflective attitude of existentialism, which paradoxically reemphasized the role of the individual's responsibility in a world of weapons of mass destruction, giant corporations, and government bureaucracy. In such existential novels as *Invisible Man*, the individual preserved a measure of autonomy and identity only by becoming invisible to society. By contrast, the neoromantic American Beats asserted themselves as individuals through intoxicated imagery and impromptu journeys in search of America.

Up from existential exhaustion, storytellers like Jorge Luis Borges and Gabriel Garcia Márquez achieved a significant new expansion of narrative forms. Borges's exploration of the world as artifice enabled him to create compellingly complex imaginative worlds in stories of the smallest possible dimensions. In postmodern fiction like Borges's, all the forms of human discourse—science, history, myth, fiction— formed different levels of the same hyperreality.

At the same time, the literary boundaries of Western civilization were redefined by women, minorities, and national poets from Africa and Asia. Poets such as Anne Sexton and Wole Soyinka were less interested in formal experimentation than in drawing on the imaginative resources of their personal or national experience. Beginning in anguish with the threat of universal destruction, the contemporary era may become more like the Renaissance, an age that creates a whole new cultural geography and a redefinition of the human self.

JEAN-PAUL SARTRE

The existentialist Jean-Paul Sartre (1905–1980) was a well-known public figure, whom Parisians might glimpse sitting at his favorite café, dining with Simone de Beauvoir, the feminist philosopher, or marching in a demonstration. As a philosopher, Sartre attempted one of the most comprehensive philosophical analyses of modern life. His *Being and Nothingness* (1943) analyzed the basis of human freedom in a world devoid of transcendent values, while his *Critique of Dialectical Reason* (1960) examined minutely the individual in modern society. In the essay excerpted here, Sartre rejects the traditional philosophical notion that humanity has a predefined nature, an "essence" that precedes and determines any particular human existence. His defense of a radically existential human freedom places all responsibility for human action squarely on the individual. The goal of human life, according to Sartre, must be to affirm this responsibility despite the anguish it brings, and to live authentically as a free actor in society.

For analysis and interpretation:

    1. Compare Sartre's dictum, "Man is nothing else but what he makes of himself" to the philosophical positions of such Christian philosophers as Pico della Mirandola, Montaigne, and Erasmus. Where might these philosophers agree concerning the nature of human freedom and the purpose of life?

    2. Apply Sartre's notion of the "anguish" of human freedom to Dostoevsky's figure of the Grand Inquisitor. What action has the Inquisitor taken, and what anguish does he therefore suffer?

    3. Explain Sartre's assertion that humans are "condemned to be free" in existential terms. Judging from the tone of this excerpt, do you believe Sartre was optimistic or pessimistic about the outcome of this freedom?

From *Existentialism is a Humanism*

In the eighteenth century, the atheism of the *philosophers* discarded the idea of God, but not so much for the notion that essence precedes existence. To a certain extent, this idea is found everywhere; we find it in Diderot, in Voltaire, and even in Kant. Man has a human nature; this human nature, which is the concept of the human, is found in all men, which means that each man is a particular example of a universal concept, man. In Kant, the result of this universality is that the wild-man, the natural man, as well as the bourgeois, are circumscribed by the same definition and have the same basic qualities. Thus, here too the essence of man precedes the historical existence that we find in nature.

    Atheistic existentialism, which I represent, is more coherent. It states that if God does not exist, there is at least one being in whom existence precedes essence, a being who exists before he can be defined by any concept, and that this being is man, or, as Heidegger says, human reality. What is meant here by saying that existence precedes essence? It means that, first of all, man exists, turns up, appears on the scene, and, only afterwards, defines himself. If man, as the existentialist conceives him, is indefinable, it is because at first he is nothing. Only afterward will he be something, and he himself will have made what he will be. Thus, there is no human nature, since there is no God to conceive it. Not only is man what he conceives himself to be, but he is also only what he wills himself to be after this thrust toward existence.

Man is nothing else but what he makes of himself. Such is the first principle of existentialism. It is also what is called subjectivity, the name we are labeled with when charges are brought against us. But what do we mean by this, if not that man has a greater dignity than a stone or table? For we mean that man first exists, that is, that man first of all is the being who hurls himself toward a future and who is conscious of imagining himself as being in the future. Man is at the start a plan which is aware of itself, rather than a patch of moss, a piece of garbage, or a cauliflower; nothing exists prior to this plan; there is nothing in heaven; man will be what he will have planned to be. Not what he will want to be. Because by the word "will" we generally mean a conscious decision, which is subsequent to what we have already made of ourselves. I may want to belong to a political party, write a book, get married; but all that is only a manifestation of an earlier, more spontaneous choice that is called "will." But if existence really does precede essence, man is responsible for what he is. Thus, existentialism's first move is to make every man aware of what he is and to make the full responsibility of his existence rest on him. And when we say that a man is responsible for himself, we do not only mean that he is responsible for his own individuality, but that he is responsible for all men.

The word subjectivism has two meanings, and our opponents play on the two. Subjectivism means, on the one hand, that an individual chooses and makes himself; and, on the other, that it is impossible for man to transcend human subjectivity. The second of these is the essential meaning of existentialism. When we say that man chooses his own self, we mean that every one of us does likewise; but we also mean by that that in making this choice he also chooses all men. In fact, in creating the man that we want to be, there is not a single one of our acts which does not at the same time create an image of man as we think he ought to be. To choose to be this or that is to affirm at the same time the value of what we choose, because we can never choose evil. We always choose the good, and nothing can be good for us without being good for all.

If, on the other hand, existence precedes essence, and if we grant that we exist and fashion our image at one and the same time, the image is valid for everybody and for our whole age. Thus, our responsibility is much greater than we might have supposed, because it involves all mankind. If I am a workingman and choose to join a Christian trade-union rather than be a communist, and if by being a member I want to show that the best thing for man is resignation, that the kingdom of man is not of this world, I am not only involving my own case—I want to be resigned for everyone. As a result, my action has involved all humanity. To take a more individual matter, if I want to marry, to have children; even if this marriage depends solely on my own circumstances or passion or wish, I am involving all humanity in monogamy and not merely myself. Therefore, I am responsible for myself and for everyone else. I am creating a certain image of man of my own choosing. In choosing myself, I choose man.

This helps us understand what the actual content is of such rather grandiloquent words as anguish, forlornness, despair. As you will see, it's all quite simple.

First, what is meant by anguish? The existentialists say at once that man is anguish. What that means is this: the man who involves himself and who realizes that he is not only the person he chooses to be, but also a lawmaker who is, at the same time, choosing all mankind as well as himself, can not help escape the feeling of his total and deep responsibility. Of course, there are many people who are not anxious; but we claim that they are hiding their anxiety, that they are fleeing from it. Certainly, many people believe that when they do something, they themselves are the only ones involved, and when someone says to them, "What if everyone acted that way?" they shrug their shoulders and answer, "Everyone doesn't act that way." But really, one should always ask himself, "What would happen if everybody looked at things that way?" There is no escaping this disturbing thought except by a kind of double-dealing. A man who lies and makes excuses for himself by saying "Not everybody does that," is someone with an uneasy conscience, because the act of lying implies that a universal value is conferred upon the lie.

Anguish is evident even when it conceals itself. This is the anguish that Kierkegaard called the anguish of Abraham. You know the story: an angel has ordered Abraham to sacrifice his son; if it really were an angel who has come and said, "You are Abraham, you shall sacrifice your son," everything would be all right. But everyone might first wonder, "Is it really an angel, and am I really Abraham? What proof do I have?"

There was a madwoman who had hallucinations; someone used to speak to her on the telephone and give her orders. Her doctor asked her, "Who is it who talks to you?" She answered, "He says it's God." What proof did she really have that it was God? If an angel comes to me, what proof is there that it's an angel? And if I hear voices, what proof is there that they come from heaven and not from hell, or from the subconscious, or a pathological condition? What proves that they are addressed to me? What proof is there that I have been appointed to impose my choice and my conception of man on humanity? I'll never find any proof or sign to convince me of that. If a voice addresses me, it is always for me to decide that this is the angel's voice; if I consider that such an act is a good one, it is I who will choose to say that it is good rather than bad.

Now, I'm not being singled out as an Abraham, and yet at every moment I'm obliged to perform exemplary acts. For every man, everything happens as if all mankind had its eyes fixed on him and were guiding itself by what he does. And every man ought to say to himself, "Am I really the kind of man who has the right to act in such a way that humanity might guide itself by my actions?" And if he does not say that to himself, he is masking his anguish.

There is no question here of the kind of anguish which would lead to quietism, to inaction. It is a matter of a simple sort of anguish that anybody who has had responsibilities is familiar with. For example, when a military officer takes the responsibility for an attack and sends a certain number of men to death, he chooses to do so, and in the main he alone makes the choice. Doubtless, orders come from above, but they are too broad; he interprets them, and on this interpretation depend the lives of ten or fourteen or twenty men. In making a decision he can not help having a certain anguish. All leaders know this anguish. That doesn't keep them from acting; on the contrary, it is the very condition of their action. For it implies that they envisage a number of possibilities, and when they choose one, they realize that it has value only because it is chosen. We shall see that this kind of anguish, which is the kind that existentialism describes, is explained, in addition, by a direct responsibility to the other men whom it involves. It is not a curtain separating us from action, but is part of action itself.

When we speak of forlornness, a term Heidegger was fond of, we mean only that God does not exist and that we have to face all the consequences of this. The existentialist is strongly opposed to a certain kind of secular ethics which would like to abolish God with the least possible expense. About 1880, some French teachers tried to set up a secular ethics which went something like this: God is a useless and costly hypothesis; we are discarding it; but, meanwhile, in order for there to be an ethics, a society, a civilization, it is essential that certain values be taken seriously and that they be considered as having an *a priori* existence. It must be obligatory, *a priori*, to be honest, not to lie, not to beat your wife, to have children, etc., etc. So we're going to try a little device which will make it possible to show that values exist all the same, inscribed in a heaven of ideas, though otherwise God does not exist. In other words— and this, I believe, is the tendency of everything called reformism in France—nothing will be changed if God does not exist. We shall find ourselves with the same norms of honesty, progress, and humanism, and we shall have made of God an outdated hypothesis which will peacefully die off by itself.

The existentialist, on the contrary, thinks it very distressing that God does not exist, because all possibility of finding values in a heaven of ideas disappears along with Him; there can no longer be an *a priori* Good, since there is no infinite and perfect consciousness to think it. Nowhere is it written that the Good exists, that we must be honest, that we must not lie; because the fact is we are on a plane where there are only men. Dostoievsky said, "If God didn't exist, everything would be possible." That is the very starting point of existentialism. Indeed, everything is permissible if God does not exist, and as a result man is forlorn, because neither within him nor without does he find anything to cling to. He can't start making excuses for himself.

If existence really does precede essence, there is no explaining things away by reference to a fixed and given human nature. In other words, there is no determinism, man is free, man is freedom. On the other hand, if God does not exist, we find no values or commands to turn to which legitimize our conduct. So, in the bright realm of values, we have no excuse behind us, nor justification before us. We are alone, with no excuses.

That is the idea I shall try to convey when I say that man is condemned to be free. Condemned, because he did not create himself, yet, in other respects is free; because, once thrown into the world, he is responsible for everything he does. The existentialist does not believe in the power of passion. He will never agree that a sweeping passion is a ravaging torrent which fatally leads a man to certain acts and is therefore an excuse. He thinks that man is responsible for his passion.

The existentialist does not think that man is going to help himself by finding in the world some omen by which to orient himself. Because he thinks that man will interpret the omen to suit himself. Therefore, he thinks that man, with no support and no aid, is condemned every moment to invent man. Ponge, in a very fine article, has said, "Man is the future of man." That's exactly it. But if it is taken to mean that this future is recorded in heaven, that God sees it, then it is false, because it would really no longer be a future. If it is taken to mean that, whatever a man may be, there is a future to be forged, a virgin future before him, then this remark is sound. But then we are forlorn. . . .

RALPH ELLISON

In his novel *Invisible Man*, Ralph Ellison (1914–1994) made a young black man's search for identity into a metaphor for existential alienation. Each time he encounters the institutions and authority figures of a racist society, the nameless black hero finds his authentic self denied and degraded. In the novel's first episode, the "Battle Royal," the humiliating entertainment provides an ironic counterpoint to the platitudes of the hero's speech. In subsequent episodes, the hero encounters the hypocrisy of a college president, a wealthy business person, and the leaders of the Black Nationalist Party. Ellison's young hero thus is subject to an "enlightenment" that resembles Voltaire's *Candide*; rather than cultivate a garden, however, the invisible man lives an anonymous existence in a basement illuminated by thousands of light bulbs. Ellison's figure of the invisible man was one of the contemporary age's most powerful protests against the racism in the modern world.

For analysis and interpretation:

1. Analyze the irony of the Battle Royal, especially its contrasting portrayal of the white members of the civic club and the young black men fighting for the money. Compare Ellison's tone to such satirists as Jonathan Swift and Voltaire.

2. What is the effect of the hero's speech on the audience? How might the speech be seen as a satire on American political values?

3. What ominous and ironic note is sounded by the hero's dream? To what extent does the hero, at this point, fail to understand the dream's significance?

From *Invisible Man*

[*Battle Royal*]

It goes a long way back, some twenty years. All my life I had been looking for something, and everywhere I turned someone tried to tell me what it was. I accepted their answers too, though they were often in contradiction and even self-contradictory. I was naïve. I was looking for myself and asking everyone except myself questions which I, and only I, could answer. It took me a long time and much painful boomeranging of my expectations to achieve a realization everyone else appears to have been born with: That I am nobody but myself. But first I had to discover that I am an invisible man!

And yet I am no freak of nature, nor of history. I was in the cards, other things having been equal (or unequal) eighty-five years ago. I am not ashamed of my grandparents for having been slaves. I am only ashamed of myself for having at one time been ashamed. About eighty-five years ago they were told that they were free, united with others of our country in everything pertaining to the common good, and, in everything social, separate like the fingers of the hand. And they believed it. They exulted in it. They stayed in their place, worked hard, and brought up my father to do the same. But my grandfather is the one. He was an odd old guy, my grandfather, and I am told I take after him. It was he who caused the trouble. On his deathbed he called my father to him and said, "Son, after I'm gone I want you to keep up the good fight. I never told you, but our life is a war and I have been a traitor all my born days, a spy in the enemy's country ever since I give up my gun back in the Reconstruction. Live with your head in the lion's mouth. I want you to overcome 'em with yeses, undermine 'em with grins, agree 'em to death and destruction, let 'em swoller you till they vomit or bust wide open." They thought the old man had gone out of his mind. He had been the meekest of men. The younger children were rushed from the room, the shades drawn and the flame of the lamp turned so low that it sputtered on the wick like the old man's breathing. "Learn it to the younguns," he whispered fiercely; then he died.

But my folks were more alarmed over his last words than over his dying. It was as though he had not died at all, his words caused so much anxiety. I was warned emphatically to forget what he had said and, indeed, this is the first time it has been mentioned outside the family circle. It had a tremendous effect upon me, however. I could never be sure of what he meant. Grandfather had been a quiet old man who never made any trouble, yet on his deathbed he had called himself a traitor and a spy, and he had spoken of his meekness as a dangerous activity. It became a constant puzzle which lay unanswered in the back of my mind. And whenever things went well for me I remembered my grandfather and felt guilty and uncomfortable. It was as though I was carrying out his advice in spite of myself. And to make it worse, everyone loved me for it. I was praised by the most lily-white men of the town. I was considered an example of desirable conduct—just as my grandfather had been. And what puzzled me was that the old man had defined it as *treachery*. When I was praised for my conduct I felt a guilt that in some way I was doing something that was really against the wishes of the white folks, that if they had understood they would have desired me to act just the opposite, that I should have been sulky and mean, and that that really would have been what they wanted, even though they were fooled and thought they wanted me to act as I did. It made me afraid that some day they would look upon me as a traitor and I would be lost. Still I was more afraid to act any other way because they didn't like that at all. The old man's words were like a curse. On my graduation day

I delivered an oration in which I showed that humility was the secret, indeed, the very essence of progress. (Not that I believed this—how could I, remembering my grandfather?—I only believed that it worked.) It was a great success. Everyone praised me and I was invited to give the speech at a gathering of the town's leading white citizens. It was a triumph for our whole community.

It was in the main ballroom of the leading hotel. When I got there I discovered that it was on the occasion of a smoker, and I was told that since I was to be there anyway I might as well take part in the battle royal to be fought by some of my schoolmates as part of the entertainment. The battle royal came first.

All of the town's big shots were there in their tuxedoes, wolfing down the buffet foods, drinking beer and whiskey and smoking black cigars. It was a large room with a high ceiling. Chairs were arranged in neat rows around three sides of a portable boxing ring. The fourth side was clear, revealing a gleaming space of polished floor. I had some misgivings over the battle royal, by the way. Not from a distaste for fighting, but because I didn't care too much for the other fellows who were to take part. They were tough guys who seemed to have no grandfather's curse worrying their minds. No one could mistake their toughness. And besides, I suspected that fighting a battle royal might detract from the dignity of my speech. In those pre-invisible days I visualized myself as a potential Booker T. Washington. But the other fellows didn't care too much for me either, and there were nine of them. I felt superior to them in my way, and I didn't like the manner in which we were all crowded together into the servant's elevator. Nor did they like my being there. In fact, as the warmly lighted floors flashed past the elevator we had words over the fact that I, by taking part in the fight, had knocked one of their friends out of a night's work.

We were led out of the elevator through a rococo hall into an anteroom and told to get into our fighting togs. Each of us was issued a pair of boxing gloves and ushered out into the big mirrored hall, which we entered looking cautiously about us and whispering, lest we might accidentally be heard above the noise of the room. It was foggy with cigar smoke. And already the whiskey was taking effect. I was shocked to see some of the most important men of the town quite tipsy. They were all there— bankers, lawyers, judges, doctors, fire chiefs, teachers, merchants. Even one of the more fashionable pastors. Something we could not see was going on up front. A clarinet was vibrating sensuously and the men were standing up and moving eagerly forward. We were a small tight group, clustered together, our bare upper bodies touching and shining with anticipatory sweat; while up front the big shots were becoming increasingly excited over something we still could not see. Suddenly I heard the school superintendent, who had told me to come, yell, "Bring up the shines, gentlemen! Bring up the little shines!"

We were rushed up to the front of the ballroom, where it smelled even more strongly of tobacco and whiskey. Then we were pushed into place. I almost wet my pants. A sea of faces, some hostile, some amused, ringed around us, and in the center, facing us, stood a magnificent blonde—stark naked. There was dead silence. I felt a blast of cold air chill me. I tried to back away, but they were behind me and around me. Some of the boys stood with lowered heads, trembling. I felt a wave of irrational guilt and fear. My teeth chattered, my skin turned to goose flesh, my knees knocked. Yet I was strongly attracted and looked in spite of myself. Had the price of looking been blindness, I would have looked. The hair was yellow like that of a circus kewpie doll, the face heavily powdered and rouged, as though to form an abstract mask, the eyes hollow and smeared a cool blue, the color of a baboon's butt. I felt a desire to spit upon her as my eyes brushed slowly over her body. Her breasts were firm and round as the domes of East Indian temples, and I stood so close as to see the fine skin texture and beads of pearly perspiration glistening like dew around the pink and erected buds of her nipples. I wanted at one and the same time to run from the room, to sink through the floor, or go to her and cover her from my eyes and the eyes of the others with my body; to feel the soft thighs, to caress her and destroy her, to love her and murder her, to hide from her, and yet to stroke where below the small American flag tattooed upon her belly her thighs formed a capital V. I had a notion that of all in the room she saw only me with her impersonal eyes.

And then she began to dance, a slow sensuous movement; the smoke of a hundred cigars clinging to her like the thinnest of veils. She seemed like a fair bird-girl girdled in veils calling to me from the angry surface of some gray and threatening sea. I was transported. Then I became aware of the clarinet playing and the big shots yelling at us. Some threatened us if we looked and others if we did not. On my right I saw one boy faint. And now a man grabbed a silver pitcher from a table and stepped close as he dashed ice water upon him and stood him up and forced two of us to support him as his head hung and moans issued from his thick bluish lips. Another boy began to plead to go home. He was the largest of the group, wearing dark red fighting trunks much too small to conceal the erection which projected from him as though in answer to the insinuating low-registered moaning of the clarinet. He tried to hide himself with his boxing gloves.

And all the while the blonde continued dancing, smiling faintly at the big shots who watched her with fascination, and faintly smiling at our fear. I noticed a certain merchant who followed her hungrily, his lips loose and drooling. He was a large man who wore diamond studs in a shirtfront which swelled with the ample paunch underneath, and each time the blonde swayed her undulating hips he ran his hand through the thin hair of his bald head and, with his arms upheld, his posture clumsy like that of an intoxicated panda, wound his belly in a slow and obscene grind. This creature was completely hypnotized. The music had quickened. As the dancer flung herself about with a detached expression on her face, the men began reaching out to touch her. I could see their beefy fingers sink into the soft flesh. Some of the others tried to stop them and she began to move around the floor in graceful circles, as they gave chase, slipping and sliding over the polished floor. It was mad. Chairs went crashing, drinks were spilt, as they ran laughing and howling after her. They caught her just as she reached a door, raised her from the floor, and tossed her as college boys are tossed at a hazing, and above her red, fixed-smiling lips I saw the terror and disgust in her eyes, almost like my own terror and that which I saw in some of the other boys. As I watched, they tossed her twice and her soft breasts seemed to flatten against the air and her legs flung wildly as she spun. Some of the more sober ones helped her to escape. And I started off the floor, heading for the anteroom with the rest of the boys.

Some were still crying and in hysteria. But as we tried to leave we were stopped and ordered to get into the ring. There was nothing to do but what we were told. All ten of us climbed under the ropes and allowed ourselves to be blindfolded with broad bands of white cloth. One of the men seemed to feel a bit sympathetic and tried to cheer us up as we stood with our backs against the ropes. Some of us tried to grin. "See that boy over there?" one of the men said. "I want you to run across at the bell and give it to him right in the belly. If you don't get him, I'm going to get you. I don't like his looks." Each of us was told the same. The blindfolds were put on. Yet even then I had been going over my speech. In my mind each word was as bright as flame. I felt the cloth pressed into place, and frowned so that it would be loosened when I relaxed.

But now I felt a sudden fit of blind terror. I was unused to darkness. It was as though I had suddenly found myself in a dark room filled with poisonous cotton-mouths. I could hear the bleary voices yelling insistently for the battle royal to begin.

"Get going in there!"

"Let me at that big nigger!"

I strained to pick up the school superintendent's voice, as though to squeeze some security out of that slightly more familiar sound.

"Let me at those black sonsabitches!" someone yelled.

"No, Jackson, no!" another voice yelled. "Here, somebody, help me hold Jack."

"I want to get at that ginger-colored nigger. Tear him limb from limb," the first voice yelled.

I stood against the ropes trembling. For in those days I was what they called ginger-colored, and he sounded as though he might crunch me between his teeth like a crisp ginger cookie.

Quite a struggle was going on. Chairs were being kicked about and I could hear voices grunting as with a terrific effort. I wanted to see, to see more desperately than ever before. But the blindfold was tight as a thick skin-puckering scab and when I raised my gloved hands to push the layers of white aside a voice yelled, "Oh, no you don't, black bastard! Leave that alone!"

"Ring the bell before Jackson kills him a coon!" someone boomed in the sudden silence. And I heard the bell clang and the sound of the feet scuffling forward.

A glove smacked against my head. I pivoted, striking out stiffly as someone went past, and felt the jar ripple along the length of my arm to my shoulder. Then it seemed as though all nine of the boys had turned upon me at once. Blows pounded me from all sides while I struck out as best I could. So many blows landed upon me that I wondered if I were not the only blindfolded fighter in the ring, or if the man called Jackson hadn't succeeded in getting me after all.

Blindfolded, I could no longer control my motions. I had no dignity. I stumbled about like a baby or a drunken man. The smoke had become thicker and with each new blow it seemed to sear and further restrict my lungs. My saliva became like hot bitter glue. A glove connected with my head, filling my mouth with warm blood. It was everywhere. I could not tell if the moisture I felt upon my body was sweat or blood. A blow landed hard against the nape of my neck. I felt myself going over, my head hitting the floor. Streaks of blue light filled the black world behind the blindfold. I lay prone, pretending that I was knocked out, but felt myself seized by hands and yanked to my feet. "Get going, black boy! Mix it up!" My arms were like lead, my head smarting from blows. I managed to feel my way to the ropes and held on, trying to catch my breath. A glove landed in my mid-section and I went over again, feeling as though the smoke had become a knife jabbed into my guts. Pushed this way and that by the legs milling around me, I finally pulled erect and discovered that I could see the black, sweat-washed forms weaving in the smoky-blue atmosphere like drunken dancers weaving to the rapid drum-like thuds of blows.

Everyone fought hysterically. It was complete anarchy. Everybody fought everybody else. No group fought together for long. Two, three, four, fought one, then turned to fight each other, were themselves attacked. Blows landed below the belt and in the kidney, with the gloves open as well as closed, and with my eye partly opened now there was not so much terror. I moved carefully, avoiding blows, although not too many to attract attention, fighting from group to group. The boys groped about like blind, cautious crabs crouching to protect their mid-sections, their heads pulled in short against their shoulders, their arms stretched nervously before them, with their fists testing the smoke-filled air like the knobbed feelers of hypersensitive snails. In one corner I glimpsed a boy violently punching the air and heard him scream in pain as he smashed his hand against a ring post. For a second I saw him bent over holding his hand, then going down as a blow caught his unprotected head. I played one group against the other, slipping in and throwing a punch then stepping out of range while pushing the others into the melee to take the blows blindly aimed at me. The smoke was agonizing and there were no rounds, no bells at three minute intervals to relieve our exhaustion. The room spun round me, a swirl of lights, smoke, sweating bodies surrounded by tense white faces. I bled from both nose and mouth, the blood spattering upon my chest.

The men kept yelling, "Slug him, black boy! Knock his guts out!"

"Uppercut him! Kill him! Kill that big boy!"

Taking a fake fall, I saw a boy going down heavily beside me as though we were felled by a single blow, saw a sneaker-clad foot shoot into his groin as the two who had knocked him down stumbled upon him. I rolled out of range, feeling a twinge of nausea.

The harder we fought the more threatening the men became. And yet, I had begun to worry about my speech again. How would it go? Would they recognize my ability? What would they give me?

I was fighting automatically when suddenly I noticed that one after another of the boys was leaving the ring. I was surprised, filled with panic, as though I had been left alone with an unknown danger. Then I understood. The boys had arranged it among themselves. It was the custom for the two men left in the ring to slug it out for the winner's prize. I discovered this too late. When the bell sounded two men in tuxedoes leaped into the ring and removed the blindfold. I found myself facing Tatlock, the biggest of the gang. I felt sick at my stomach. Hardly had the bell stopped ringing in my ears than it clanged again and I saw him moving swiftly toward me. Thinking of nothing else to do I hit him smash on the nose. He kept coming, bringing the rank sharp violence of stale sweat. His face was a black blank of a face, only his eyes alive—with hate of me and aglow with a feverish terror from what had happened to us all. I became anxious. I wanted to deliver my speech and he came at me as though he meant to beat it out of me. I smashed him again and again, taking his blows as they came. Then on a sudden impulse I struck him lightly and as we clinched, I whispered, "Fake like I knocked you out, you can have the prize."

"I'll break your behind," he whispered hoarsely.

"For *them*?"

"For *me*, sonofabitch!"

They were yelling for us to break it up and Tatlock spun me half around with a blow, and as a joggled camera sweeps in a reeling scene, I saw the howling red faces crouching tense beneath the cloud of blue-gray smoke. For a moment the world wavered, unraveled, flowed, then my head cleared and Tatlock bounced before me. That fluttering shadow before my eyes was his jabbing left hand. Then falling forward, my head against his damp shoulder, I whispered,

"I'll make it five dollars more."

"Go to hell!"

But his muscles relaxed a trifle beneath my pressure and I breathed, "Seven?"

"Give it to your ma," he said, ripping me beneath the heart.

And while I still held him I butted him and moved away. I felt myself bombarded with punches. I fought back with hopeless desperation. I wanted to deliver my speech more than anything else in the world, because I felt that only these men could judge truly my ability, and now this stupid clown was ruining my chances. I began fighting carefully now, moving in to punch him and out again with my greater speed. A lucky blow to his chin and I had him going too—until I heard a loud voice yell, "I got my money on the big boy."

Hearing this, I almost dropped my guard. I was confused: Should I try to win against the voice out there? Would not this go against my speech, and was not this a moment for humility, for nonresistance? A blow to my head as I danced about sent my right eye popping like a jack-in-the-box and settled my dilemma. The room went red as I fell. It was a dream fall, my body languid and fastidious as to where to land, until the floor became impatient and smashed up to meet me. A moment later I came to. An hypnotic voice said FIVE emphatically. And I lay there, hazily watching a dark red spot of my own blood shaping itself into a butterfly, glistening and soaking into the soiled gray world of the canvas.

When the voice drawled TEN I was lifted up and dragged to a chair. I sat dazed. My eye pained and swelled with each throb of my pounding heart and I wondered if now I would be allowed to speak. I was wringing wet, my mouth still bleeding. We were grouped along the wall now. The other boys ignored me as they congratulated Tatlock and speculated as to how much they would be paid. One boy whimpered over his smashed hand. Looking up front, I saw attendants in white jackets rolling the portable ring away and placing a small square rug in the vacant space surrounded by chairs. Perhaps, I thought, I will stand on the rug to deliver my speech.

Then the M.C. called to us, "Come on up here boys and get your money."

We ran forward to where the men laughed and talked in their chairs, waiting. Everyone seemed friendly now.

"There it is on the rug," the man said. I saw the rug covered with coins of all dimensions and a few crumpled bills. But what excited me, scattered here and there, were the gold pieces.

"Boys, it's all yours," the man said. "You get all you grab."

"That's right, Sambo," a blond man said, winking at me confidentially.

I trembled with excitement, forgetting my pain. I would get the gold and the bills, I thought. I would use both hands. I would throw my body against the boys nearest me to block them from the gold.

"Get down around the rug now," the man commanded, "and don't anyone touch it until I give the signal."

"This ought to be good," I heard.

As told, we got around the square rug on our knees. Slowly the man raised his freckled hand as we followed it upward with our eyes.

I heard, "These niggers look like they're about to pray!"

Then, "Ready," the man said. "Go!"

I lunged for a yellow coin lying on the blue design of the carpet, touching it and sending a surprised shriek to join those rising around me. I tried frantically to remove my hand but could not let go. A hot, violent force tore through my body, shaking me like a wet rat. The rug was electrified. The hair bristled up on my head as I shook myself free. My muscles jumped, my nerves jangled, writhed. But I saw that this was not stopping the other boys. Laughing in fear and embarrassment, some were holding back and scooping up the coins knocked off by the painful contortions of the others. The men roared above us as we struggled.

"Pick it up, goddamnit, pick it up!" someone called like a bass-voiced parrot. "Go on, get it!"

I crawled rapidly around the floor, picking up the coins, trying to avoid the coppers and to get greenbacks and the gold. Ignoring the shock by laughing, as I brushed the coins off quickly, I discovered that I could contain the electricity—a contradiction, but it works. Then the men began to push us onto the rug. Laughing embarrassedly, we struggled out of their hands and kept after the coins. We were all wet and slippery and hard to hold. Suddenly I saw a boy lifted into the air, glistening with sweat like a circus seal, and dropped, his wet back landing flush upon the charged rug, heard him yell and saw him literally dance upon his back, his elbows beating a frenzied tattoo upon the floor, his muscles twitching like the flesh of a horse stung by many flies. When he finally rolled off, his face was gray and no one stopped him when he ran from the floor amid booming laughter.

"Get the money," the M.C. called. "That's good hard American cash!"

And we snatched and grabbed, snatched and grabbed. I was careful not to come too close to the rug now, and when I felt the hot whiskey breath descend upon me like a cloud of foul air I reached out and grabbed the leg of a chair. It was occupied and I held on desperately.

"Leggo, nigger! Leggo!"

The huge face wavered down to mine as he tried to push me free. But my body was slippery and he was too drunk. It was Mr. Colcord, who owned a chain of movie houses and "entertainment palaces." Each time he grabbed me I slipped out of his hands. It became a real struggle. I feared the rug more than I did the drunk, so I held on, surprising myself for a moment by trying to topple *him* upon the rug. It was such an enormous idea that I found myself actually carrying it out. I tried not to be obvious, yet when I grabbed his leg, trying to tumble him out of the chair, he raised up roaring with laughter, and, looking at me with soberness dead in the eye, kicked me viciously in the chest. The chair leg flew out of my hand and I felt myself going and rolled. It was as though I had rolled through a bed of hot coals. It seemed a whole century would pass before I would roll free, a century in which I was seared through the deepest levels of my body to the fearful breath within me and the breath seared and heated to the point of explosion. It'll all be over in a flash, I thought as I rolled clear. It'll all be over in a flash.

But not yet, the men on the other side were waiting, red faces swollen as though from apoplexy as they bent forward in their chairs. Seeing their fingers coming toward me I rolled away as a fumbled football rolls off the receiver's fingertips, back into the coals. That time I luckily sent the rug sliding out of place and heard the coins ringing against the floor and the boys scuffling to pick them up and the M.C. calling, "All right, boys, that's all. Go get dressed and get your money."

I was limp as a dish rag. My back felt as though it had been beaten with wires.

When we had dressed the M.C. came in and gave us each five dollars, except Tatlock, who got ten for being last in the ring. Then he told us to leave. I was not to get a chance to deliver my speech, I thought. I was going out into the dim alley in despair when I was stopped and told to go back. I returned to the ballroom, where the men were pushing back their chairs and gathering in groups to talk.

The M.C. knocked on a table for quiet. "Gentlemen," he said, "we almost forgot an important part of the program. A most serious part, gentlemen. This boy was brought here to deliver a speech which he made at his graduation yesterday . . ."

"Bravo!"

"I'm told that he is the smartest boy we've got out there in Greenwood. I'm told that he knows more big words than a pocket-sized dictionary."

Much applause and laughter.

"So now, gentlemen, I want you to give him your attention."

There was still laughter as I faced them, my mouth dry, my eye throbbing. I began slowly, but evidently my throat was tense, because they began shouting, "Louder! Louder!"

"We of the younger generation extol the wisdom of that great leader and educator," I shouted, "who first spoke these flaming words of wisdom: 'A ship lost at sea for many days suddenly sighted a friendly vessel. From the mast of the unfortunate vessel was seen a signal: "Water, water; we die of thirst!" The answer from the friendly vessel came back: "Cast down your bucket where you are." The captain of the distressed vessel, at last heeding the injunction, cast down his bucket, and it came up full of fresh sparkling water from the mouth of the Amazon River.' And like him I say, and in his words, 'To those of my race who depend upon bettering their condition in a foreign land, or who underestimate the importance of cultivating friendly relations with the Southern white man, who is his next-door neighbor, I would say: "Cast down your bucket where you are"—cast it down in making friends in every manly way of the people of all races by whom we are surrounded . . .' "

I spoke automatically and with such fervor that I did not realize that the men were still talking and laughing until my dry mouth, filling up with blood from the cut, almost strangled me. I coughed, wanting to stop and go to one of the tall brass, sand-filled spittoons to relieve myself, but a few of the men, especially the superintendent, were listening and I was afraid. So I gulped it down, blood, saliva and all, and continued. (What powers of endurance I had during those days! What enthusiasm! What a belief in the rightness of things!) I spoke even louder in spite of the pain. But still they talked and still they laughed, as though deaf with cotton in dirty ears. So I spoke with greater emotional emphasis. I closed my ears and swallowed blood until I was nauseated. The speech seemed a hundred times as long as before, but I could not leave out a single word. All had to be said, each memorized nuance considered, rendered. Nor was that all. Whenever I uttered a word of three or more syllables a group of voices would yell for me to repeat it. I used the phrase "social responsibility" and they yelled:

"What's that word you say, boy?"

"Social responsibility," I said.

"What?"

"Social . . ."

"Louder."

". . . responsibility."

"More!"

"Respon—"

"Repeat!"

"—sibility."

The room filled with the uproar of laughter until, no doubt, distracted by having to gulp down my blood, I made a mistake and yelled a phrase I had often seen denounced in newspaper editorials, heard debated in private.

"Social . . ."

"What?" they yelled.

". . . equality—"

The laughter hung smokelike in the sudden stillness. I opened my eyes, puzzled. Sounds of displeasure filled the room. The M.C. rushed forward. They shouted hostile phrases at me. But I did not understand.

A small dry mustached man in the front row blared out, "Say that slowly, son!"

"What, sir?"

"What you just said!"

"Social responsibility, sir," I said.

"You weren't being smart, were you, boy?" he said, not unkindly.

"No, sir!"

"You sure that about 'equality' was a mistake?"

"Oh, yes, sir," I said. "I was swallowing blood."

"Well, you had better speak more slowly so we can understand. We mean to do right by you, but you've got to know your place at all times. All right, now, go on with your speech."

I was afraid. I wanted to leave but I wanted also to speak and I was afraid they'd snatch me down.

"Thank you, sir," I said, beginning where I had left off, and having them ignore me as before.

Yet when I finished there was a thunderous applause. I was surprised to see the superintendent come forth with a package wrapped in white tissue paper, and, gesturing for quiet, address the men.

"Gentlemen, you see that I did not overpraise this boy. He makes a good speech and some day he'll lead his people in the proper paths. And I don't have to tell you that that is important in these days and times. This is a good, smart boy, and so to encourage him in the right direction, in the name of the Board of Education I wish to present him a prize in the form of this . . ."

He paused, removing the tissue paper and revealing a gleaming calfskin brief case.

". . . in the form of this first-class article from Shad Whitmore's shop."

"Boy," he said, addressing me, "take this prize and keep it well. Consider it a badge of office. Prize it. Keep developing as you are and some day it will be filled with important papers that will help shape the destiny of your people."

I was so moved that I could hardly express my thanks. A rope of bloody saliva forming a shape like an undiscovered continent drooled upon the leather and I wiped it quickly away. I felt an importance that I had never dreamed.

"Open it and see what's inside," I was told.

My fingers a-tremble, I complied, smelling the fresh leather and finding an official-looking document inside. It was a scholarship to the state college for Negroes. My eyes filled with tears and I ran awkwardly off the floor.

I was overjoyed; I did not even mind when I discovered that the gold pieces I had scrambled for were brass pocket tokens advertising a certain make of automobile.

When I reached home everyone was excited. Next day the neighbors came to congratulate me. I even felt safe from grandfather, whose deathbed curse usually spoiled my triumphs. I stood beneath his photograph with my brief case in hand and smiled triumphantly into his stolid black peasant's face. It was a face that fascinated me. The eyes seemed to follow everywhere I went.

That night I dreamed I was at a circus with him and that he refused to laugh at the clowns no matter what they did. Then later he told me to open my brief case and read what was inside and I did, finding an official envelope stamped with the state seal; and inside the envelope I found another and another, endlessly, and I thought I would fall of weariness. "Them's years," he said. "Now open that one." And I did and in it I found an engraved document containing a short message in letters of gold. "Read it," my grandfather said. "Out loud!"

"To Whom It May Concern," I intoned. "Keep This Nigger-Boy Running."

I awoke with the old man's laughter ringing in my ears.

(It was a dream I was to remember and dream again for many years after. But at that time I had no insight into its meaning. First I had to attend college.)

CONTEMPORARY POETRY

Allen Ginsberg (born 1926) was the leading poetic voice of the Beat movement, whose loosely structured verse and eccentric imagery suited the improvisational spirit of the Beat sensibility. Like Baudelaire, Ginsberg experimented with drugs and faced obscenity charges for his first major collection of poems, *Howl* (1956). "A Supermarket in California" announces Ginsberg's kinship with Walt Whitman and expresses his misgivings about post-World War II American civilization.

Gwendolyn Brooks (born 1917) rose to prominence as a poet depicting sympathetically the lives of African-Americans in her native Chicago. Brooks succinctly characterized ordinary lives, like the old couple in "Bean Eaters" or the reckless youths of "We Real Cool." Brooks's poetry became more explicitly concerned with racial equality in the 1960s, although her poetic voice kept the gentle tone of the poems reprinted here.

Anne Sexton (1928–1974) is especially notable for the personal frankness of her poetry, which seemed almost to be a journal of her anguished personal odyssey. Her intimate poetry attracted an enthusiastic popular audience, who sympathized with Sexton's personal frustrations and occasional despair. The poems reprinted here typify the self-affirmative tone that underlies many of Sexton's confessional poems.

Wole Soyinka (born 1934), the Nigerian playwright, poet, and essayist, is one of the greatest literary talents of contemporary Africa. In the two poems here, from *Idanre and Other Poems* (1967), the hopeful mood of the day's beginning is darkened by the dangers of traveling on crowded, narrow highways. The road is a "famished" god, perhaps an incarnation of the Nigerian deity Ogun, whose dual nature encompasses both the capacity for sudden violence and the protection of orphans and the homeless.

For analysis and interpretation:

1. How does Allen Ginsberg employ the supermarket as a metaphor for contemporary America? Compare the searching, anguished tone of Ginsberg's poem to Walt Whitman's romantic confidence in *Song of Myself*. What changes in historical circumstances and intellectual perspective might account for the differences?

2. In what ways are the characters in Gwendolyn Brooks's poems heroic? What seems to be the poet/speaker's attitude toward the characters? Is it important to understanding the poems that both the poet and her subject are African-American?

3. Describe the unconventional images of women Anne Sexton accumulates in "Her Kind." Explain how these images are a pointed alternative to such views of women as Andrew Marvell's "To His Coy Mistress." Contrast how the comforting domestic symbol of the house is depicted in the startling imagery of Sexton's "Housewife."

4. Analyze the nature imagery of Soyinka's "Dawn," especially the heroic symbolism of the palm tree that receives the first rays of the dawning sun. Compare the poem's mood to the menace of dawn in "Death in the Dawn." How does this contrast express the nature of modern life?

Allen Ginsberg

Supermarket in California

What thoughts I have of you tonight, Walt Whitman, for I walked down the sidestreets under the trees with a headache self-conscious looking at the full moon.

In my hungry fatigue, and shopping for images, I went into the neon fruit supermarket, dreaming of your enumerations!

What peaches and what penumbras! Whole families shopping at night! Aisles full of husbands! Wives in the avocados, babies in the tomatoes!—and you, Garcia Lorca, what were you doing down by the watermelons?

I saw you, Walt Whitman, childless, lonely old grubber, poking among the meats in the refrigerator and eyeing the grocery boys.

I heard you asking questions of each: Who killed the pork chops? What price bananas? Are you my Angel?   10

I wandered in and out of the brilliant stacks of cans following you, and followed in my imagination by the store detective.

We strode down the open corridors together in our solitary fancy tasting artichokes, possessing every frozen delicacy, and never passing the cashier.

Where are we going, Walt Whitman? The doors close in an hour. Which way does your beard point tonight?

(I touch your book and dream of our odyssey in the supermarket and feel absurd.)

Will we walk all night through solitary streets? The trees add shade to shade, lights out in the houses, we'll both be lonely.   20

Will we stroll dreaming of the lost America of love past blue automobiles in driveways, home to our silent cottage?

Ah, dear father, graybeard, lonely old courage-teacher, what America did you have when Charon quit poling his ferry and you got out on a smoking bank and stood watching the boat disappear on the black waters of Lethe?

Gwendolyn Brooks

The Bean Eaters

They eat beans mostly, this old yellow pair.
Dinner is a casual affair.

Plain chipware on a plain and creaking wood,
Tin flatware.

Two who are Mostly Good.
Two who have lived their day,
But keep on putting on their clothes
And putting things away.

And remembering . . .
Remembering, with twinklings and twinges,   10
As they lean over the beans in their rented back room that is full of beads and re-
    ceipts and dolls and cloths, tobacco crumbs, vases and fringes.

We Real Cool

The Pool Players.
Seven at the Golden Shovel.

We real cool. We
Left school. We

Lurk late. We
Strike straight. We

Sing sin. We
Thin gin. We

Jazz June. We
Die soon.

Anne Sexton

Her Kind

I have gone out, a possessed witch,
haunting the black air, braver at night;
dreaming evil, I have done my hitch
over the plain houses, light by light:
lonely thing, twelve-fingered, out of mind.
A woman like that is not a woman, quite.
I have been her kind.

I have found the warm caves in the woods,
filled them with skillets, carvings, shelves,
closets, silks, innumerable goods;   10
fixed the suppers for the worms and the elves:

whining, rearranging the disaligned.
A woman like that is misunderstood.
I have been her kind.

I have ridden in your cart, driver,
waved my nude arms at villages going by,
learning the last bright routes, survivor
where your flames still bite my thigh
and my ribs crack where your wheels wind.
A woman like that is not ashamed to die.   20
I have been her kind.

Housewife

Some women marry houses.
It's another kind of skin; it has a heart,
a mouth, a liver and bowel movements.
The walls are permanent and pink.
See how she sits on her knees all day,
faithfully washing herself down.
Men enter by force, drawn back like Jonah
into their fleshy mothers.
A woman *is* her mother.
That's the main thing.

Wole Soyinka

Dawn

Breaking earth upon
A spring-haired elbow, lone
A palm beyond head-grains, spikes
A guard of prim fronds, piercing
High hairs of the wind

As one who bore the pollen highest

Blood-drops in the air, above
The even belt of tassels, above
Coarse leaf teasing on the waist, steals
The lone intruder, tearing wide   10

The chaste hide of the sky

O celebration of the rites of dawn
Night-spread in tatters and a god
Received, aflame with kernels.

Death in the Dawn

*Driving to Lagos one morning a white cockerel flew out of the dusk and smashed it-
self against my windscreen. A mile further I came across a motor accident and a
freshly dead man in the smash.*

Traveller, you must set out
At dawn. And wipe your feet upon
The dog-nose wetness of earth.

Let sunrise quench your lamps, and watch
Faint brush pricklings in the sky light
Cottoned feet to break the early earthworm
On the hoe. Now shadows stretch with sap
Not twilight's death and sad prostration

This soft kindling, soft receding breeds
Racing joys and apprehensions for   10
A naked day, burdened hulks retract,
Stoop to the mist in faceless throng
To wake the silent markets—swift, mute
Processions on grey byways. . . .

On this
Counterpane, it was—
Sudden winter at the death
Of dawn's lone trumpeter, cascades
Of white feather-flakes, but it proved
A futile rite. Propitiation sped
Grimly on, before.   20

The right foot for joy, the left, dread
And the mother prayed, Child
May you never walk
When the road waits, famished.

Traveller you must set forth
At dawn
I promise marvels of the holy hour
Presages as the white cock's flapped
Perverse impalement—as who would dare
The wrathful wings of man's Progression. . . .   30

> But such another Wraith! Brother,
> Silenced in the startled hug of
> Your invention—is this mocked grimace
> This closed contortion—I?

JORGE LUIS BORGES

The fiction of Jorge Luis Borges (1899–1986) is an intellectual tangle of puzzles, mirrors, and twisting paths, populated by characters who seem as bemused by the shifting levels of "reality" as Borges's own readers. Borges creates a metaphor for his own work in the "garden of forking paths," a fictional world where the possibilities of multiple, simultaneous worlds are infinite. The story "The Garden of Forking Paths" (1944) is typical of Borges's works in absorbing historical reality into its shifting boundaries. The events and book of military history referred to in the opening paragraph are authentic. But this supposedly reliable "history" is questioned by the fictional confession of Yu Tsun, which takes on the tone of a detective story or thriller. By apparent coincidence, Yu Tsun's choice of a man named Albert leads him into the novelistic labyrinth created by his own ancestor. The story itself is evidence that, as Dr. Albert explains, the world consists of a "growing, dizzying net of divergent, convergent and parallel times." The dizzying perspective of Borges's fiction, with its concentric or overlapping fictions, emphasizes the artifice of storytelling and rests on the philosophical belief that reality is actually a bundle of perceptions, not the unchanging factuality that we sometimes believe.

For analysis and interpretation:
　　1. What is the significance of the story's opening, which refers to verifiable historical events and an actual military history? Does the narration present these as more reliable than the confession that follows?
　　2. Analyze the theme of the maze in the story (the path to Dr. Albert's, Albert's garden, the novel of Ts'ui Pen). How does this theme demonstrate the story's own course?
　　3. Compare Borges's dizzying view of multiple worlds to the reasoning of Descartes. How does the philosophy of the "garden of forking paths" undermine the premises of modern science?

The Garden of Forking Paths

On page 22 of Liddell Hart's *History of World War I* you will read that an attack against the Serre-Montauban line by thirteen British divisions (supported by 1,400 artillery pieces), planned for the 24th of July, 1916, had to be postponed until the morning of the 29th. The torrential rains, Captain Liddell Hart comments, caused this delay, an insignificant one, to be sure.

The following statement, dictated, reread and signed by Dr. Yu Tsun, former professor of English at the *Hochschule* at Tsingtao, throws an unsuspected light over the whole affair. The first two pages of the document are missing.

". . . and I hung up the receiver. Immediately afterwards, I recognized the voice that had answered in German. It was that of Captain Richard Madden. Madden's presence in Viktor Runeberg's apartment meant the end of our anxieties and—but this seemed, *or should have seemed*, very secondary to me—also the end of our lives. It meant that Runeberg had been arrested or murdered.[1] Before the sun set on that day, I would encounter the same fate. Madden was implacable. Or rather, he was obliged to be so. An Irishman at the service of England, a man accused of laxity and perhaps of treason, how could he fail to seize and be thankful for such a miraculous opportunity: the discovery, capture, maybe even the death of two agents of the German Reich? I went up to my room; absurdly I locked the door and threw myself on my back on the narrow iron cot. Through the window I saw the familiar roofs and the cloud-shaded six o'clock sun. It seemed incredible to me that that day without premonitions or symbols should be the one of my inexorable death. In spite of my dead father, in spite of having been a child in a symmetrical garden of Hai Feng, was I—now—going to die? Then I reflected that everything happens to a man precisely, precisely *now*. Centuries of centuries and only in the present do things happen; countless men in the air, on the face of the earth and the sea, and all that really is happening is happening to me . . . The almost intolerable recollection of Madden's horselike face banished these wanderings. In the midst of my hatred and terror (it means nothing to me now to speak of terror, now that I have mocked Richard Madden, now that my throat yearns for the noose) it occurred to me that that tumultuous and doubtless happy warrior did not suspect that I possessed the Secret. The name of the exact location of the new British artillery park on the River Ancre. A bird streaked across the gray sky and blindly I translated it into an airplane and that airplane into many (against the French sky) annihilating the artillery station with vertical bombs. If only my mouth, before a bullet shattered it, could cry out that secret name so it could be heard in Germany . . . My human voice was very weak. How might I make it carry to the ear of the Chief? To the ear of that sick and hateful man who knew nothing of Runeberg and me save that we were in Staffordshire and who was waiting in vain for our report in his arid office in Berlin, endlessly examining newspapers . . . I said out loud: *I must flee.* I sat up noiselessly, in a useless perfection of silence, as if Madden were already lying in wait for me. Something—perhaps the mere vain ostentation of proving my resources were nil—made me look through my pockets. I found what I knew I would find. The American watch, the nickel chain and the square coin, the key ring with the incriminating useless keys to Runeberg's apartment, the notebook, a letter which I resolved to destroy immediately (and which I did not destroy), a crown, two shillings and a few pence, the red and blue pencil, the handkerchief, the revolver with one bullet.

---

[1] An hypothesis both hateful and odd. The Prussian spy Hans Rabener, alias Viktor Runeberg, attacked with drawn automatic the bearer of the warrant for his arrest, Captain Richard Madden. The latter, in self-defense, inflicted the wound which brought about Runeberg's death. (Editor's note.) [Borges's note]

Absurdly, I took it in my hand and weighed it in order to inspire courage within myself. Vaguely I thought that a pistol report can be heard at a great distance. In ten minutes my plan was perfected. The telephone book listed the name of the only person capable of transmitting the message; he lived in a suburb of Fenton, less than a half hour's train ride away.

I am a cowardly man. I say it now, now that I have carried to its end a plan whose perilous nature no one can deny. I know its execution was terrible. I didn't do it for Germany, no. I care nothing for a barbarous country which imposed upon me the abjection of being a spy. Besides, I know of a man from England—a modest man—who for me is no less great than Goethe. I talked with him for scarcely an hour, but during that hour he was Goethe . . . I did it because I sensed that the Chief somehow feared people of my race—for the innumerable ancestors who merge within me. I wanted to prove to him that a yellow man could save his armies. Besides, I had to flee from Captain Madden. His hands and his voice could call at my door at any moment. I dressed silently, bade farewell to myself in the mirror, went downstairs, scrutinized the peaceful street and went out. The station was not far from my home, but I judged it wise to take a cab. I argued that in this way I ran less risk of being recognized; the fact is that in the deserted street I felt myself visible and vulnerable, infinitely so. I remember that I told the cab driver to stop a short distance before the main entrance. I got out with voluntary, almost painful slowness; I was going to the village of Ashgrove but I bought a ticket for a more distant station. The train left within a very few minutes, at eight-fifty. I hurried; the next one would leave at nine-thirty. There was hardly a soul on the platform. I went through the coaches; I remember a few farmers, a woman dressed in mourning, a young boy who was reading with fervor the *Annals* of Tacitus, a wounded and happy soldier. The coaches jerked forward at last. A man whom I recognized ran in vain to the end of the platform. It was Captain Richard Madden. Shattered, trembling, I shrank into the far corner of the seat, away from the dreaded window.

From this broken state I passed into an almost abject felicity. I told myself that the duel had already begun and that I had won the first encounter by frustrating, even if for forty minutes, even if by a stroke of fate, the attack of my adversary. I argued that this slightest of victories foreshadowed a total victory. I argued (no less fallaciously) that my cowardly felicity proved that I was a man capable of carrying out the adventure successfully. From this weakness I took strength that did not abandon me. I foresee that man will resign himself each day to more atrocious undertakings; soon there will be no one but warriors and brigands; I give them this counsel: *The author of an atrocious undertaking ought to imagine that he has already accomplished it, ought to impose upon himself a future as irrevocable as the past.* Thus I proceeded as my eyes of a man already dead registered the elapsing of that day, which was perhaps the last, and the diffusion of the night. The train ran gently along, amid ash trees. It stopped, almost in the middle of the fields. No one announced the name of the station. "Ashgrove?" I asked a few lads on the platform. "Ashgrove," they replied. I got off.

A lamp enlightened the platform but the faces of the boys were in shadow. One questioned me, "Are you going to Dr. Stephen Albert's house?" Without waiting for my answer, another said, "The house is a long way from here, but you won't get lost if you take this road to the left and at every crossroads turn again to your left." I tossed them a coin (my last), descended a few stone steps and started down the solitary road. It went downhill, slowly. It was of elemental earth; overhead the banches were tangled; the low, full moon seemed to accompany me.

For an instant, I thought that Richard Madden in some way had penetrated my desperate plan. Very quickly, I understood that that was impossible. The instructions to turn always to the left reminded me that such was the common procedure for discovering the central point of certain labyrinths. I have some understanding of labyrinths: not for nothing am I the great grandson of that Ts'ui Pên who was governor of Yunnan and who renounced worldly power in order to write a novel that might be even more populous than the *Hung Lu Meng* and to construct a labyrinth in which all men would become lost. Thirteen years he dedicated to these heterogeneous tasks, but the hand of a stranger murdered him—and his novel was incoherent and no one found the labyrinth. Beneath English trees I meditated on that lost maze: I imagined it inviolate and perfect at the secret crest of a mountain; I imagined it erased by rice fields or beneath the water; I imagined it infinite, no longer composed of octagonal kiosks and returning paths, but of rivers and provinces and kingdoms . . . I thought of a labyrinth of labyrinths, of one sinuous spreading labyrinth that would encompass the past and the future and in some way involve the stars. Absorbed in these illusory images, I forgot my destiny of one pursued. I felt myself to be, for an unknown period of time, an abstract perceiver of the world. The vague, living countryside, the moon, the remains of the day worked on me, as well as the slope of the road which eliminated any possibility of weariness. The afternoon was intimate, infinite. The road descended and forked among the now confused meadows. A high-pitched, almost syllabic music approached and receded in the shifting of the wind, dimmed by leaves and distance. I thought that a man can be an enemy of other men, of the moments of other men, but not of a country: not of fireflies, words, gardens, streams of water, sunsets. Thus I arrived before a tall, rusty gate. Between the iron bars I made out a poplar grove and a pavilion. I understood suddenly two things, the first trivial, the second almost unbelievable: the music came from the pavilion, and the music was Chinese. For precisely that reason I had openly accepted it without paying it any heed. I do not remember whether there was a bell or whether I knocked with my hand. The sparkling of the music continued.

From the rear of the house within a lantern approached: a lantern that the trees sometimes striped and sometimes eclipsed, a paper lantern that had the form of a drum and the color of the moon. A tall man bore it. I didn't see his face for the light blinded me. He opened the door and said slowly, in my own language: "I see that the pious Hsi P'êng persists in correcting my solitude. You no doubt wish to see the garden?"

I recognized the name of one of our consuls and I replied, disconcerted, "The garden?"

"The garden of forking paths."

Something stirred in my memory and I uttered with incomprehensible certainty, "The garden of my ancestor Ts'ui Pên."

"Your ancestor? Your illustrious ancestor? Come in."

The damp path zigzagged like those of my childhood. We came to a library of Eastern and Western books. I recognized bound in yellow silk several volumes of the Lost Encyclopedia, edited by the Third Emperor of the Luminous Dynasty but never printed. The record on the phonograph revolved next to a bronze phoenix. I also recall a *famille rose* vase and another, many centuries older, of that shade of blue which our craftsmen copied from the potters of Persia . . .

Stephen Albert observed me with a smile. He was, as I have said, very tall, sharp-featured, with gray eyes and a gray beard. He told me that he had been a missionary in Tientsin "before aspiring to become a Sinologist."

We sat down—I on a long, low divan, he with his back to the window and a tall circular clock. I calculated that my pursuer, Richard Madden, could not arrive for at least an hour. My irrevocable determination could wait.

"An astounding fate, that of Ts'ui Pên," Stephen Albert said. "Governor of his native province, learned in astronomy, in astrology and in the tireless interpretation of the canonical books, chess player, famous poet and calligrapher—he abandoned all this in order to compose a book and a maze. He renounced the pleasures of both tyranny and justice, of his populous couch, of his banquets and even of erudition—all to close himself up for thirteen years in the Pavilion of the Limpid Solitude. When he died, his heirs found nothing save chaotic manuscripts. His family, as you may be aware, wished to condemn them to the fire; but his executor—a Taoist or Buddhist monk—insisted on their publication."

"We descendants of Ts'ui Pên," I replied, "continue to curse that monk. Their publication was senseless. The book is an indeterminate heap of contradictory drafts. I examined it once: in the third chapter the hero dies, in the fourth he is alive. As for the other undertaking of Ts'ui Pên, his labyrinth . . ."

"Here is Ts'ui Pên's labyrinth," he said, indicating a tall lacquered desk.

"An ivory labyrinth!" I exclaimed. "A minimum labyrinth."

"A labyrinth of symbols," he corrected. "An invisible labyrinth of time. To me, a barbarous Englishman, has been entrusted the revelation of this diaphanous mystery. After more than a hundred years, the details are irretrievable; but it is not hard to conjecture what happened. Ts'ui Pên must have said once: *I am withdrawing to write a book.* And another time: *I am withdrawing to construct a labyrinth.* Every one imagined two works; to no one did it occur that the book and the maze were one and the same thing. The Pavilion of the Limpid Solitude stood in the center of a garden that was perhaps intricate; that circumstance could have suggested to the heirs a physical labyrinth. Hs'ui Pên died; no one in the vast territories that were his came upon the labyrinth; the confusion of the novel suggested to me that *it* was the maze. Two circumstances gave me the correct solution of the problem. One: the curious legend that Ts'ui Pên had planned to create a labyrinth which would be strictly infinite. The other: a fragment of a letter I discovered."

Albert rose. He turned his back on me for a moment; he opened a drawer of the black and gold desk. He faced me and in his hands he held a sheet of paper that had once been crimson, but was now pink and tenuous and cross-sectioned. The fame of Ts'ui Pên as a calligrapher had been justly won. I read, uncomprehendingly and with fervor, these words written with a minute brush by a man of my blood: *I leave to the various futures (not to all) my garden of forking paths.* Wordlessly, I returned the sheet. Albert continued:

"Before unearthing this letter, I had questioned myself about the ways in which a book can be infinite. I could think of nothing other than a cyclic volume, a circular one. A book whose last page was identical with the first, a book which had the possibility of continuing indefinitely. I remembered too that night which is at the middle of the Thousand and One Nights when Scheherazade (through a magical oversight of the copyist) begins to relate word for word the story of the Thousand and One Nights, establishing the risk of coming once again to the night when she must repeat it, and thus on to infinity. I imagined as well a Platonic, hereditary work, transmitted from father to son, in which each new individual adds a chapter or corrects with pious care the pages of his elders. These conjectures diverted me; but none seemed to correspond, not even remotely, to the contradictory chapters of Ts'ui Pên. In the midst of this perplexity, I received from Oxford the manuscript you have examined. I lingered, naturally, on the sentence: *I leave to the various futures (not to all) my garden of forking paths.* Almost instantly, I understood: 'the garden of forking paths' was the chaotic novel; the phrase 'the various futures (not to all)' suggested to me the forking in time, not in space. A broad rereading of the work confirmed the theory. In all fictional works, each time a man is confronted with several alternatives, he chooses one and eliminates the others; in the fiction of Ts'ui Pên, he chooses—simultaneously—all of them. *He creates,* in this way, diverse futures, diverse times which themselves also proliferate and fork. Here, then, is the explanation of the novel's contradictions. Fang, let us say, has a secret; a stranger calls at his door; Fang resolves to kill him. Naturally, there are several possible outcomes: Fang can kill the intruder, the intruder can kill Fang, they both can escape, they both can die, and so forth. In the work of Ts'ui Pên, all possible outcomes occur; each one is the point of departure for other forkings. Sometimes, the paths of this labyrinth converge: for example, you arrive at this house, but in one of the possible pasts you are my enemy, in another, my friend. If you will resign yourself to my incurable pronunciation, we shall read a few pages."

His face, within the vivid circle of the lamplight, was unquestionably that of an old man, but with something unalterable about it, even immortal. He read with slow precision two versions of the same epic chapter. In the first, an army marches to a battle across a lonely mountain; the horror of the rocks and shadows makes the men undervalue their lives and they gain an easy victory. In the second, the same army traverses a palace where a great festival is taking place; the resplendent battle seems to them a continuation of the celebration and they win the victory. I listened with proper veneration to these ancient narratives, perhaps less admirable in themselves than the fact that they had been created by my blood and were being restored to me by a man of a remote empire, in the course of a desperate adventure, on a Western isle. I remember the last words, repeated in each version like a secret commandment: *Thus fought the heroes, tranquil their admirable hearts, violent their swords, resigned to kill and to die.*

From that moment on, I felt about me and within my dark body an invisible, intangible swarming. Not the swarming of the divergent, parallel and finally coalescent armies, but a more inaccessible, more intimate agitation that they in some manner prefigured. Stephen Albert continued:

"I don't believe that your illustrious ancestor played idly with these variations. I don't consider it credible that he would sacrifice thirteen years to the infinite execution of a rhetorical experiment. In your country, the novel is a subsidiary form of literature; in Ts'ui Pên's time it was a despicable form. Ts'ui Pên was a brilliant novelist, but he was also a man of letters who doubtless did not consider himself a mere novelist. The testimony of his contemporaries proclaims—and his life fully confirms—his meta-physical and mystical interests. Philosophic controversy usurps a good part of the novel. I know that of all problems, none disturbed him so greatly nor worked upon him so much as the abysmal problem of time. Now then, the latter is the only problem that does not figure in the pages of the *Garden*. He does not even use the word that signifies *time*. How do you explain this voluntary omission?"

I proposed several solutions—all unsatisfactory. We discussed them. Finally, Stephen Albert said to me:

"In a riddle whose answer is chess, what is the only prohibited word?"

I thought a moment and replied, "The word *chess*."

"Precisely," said Albert. "*The Garden of Forking Paths* is an enormous riddle, or parable, whose theme is time; this recondite cause prohibits its mention. To omit a word always, to resort to inept metaphors and obvious periphrases, is perhaps the most emphatic way of stressing it. That is the tortuous method preferred, in each of the meanderings of his indefatigable novel, by the oblique Ts'ui Pên. I have compared hundreds of manuscripts, I have corrected the errors that the negligence of the copyists has introduced, I have guessed the plan of this chaos, I have re-established—I believe I have re-established—the primordial organization, I have translated the entire work: it is clear to me that not once does he employ the word 'time.' The explanation is obvious: *The Garden of Forking Paths* is an incomplete, but not false, image of the universe as Ts'ui Pên conceived it. In contrast to Newton and Schopenhauer, your ancestor did not believe in a uniform, absolute time. He believed in an infinite series of times, in a growing, dizzying net of divergent, convergent and parallel times. This network of times which approached one another, forked, broke off, or were unaware of one another for centuries, embraces *all* possibilities of time. We do not exist in the majority of these times; in some you exist, and not I; in others I, and not you; in others, both of us. In the present one, which a favorable fate has granted me, you have arrived at my house; in another, while crossing the garden, you found me dead; in still another, I utter these same words, but I am a mistake, a ghost."

"In every one," I pronounced, not without a tremble to my voice, "I am grateful to you and revere you for your re-creation of the garden of Ts'ui Pên."

"Not in all," he murmured with a smile. "Time forks perpetually toward innumerable futures. In one of them I am your enemy."

Once again I felt the swarming sensation of which I have spoken. It seemed to me that the humid garden that surrounded the house was infinitely saturated with invisible persons. Those persons were Albert and I, secret, busy and multiform in other dimensions of time. I raised my eyes and the tenuous nightmare dissolved. In the yellow and black garden there was only one man; but this man was as strong as a statue . . . this man was approaching along the path and he was Captain Richard Madden.

"The future already exists," I replied, "but I am your friend. Could I see the letter again?"

Albert rose. Standing tall, he opened the drawer of the tall desk; for the moment his back was to me. I had readied the revolver. I fired with extreme caution. Albert fell uncomplainingly, immediately. I swear his death was instantaneous—a lightning stroke.

The rest is unreal, insignificant. Madden broke in, arrested me. I have been condemned to the gallows. I have won out abominably; I have communicated to Berlin the secret name of the city they must attack. They bombed it yesterday; I read it in the same papers that offered to England the mystery of the learned Sinologist Stephen Albert who was murdered by a stranger, one Yu Tsun. The Chief had deciphered this mystery. He knew my problem was to indicate (through the uproar of the war) the city called Albert, and that I had found no other means to do so than to kill a man of that name. He does not know (no one can know) my innumerable contrition and weariness.

For Victoria Ocampo

—Translated by John M. Fein